ALL SHE WANTS

Jonathan Harvey comes from Liverpool and is a multi-award winning writer of plays, films, sitcoms and Britain's longest running drama serial.

Jonathan's theatre work includes the award winning *Beautiful Thing* (Bush Theatre, Donmar Warehouse, Duke of York's – winner: John Whiting Award. Nominated: Olivier Award for Best Comedy), *Babies* (Royal Court Theatre – winner: *Evening Standard* Award for Most Promising Playwright; winner: George Devine Award), *Rupert Street Lonely Hearts Club* (English Touring Theatre, Donmar Warehouse, Criterion Theatre – winner: *Manchester Evening News* Award for Best New Play; winner: Best New Play – *City Life Magazine*). Other plays include *Corrie!* (Lowry Theatre and National Tour – winner: *Manchester Evening News* Award for Best Special Entertainment), *Canary* (Liverpool Playhouse, Hampstead Theatre and English Touring Theatre), *Hushabye Mountain* (English Touring Theatre, Hampstead Theatre), *Guiding Star* (Everyman Theatre, Royal National Theatre), *Boom Bang a Bang* (Bush Theatre), *Mohair* (Royal Court Theatre Upstairs) and *Wildfire* (Royal Court Th̶ ̶stairs). Jonathan also co-wrote the musical C̶ ̶h Pet Shop Boys.

For tel̶ ̶wrote three series of the BA̶ ̶*Gimme* for the BBC, two ser̶ ̶Best Comedy, Banff TV Festi̶ ̶nominated *Best Friends*, *Von Trapped!* ̶ ̶*Girl*.

Jonathan has also written for the shows *Rev* (winner: BAFTA, Best Sitcom) *Shameless*, *The Catherine Tate Show*, *At Home With The Braithwaites*, *Lilies* and *Murder Most Horrid*. To date he has written over a hundred episodes of *Coronation Street*.

Jonathan's film work includes: *Beautiful Thing* for Film Four (Outstanding Film, GLAAD Awards, New York; Best Film: London Lesbian and Gay Film Festival; Best Screenplay, Fort Lauderdale Film Festival; *Grand Prix*, Paris Film Festival; San Paolo International Film Festival, Jury Award).

But perhaps most telling of all, he also won the Spacehopper Championships at Butlins Pwhelli in 1976.

JONATHAN HARVEY

All She WANTS

PAN BOOKS

First published 2012 by Pan Books
an imprint of Pan Macmillan, a division of Macmillan Publishers Limited
Pan Macmillan, 20 New Wharf Road, London N1 9RR
Basingstoke and Oxford
Associated companies throughout the world
www.panmacmillan.com

ISBN 978-0-330-54427-6

1 3 5 7 9 8 6 4 2

A CIP catalogue record for this book is available from
the British Library.

Printed and bound by CPI Group (UK) Ltd, Croydon, CR0 4YY

*This book is dedicated to anyone who ever woke up
with the horrors, the morning after the night before,
and thought 'Oh God. What did I do last night?'*

ACKNOWLEDGEMENTS

Thank you to all those who were so encouraging when I first said I wanted to write a book and offered invaluable, sage advice in the early stages: Marian Keyes, Paul Burston and David Nicholls, who didn't even bat an eyelid but told me to go for it, and Kathy Burke for her continuing unconditional positive regard.

To my agent Gordon Wise and all at Curtis Brown for holding my hand through the experience and for explaining the whys and wherefores of this brave new world. Also to Michael McCoy and Alec Drysdale at Independent for everything they do with all my *other* writing. Thank you so much for never balking, no matter how demanding I might be!

Thank you to my editor Wayne Brookes for taking a punt, laughing at my jokes, the boozy lunches, and for being my literary sat nav. And to Jeremy Trevathan and all the sales, marketing and publicity teams at my new home Pan Macmillan.

To all the cast and crew of *Coronation Street*, my day job, for making it such a special place to work. To my fellow writers there for always making me laugh and inspiring me with their talent. Special thanks also to Kieran Roberts and Phil Collinson for being so supportive when I said I wanted to write a novel set in the world of a soap opera.

Thank you to all the actors who took the time to discuss their experiences of drama school with me: Sarah Dorsett, Philip McGinley, Morgan Jones, Jordan Cluroe, Sue Vincent, Ken Christiansen, Ian Connop, Jane Slavin, Maria McErlane, Dan Crowder and Ruth Jarvis. Special thanks to Kate Kelly who let me bend her ear a bit more than was really necessary.

Thank you particularly to Jodie McNee for letting me, almost, steal her name.

To Richard Foord for some very special memories, good laughs and continuing support. Likewise to all my friends who have given me nothing but encouragement along the way, but particularly Angela Sinden, Steven Doherty, Damon Rochefort, Debbie Rodaway and Hayley Johnson. Thanks again to my old flatmate and long-term soulmate Julie Graham for reading and squealing and the laughs around the camp fire.

To Antony Cotton and Peter Eccleston for listening in times of trouble, never judging, and pouring copious amounts of alcohol down my neck. Likewise to Jennie, Geoff and Wendy for taking me in and looking after me when I most needed it.

To my Mum and Dad, Maureen and Brian Harvey, who as well as teaching me to read and write, taught me that it was always okay to be myself. They would never admit it, but they really are the best mum and dad in the world.

PROLOGUE

1994

We must have looked an odd sight, the three of us: me, Our Joey and Mum, scuttling along the pavement of an industrial estate in South Liverpool carrying deckchairs and packed lunch boxes in the middle of December.

'Jodie, your shoes are really getting on my tits,' moaned Our Joey.

'Don't say tits, Joey,' Mum said sternly.

'Why not?'

He knew why not. 'It's not becoming for an eight-year-old.'

'Can I say it?' I asked. I was ten. AKA dead grown up.

'No.'

Our Joey tried again. 'Jodie your shoes are really getting on my *nerves*.'

He meant the noise they were making. I'd recently looped some *Friends* fridge magnets into the laces of my shoes, so with every hurried step I took, Chandler and Joey clunked against my burgundy patent leather T-bars.

The air was heavy with the acrid tang of chemicals wafting on the breeze from the Mersey. We passed the cigarette factory where Mum worked. We passed the boarded-up bank. We passed the faded old sign that said, 'Welcome To Liverpool, A Socialist Council', onto which someone had graffitied 'anti' before the 'socialist' and then crossed out the 'ist'. Hilarious. And then suddenly Mum stopped, snapped her deckchair out and sat down. Me and Our Joey followed suit, and wondered what on earth was going on.

We appeared to be sitting outside some gates. There was a barrier that looked like it might go up to let traffic through, a glass-fronted booth with a security guard in it and two brick walls on either side. It looked just like the entrance to Mum's work, except there were a few purple flags on each side of the gates, which I felt was a bit showy offy for a factory.

'Mum? Why are we here?'

'Shut up and have a sandwich, Jodie.'

I opened the red plastic *Friends* lunchbox I held in my shivering hand and prised apart the Slimcea slices within to inspect their contents. Tuna paste. I pulled a face and looked at Mum. She smiled apologetically.

'I haven't had time to go up Kwik Save,' she explained.

I rolled my eyes and shut the box in disgust.

'Where are we, Mum?' moaned Our Joey, toying with the clasp on his Polly Pocket lunchbox. 'I don't understand.'

Mum allowed herself a mischievous chuckle and my heart sank.

'This, kids' – I rolled my eyes again and tutted. I wasn't a kid. I was TEN – 'is where dreams are made!'

I looked at her like she was mad.

Let me explain. This was meant to be a Big Day Out for us. It was the school holidays, and to spare the monotony of just 'playing out' each day, Mum would occasionally wake us up with the thrilling announcement, 'Right! We're having a day . . . *out*!' At which me and my brother would squeal, jump like lemmings from our bunk beds, then run to the bathroom to wash and brush our teeth together, fizzing with excitement. We did everything together, me and Our Joey, bar going to the loo. Mind you, we did that too sometimes, just to wind Mum up.

'Get out of there, the pair of you! It's not natural!' she'd holler, banging on the door. 'If you're showing each other your bits I'll hit the roof,' which, bearing in mind she always wore impossibly high heels, was not outside the realms of possibility. Though she needn't have worried. We never showed each other our bits. For my part I'd already seen Sean McEvoy's todger when he waggled it around in show and tell, and whenever I mentioned fannies to Our Joey he went a bit pale, said, 'I feel sick,' and waggled his hand around, which was drama queen sign language for 'change the subject'.

Anyway. Where was I? Oh yes! Big Days Out. So there's me and Our Joey, full of the joys of spring, or summer, or Christmas, or whichever half term it might be. But then, within an hour or so, as reality set in, we'd become less enamoured with what constituted Mum's idea of 'a holiday in a day':

One day in the summer holidays we went to watch the planes take off at Liverpool airport.

One day in the Easter half term we got a train to Southport to go and see some red squirrels in a forest, only instead we found a trampy bloke playing with himself and ended up catching the first train back. When Our Joey asked Mum what he was doing, she kept saying he was 'very itchy'.

Another day Mum took us to the local cats' home to stare at a bunch of moggies lying behind Perspex. At the end of the visit me and Our Joey wanted to take one home, but Mum claimed Dad was allergic.

So as you can imagine, my hopes weren't high for this

particular day out. Particularly as we were sitting in deckchairs outside a factory three bus stops away from home.

However, the next thing she said made my heart literally skip a beat.

'This, kids, is where they film *Acacia Avenue*.'

'WHAT?!' That was me and Our Joey speaking in unison.

We looked at each other, then peered back at the gates. It was now I realized that written on the purple flags on either side of the gates were the words 'Crystal TV'. I had seen those words before. They came up on the telly at the end of every episode of our favourite soap opera.

Every Monday and Wednesday *Acacia Avenue* was religious viewing in our house. Me, Our Joey, Mum and Dad would sit watching it through a fog of smoke, courtesy of the free cigarettes Mum got from work, Mum and Dad sucking away like they were getting the elixir of youth from every little drag; me and Our Joey hacking our guts up and wafting the smoke away dramatically. We were completely gripped when Nona Newman from the corner shop began her illicit affair with Harry from the factory behind her street-sweeper hubby Tex's back. And there was that heart-stopping moment when Tex saw Nona's handbag on the back seat of Harry's Ford Capri. But when he referred to it as 'My Nona's handbag', Our Joey hit the roof.

'It's not a handbag it's a clutchbag!' he screamed, knocking some Wotsits onto the carpet and getting an arched-eyebrow glare from my dad. It really wasn't becoming for an eight-year-old boy in Liverpool to know the difference between a handbag and a clutchbag. Our Joey caught the glare, looked wounded and muttered to himself, 'Any idiot can see that.' Mum seemed to consider this, then nodded her head in agreement. Not knowing what to say, Dad just pointed to the Wotsits on the floor and Our Joey curtly picked them up.

Our Joey and me used to play *Acacia Avenue* in the bedroom of our dormer bungalow. My dressing table became the counter of the Sleepy Trout pub and I was sneering barmaid Sorrel while Our Joey was her ditzy sidekick Cheryl. Together we'd serve imaginary pints of bitter to a selection of Barbies, Tiny Tears and teddy bears. Sometimes our back garden became the avenue itself and we'd re-enact one of the catfights that regularly ensued after kicking-out time. Mum and Dad had often commented that it was filmed 'just down the road', but I'd never quite believed them. To me it was a real world, real life; it just happened to take place inside a box in the corner of our lounge with really little people twice a week.

'Can we go in and look?' asked Joey, peering at the security guard.

'No.'

'Ah go on, Mum,' I joined in.

'No, Jodie. It's against the law.' And she clicked out the nib of her twelve-colour biro and started having a crack at a wordsearch in her *Puzzler* magazine. I looked at her, and in that instant decided she was the most brilliant, most lovely, most beautiful mum in the whole wide world. For once I thought it was fab the way she thought she looked a bit like Princess Di, side-flicking her hair accordingly, peeking out from behind her bottle-blonde fringe with an air of coyness that didn't quite suit her. I thought – possibly for the first time – that it was great she still took care of herself and her figure and that, at the grand old age of thirty-two, she still got wolf whistles whenever she past a building site. 'Best legs in Liverpool,' my dad always said. I looked at them now, resplendent in their morello cherry woollen tights. I'd always been slightly mortified by her propensity to show them off all the time by wearing skirts that were far too short for her, but today I decided she had every right. Those legs were just so . . . leggy. Both of them. So why not wear miniskirts at the really old age of thirty-two and make a show of yourself and your family? She was my mum. She could do anything she wanted. She had brought me and Our Joey to *Acacia Avenue*!

I looked at Our Joey and it seemed like he was having similar thoughts. His little snub nose with the smattering of freckles, which I had too but covered in the powder from Mum's compact whenever she wasn't looking, rose skyward, like one of the Bisto kids smelling something wonderful on the other side of the gates. It was as if the magic of *Acacia Avenue* was wafting towards us in a glittery line of fairy dust, completely blocking out the smell from the factories. His green eyes, which I hated with an envy only a sibling can understand – one of mine was blue, the other brown; I was a freak – were half closed in an affectation of contentment that he usually only saved for the Eurovision Song Contest and whenever Madonna was on *Top of the Pops*. While I watched him, his eyes flicked open like a startled china doll as a shadow crossed our path. Someone else had joined our party.

A fat man in a dirty parka with matted fur trim and a plaster on his glasses was standing nearer the gates than our deck-chairs. He had a camera in one hand and an autograph book in the other. At first I thought he was the trampy bloke from the forest near Southport, but when Mum gave him a cheery, 'Hiya!' I thought he mustn't be. There was definitely something weird about him, though. If he lived on our street, Mum would probably have told us to hurry past his house whenever we went by. The fat man nodded and started flicking through his autograph book.

'Who's that?' asked Joey. But Mum gave him one of her looks, so he tutted and looked away, muttering, 'Well you were talking to him,' under his breath.

The fat guy had a weird habit of licking his thumb and turning the pages of his autograph book quickly, almost tearing the paper in his brusqueness. I could tell he was showing off, so I ignored him. I saw Joey looking at the weird guy, so I coughed and he looked at me.

'He loves that book,' I said quietly, cocking my head in the direction of the fat bloke.

Joey giggled. 'I know.'

'He's made up with it.'

'I know.'

'He's like, going with it.'

'I know.'

Our Joey could hardly get his words out because he was laughing so much. I loved it when I made Our Joey laugh. But then we jumped as Fat Bloke said something.

'How long you been here?' he was talking to Mum.

'Just got here, love.' Mum was calling him love. I looked to Our Joey.

'She fancies him,' he mouthed to me and I giggled.

'Seen anyone?'

'Not yet, love.'

And because she said love again, me and Our Joey creased up. Mum gave us a look, so we settled down.

'I've seen them all here,' the bloke carried on, and reeled off a list of names that meant nothing to me but everything to my mum, because she oo'd and ah'd throughout the extensive list. When he finished she took a cigarette out of her handbag and lit up, like she did after a good movie or a long phone conversation. She breathed the smoke out of her nose like a dragon and shook her head, impressed. I was just about to ask her who all those people were when Fat Bloke jumped to attention and Mum swivelled her head to look down the street. I looked. Our Joey looked.

A car was approaching. I'm not sure what sort of car it was – I've never been into cars – but it was black and the windows were black, too. Fat Bloke was getting very excited, hopping from one foot to the other like some sort of sumo morris dancer.

'It's Yvonne Carsgrove! It's Yvonne Carsgrove!' he squealed. 'That's her car, I'd know it anywhere!' Mum stood up, letting her *Puzzler* fall into her deckchair.

'Go'way, you're joking!' she was getting excited, too. She flicked her ciggie into the road and reflicked her hair with her hands. 'Get up, kids!'

Kids! I was TEN! I got up anyway as the black car slowed down as it approached the gates. Fat Bloke was waving at it like we were stranded in the desert and he was flagging down the first vehicle in ages that might take us to the next town. As the car ground to a halt – it had little choice as Fat Bloke had flung himself into its path, so it was either stop or the fat guy gets it – the driver's window lowered. I looked in.

All I could see was a head. Not severed or anything, but a woman's head. She had a fur hat thing on and *massive* sunglasses. And it wasn't even sunny. For a second I thought it was Shirley Bassey, because that's what she looked like on the back of one of my dad's LPs (the one that described her as 'the Lily of Tiger Bay'), but as Fat Bloke was rushing to the open car window waggling his autograph book in this vision's face, I realized it must be someone from *Acacia Avenue*. But who? He thrust the book through the open window and I saw the vision scribble something inside.

Mum started poking me. 'Say hello, Jodie!' And she pushed me forward. Our Joey fell in alongside me: she must have been poking him, too.

'Who is it?' Our Joey asked.

Mum rolled her eyes like he was stupid. 'It's Nona Newman!'

I gulped and looked again. Could it really be? No! Nona Newman? The lady who worked in the corner shop who'd had an affair with the factory foreman behind her street-sweeper husband's back? That wasn't Nona Newman. Nona Newman was dead ordinary looking. She worked in a shop. She wore a mac when it rained and always moaned that she 'didn't have enough money for a pair of shoes that wouldn't let the rain in'. Why would she be driving round in a big black car, wearing fur hats and sunglasses? Nona was a bit . . . dull. So dull me and Our Joey used to row over who would play her when we were playing corner shop in our bedroom. But this lady. Well, this lady looked like a star!

'Excuse me, Nona,' I heard Mum saying. 'Only these are my kids. Our Jodie and Our Joey. And they're both big fans of yours.'

At which the vision slipped off her sunglasses to reveal that – oh my God, Mum was right – it was indeed Nona Newman. She smiled. We both stood there in stunned silence. She was a lot bigger than when she was in the corner of our lounge.

'But he said your name was something else,' I said, confused.

The vision smiled, like a kindly teacher who was going to teach you a big word you didn't understand but they did and they loved showing off about it.

'Darling, I'm an actress. My real name is Yvonne, but I play Nona. It's my job.'

I nodded.

'Kids, eh?' Fat Bloke muttered. Nona shot him a look of contempt, which made me warm to her.

'Anyway,' said Nona. She sounded posher than she did on the telly. 'Have you two cherubs decided what you want for Christmas yet?'

I had. I'd written to Santa and asked for a night of passion with Joey from *Friends*. I had no idea what it meant, but I'd heard Mum's friend Maureen saying she'd had a night of passion with Ged from the Elephant and not to tell their Tony. Something told me that if I said this now Mum'd protest that it wasn't becoming for a ten-year-old, so I just shook my head and shrugged. Our Joey stepped forward and opened his mouth. Surely he wasn't going to tell her the truth, was he? He'd confided in me only the night before that all he wanted for Christmas was a horse-riding Barbie. He'd sworn me to secrecy over it, because if anyone found out he would a) get his head kicked in and b) get his head kicked in again. But he opened his mouth and instead of telling the truth and saying, 'I might only be eight, but I'm the biggest poofter on the block and would therefore like a horse-riding Barbie with a poseable body and moveable arms,' he said:

'All I want for Christmas is a kiss from Nona Newman.'

Oh God. I actually felt physically sick. My brother, much as I loved him, and much as he was kind of my best friend in the whole wide world, always knew which buttons to press to get people on his side. I knew now that Nona Newman would be putty in his hands.

And indeed she was. She stretched out both her arms – no mean feat through a car window – and beckoned my little brother towards her with a very theatrical cry of, 'Come here, my little soldier!' Which he did. Though how many soldiers were known to skip rather than march I didn't know. Mum was bubbling with excitement and pride as she watched her youngest being kissed by none other than Nona Newman. Problem was, Our Joey was a bit too tiny to reach up through her window.

'Lift him up, Mum,' Nona encouraged. Mum stepped forward and hoisted Our Joey aloft so he came in line with Nona's lips, and when she eventually put him down again he had an orange lip mark on his forehead. I jealously saw that she was now holding his hand through the window. It looked quite awkward, but neither of them seemed to mind. She had this weird black velvet coat thing on with a wizard's sleeve effect, which would have looked hideous on Mum or me, but sort of worked on her.

'What do you want to be when you grow up, kid?' Nona asked.

'Like you,' he bleated. And again I felt sick. He didn't want to be her. He wanted to be Madonna in her 'True Blue' outfits. But Nona nodded as if it was perfectly normal.

'Well, kid. If I can offer you one piece of advice, it's this.'

I glanced over at Fat Bloke. He was seething with jealousy. Nona Newman had obviously never kissed him or given him advice. Mum was almost crying by now.

'What, Nona?' asked Our Joey. Blimey, he was on first-name terms with her now.

'That's not her real name!' barked Fat Bloke. 'That's her character's name. Her real name's Yvonne Carsgrove, God! GET IT RIGHT!'

Mum looked like she might punch him and said, 'All right, Tubby love. Wind your neck in!'

Nona clasped Our Joey's hand so tight I could see the colour draining out of her knuckles, then she offered her words of wisdom.

'Reach for the stars, kid. But remember, be nice to the people you meet on the way up, coz you only meet the same people on the way back down. OK?'

Our Joey nodded, though I could tell he had no idea what she was on about. Mum was nodding her head vehemently, as if she'd been entrusted with the meaning of life itself. I saw her lips move as she mouthed the words back to herself, in case she was asked to repeat it at a later date.

And then Nona's hand slipped away from Our Joey's and disappeared back into the car. As the colour returned to Our Joey's hand, so the window silently slid closed and the car started up again. Nona Newman/Yvonne Carsgrove drove through the gates into Crystal TV and Our Joey stood on the pavement gloating like the cat who'd got the cream.

We hung around for another hour. A few cars came and went, but no one else stopped to say hello and Fat Bloke was convinced they were 'only extras' – whatever that meant – then when it started to rain Mum decided it was time to go home. As we dragged our deckchairs to the bus stop Mum kept wittering on about what a special day it had been and how lovely Nona Newman was. Our Joey kept his mouth shut, which was almost more irritating than if he'd not shut up about his 'special moment'. I thought he was still gloating until he said, 'Nona Newman's breath smells of poo.'

'Joey!' snapped Mum.

'What?'

'That's very unbecoming!'

'Why? I never said shite!'

'JOEY!'

We carried on walking. God the deckchairs were heavy.

'Nona Newman was lovely to you then and that's how you repay her? Joey McGee I am disappointed in you. Very disappointed in you. You had to go and spoil an otherwise perfect day.'

As we waited at the bus stop, Mum took out a cigarette and lit it up. Again the dragon nose. She saw me staring and smiled. I smiled back.

'Mum?'

'What?'

'When I grow up,' I said, 'I'm gonna be an actress. And I'm gonna be in *Acacia Avenue*.'

Mum chuckled, letting the ciggie hang out of the corner of her mouth as she looked in her handbag for her little compact mirror. She got it out and checked her face.

'You daft sod,' she said, but she said it fondly.

I looked out at the empty street. There was nothing to be seen for miles but factory gates and boarded-up buildings. And I thought, Why not? It was only three bus stops away. Why shouldn't I? The teachers at school were always asking us what we wanted to be when we grew up. Everyone else in my class used to say they wanted to work at the ciggie factory like their mams and dads, but I was going to be different. From now on I'd say I was going to be like Nona Newman and be an actress in *Acacia Avenue*. What was so weird about that?

And maybe, if I wished for it hard enough, one day it would actually come true.

PART ONE

ONE

2012

Keep it all in, Jodie. Keep it all in. Deep breaths, you're going to be fine. Just get through this and then the rest of your life can begin.

I opened my eyes. I'd arrived.

The noise from the screaming fans outside the Royal Albert Hall was so high-pitched I thought my eardrums might explode. Thank God I wasn't epileptic or the constant flash of paparazzi bulbs would surely have sparked a seizure. I squinted my way through the melee, convinced that every picture being taken would show me blinded by the glare, a hostage seeing daylight for the first time. It had only just stopped bucketing it down, so with every step my heels dug further and further into the squidgy red carpet that felt like it was actually sucking me in. What a great look. Jeez. What was I doing? Pressing grapes or arriving at the National Soap Awards? Hands punched forwards from the barriers on either side of the carpet, waving scraps of paper, autograph books, pens and camera phones. It would have been quite scary if I wasn't so dazed.

'Jodie! Jodie! Over here, Jodie!'

I turned towards the voice and stopped side on to the

cameraman, maintaining the fixed smile I'd had on my face since stepping out of the limo.

'You look gorgeous, Jodie!' someone screamed.

And so would you, I thought, if you'd spent three hours in a hotel room being primped, plucked and backcombed to within an inch of your life. I'd had little say over my look, Crystal TV provided the hair and make-up artists and some top designers had donated the dress and jewellery for free publicity. They'd delivered a van load of stuff to the hotel, and me and my fellow cast mates had fought over who'd wear what. I'm not saying blood was drawn, but a couple of the girls had had to lie down with steaks on their eyes for half an hour afterwards.

Our producer Eva had been adamant that I should look as unlike my character Sister Agatha as possible. And as Sister Agatha was a nun I'd ended up wearing what can best be described as a dwarf's tinfoil hankie with gladiatorally laced high heels. Setting off the look was a diamond-encrusted headband with matching bracelet. I looked like an anaemic Tina Turner entering the Thunderdome.

'We love you, Sister Aggie!' someone screamed.

'Bless you, my child!' I giggled, before being herded inside by an over-enthusiastic runner who got her clipboard caught in my bracelet.

'Sorry, Sister.'

Blimey. Even when I was wearing little more than tit tape, people still thought I was a nun. I looked again and saw that it wasn't a runner but our press officer, Ming.

(Ming rhymed with Sting. Yes, I'd made that mistake, too. She was Chinese, but sounded like Cilla Black.)

'Ming! How many times? I'm not a nun. I'm an actress

who *plays* a nun,' I said as she did a fetching 'disentangling a clipboard from a bracelet' dance I'd not seen before and wasn't likely to ever see again.

'Oh gerrover yourself, Jodie, am only pullinya leg. Now there's looooadsa press hoove gorra lorra questions for you. Come on chuck. And DON'T mention the war. Please.'

(OK, so I'm exaggerating her voice, but she was totally annoying.)

OK. The war. I wasn't to mention what I'd done only this morning. And if anyone did ask I was to answer with a polite, 'Not now, sorry . . .'

'I'm warning you, Jozie,' Ming said as she thrust me forward, 'you've shown us up enough these past twenny-four hours.'

Anyway. I wasn't going to let someone as energy sucking as miserable Ming spoil my fun tonight. I was determined this was going to be the best night of my life. And that included the night I'd found back-to-back reruns of *Hart to Hart* on some cable channel *and* a twenty pound note down the back of the settee.

I, Jodie McGee, had been nominated for Best Actress at the National bloody Soap Awards. *ARGH!*

It was pandemonium in the foyer. Ming pushed me through a cattle market of emaciated babes in too much make-up and too little clothing and identikit muscled hunks bursting out of their dinner jackets. God I wanted a drink. I had promised myself I wouldn't touch a drop till after my award was announced. I was 90 per cent sure I wouldn't get it and that heifer from *EastEnders* would, but I thought I'd better steer clear of the sauce just in case.

Ming steered me into a side room, which had a bank of besuited and be-ballgowned radio and TV journos penned in behind a cordon, cameras and microphones at the ready.

'Remember,' Ming whispered in my ear, 'there's no competition between us, *Corrie* and *EastEnders*. There's a lorra lovintharoom.'

I rolled my eyes, stepped into the pen and beamed at the gurning simpleton from *On The Sofa with Colin and Carol*, who'd decided to dress as a big bar of pink soap for the occasion.

'Everybody, look, it's Jodie McGee who plays Sister Agatha in *Acacia Avenue*!' She beamed into the camera, then turned to me with all the fluidity and grace of the tin man. 'So, Jodie, can I just say you look amazing.'

I fluttered my eyelashes and shot a 'What, these old rags?' grimace to camera.

'Thanks . . .' But I couldn't remember her name. I couldn't say Gurning Simpleton, so I just gurned back at her and said it again: 'Thanks,' which made it sound like I was being uber sincere. Back of the net!

'So, Jodie. Great piece on *Brunch With Bronwen* this morning. You've had a lot of hits on YouTube already. Have you got the police involved yet?'

'No comment. Sorry.'

She could see it would be like getting blood out of a stone, so . . .

'So, Jodie. Who's going to win Best Actress?'

'Well' – Damn, if only I could remember her name – 'it's a really tough year and a really tough category, but I thought Colette Court was *to die for* in those wonderful rape scenes.'

Oh God. Did I really say that? Gurning Simpleton was poking me with her mic again.

'So the rivalry between *Corrie*, *EastEnders* and *Acacia Avenue*. That's just something that's made up by the press?'

I smiled my best Sister Agatha beatific smile and suddenly remembered the interviewer's name.

'Stephanie. Colette Court and I really are best buddies.'

The words almost choked me. I was desperate to add, Even if she does sound like a block of flats. I clocked Gurning Simpleton frowning and miming a hacking movement at her throat.

'OK, can we re-record that?' she said to her cameraman, then looked to me. 'My name's Penny?'

Suitably humbled, or at least pretending to be, we continued.

Twenty minutes later I was in the bar.

'It's not going your way. I know it's not going your way. Don't ask how I know.' Eva Hart the producer of *Acacia Avenue* (AKA my boss) took a big swig of her champagne and my balloon of pride was burst. She'd poked it with a pin, and now she was poking me with a finger. What was it with all the poking tonight?

'OK, you dragged it out of me. Lisa in the office's boyfriend knows someone who knows someone who actually does thingy.' She snapped her fingers, searching for the word. 'ENGRAVES!' she screamed. 'He engraves . . . the awards. He's an engraver, he does ENGRAVING. And she swears blind he had to ask if there was one or two 'L's in Colette. What do you think of THAT?'

Eva had a very annoying habit of shouting words she wanted to emphasize. I shrugged coyly.

'She was really good at getting raped.'

Eva practically spat out her champagne.

'BOLLOCKS! She was just lit well.' I didn't dare disagree. This was my boss after all. She leaned in conspiratorially.

'Anyway, fuck Colette Court, I've got big plans for you, Jodie. Big, big plans. The writers heart you. They do, they HEART you. And they have got VERY big plans for Sister Agatha.'

'Ooh that sounds fun. Like what?'

Eva leaned in even further. 'I suppose you've heard there's a serial killer hitting the Avenue?'

I had. It was all we'd discussed in the green room for weeks. Rumours were spreading like wildfire about who'd be killed off. Every day a cast member would come in to work and be convinced they'd seen an early draft of a script in which they were for the chop, or someone else was for the chop. Maybe if I won the award tonight I'd be saved the chop.

'Well, people have been talking.'

Eva's eyes narrowed.

'Shit! Did anyone from *EastEnders* hear?' She looked around furtively as she raised her champagne flute to her lips. 'Who told you we were planning a serial-killer story? Who's leaking stuff to the actors? Oh, this won't do, this WON'T do.'

'No, Eva, I didn't know for—'

'I can't possibly tell you who's going to be the killer or who's going to be KILLED.'

'Eva, no one's leaking stories.'

Eva rearranged the collar on her electric-blue Bacofoil two-piece.

'Suffice it to say I want you in my office tomorrow at TEN,' Eva continued.

'Eva. About this morning. When I was on *Brunch With Bronwen*. I—'

'Don't piss on my chips, Jodie! We'll discuss it tomorrow at TEN.'

Ten? Blimey, I'd better not have a hangover and oversleep, I thought. Getting back to Liverpool for ten meant getting a train at some ungodly hour. Was it even worth going to bed?

'We're gonna make sure Sister Agatha keeps on growing and stays right at the heart of the show as an FCC.'

'FCC?'

'Front Cover Character. I want you on all of them, darling, ALL of them.'

'OK, Eva. Great.'

But how would I be at the centre of the show? Were they going to make *me* the serial killer? Or have me bumped off by said killer? I started to shake with nerves. Just then Eva's handbag vibrated and she yanked out her phone. She jabbed it a couple of times, then threw her head back and guffawed.

'Look at that. Look at THAT.' She shoved her phone in front of my nose. 'Aren't my kids ADORABLE?'

I really wanted to push her away from me and say, 'Actually, can I just have five minutes? I've been really looking forward to tonight. It's a really big deal for me to be nominated for this award and yet you've just told me in no uncertain terms that I haven't won it. I just need five minutes to process that. Plus you're confusing me with your serial killer musings . . .'

But instead I was looking at an image on her phone of three toddlers holding up a sign saying, 'We Miss You, Mummy'. They weren't adorable, even if Eva had signed them up with a kiddies modelling agency, but then I wasn't really the maternal sort. I got into trouble last year when a former cast member paraded her new baby up and down *Acacia Avenue* to adoring wails from present cast members about how cute and angelic-looking he was. I spoke before I thought and said, 'Ooh, isn't she fat?', which had triggered the former cast member to burst into tears and run to the green room, clutching her baby to her bosom.

On the back of that I guessed honesty wasn't the best policy with my boss. Eva's kids were very important to her. I knew every mother would say the same about their kids, but Eva had adopted hers from Lithuania. It had been all over the papers at the time because Eva was in her early sixties, so her biological clock had ticked itself out decades earlier and no British adoption agency would touch her with a very long bargepole. Plus she was single, all of which meant she was the devil incarnate as far the press was concerned. Eva was, in her own words, 'a ball-busting media bitch who took no prisoners,' so I heard myself saying, 'God, Eva, I want your kids.'

'You can have them. An episode fee each. Only KIDDING!' And she poked me again. I'd been Eva'd.

'I think you've done something really amazing there, Eva.' I smiled and she smiled back.

'I've got it all, Jodie. Got it all. And I just wanna share it with someone, you know?'

She had lowered her voice and in that moment she sounded almost human. But then she saw someone more important than me and sprinted over to speak to them.

Left alone in the melee, I looked across the room and saw none other than Colette Court sweep into the room in lots of mushroom-coloured tulle, a tiara perched on her jet black beehive, looking like the queen of all she surveyed. And with that lazy eye she surveyed a lot. I smiled and when I thought she was looking over at me I raised my glass of orange to her, which is when I realized she wasn't looking at me, she was looking at a tray of mini burgers, which were heading her way on the arm of a spotty-necked waiter. She appeared to snort the lot. One minute the tray was full, the next it was empty and Colette Court was chewing away like Ermintrude the cow in *The Magic Roundabout*. A voice cooed in my ear, 'I know, babe. How does she stay so slim? She totes has an eating disorder.'

I looked to see who it was. It was my best friend on the show, Trudy. She laughed her head off to show she was being sarcastic, then pecked me fondly on the cheek.

'You look fabulous, babe.'

'Thanks, Trude.'

'Who cares what the papers say? I think you dress really well.'

She cocked her head to one side and rubbed my arm.

'Everyone's saying you haven't won, babe,' and then she quickly added, 'I'm just saying coz I'm your friend, babe. Don't want you to be too disappointed if you don't.'

I gulped and realized I wanted to cry. I looked around the room. Was everyone laughing at me for coming this evening?

I'd looked forward to this night for ages. I was going to be the first person to win Best Actress at the National Soap Awards and then go on to win an Oscar. Fat chance of that now.

I know it sounds daft. But I once met a gypsy in Blackpool who told me that one day I would win an Oscar. Mum reckoned Our Joey had put her up to it, but I had an inkling Gypsy Donna Marie could see the future.

'Anyway,' added Trudy. 'It's the taking part that counts, babe.'

I was starting to cry.

'I have to go the toilet,' I said.

And I legged it.

I sat on the loo for what felt like an eternity and quietly cried my eyes out. I went to text Stu, then realized I couldn't. Not any more. Then I heard some rustling in the cubicle next to me and wondered if it was Colette Court from *EastEnders* chopping out a line of coke. Rumours abounded that she had a drug problem, though I found it hard to believe: she certainly didn't have the figure of a drug addict. Not that it did her any harm, audiences loved her, presumably unthreatened by her ample shape. Just then I heard Eva's voice.

'Can you put me on speakerphone, Ivanka? I want to sing them a LULLABYE.'

Oh no. My boss was phoning her kids from inside a toilet. I heard Eva strain quietly then start to sing, 'Hush Little Baby Don't You Cry'. As she did I heard something falling into water.

Oh God. My boss was singing her kids to sleep while taking a dump. I felt sick. Talk about multitasking. I got up, flushed, unbolted the door and went out to do some damage-repair to my panda eyes. Trudy stood by the basins, touching up her lippy.

'Isn't Stu with you tonight?' she fished.

'No.'

'Why?'

'Did you not see *Brunch With Bronwen*?'

Trudy looked at me. 'God, babe. I've watched it like eighty times on YouTube. So it was true?'

'Well, I wasn't making it up.'

She rubbed my arm and cocked her head to one side again.

'Oh, babe. It was really brave of you to try and have a boyfriend who wasn't in the business. But, babe, people like us aren't meant to date civilians.'

She turned back to her other best friend, the mirror, and added, 'So, did he find out about your little . . . affair and stuff?'

I was about to argue with her – I had not been having an affair – but before I could say anything she was talking again.

'You know what you need, babe?'

I chuckled and examined my chest in the mirror. 'A boob job?'

Trudy laughed. 'Apart from that, babe!' And she opened her massive handbag. I peered inside. It was completely full of miniatures. (Drinks. Not miniature anything else, like miniature furniture. That would have been weird.)

She winked at me.

'A drink.'

I smiled. Maybe she was right.

An hour later and boy was I feeling a lot better. I think I'd had five miniatures by then. Or maybe six. Enough to feel nice and warm. Like on Christmas Day. But a nice Christmas Day. Not the sort of Christmas Day where your husband beats you up or your dog eats the turkey. You know, the sort of Christmas Day you might get on *Acacia Avenue* – a nice nostalgic Christmas Day where you've got all the presents you want and you've eaten too much turkey and the dog doesn't fart and your boyfriend isn't, like, 'Give me a blow job during *Victoria Wood*' etc. 'Coz it's, like, women's comedy and it'll help me get into it.'

Like. Go fuck yourself, Stu.

And then I remembered. I wasn't with Stu any more.

God this was a long night. And the seats were really uncomfortable. I was wedged in between that new girl who played the chip shop assistant with OCD whose name I could never remember, and the sweet one who played tearaway Asian teenager Supjit (I was convinced Supjit was a made-up name, invented by lazy/racist storyliners). There was a tribal-istic feeling in the hall, with each quarter of the stalls area holding cast members of the different soaps, penned in like horses on slaughter day, each team power-screaming for their representative nominee as the names were read out. It was getting so heated I half expected to see loo roll and chairs come flying above our heads every time *Acacia Avenue* was name-checked.

I felt my mobile pulse in my bag and pulled it out to check for texts, hoping against hope that it might be from Our Joey.

But no, it was from Jason, who played Dodgy Rog, *Acacia Avenue*'s much loathed drug dealer.

'Nice rack.'

I looked round and saw him sat a few rows behind. He winked and took a swig from a bottle of lager he'd snuck in. I shook my head playfully, then turned back round to see Trudy mouthing, 'D'you want another Absinthe?' I didn't realize how good I was at lip-reading till then and nodded eagerly. She handed me another miniature and I unscrewed the top and glugged it greedily. This stuff was great, it had almost made me forget all my worries over the past few weeks and the upcoming serial-killer story. They were just announcing Best Storyline. As *Acacia Avenue* was declared victorious for its 'evil Pippa escapes from prison and pretends to be her nice identical twin (with tragic consequences for the Nandras)' storyline, the entire cast and crew leapt to their feet in a frenzy of self-congratulation. Cameras zoomed up the aisle towards us and I found myself performing for them, suddenly bursting into tears with pride. The two actresses on either side of me caught on quickly and followed suit. It had the desired effect: a camera jabbed in our faces, beaming our tears into millions of living rooms. Eva, some of the writers and the actresses who played Pippa and Feroza Nandra practically flew towards the stage, with Eva screaming, 'Can you BELIEVE this? This is SO deserved. SO deserved,' to the wrong area of seating. She was shouting it to *EastEnders*.

'Well done, guys. Well DONE, guys!'

She clearly hadn't put her contacts in. When she reached the stage she screamed into the mic, 'GOD, YOU GUYS GET IT RIGHT SOMETIMES! WOWZER!'

I thought I might be a little bit tipsy because I started to zone out and wonder if Stu might be watching me. Yeah right, Jodie, dream on. If he was watching this he'd probably be sticking pins in a doll of you. I tried to think of something else.

I wondered if Mrs Mendelson might be watching. Mrs Mendelson was my drama teacher in the Nineties. She ran the Myrtle Mendelson School of Drama and Disco, South Merseyside with a rod of iron and a well-oiled metronome in a couple of rooms above a betting shop two nights a week and all day Saturdays. I was her star pupil. No mean feat when, according to Mrs Mendelson, 'South Merseyside is a breeding ground for stars. They've all come from here. Smile!'

At which point her thirty eager students, standing straight backed in rows of five facing her, smiled as though we were on dangerously strong anti-depressants.

'And . . . Look worried!'

The thirty wannabes switched from beaming grins to furrowed brows and lip biting in an instant.

This was one of Mrs Mendelson's techniques: instant emotion.

'You never know when you're going to be called upon to instantly emote. When you are arrested on *The Bill*, when you have to choose which conjoined twin to lose on *Casualty*, even selecting a sweet at The Kabin on *Coronation Street*. Will you have hours to get into character and practice 'the Method'? No. You will have to instantly emote. And . . . be scared!'

The furrowed brows gave way to wide-eyed terror, hands jumped to faces. I whimpered out loud like a kicked puppy.

'Very good, Miss McGee. Never be frightened to make a noise. They can always switch the boom off if they no likey. And relax!'

We relaxed. Mrs Mendelson grabbed her stick and crab-walked to the toilet. This was a little ritual of hers, disappearing to the ladies' room every twenty minutes with her lorry-sized handbag to 'powder my accoutrements'. She was a strange woman, Mrs Mendelson, with her victory-roll hairdo and clip-on earrings that looked like sucked boiled sweets. She had a habit of unclipping them during a lesson and then putting them back on later with not so much as a glance towards a mirror, leaving the earrings at mismatching levels on her ears. She always spoke as if playing to the back row, and had a habit of rolling her Rs so aggressively that strangers passing the Myrtle Mendelson School of Drama and Disco, South Merseyside, might have mistaken it for machine-gun fire. She would return from the toilet cherry red of face, having secretly knocked back some vodka from a hip flask. After each comfort break she'd flop into a chair, come over a bit misty-eyed and regale us with tales of her life in weekly rep in the Fifties and how Sir John Gielgud once made a pass at her then boyfriend when they were in *Salad Days* in Chipping Norton. I loved these tales and would hurry home to repeat them at the dinner table to Our Joey and Mum and Dad. I was really good at taking her off, so even though the family rarely met Mrs Mendelson, they felt they knew her intimately.

I hoped she could see me tonight and be proud. Purists might have poo-pooed her instant emotion technique – I could hardly imagine Fiona Shaw employing it when performing *Medea* – but on a soap like *Acacia Avenue* it was an invaluable tool. I had a reputation at work for being able to cry buckets on cue. When the writers saw how good I was they started writing tears into nearly every episode. Sister Agatha was frequently sobbing over the Godlessness of the world, her ill-fated kiss, and in a recent episode I'd even had to bawl about finding some litter on *Acacia Avenue*, whilst uttering the immortal line, 'Why, dear Lord? Why do they do it?' The memory made me shiver.

Trudy slipped me another Absinthe and again I found my mind wandering back to Stu. In the big scheme of things I should have been married by now. I should have had seven children, three dogs, annual holidays somewhere fancy and a macrobiotic chef. Instead I was twenty-eight, and already washed up and over the hill. I felt like crying.

Suddenly I was being nudged. The Supjit girl leaned in.

'You next, Jodie. Good luck!'

I appeared to have slumped down in my seat. I could see two Trudies and they were both mouthing, 'You OK, babe?'

I tried to sit up. Straight back, eye on the sky, as Mrs Mendelson used to say. Some cheesy pop presenter walked onstage and said, 'And now the award for best dramatic performance by an actress. Let's have a look at the nominations.'

For some reason, I started to giggle uncontrollably.

TWO

The next thing I remember I was waking up. Judging by the strain it took to prise my eyelids apart I guessed correctly that I hadn't taken my false eyelashes off. And judging by the pain in my forehead, something was digging into it – it would appear I still had my diamond-encrusted headband on. I was lying face down on a bed, not my bed. I looked around the room. Oh yes, I was in a hotel. This was the room I'd checked into a few days ago; this was my room in a hotel in central London with a bed and a couch and products in the bathroom. It had a number and I'd ordered a paper for the morning. So far so good. So I couldn't remember going to bed, so what? Lifting my head off the pillow – lilac with black stripes from my mascara, nice – I pushed myself up and looked round the room. There were a few empty glasses on the coffee table and . . .

Oh NO!

There was a brown stain on the bed sheet. What had I . . . then I relaxed when I realized it was just the chocolates they must have put on the pillow the night before in an attempt to be chichi. I turned myself over and sat up and . . .

Shit. Shit shit shit shit shit shit shit.

There was a sleeping man in the bed beside me. And he wasn't Stu.

Shit shittety shittery shit!

Then I remembered that Stu and I had broken up. Still, this was the behaviour of a loose lady, and I was not a loose lady.

SHIT!

I immediately jumped out of bed and . . . whooo . . . started relaxing a little bit more when I realized I was fully clothed. I even had my shoes on, so how much funny business could really have gone on with this strange man? I crept around the room, hoping no floorboards would creak and wake him, and slipped onto the other side of the bed to align my face with his. I approached the task with as much caution as if I were reverse parking. His face was covered with a flipped-up corner of the duvet. As I stepped over his shoes – maybe he'd been less pissed than me; his DJ was hanging on the back of the door, too, most neat – I pulled down the duvet and saw his face.

Oh shit. Shit shit shit shit shit shit SHIT!

I had shared a bed with Jason. He who sent me the text the night before saying, 'Nice rack.' Jason who played drug dealer Dodgy Rog in the show.

Oh BOLLOCKS!

Who knew? Who might have seen us coming back to my room together? Did Trudy see? Did Eva? Oh Christ, Eva! What time was it?! And where was my phone? My bag? I started running round the room in a zigzag fashion, trying to locate both items. If I'd been so drunk I didn't remember getting back to the hotel, was it not also possible that I'd lost everything I had bar the clothes – and diamond-encrusted headband – I stood up in? The noise of gladiatorially laced high heels on Axminster carpet made Jason stir. Then . . . Hallelujah! My handbag, with my phone inside, was on the bathroom floor. I checked the time.

Nine forty-six.

NINE FORTY-SIX!

I was in London. It was nine forty-six. And in exactly four-teen minutes' time I was meant to be having a face-to-face meeting with my boss in Liverpool. Liverpool was a million miles away from London; it would be impossible to get there on time unless I had a tardis.

Shit!

Panic rose in my chest and I saw the phone shake in my hand as I jabbed in a number. Oh well, best to be honest in these situations. Or was it? As I was calling Eva I clocked something on top of the toilet cistern that completely floored me. An oblong of glass about a foot high and engraved, 'The National Soap Award for Best Actress'. Oh no. I had clearly got hammered and stolen it from Colette Court for a laugh. Some joke! How would I get it back to her?

Then on closer inspection I noticed something that made me sink to my knees.

Two words were engraved on the award: Jodie McGee. My eyes flickered between the two words like a spectator at Wimbledon. Yup. The first word said Jodie and the one on the right said McGee. Together that made Jodie McGee. That was my name. I had won the bloody award. I dropped my phone. I grabbed it back and checked my text messages. I had thirty-six unread texts. The earlier ones said things like, 'Well done', 'About time, too' and 'Congrats hun!' The latter ones said, 'How pissed were you?', 'You were hilarious LOL', 'Pisshead!' and 'You showed them!'

I felt sick. Still kneeling in front of the toilet I phoned Eva. After a few rings she answered. Curtly.

'Jodie.'

'Hi, Eva.'

'How's your head?'

'Oh God, I think I've got really bad twenty-four-hour flu or something.'

'Congratulations.'

She said it the way Adolf Hitler might have said it to Winston Churchill when he won the war (or was he dead by then?).

'Thanks,' I replied uneasily.

'I take it you're cancelling our meeting?'

'Oh. Well . . .'

'Well, tough. I don't care what time you get here, just get here and come straight up and see me.'

'Erm.'

'I've got a call waiting from my nanny.' And she hung up.

I hoiked myself to my feet and steadied myself on the sink. I stared in the mirror and got a fright. I looked like a Transylvanian drag queen with bad surgery. I had lipstick all over my chin, panda eyes and, worse still, my hair looked like Melanie Griffiths' in *Working Girl*. I staggered back into the bedroom. Jason was awake now and stretching his arms. He still had his white shirt on and it appeared to have red wine stains all over it.

'Morning.' He yawned and I nodded, saying nothing. 'Jeez, you look shocking.'

I rolled my eyes. He pulled himself up in bed, looking round the room.

'Are you in today?' I asked, as if it was completely normal for us to have shared a bed in a hotel room and be discussing work. He scratched his hair and nodded.

'Not till three. You?'

I shook my head. 'But I've got to go and see Eva.'

He giggled. 'I'm not fucking surprised.'

What did he mean? WHAT DID HE MEAN? OH GOD!

'Anyway. I'd better get back to my room for a shower,' he

said, jumping out of bed. It was then that I saw he was wearing his dress shirt. AND NOTHING ELSE. I felt sick. He shyly turned away so I would only see his (rather pert, it has to be said) buttocks. I turned coyly in the opposite direction and looked up, as if inspecting for cobwebs. Which is when I saw something that put the fear of God into me.

My knickers were hanging from the ceiling fan.

On the train back to Liverpool I got my iPad out and decided to write some lists. God I felt sick. I was fully aware that people were staring at me. At first I thought it was because they recognized me as Sister Agatha, even though I was wearing shades and a baseball cap, but then I discovered I had a Tampax stuck to my Mulberry handbag. I flicked it off. Today was not going well.

So. That list. Life felt more achievable when you made lists. OK, so:

Bad Things About Last Night
- I got very drunk on live TV and don't remember anything.
- I slept with Jason. Although Jason is fit he is a dirty get and will shag anything that moves. He even shagged Morag in Costume and she's the double of Jeanette Krankie (as a little boy) so this is not good. (Slept = sharing a bed. Have decided that just coz not wearing knickers, doesn't mean sex was had. Even if knickers were on ceiling fan as if thrown off lasso style as part of high-jinks jiggery-pokery business.)

Good Things About Last Night
- I won an award.
- I beat Colette Court.
- I did not lose my handbag.

- I did not lose my phone.
- I did not lose my award.
- I did not lose the free clothes given to me by top designers.
- I did not lose jewels.
- Nobody thought I was a bad person because of what I did on *Brunch With Bronwen*.
- Mind you, they might have, but I can't really remember.

OK, so I was trying to make the second list longer in a desperate attempt to feel good about myself, but guess what? It worked. My positive list outshone my negative list. The pros outweighed the cons. Hoorah! A good night then!

My phone flashed to say I had an answerphone message. I listened to it. It was Dad. In a very sombre tone he said, 'I don't care what the extenuating circumstances are. You have brought shame on me, on the family and on nuns.'

Shit, what did I say? Stu had said I should look at YouTube. Maybe tomorrow. Stu was quite sweet when I'd called. I'd waited till Jason had left my room before trying and had reached him at work.

'Hello?'

Usually he'd answer and go, 'Ryan Phillipe speaking?' Not today.

'Stu, it's me. What did I do?'

'Jodie?'

As soon as he said my name I could hear laughter in the background.

'Is that Jodie, Stu?'

'Is she still pissed, dude?'

'Piss off, knobheads!' Stu shouted in his own inimitable cockney brogue. (Unless you are from London, or are good at accents, in which case it was imitable.)

'Stu, what did I do?' I repeated, more insistent.

'Jodie, I can't really speak now,' he whispered. 'Why don't you have a look at YouTube?'

'YouTube?!' I cried. 'Am I on YouTube?'

'Do you not remember phoning me?'

I gulped. No. Oh God, I must have done drunk dialling. It's almost as dangerous as drunk driving, except that the only thing it damages is your ego.

'Yeah, you phoned me about midnight, crying?'

'What was I saying?'

'You were like, "They love me", "Everyone's so nice".'

'OK.' God I sounded like a complete and utter *actress*.

'But, Jodie, you made your feelings quite clear the other day. It's not my responsibility to make you feel better any more. You completely showed me up, I've got the police on my back and I think that's really unfair. I did apologize. I did try to make it up to you.'

'I'm sorry,' I bleated. I really did. I sounded like a sheep. I cleared my throat and said it again a bit louder, as though I meant it. I heard him sigh.

'Jodie, I've gotta go. We've got a big meeting at half past.'

'OK,' I said, with more than a hint of desperation, and he hung up. Oh well, I left him. He had every right to not say goodbye. Or congratulations, come to think of it. And then I remembered something, and I wondered why I was being so reasonable with him. I must still have been drunk. I texted him angrily:

Jodie: 'I found the bag in the loft.'

He texted back.

Stuart: 'I have no idea what you're talking about.'
Jodie: 'Have a nice life, liar.'

A woman walked past me on the train. She did a double take, realizing who I was, then burst out laughing. I was determined to ignore this. If I thought everything was fine, then everything would be fine. It was a philosophical thingamajig. Think something hard enough and it will happen. You might call it burying your head in the sand; I call it something intellectual, so it sounds better and more plausible. Ish.

I looked down at my iPad and deleted the two lists. The press office kept phoning and leaving messages, but I didn't listen to them. Not yet. I also averted my eyes every time I saw someone in the carriage holding a tabloid.

My phone started vibrating again. I saw it was a call from Trudy so I answered it.

'Babe, do you feel like killing yourself?'

'Er . . . No. I just . . . can't remember what happened.'

'You won, babe. We were all so amazed. I would never have given you all that drink you kept asking me for if I'd thought you were going to win. I feel so bad. Forgive me?'

'Of course I forgive you, Trudy.'

'Did you sleep with Jason last night?'

I wanted the ground to open and swallow me up for about the 398th time that day.

'No. I don't know. What do you know?'

'He's saying you did, babe. He said you were, like, really out of it.'

'What? He's going round telling people?'

'No, he only told me, babe. As far as I know.'

'What? He called you?'

'No, he texted.'

'He just decided to send you a text saying he'd slept with me?'

'No, babe, I texted him. I wanted to check you were OK, babe. You were so out of it last night and I feel responsible.' She sounded quite sweet really. Until she added, 'Although an expert would probably say, you know, an alcoholic is responsible for their own drinking problem.' Then she added brightly, 'Not that I'm saying you're an alkie, babe!'

'I had eight miniature absinthes. I got drunk. I'm not Carrie Fisher.'

'Oh, babe, do you remember dancing on the bar at the Club at the Ivy?' She laughed her head off. 'Is it any wonder you were thrown out?' And she laughed her head off again. 'God you are hilarious, Jodie. I love you so much, babes.'

The list of the previous night's misdemeanours was growing by the minute.

'What's Eva said?'

'She wants me to go in this afternoon.'

'Babe. I don't think she'll fire you. I think she kind of quite likes you deep down. And anyway, it would make no sense to fire you. You're the best actress in a soap.'

I was about to ask Trudy what I'd actually done last night, but I stopped myself. I suddenly got the feeling she'd enjoy telling me too much. And besides, I didn't want to know. I found myself mimicking her voice.

'Babe? I've really gotta shoot. I've got, like, twenty odd people queuing for an autograph.'

I looked up the empty aisle and was surprisingly pleased to hear the sting in Trudy's voice.

'Babe that's fine. I'm really proud of you winning Best Dramatic Performance. I'm just really jealous coz, like, my character's a comedy character? And comedy's, like, the *hardest*? But well done you, babe. You totes deserve it. Kisses!'

'Kisses!' and I hung up.

I tried to think back to other times that I'd showed myself up on booze. I made another list on my iPad.

Times I Have Shown Myself Up on Booze

1   Last year. Got steaming at Tom Turner's eightieth birthday party (Tom Turner played one of the old men on *Acacia Avenue;* he was one of the first people to appear on the show a zillion years ago). I nicked his walking stick and did a dance to 'Thank You For The Music', then wheeled him round in his wheelchair in time to the music whilst high kicking. NB. I remember everything and Tom thought it was hilarious, despite the coughing fit, and said he hadn't laughed so much in years. When he died suddenly a week later people said at his funeral how excitable he'd seemed that day.

2   When I was about twenty-five (well, it was about three years ago) I got wrecked at Creamfields with Stu and neither of us can remember getting home. But we did. NB. Stu was as bad as me that night.

3   My first year at drama school I once drank a whole bottle of gin and passed out on a piece of grass in King's Cross. NB. Am amazed there was actually a piece of grass in King's Cross.

So all in all I'd had, like, four bad experiences on the booze. Or was I in denial? Was I ignoring other incidents where I'd felt bad about my level of drinking? As I racked my brains I fell asleep. When I woke, the train was pulling into Lime Street Station. I had a thread of saliva linking my mouth to my cardigan, and someone had stuck the Tampax that had been on my bag onto my forehead.

I took a cab straight from the station to the TV studios. And even though I was in the back of a minicab driven by a Nigerian guy who kept telling me that Jesus forgave me, I still savoured the feeling of excitement as I drove into Crystal Studios. As we glided towards the barrier it magically rose, allowing me to sail through, past all the autograph hunters at the gates. Those people who believe they love you, even though they don't know you. I felt a pang of guilt that we hadn't stopped to sign their books – I had been one of them once – but today I was a woman on a mission. I paid the driver, hopped out and ran towards the green room entrance, waving quickly to the security guard who'd raised the barrier for me before diving inside amidst shouts of, 'Jodie! Can I have your autograph, Jodie? Jodie!'

I avoided the green room itself – too many colleagues ready to gloat no doubt – and hurried through the maze of corridors towards my dressing room. From the teal walls, black and white photographs of former cast members looked down on me, each of them looking more and more furious. The familiar studio smell of burning charcoal and disinfectant got stronger and weaker as the maze of corridors took me closer and then further away from the studio floor. At one sharp corner I turned and bumped into someone hurrying towards me, not looking where he was going. As we collided and he squealed like a girl I realized it was Jason.

'All right?'

He got his composure back and gave me daggers, as if he was chastizing me for not looking where I was going.

'Why did you tell Trudy we slept together?' I asked. He looked taken aback. 'Coz she asked if you were OK and I said

I'd made sure you'd got to bed, and then she went on and on about it.'

I looked up the corridor. There was nobody about. I heard a catch in my voice as I asked, 'Jason, what did we do? Did we shag?'

He chuckled and pushed his hand forward. I thought he was going to smooth my hair away from my face, but he missed my head and I realized he was moving to lean against the wall.

'That memorable, huh?'

I rolled my eyes and felt like slapping him. 'Just answer the bloody question. I've got to see Eva Braun in ten minutes.'

'Jodie. Relax. We didn't do anything.'

'But you didn't have any undercrackers on and my knickers were hanging off the ceiling fan. That doesn't say "nothing" to me.'

'Jodie, we were too pissed to do anything. We were just messing about. You put Ace of Base on the stereo and we did competitive dirty dancing before collapsing in hysterics on the bed. The next thing I knew I woke up.'

'We did what?'

'Competitive dirty dancing. It's like stripping. Only we didn't manage to get much off as we were pissing ourselves so much.'

I felt almost disappointed. 'So we didn't kiss?'

He shook his head. 'I'm a bit gutted about that.'

'Jason, I've got a boyfriend.' Then I realized that wasn't true and corrected myself. 'OK. I haven't, any more. Sorry.'

It felt so weird saying it. It was all so new to me. I carried on, 'Anyway, you've got . . .'

'Two girlfriends, I know. Still, it's nice to have memories.'

I suddenly found myself warming to him. He was quite sweet really, and his smile was adorable. I leaned forward and ruffled his hair. He seemed to like it; he was one of the few guys

I've done it to that didn't flinch. I was so relieved we'd not done naughties I leaned forward and pecked him on the cheek.

'Thanks, Jase,' I said and headed for my dressing room. When I was further up the corridor I heard him call after me.

'You give great head, Jode. You just need to work on your anal.'

I stopped dead in my tracks, then heard him burst out laughing. I rolled my eyes, stuck the key in my dressing room door and disappeared inside.

My dressing room wasn't big enough to swing a gerbil in, never mind a cat, but the even bigger pisser was I had to share it with Precious O'Dowd, who played ex-hooker turned foster carer Hattie on the show. Three of her wigs sat on stands on the dressing table. The only decent thing about sharing these tiny cubicles was that the assistant director, who was in charge of dressing rooms, always tried to link up sharers who were rarely in scenes together, so they were less likely to be filming at the same time. I was quite lucky with Precious, who was prone to leaving me little presents on the tiny settee – magazines, cupcakes, make-up samples – and her personal hygiene was second to none. Trudy, on the other hand, had to share with Julie Jackson, who claimed she'd not washed her hair for fifteen years. Trudy reckoned when Julie took her tights off at the end of a day's filming, they walked themselves to the wardrobe before dying from her gusset fumes. Julie also had the annoying habit of graffiti-ing on her own walls. Trudy wasted no time in spreading it round that Julie was on smack. I knew how lucky I was sharing with someone as thoughtful as Precious. The only presents Julie left Trudy were, let's just say, located in the toilet. Nice.

I always kept an emergency smart outfit in the dressing room in case I was called away at a minute's notice to go and open a new hospice or something, and it was this that I changed into now. OK, so it made me look a bit like Maggie Thatcher in the early days, but the slit skirt at least made me a rather slutty Maggie. I spritzed myself with some of Precious's fancy spray from Liberty's, then stepped into her very elegant navy high heels. It was pointless borrowing any of my frumpy costume. Two slate-grey habits hung on a rail behind me. Neither was going to show the boss I meant business.

As I stepped before my full-length mirror looking as if I was about to address a Tory party conference, the idea of competitive dirty dancing re-entered my head. The relief of discovering Jason and I had shared this rather than bodily fluids was sweeter than wine. I found myself chuckling. You see, this was the problem with the dreaded booze. You thought you'd done all sorts of shocking things when actually you'd been quite sensible. Well, as sensible as you can be when you're stripping to Ace of Base and chucking your knickers skyward.

I checked my watch. I'd emailed Eva and suggested I see her at two, and she'd agreed. I had ten minutes to kill. A small pile of fan mail was sitting on the dressing table. I opened the first letter to find a childish scrawl.

Dear Sister Agatha,
    I like you coz you like Jesus. I like it when you cry and that.
You should marry Father Ricky. Lol.
    Matthew Graham.
    PS Please can I have a photo and that.

I stuck it in my in-tray and opened another.

Dear Ms McGee,
    I love the carpet you have in the prayer meeting room at
the church hall. Please can you advise me whence it came?

Again, in-tray. Another.

Dear Jodie,

I have now written you three letters and each one you have
ignored. I don't see what your problem is, bitch. All I want is a
picture of your snatch.

I crumpled it up and chucked it in the bin, then checked my
watch again. OK, so if the next letter was sweet . . . it meant
that everything was going to be OK. I ripped it open.

Dear Jodie McGee,

I am writing to you from Broadmoor Security Hospital.
Don't worry, I'm not in for anything too bad! I'm not a
paedophile. Well, I guess it depends how you define paedophile.

Straight in the bin.

I wasn't filming today, everyone else was shooting the
scenes for Supjit's Hindu Hen-do, and Sister Agatha hadn't
been invited since their contretemps over the tinned peaches
in the late-night grocer's.

I checked my watch. Ergh. Time to go down. And not in a
good way.

Eva's assistant did something she'd never done before. She let
me wait in Eva's office till she arrived. So this is what happened
when you'd won a major award – bring it on! Usually no one
was allowed through those hallowed portals unless Eva was
there, larger than life with her Eighties gelled perm. I tiptoed
round the room and looked at the various family photos
adorning the walls. There were a few other shots, too, from
her days on *Pets Win Prizes* – Eva grinning maniacally with her

arms round a reluctant dachshund; Eva holding a Hula Hoop up while a rabbit jumped through it. Suddenly the door swung open and Eva bustled in, clouds of Chloé swishing before her.

'God I feel like shit. My cheeky bitch of a NANNY decided to have a day off. Can you BELIEVE that? Two ticks,' she said and angrily jabbed at her BlackBerry a few times. She kicked off her shoes and yawned. It was then I noticed someone else entering the room. Ming.

'I asked Ming to join us.'

'Hiya, Jodie. Yarice?'

I nodded.

'I've been calling you all zay,' Ming continued.

'My phone! It's, like, completely screwed.'

'Phones! Warradee like?'

'I know.'

It was then that Ming looked me up and down and took in my Thatcheresque look. I dared her to say something. What was wrong with trying to look professional at a meeting with your boss? She giggled and shook her head.

'Jesus. Worruv you come as?'

While Ming and Eva sat tapping in unison on their Black-Berries I looked at the photos again. God, Eva was facially challenged. I looked back at my boss, who was now spraying her mouth with breath freshener.

'Ah. That's a lovely picture of you, Eva,' I said, pointing to one of the photos on the wall. 'You really suit glasses.'

Eva's face froze.

'That's my ex-husband.'

Ming nodded. 'Before the gastric banz.'

I wanted the ground to open up and swallow me.

'Sorry. It's me who needs the glasses. Course it is.' And then I added, 'He's really handsome.'

Ming looked like I was mad while Eva nodded. She was certainly thick-skinned.

'Was,' she corrected. 'He's dead now.'

'Oh. He doesn't look it in the picture.' I heard my voice trail off mid-sentence.

Eva pointed to a chaise longue at the side of the room. I sat on it awkwardly while Eva took a deep breath.

'Here's the thing.'

I smiled my best Sister Agatha smile.

'As you know, Jodie. We had big plans for Sister Agatha.'

Oh God. Did she just say *had*?

'People love you, Jodie. They LOVE you. And the writers had come up with a story that was going to build on your wonderful news from last night and really THRUST you to the centre of the show.'

I nodded, excited. Suddenly the sleep-free anxiety from the night before was extinguished like a ciggie in the snow.

'You said last night—'

'They wanted to make you a serial killer. As you know, on *Acacia Avenue* we like to keep it real. So . . .'

Oh yeah, really real. A serial killing nun?

'Let's be honest, Jodie. You're were never going to stay on this show for ever.'

True. Did someone mention Hollywood?

'I'm not asking to leave, Eva.'

'You probably had two years MAX left with us, before you went and became a cardiothoracic specialist on some piece of medical GARBAGE.'

Er no, I was going to crack America? I was going to be the new Angelina Jolie or Cameron Diaz.

'And then you'd've got bored and wanted to come back here when they fired you coz . . . oh I dunno, you got completely PISSED at some AWARDS ceremony and make a total TIT of yourself and the SHOW and everything it STANDS for . . .'

She sounded bitter. Or should that be BITTER?

'. . . and the work dried up. Do you understand what I'm saying?'

I shrugged. 'Well . . .'

'Making you a serial killer – a nun with a screw loose – meant we could bump off all the actors that were getting on my TITS, Jodie, and give you a really interesting story to play. After two years you'd go to PRISON and we'd look away from Sister Agatha. And then a few years later, when you were DESPERATE FOR MONEY, Nun Features would be released for good behaviour, BLAH BLAH BLAH. And you could come back to the show.'

I have to admit, I was struggling to get my head round the rationale.

'The story was going to get everyone TALKING. It was going to make you HUGE, darling. If I was you I'd've been THRILLED. Wouldn't she have been thrilled, Ming?'

Ming nodded. 'Maze up, like.'

I wasn't really sure what Eva was saying. It sounded like this wasn't a story that was any longer on offer. I played dumb.

'I think I need to let it settle in,' I said.

Eva shook her head. 'That was all on the table till last night. Today, I have different news for you.'

She smiled. She was enjoying this.

'Now. Because of your APPALLING, UNFORGIVABLE, TWATTY behaviour last night, you will no longer be the serial killer.'

I relaxed. Every cloud!

'You will be the serial killer's first victim.'

I felt faint suddenly.

'I'm going to . . . die?'

Eva nodded.

'Next week. The writers are reworking the scripts as we speak. If I were you I'd start packing your bags.'

'You're firing me?'

'Firing's a dead strong werd,' said Ming.

'But I've just won Best Actress in a Soap. Wouldn't it make more sense to keep me here for—'

Eva cut in. 'Jodie, do you actually know what you did last night?'

'Well . . .'

'Hmm?'

'No.'

She nodded. 'Then before you start arguing with me, I suggest you have a little look on YouTube.'

'Right.'

'Leave.'

I headed to the door.

'I've . . . been under a lot of strain recently,' I tried.

'I know, which is why I gave you two weeks off and a written warning. I don't give a shit what's going on at home, Jodie. You don't bring it to the office. Or the awards ceremony.'

'Or *Brunch With Bronwen*,' agreed Ming, nodding.

Eva smiled. 'Oh, and Jodie. About what you said last night.'

I turned round to see what she was going to say. She was still smiling, like one of the dreadful baddies on the show.

'Embarrass me again and I'll hunt you down and . . .' the smile broadened.

'Yes?'

'I'll kill you.'

*

I phoned for a cab. Driving out of the studios I decided to stop and sign some autographs for the fans. After all, I'd been one of them once upon a time. And this might be one of my last ever chances. One of them thrust a leaflet into my hand. I opened it to find an advert for Alcoholics Anonymous. I looked back at him.

'It helped me,' he mouthed.

I looked away and told the driver to go to Mum's. I phoned her and she answered.

'Hello?'

'Mum, it's me.'

'Oh, Jodie.' She sighed, uber disappointed. I burst out crying.

'Mum? Can I come home? I've been fired!'

'Oh, Jodie.' And she sounded even more uber disappointed. Kids. Always a disappointment, eh? Or maybe it was just me.

THREE

I was born in a Spam-coloured dormer bungalow on a Spam-coloured street. My dad is called Alan and my mum is called Sandra. Our dormer bungalow had a name: Sandalan – a mixture of their names. They thought it made the dormer bungalow sound exotic. Me and my brother were just plain mortified by it. Whereas other people would say, 'Oh, we live at thirty-nine Flaxton Road,' our parents would insist on saying, 'Oh, we live at Sandalan, Flaxton Road.' The dormer bungalow also sported a wagon wheel on the front of the house. (Not the chocolate biscuit, an actual wooden wheel painted white with a hint of Spam.)

OK, so you might be wondering what a dormer bungalow is. It's a bungalow, but it has an upstairs. In reality what we lived in was a house, but Mum always insisted on calling it a dormer bungalow. This, she felt, made it sound classier.

You see, my Mum had 'opinions' and she was pretty much immovable where they were concerned. No matter how I tried to chip away at them, they remained resolute. Any challenges I made bounced off her like hailstones off a windscreen. It's not that she was hard-faced, she was too soft and mumsy for that, it's just that she knew her own mind. Her opinions were like mantras and she'd chuck them at anyone who'd listen, taking a kind of scattergun approach to making her point. Her opinions included:

1 Anything vulgar, lewd or obscene is 'unbecoming'. (As in, 'I do not like this dirty lady dancing in her altogether at the beginning of *Tales of the Unexpected*. I find her, on the whole, unbecoming.')

2 People are either nice or not nice. There is no in between, i.e., Terry Wogan is nice. Bette Midler is not nice.

3 Nuns are bad luck, and you must always cross the road when you see one coming. Woe betide you if you see more than one. This might actually signal the end of the world.

4 Small people (or PORGs – Persons of Restricted Growth – as she called them) are good luck charms and you should always try to touch one if you see one out and about.

5 Gay men were women in a past life and now the femininity in them is coming out. Vice versa for lesbians (though she often got this wrong and called them Libyans).

6 Women who wear harem pants look like they have bowel issues and are not to be trusted, particularly in the refrigerated aisle of Kwik Save.

7 We must always avoid all things common: processed cheese, acrylic jumpers, her from number 8 who sweeps the path in her slippers. My Mother was basically a small town snob, which is ironic, considering she came from such a big city.

8 Everything is good in moderation. Too much of a good thing is showing off.

9 The demise of Johnny Matthis's career is one of the tragedies of modern history.

10 The women on *Loose Women* are all sluts (this was a more recent addition).

When I got to Flaxton Road, Sandalan's curtains were drawn, as if the family was in mourning.

As I walked up the path I could see me and Our Joey playing in the front garden all those years before. Him click clacking around in my mother's wedge heels, hands on hips, pretending to be someone from *Acacia Avenue*. Me laughing in his face, insisting that one day I would be in the real thing, not some pretend version in a crappy front garden. And then I had been. And now I wasn't. As I tried to take in this information, our nine-year-old Joey stepped forward and held something out to me. It was a little brown twig with bright green leaves. It was quite, quite beautiful. I looked at it, then looked at him.

'What's that?'

'It's an olive branch,' he said. And he said it so sweetly I could have cried. 'Jodie, I'm sorry we fell out.'

I felt a lump in my throat. All I could think to say was, 'You were my best friend.'

He nodded and I heard the front door opening, then Mum shouting in a whisper, 'For God's sake, Jodie, get inside. You're talking to yourself!'

I looked at her. She was stood on the step, pulling the flaps of her wrapover cardi round herself and checking up and down the street in case any nosey neighbour had seen. Confused, I looked back at the garden. It was empty. I had, of course, been seeing things, imagining Our Joey making a peace offering. All of a sudden a tsunami of tears cascaded down my face. Mum dragged me towards the door and I collapsed in her arms, sobbing my heart out. I felt her freeze beneath me; she wasn't brilliant at dealing with – in her eyes – drama queen daughters, never mind emotions. She pushed me away and I saw I'd stained her cardigan with my mascara. She didn't look happy. I sniffed.

'I think you'd better go in the through lounge.' She sounded so icy. I looked into the lounge. The lighting looked weird, but I ventured in anyway.

Dad was standing by the telly. It was on, but none of the ceiling lights were. The picture on the screen was frozen on an image that was at once familiar and alien. It was the bloody Royal Albert Hall. Mum shut the living room door behind me and they both stared at me. Oh God. They were staging an intervention. They were going to make me watch myself accept my award. Without speaking, I groaned, accepted my fate and sank into an armchair. Suddenly I realized I was sitting on Archie, the family dog. He squealed and scratched my arse, so I moved to the next chair, muttering something about 'the bloody lights in here' while Dad pressed play.

Why the hell did I get them Sky Plus for Christmas? And how on earth did they become so good at using it?

Loud, sweeping music blasted out from the telly, the sort that would accompany a dramatic helicopter ride across the tundra in a Hollywood movie. On screens dotted around the hall you could see the four actresses up for the award. There was a fat girl from *Emmerdale* giving birth to what I took (from the startled looks on the medics' faces) to be a Down's Syndrome baby. Then someone from a medical soap pretending to be a consultant gynaecologist in far too much make-up and fantastic hair (lucky cow), who seemed to be talking a mad axe man out of running riot in ITU. Next up was that really nice actress from *EastEnders* – well, she seemed nicer in defeat – who got a huge roar from the crowd. She was in a shower, made up to look battered and bruised, possibly washing the smell of a rapist off her. Next up was a shot of me, crying, in the middle of the burning church, attempting to douse the flames with some holy water. Again, the audience roared their approval. There was a close-up of me in the audience, clapping myself and smiling for the camera, then raising my hands with my fingers crossed.

'God, I don't look too bad, do I?' I bleated. I heard Mum tut.

The presenter ripped open his golden envelope.

'And the winner is . . .'

Silence. Oh God. I wanted so much to jump up and switch the TV off. What on earth did I do to merit this? But another part of me wanted to savour my moment of glory. And at least see the smirk wiped off Colette Court's face.

'Jodie McGee for *Acacia Avenue*.'

The camera cut back to me again and I appeared to be applying my lipstick. Rather generously. I didn't appear to have realized I'd won. I got nudged by Supjit whatsername, which smudged the lipstick across my cheek. How dare she! And then Trudy leaned in and whispered something in my ear. I looked genuinely dazed and then stood, albeit rather shakily, kicking Supjit's legs so I could get past her. Once in the aisle – needless to say the audience was going wild. Wow! – I did a little victory bum wiggle. I've been known to do this a lot. I'd always thought it made me look like Beyoncé. It didn't. I looked more like Susan Boyle. Except Susan Boyle wouldn't have lipstick all over her face like a mad woman. I then walked down the aisle, smugly high-fiving my fellow cast members, before swapping sides and trying to high-five the cast members from *EastEnders*. They weren't playing ball, and I actually slapped one of them in the face. Oh dear. It was Colette Court. As I pulled my hand back I had her tiara stuck to my hand, but didn't appear to have noticed. Oh but now I had. I suddenly saw it, shrieked and flicked it away like it was a poisonous insect. It flew into the audience and hit someone in the face.

Jesus. And I'd not even reached the stage yet.

It looked like I might not make it that far as I tripped over some camera cables and went base over apex. I disappeared from view and they kindly cut to the other nominees. Usually at this point in the proceedings the other nominated actresses would be looking faux congratulatory, trying to mask their disappointment. These girls weren't, though. Each and every one of them was pissing herself laughing. Even the tiara-less Colette Court. For they knew Sister Agatha was making a holy show of herself.

The next time you saw me I was onstage, hugging the presenter like I'd known him all my life. (I couldn't stand him usually. Too many teeth.) Just as I started dry humping him he pushed me away and practically threw the award at me. Surely it was going to get better from here on in. I started to relax.

But then I opened my mouth and burst out crying. I looked ridiculous. The bottom half of my face was covered in bright red lipstick and now mascara was drenching the top half. Basically, my acceptance speech went something like this:

Me: Through tears, of course.'I am not worthy. I am not worthy. I'm just a little girl from the back streets of Liverpool who dragged herself up by her bra straps.'

I could feel poisonous looks darting from Mum and Dad.

Me: 'So this, this is the stuff of fairytales.'

Oh God. I realized now what I was going to say. Not because I remembered, but because this was a speech I'd written a very long time ago. And not for the National Soap Awards.

Me: 'I'd like to thank my wonderful husband, Tom Cruise.'

I heard Dad wriggle in his seat.

Me: 'Our divine daughters, Tammy-Faye and Honey-Jaye. My bikini waxer. My dog walker. The inspirational Mr Steven Spielberg.'

I wanted the ground to open up and swallow me whole.

Me: 'And to any lonely, ugly little girls out there. Take courage. I used to be you. And look at me now. I'm amazing.'

I needed to kill myself. Now.

Me: 'I stand before you today, proud. Proud of myself and proud of the human race that helped me become . . .

NOW!

Me: 'The worthy winner of an Academy Award.'

And then I waggled the soap award in the air.

Me: 'I love you Oscar!'

The audience roared their approval. Phew, it was over. But then instead of leaving the stage I returned to the microphone.

Me: 'Sorry. One last thing. Our producer, Eva. Eva thingy.

There was a close-up on Eva in the audience, trying to smile.

Me: 'You know? The old-age pensioner who's just bought some kids off the internet?'

Eva's face really had dropped by now.

Me: 'I just want to say. We all call you Eva Braun.'

The audience laughed as the fury froze on Eva's face. Then I raised my right arm, placed a finger over my lips and shouted:

Me: 'Heil Hitler!'

Then I high-kicked off the stage, leaving the award on the lectern. The presenter ran after me with it.

OK, so now I understood why I'd been fired.

Dad switched off the TV. Mum switched on the light. Three pairs of eyes were on me (I'm including the dog there). Mum took my hand, the way people did on *Jeremy Kyle*.

'Jodie, I think you need to do something about your drinking.'

How on earth did I get into this mess? Why had I got myself into such a state on such an important night? What was so bad about my life that I had to run away to the island of annihilation to deal with it? How had I managed to put myself in a position where I'd let down myself, my parents, my friends and got myself the sack to boot?

I excused myself and offered to take the dog for a walk. Sometimes walking round the streets of my childhood could make me feel better. Not this day. I walked and walked for what felt like hours. It felt like an out-of-body experience, seeing the landmarks of my youth: the chippy outside of which I'd had my first snog; the corner where two lads set upon me and nicked my dinner money; the level crossing where the people from number fourteen's dog was run over. But seeing those places today left me unmoved, numb. It was as if they'd never really happened to me, but to somebody else. A while later, the dog stopped to drink some water from a puddle and I realized I must have walked too far, or for too long. I looked up. I was outside my old secondary school. I stared up at the boarded-up windows where once there was bustling life. The dog sat at my feet as if to say, 'Jesus, Jodie. Where the frig have you brought me?'

And I looked down at him and said, 'Archie, this is where it all started to go wrong.'

He looked up at me with those beguiling eyes and said, 'Really, Jodie? Wanna tell me all about it?'

Well, actually, he didn't. Dogs can't speak. But he may as well have done. I knelt beside him and ruffled the top of his head. I looked back up at the boarded-up windows. It had been considered a problem school, and its pupils had long since dispersed to other nearby comps. It was due for demolition and apparently the land was going to be used for a new shopping mall. Right now, though, it looked sad, abandoned and forlorn. Some foliage grew out of the old maths classroom window. That tree knew nothing of the building's past. And yet . . . I remembered . . . I remembered . . . well, I remembered so much.

FOUR

1999

'Donna-Marie Kilpatrick says there's a new lad started today in Mr Taylor's class and he's, like, really, really, fit,' said my best mate Hayls as we touched up our make-up in the girls' loos instead of going to Chemistry.

My other best mate Debs tutted, 'Donna-Marie Kilpatrick's got posters of Philip Schofield in her locker; I'm not gonna listen to her.'

'What colour's that eyeshadow, Debs?' God, I was completely coveting it.

'Azure sunset. Isn't it fab?'

'It's gorge. I heart it.'

'I heart it an' all,' agreed Hayls.

'So what else do we know about this new lad?' I asked as I dusted the finest trace of body glitter onto my cheekbones.

'He's a bit of a bad boy,' said Hayls, excited. 'He's been excluded from St Eddie's for setting fire to something.'

'Ooh, what?' asked Debs.

'Dunno. I think it was, like, a classroom. Or a teacher.'

'Ergh,' I said. 'He'll probably be some full-on scally in a shell suit and trainees.' (We didn't call them trainers, we called them trainees.) The girls nodded in agreement.

On one level I was right. When we first caught sight of him in the canteen at dinner time, Greg Valentine was wearing something approaching sports casual rather than the standard school uniform, and his trainees were Adidas, multicoloured, which some of the lads in the canteen eyed with something approaching lust. What I wasn't prepared for was that he had the face of an angel. Charlotte Church may have had the voice, but Gregory Valentine definitely had the face.

For a start he didn't look English. I'm not being racist pointing that out, it's just he had this sun-kissed mop of blond curls, cut into an attempt at a wedge. The mop fell flatteringly into his eyes, which looked dark and brown, and his eyebrows were similarly at odds with his blonde hair. And the dimples. Oh the dimples! They hadn't just tickled Gregory Valentine with the pretty stick, they'd poked him in either cheek with it, and it had stuck. On paper it sounded so wrong. Blond curly hair. On a bloke. But the reality seemed to be making every girl in the canteen swoon. It was like he walked in and we toppled over in rapid succession, like dominoes.

'He looks like thingy,' said Hayls. 'That fella in *The Blue Lagoon*.'

'I've never been to the Blue Lagoon,' said Debs.

'Not the wine bar on Rose Lane, y'knob, the film. On the desert island. Where they keep shagging.'

Neither of us had seen it. Though from the look on Debs' face, you could tell she thought it sounded good.

'She's in it,' Hayls continued. 'South Shields. Our Andy's got the video.'

We weren't really listening, though. We were too busy staring at Greg. He even had tanned skin. I later found out this was natural; he only had to hear there was a bit of sun outside for him to go the same colour as a mug of Mellow Birds. That's why I thought he didn't look particularly English. Not that we did either, I suppose. Liverpool is practically the capital of Ireland so, in the Caucasian population at least, there's a lot of fair skin, freckles and dark brown hair everywhere.

'He looks like he should be in Abba or something,' Debs said, and she was so right.

'Scandinavian,' I said.

'But with a tan,' pointed out Hayls.

'Tandinavian,' I added, and they both smiled. Suddenly Hayls laughed her head off really loudly, and Greg looked over. So me and Debs laughed our heads off, too, almost crying, clutching onto each other for dear life, such was the force of our hilarity. You see, this was Rule Number One in our flirting book. In order to grab a man's attention, make out you're having the BEST (and noisiest) time. And it worked. Greg bought a sausage roll from the counter – cue Hayls stopping howling with laughter in order to say, 'Sausage rolls. I *love* sausage rolls!' before recommencing with the laughter – checked us out again, possibly thinking we were mad women, and scarpered from the canteen. Which is when our laughter ended as abruptly as it had begun, and everyone else in the canteen eyed us suspiciously, as if they totally knew what we were up to. The three of us sighed, knackered from the exertion.

'He looked straight at me,' said Debs.

'He was like, mentally undressing me,' echoed Hayls.

Whereas actually, I couldn't help but think – I'm not blowing my own trumpet or anything. Why should I? I can't read music – that that young man was *defo* looking straight at me.

It wasn't the most romantic of first encounters. I wished it had been. Like my mum and dad. They'd met on the steps of the Anglican cathedral when he'd been going in for midnight mass and Mum had been collecting money for Dr Barnardo's on the steps on the way in. He was a bit pissed – he'd been on a pub crawl with some of the fellas from work – but he took a bit of a shine to her and tried to put a fifty pence piece in the slot of her box, only he was a bit fingers and thumbs because of the extent of his inebriation and they had a laugh about it. When the service was over he saw her again and slipped her what she thought was a five pound note. But when she looked again it was a corner of the order of service he'd ripped off and scribbled his phone number on. She phoned him a few days later and he took her to a dance at the Rialto. They really hit it off, but there was a spanner in the works because Dad had to go away for two weeks on a training course, so Mum made him promise to write every day. He said he would, but she didn't believe him for one minute. Still, he came up trumps and she still has the fourteen letters to this day. I was always amazed when I read them. He's a man of such few words usually, and yet on paper he was articulacy itself. One day, I decided, I wanted fourteen letters of my own.

The first time I spoke to Greg we were in between classes on the Maths corridor and he was walking behind me. He tapped me on the shoulder and I turned round and feigned surprise with a, 'Oh. You. Hi. Greg, isn't it? Did you want something?'

And he sort of smiled, embarrassed, and said, 'You've got something on your back.'

'Duh!' I joked. 'It's my blazer!'

'No. On your blazer.'

And he ripped off a piece of paper onto which someone had written, 'I AM A SLAG'. I went the colour of beetroot and quickly said, 'I'm not a slag! That's just people messing about.'

To which he shrugged and went, 'Well, I never wrote it. I don't even know you.'

WHY? Why couldn't he finish it off with, 'But I'd like to get to know you better,' like they did in the movies or on *Byker Grove*? But no, this wasn't fantasy land, this was my life. And so he walked off, hands in pockets, head down. An Adonis with a complex about his height perhaps. Because it was at that moment that I realized he was a lot taller than the other lads in our year. I'd not noticed it in the canteen as there'd been so many older kids about, but now we were alone in the corridor he looked ginormous. Just as I was idly wondering whether he might have gigantism disorder I saw him peer into one of the classrooms, falter, then look back to me.

'Sorry. Can you help me? I'm completely lost.'

Yes! There was a God!

Turned out he was looking for the metalwork room, so I showed him the way. OK, so I went a very circuitous route so that we'd get to spend more time together, and I remembered the guidelines set out in my *Sugar* magazine about how to impress a boy if you didn't have big boobs – it was mostly to do with smiling a lot, cracking jokes and chewing the end of your hair. As my hair was scraped back, I skipped the chewing-hair bit and, on the whole, it seemed to work as he laughed affably, although I wasn't sure how much was out of politeness as opposed to finding me hilarious. But he laughed all the same. And when, three days later – well, that's what it felt like – we arrived at the metalwork room he turned to me and said, 'Cheers, Jodie. You're a star. I really appreciate it.'

How could a lad who'd been kicked out of another school be so polite? It didn't make sense. Maybe he'd been polite when setting fire to the classroom/teacher. 'Sorry, mate, I hate to have to do this, but it's for the best, what with me pyromaniacal tendencies and all that, you know?' Not that he looked like a fire starter, twisted fire starter. But then again, maybe still, fiery waters really did run deep. Then I realized something else. He knew my name and I hadn't even told him it. That, surely, was a good sign?

After our chance encounter in the corridor and subsequent ten-mile hike around the school, Greg and I often kept each other company at break and dinner time. Debs and Hayls didn't mind, they positively encouraged it, thrilled that they could bask in his reflected gorgeousness glory second hand. And truth be told I was flattered, amazed even, that Greg wasn't embarrassed to be seen with me in public.

And he knew my name without me telling him it. I must have kept banging on about this because one day Hayls said, 'Maybe he's psychic. Now can you shut your fucking cakehole, Jodie?'

So I did.

We had our first kiss when we were babysitting for this posh couple who lived in one of the big houses near the golf course. Derek was a social worker, and I loved it when I babysat for him and his wife because I'd go rooting around in his briefcase and read all the case notes about the different families he was working with. It was really interesting, and even though I knew it was wrong I justified it to myself by deciding it was educational. I learned a lot about how other people led their lives, and how horrible people can be to each other and their kids. It made me realize how lucky I was living with my mum and dad. And it made me aware that neglect and abuse didn't just happen on our estate, it happened in posh houses, too. One of his cases was a little girl of about three who'd been neglected, and part of the neglect was that her dad had left her unsupervised in their swimming pool. I didn't even know people in Liverpool had their own swimming pools. I thought everyone was like me and had to traipse down to the local municipal pool, where there were turds floating about in the deep end and you had to dive for a brick in a pair of pyjamas – God knows why. What use is that in an emergency?

'Quick! Swim for your life, the boat is sinking! But can you bob down and get us that brick first? WHADDAYA MEAN YOU HAVEN'T GOT YOUR PYJAMAS ON!?'

Derek and his wife Eileen were a pair of old hippies; their house was crammed with joss sticks and pot pourri, and she was never out of a gypsy skirt. Their kids, Molly, five, and Rufus, three, were a pair of spoilt brats, but they always nodded off when I read them their bedtime story. Not that I was boring them or anything, in fact, quite opposite. They'd told Eileen that I was really good at doing all the voices, which was one of the reasons they liked me babysitting, even if I did eat them out of house and home and help myself to their Tia Maria every now and again. They also didn't mind if I had mates over to help pass the time while I was babysitting. Not that I had that much spare time as there were so many case notes to read and lovely salads to eat – Eileen was always throwing dinner parties and insisted I helped myself to whatever leftovers were lurking under clingfilm in the fridge. So anyway, one night I'd planned on babysitting alone and getting stuck into some notes about a little girl who was being sexually abused by her mum's boyfriend. I was desperate to know what happened next, but as I opened the briefcase and pulled out the brown folder of notes the doorbell rang. I hastily shoved everything back, closed the briefcase and hot-footed it to the front door.

It was Greg. He'd come over on his BMX. It was the nicest surprise ever. He explained that he'd called round at ours and Our Joey had told him where I was, so he'd cycled over to see if I 'wanted some company'. It sounded so grown-up: 'wanted some company'. It was the sort of thing people said on the telly, not fifteen-year-old lads from round our way. He wheeled his bike into the hall and I went and fixed him a Tia Maria with ice from Derek and Eileen's special dispenser in the door of the fridge. We went and sat on their huge chunky sofa in the living room and there was an anxious silence.

'So. What were you doing before I got here?' he asked.

'Oh, I was just reading the kids a bedtime story,' I lied. 'They're spark out now.'

'What were you reading them?'

'*Forever* by Judy Blume.'

He giggled. Everyone at school knew that book was filthy because it had blow jobs in it. It was the most thumbed book in the school library.

'I'm only messing. Just some shite about a teddy bear and his pyjamas.'

He nodded. 'Nice one.'

God, I wished I'd known he was coming, I thought, I would have made more of an effort with my appearance, instead of being sat there in a granny cardigan, leggings and a scrunchy.

'Boss house this, isn't it?' he said, looking around the room.

'I know, it's off its head,' I agreed. 'So. How you finding school?'

'S'all right. Most of them are knobs, but a few are OK.'

'What, the teachers or the pupils?'

'Both. I like Your Joey, he's sound.'

I liked that about him. He'd seen Our Joey being picked on by a gang of year eleven lads on the way home from school once and he'd scared them off by threatening to set fire to them. Ever since he'd kept Our Joey company on the way home from school, riding his BMX at a snail's pace while Our Joey ambled along. God knows what they found to talk about, Our Joey's conversational repertoire was mostly about the Eurovision Song Contest, but Greg claimed Joey made him laugh. I liked to think he was doing it for me, being Our Joey's protector to show me how much he loved me, or at the very least that he had feelings for me. To be honest, I thought it impossibly romantic, though Hayls and Debs reckoned he was only doing it 'coz he had no other mates'.

We sat and chatted for ages; the conversation just flowed. I don't know whether it was because it was nearly the end of the summer term and we had imminent freedom stretching ahead of us for six weeks, but something certainly made us relax. Maybe it was the Tia Maria. He told me all about his dad's skip-hire business, which would have been totally boring if someone else had been talking about it, but with him it was interesting. I started wondering if I might one day want to work with skips. I even mooted the idea of a women-run skip-hire business called Ladyskips, which really made him laugh. I also made him laugh with all my impersonations of the different teachers at school. When eventually the conversation seemed to be drying up, as well as our Tia Marias, I hot-footed it to the kitchen and poured us both a refill. He followed me, as if nervous to be left in a strange room in a strange house on his own. It was then that I confronted the white elephant in the room and asked him why he'd been kicked out of his old school. He told me that he knew his reputation went before him, and that everyone assumed he was a fire starter, but actually he'd done no such thing. He'd been in the wrong place at the wrong time and had been caught up in a fire started by some other lads (oooh, dramatic!) and when the headmaster had asked him who'd started the blaze, which was in the music room and damaged loads of wooden instruments like cellos, violins and even a baby grand, Greg refused to say.

'I know I should've fessed up,' he said, 'but I'd only have got my head kicked in. And these lads knew where I lived and said they'd set fire to our house if I said anything. I bet you think I'm a right coward.'

'No,' I insisted. 'I'm glad you never grassed.'

I'd said it a bit quickly. I was glad he never grassed because it meant he'd ended up at our school. If he'd grassed then he wouldn't have been stood here now at Derek and Eileen's, pretending to enjoy Tia Maria on ice. But rather than sound desperate I added, 'No one likes a grass!'

He shrugged. 'Well, my dad's worked dead hard to build up the skip business. I didn't wanna see it all go up in a puff of smoke.'

'It still feels a bit tight, kicking you out just coz you were there. The head couldn't really have thought you started it, could he?'

'He was just trying to make an example out of me. He threatened me with exclusion if I didn't grass, so me ma removed me from the school anyway. She was fuming.'

'I bet she was.'

'I just . . . haven't told anyone else at school, in case they think I'm a wimp.'

'Your secret's safe with me.'

'I knew it would be.'

And he winked. Now, as far as the magazines I read were concerned, winking could definitely be bracketed in the flirting category of human behaviour. Unsure what to do, I found myself winking back. Greg was just taking a sip of his Tia Maria when I did it, and he spat it out, pissing himself. Oh well, at least I'd made him laugh. He'd got Tia Maria all down his Lacoste sweatshirt, so I went and got a cloth from the sink and dabbed it down for him. It didn't make much difference so he went, 'Come on, I'll do it.' And he took the cloth from me, with the slightest brush of skin on skin as he did so, then he brusquely rubbed the jumper and the stain started to come out.

I took the cloth back off him and went to run it under the tap. Suddenly I felt heat behind me. It wrong-footed me, but then before I could wonder what was going on I felt Greg's arms snaking round my waist and he started nuzzling the back of my neck. And although this is what I'd wanted right from the minute I'd seen him coming into the canteen to get a sausage roll, I just froze. He, of course, sensed this and backed off as soon as he'd advanced. I swung round.

'No! It's fine. I like it. I was just a bit . . .'

'Sorry.'

'No, don't be.'

'Nah, I thought . . .'

'No, you thought right.'

The relief on his face was evident.

'So can I . . .?'

'Do what you want!' That sounded a bit desperate.

'Well, I could start off by . . . kissing you, like.'

'OK. Go on then.'

And he leaned forward, cupped my face in his hands as if it was a mug of hot chocolate and . . . well . . . it's not like I hadn't kissed anyone before. I'd kissed loads of lads. I mean, I wasn't a slag or anything – despite what that sign on my back said – but I'd snogged enough people to know I wasn't that keen on the whole thing. But then, I hadn't been snogged by Greg Valentine. Until now. And, oh my God, it was amazing. He started off just kissing my lips, and while he slipped his hands down, off my hot chocolate face, he wrapped one arm around my back and put the other one on my shoulder. His breath was hot and sweet, and then, as though it was the most natural thing in the world, he pushed his tongue into my mouth. I say it like it was the most natural thing in the world because this was the first time it had felt anything other than completely weird. Usually it felt as alien as someone shoving a pickled gherkin in my mouth and waggling it about a bit. But this just felt wonderful. I even reciprocated and shoved my gherkin – I mean tongue – in his mouth, and he didn't gag or anything and go, 'Ergh! Don't do that, you dirty bitch, how do I know where it's been?!' He carried on like it was what he wanted, too. Like we were exploring each other.

He was so tall he must have started to get a stiff neck from cranking it down to kiss me, because just then he lifted me up and sat me on the sink unit so he could kiss me while standing at his full height. And he never took his tongue out of my mouth the whole time! It felt dead sexy and exciting, especially when he then poked his knee between my legs and I sort of whimpered, which was a bit mortifying. He didn't seem to mind, though, in fact it seemed to get him going somewhat. He moved his hand down and cupped my left breast. I was kind of mortified because my nipples seemed to have turned into football studs. If I was mortified he seemed even more so, and almost as soon as he'd touched me he backed off. He actually stepped back.

'Sorry, I . . .'

'No . . . I just . . .'

'Erm . . .'

He rearranged his jogging bottoms and I realized I wasn't the only one who had cause to be embarrassed.

'Listen, er. You know I . . . might get off.'

'Oh, OK.'

'Got a bit carried away with meself there.'

'It's OK.'

'Sorry, like.'

'No, it's fine. I'd better check on the kids anyway.'

He nodded. I jumped down from the sink and showed him out to the hall, where he immediately started busying himself with his bike. He looked back at me as he opened the front door.

'Listen. We should do this again some time.'

'Yeah, if you want.'

'And I'll try and go a bit slower next time.'

I nodded. I wasn't really sure what had gone wrong.

'If you're sure,' he added.

'Positive. Anyway, we've got the whole of the summer holidays to snog.'

Oh dear. He was pulling a face. I'd clearly suggested this might be a relationship and he didn't like the sound of it. Bollocks! But then he said, 'The only thing is I'm going away for the first three weeks, so we'll have to snog after that.'

Three weeks away? Usually that would have made my heart plummet to my boots, but for the fact that I'd thought he wasn't that keen. Now there was the promise of further snogging I was completely and utterly made up.

'Where you going for three weeks?'

Greg pulled a face. 'All over. Mum says posh people in the olden days went on something called the Grand Tour all over the world.'

I gasped, 'You're going all over the world? That's brilliant! Get you!' I was *so* jealous.

'Nah, we're staying a little closer to home.'

'All over the Wirral? The bright lights of Birkenhead?'

He smiled. 'Just up and down the country.'

I was less impressed and my face showed it.

'In a . . . motor home thingy.'

'Right.'

'Mum says it's a palace on wheels.'

I put myself in his shoes and could think of nothing worse. Stuck in a small space for three weeks with my mum and dad and Our Joey? Vile. But then, being stuck in close confines with this apparition before me and . . . well, that would have been a different story. I'm sure we could have found lots of things to keep ourselves amused. Well, I'm sure I could have, I couldn't speak for him. Just then I heard myself say something bizarre. I had no idea why I said it, but say it I did.

'If you want to go out with me, Greg . . .'

He looked a bit startled. 'Aha?'

'Then you're gonna have to court me the old-fashioned way.'

He nodded. 'And what's that?'

'You will have to woo me via the ancient art of letter-writing.'

He looked confused. 'I've . . . gotta write you a letter?'

I nodded, like it was the most reasonable request in the world. 'While you're away, we shall strike up a correspondence. We'll write to each other.'

He thought about it for a second, then nodded. 'OK. But . . .'

'What?'

'I'm gonna be moving around all the time. How will you know where to send your letters?'

I'd not thought of that.

'Then you shall furnish me with your itinerary.'

He looked like a startled deer. As well he might. I had turned into something out of a period drama.

'Er, I'll see if me ma's got a list.'

I nodded, as if giving my consent or approval, and with that he left. I turned and looked at myself in the hall mirror. I half expected to find I was wearing a bonnet, but no. Just me and my scrunchy and my granny cardigan. I clocked a spot on my nose that I hadn't noticed before and wondered whether Greg might be partially sighted.

FIVE

Four days into the summer holidays I was coming downstairs in my Care Bears nightie in a very bad mood. I could hear Our Joey in the through lounge, dancing and singing along to one of the many compilation tapes he'd made of Madonna's Most Fabbest Hits – well, that's what he'd written on the cassette cover. At the moment he was making the coffee table rattle to 'Borderline'. I heard the crack of slipper on glass, which meant he'd knocked said coffee table again doing a high kick, but it didn't stop him singing, not for one note.

'Idiot,' I muttered under my breath to no one in particular.

The reason I was in a bad mood was that I'd had yet another dream where Greg was hanging round a pool, surrounded by a bevy of bathing beauties, all desperate to get into his demi wave, and he was lapping up the attention and showing off about his dad's skip-hire business. At this point I would run into the holiday resort in my school uniform and shout, 'It's not a demi wave, it's natural and he's MINE!' to which the bathing beauties would all laugh their heads off and Greg would look at me from the comfort of his paisley-patterned sunlounger and go, 'I've no idea who this bizarre creature is,' in a weird posh accent. After which I'd have no other recourse but to drown myself in the kidney-shaped swimming pool.

Then I saw something on the mat. It was a postcard. I picked it up. On the front was a picture of a small horse and at the top it said, 'A New Forest Pony'. OK, so it wasn't just a small horse, it was in fact a pony. I turned it over quickly. Oh my God, it was from him!

1 August 1999

Dear Jodie,

Got here last night. All that money my dad earns and we are in this shithole on wheels. I hate him. Wish I was there with you. Greg. X

PS. It's not a shithole really, but it's dead cramped. So I have to look at our Teresa-May in her bra and knickers every morning and it's knocking me sick. I want privacy!

PPS. What are you doing the rest of your summer?

OK, so it was hardly *War and Peace*, but it was a start. He'd done what I'd asked him to do, or made a start on it anyway, which meant he took me seriously. It meant that he was interested. I got some toast and a scalding hot cup of tea – ducking my way through the lounge to avoid Our Joey's flying fists as he attempted to recreate the moves from the 'Vogue' video – and took the card back to my bedroom to read it again. I must have read it a thousand times that day. And so began the summer of the thirteen letters from Greg.

Because after that first postcard he obviously invested in a notepad and envelopes. Oh, the romance of it all!

Letter number two:

Hiya, it's me.

Have you ever been to the New Forest? I don't know why they've dragged me here as am bored out me skull. There isn't even anything to do at the campsite except look at horses

when they come by. Sorry I got off dead quick that night
I come round when you were babysitting. Just suddenly
thought I'd overstepped the mark. I got a bit carried away
with myself, sorry about that. Last night I asked Teresa-May
what 'to court' meant and she told me. Well, it's official, this
is me courting you. You crazy bitch.

Greg xx

P.S. Show this to anyone and you are completely deaded.

He called me his crazy bitch. I thought I might be falling
in love with him.

Letter number three:

Jodie,

Teresa-May was wrong. She said courting meant to go out
with someone. But I looked it up in a dictionary I found in
a bookshop in Glastonbury, where we are now, and it said
it's the period of time when a couple get to know each other
before they get engaged and then married. IT'S TOO SOON
TO MARRY. Screw you. It's over.

G x

PS. It's nothing without the festival, Dad keeps saying.

Hmmm, not sure I was that keen on his crazy 'put down'
sarcastic humour. Still, every woman wanted to change their
man, right? And if that was the only thing I needed to change
I'd better be grateful for small mercies.

Letter number four:

Hi Jodes,

We're in Wales. Or Wayulzz as Teresa-May keeps
pronouncing it and then wetting herself. And guess what? We
climbed a mountain today. Well, it was a very big hill, but it

felt like a mountain. Teresa-May was fuming because she had high heels on and all she did was moan, moan, moan non-stop. When we got to the top we looked out and it was dead nice. Dad goes, 'Stunning.' And Mum burst out crying. She's weird. She just stood there for, like, ten minutes sobbing into my dad's shoulder. I didn't know where to put myself. She keeps going, 'Ignore me Greg. Tree.' so I did. Teresa-May had a ciggie and Dad kicked off. Parents, hey. Knobs, the lot of them. You climb all that way and they just start crying? Mum's seriously disturbed in the head, I've always said it. I wish I was at home. I hate everything about this holiday.

We were meant to be going abroad to Spain, but Dad changed his mind at the last minute – well, a few months ago – and there was no arguing with him. He said we all had to tighten our belts and that Mum was scared of flying. She's never been scared of flying before. It just does my head in.

Your drama course sounds boss, I bet you're dead good at it. When you're a dead famous actress I'm gonna be, like, I know her. I courted her when she was fifteen. Always knew she'd be dead famous. She always had a certain something. This woman at the pub tonight where we went for our tea asked me if I was a model and Mum kicked off at her. He's only fifteen. I think she was flirting with us. She was old enough to be my granny. Arl Grannybags, Teresa-May called her. To her face. So there's me holiday romance bitten the dust. I told you my mum was trouble. (Hope she doesn't read this. SHIT!)

Will write soon.

Gxx

I was slowly becoming of the opinion that Greg was a genius letter writer. No other lad I had ever met would be capable of such beautiful, heartfelt prose.

Letter number five:

Dear Jodie,

Today was really embarrassing. Mum said she wanted to talk to me, so Dad and Teresa-May went out and we stayed in the motor home. She told me she loved me and was dead proud of me and I could do anything I wanted with my life and that I should always follow my dreams. She said she knew Dad wanted me to carry on with Skippy Skips, but that if that didn't make me happy I shouldn't be scared to make up my own mind about what I wanted to do. She said if I got married I should be nice to my wife and not cheat on her and treat my kids with respect and watch out for them taking drugs. The whole thing was too weird, Jodie, dead heavy, I didn't know were to look. Why is it everyone else goes on holidays and gets wrecked or has a laugh and my family treats it like an extended episode of *Oprah Winfrey*? Honestly, I am that close to getting on a train and just coming home. I hate it.

The show you're doing on the course sounds boss. But yes, I agree with you, *Say No to Date Rape* is a shit title. I think it should be called (and this is genius) *Asking For It?* The question mark is dead important, remember that. You can tell the drama teacher if you like, but make sure I get my royalties if it makes you a millionaire. I wish I could phone you, but the only phone box nearby is broken. Someone's been using it as a bog and there's even bog roll in there – can you believe that? Oh well, I'll ask for one of them mobile phones for Christmas and see where it gets me.

Best go. I can smell something vile. Mum must be cooking the tea.

And good luck with the show again.

Gx

He loved me. He did, I could tell. Although maybe he'd forgotten what an absolute dog I was. Oh well, plenty of time for a face lift before he got back.

Letter number six:

Me again,

You are my gift sent from heaven above, Jodie McGee, do you know that? I read your letters on the shittest holiday in the world and I have a right grin. It's brilliant that you cried real tears during the play, and I bet no one really minded that you swore when you were improvising on the spot. Even if you did get told off for it. I wish I'd seen you hit that lad who was pretending to rape you – bet he got a right shock! Shame he had to go to casualty to have his scratches seen to, but like you were saying, you were in character. You were being raped for God's sake!

We are now in Oxford, which Mum wanted to come to because of *Inspector Morse*. She keeps going on about the dreaming spires, but we're currently parked in a layby and can only see cars and trees. We got a Park and Ride bus into Oxford today and it was full of toffs and Americans, but Mum was walking around with a big smile on her face going, 'Isn't it gorgeous? Isn't it quaint? Oh God, Greg, I love it. Don't you, Tree?' When I said no, Dad said I was deliberately sabotaging the holiday. Mum was telling him to shut up coz a bus load of Japanese tourists were taking a picture of us – 'They think you're street theatre,' she goes – so I said he was sabotaging my holiday by taking me to shit places. He goes, 'They're the places your Mum likes.' I go, 'What about what I like? What about what our Teresa-May likes?' And he goes, 'One of these days you're gonna regret saying that.' At that point Mum burst out crying *again* and walked off in a huff and the Japanese

people gave us a round of applause. When I bowed for them
Dad cuffed me round the head, the bastard, so I came back to
the motor home, but of course I didn't have any keys so I just
had to sit here for about two whole hours till they came back.
Dad said nothing and unlocked the van and went in. Mum was
all perky as if nothing had happened. Teresa-May was dead
quiet. I feel ashamed for them, I do. I went and sat on my bed
and started writing this letter, so Dad shouts, 'Oh yer writing
to your girlfriend instead of talking to us,' so I shout back, 'I've
got nothing to say to you,' and we've not spoken since.

Teresa-May came and sat on my bed before and said, 'I
think there's something wrong with Mum.' I said, 'Yeah she's a
big knob.' Teresa-May goes, 'No, Greg, you're the knob.' And
then she flounces out. What a tit.

Mum's watching *Acacia Avenue* on the little portable
and crying coz someone's died. Someone diabetic took an
overdose of chocolate bars or something. She keeps saying,
'So young. So young.' Like it's a real person, the big meff.

I'm off out now to find a post box. Fuck 'em.

Pity me, Gxx

I was starting to hate this Teresa-May. I fashioned a doll of
her from one of my old Barbies and stuck pins in it. Our Joey
called me a loopy bitch.

Letter number seven:

Hi Jodie,

Today wasn't so bad actually. We are in Stratford Upon
Avon, so called because it is a place called Stratford, and it is
on a river called River Avon. See? You learn something new
every day with me. Stratford is where William Shakespeare
hung out. There's pictures of him everywhere. At first the

whole place bored the liver out of me – we had a look round this cottage where his Mrs lived, with Mum practically having an orgasm over every room we went in. Teresa-May showed us all up by asking the security person if she could smoke. They asked her to leave and she punched the air as she did. But then we went and looked at the theatres and that was OK coz I kept imagining coming back to see you in a play here. Acting an' all that.

We had a guided tour and they showed us the dressing rooms and the stages and backstage and everything. Mum kept going to the tour guide, 'Gregory's girlfriend's going to be an actress,' and I was blushing. 'Well, maybe one day she will perform in something here,' the tour guide said. But my dad goes, 'I doubt it. She lives on a council estate in Liverpool. Hardly Kate frigging Winslet is she?'

I'm only telling you that coz I want you to hate him as much as me. Sorry. He's an arlarse. Mum kept giving him evils for ages afterwards. Teresa-May did, too, and she doesn't even know you.

Anyway, the tour guide went, 'Some of our finest actors and actresses are from council estates.' And that told him. Though Dad did keep mouthing 'Who? Who?' behind the guide's back like a prick.

Yes I do know 'Heartbeat' by Steps, Teresa-May has it on her Walkman all the time. I don't think I have a favourite one, but as you're demanding to know I reckon Faye. She looks like a bit of a laugh. Though Teresa-May says H makes her fanny beat. Dirty bitch. Fortunately she never said it in front of Mum and Dad or they'd've ragged her. I was quite shocked when she said it, but then I think she likes to do that. (Shock I mean, not beat her fanny – mind you, I don't know. Let's just say when the caravan's rocking don't come knocking.)

We got through the whole of today without Mum crying,

so that's an improvement. But you're right, I guess it could
be the menopause, I don't really know what that involves. If
it makes you moody and emotional I think our Teresa-May's
got it as well. I can't believe she said that about H. I just wish
I could grass her up about it (even though you hate grasses),
but she's been clever, she knows I'd never mention fannies, or
her fanny specially, to Mum.

Tomorrow we're driving miles and miles and miles to
Newcastle. Bloody hell, we're seeing all the hotspots.

Miss you, Gx

Sometimes people were sent to you to show you how lucky
you are. I looked at my mum with fresh eyes. At least all she did
all day was smoke free ciggies, not lounge around crying her
eyes out all the time.

Letter number eight:

Whassssuuuuup?

Yep. I have decided. Teresa-May may only be seventeen,
but she is defo on her menopause an' all. Today Mum said she
wanted a chat with her, so me and Dad had to go for a walk.
You can imagine how much I enjoyed that. By the time we got
back Mum was making sandwiches and Teresa-May was on
her bed crying. She pretended she wasn't but I knew she was.
Maybe Mum's told her a few home truths – you're a slag innit.

Off out in a bit to see the Angel of the North. Mum's always
wanted to see it. It's all about Mum. Grrr. Plus I think you've
sent your last letter to the place we were in yesterday as Dad
changed the itinerary, so I might not hear from you for a bit.
Grrr. Maybe I should have a flaming menopause. Can fellas
get them?

Write soon. Gx

This Teresa-May. Grr. She was really getting on my tits. Letter number nine:

Hello, oh love of my life (see? You set a challenge and I do it. And no I don't think you're needy at all. You needy cow),

Sorry if the handwriting's all over the shop, we're on the move, heading for Scotland Inversomewhere. Got a kilt on specially (lies). The Angel of the North is basically a big statue in a place called Gateshead and it looks like some fella with aeroplane wings. It's what they call an icon of England, a bit like Paul Gascoigne. Personally I think they should have built it in Liverpool as it would have been a fuck of a lot easier to get to, know what I'm saying. It's as tall as four double decker buses (I measured it) and has the wingspan of a jumbo jet (do they still make jumbo jets?). Guess who read their brochure? It's stood up on top of this hill and it's weird, coz when you're up there you feel like you're in the middle of nowhere, but you know you're not coz all you can see from every main road round there for miles about is the angel looking down on you. Mum asked me if I believed in angels. I said I didn't know, I'm a bit funny about people when you can't tell if they're a bird or a fella. I was only messing, but our Teresa-May said someone at her work is going through a sex change and he's dead nice, even if he has changed his name from Simon to Simone and started dressing like a hooker. Teresa-May's been encouraging him to tone it down a bit coz everyone's laughing. But that hasn't stopped her, has it? Anyway, Mum said she believed in angels and 'just wanted us to know that'. Off. Her. Cake.

Anyway. Less of the Angel of the North and more of the Angel of Liverpool. It was so boss to finally talk to you last night and hear your voice. I'm sorry I didn't have enough money to call you back again, and it didn't seem to take

incoming calls, so when you were probably trying to get
through it wasn't ringing. And after all that time of not
speaking to you and writing I didn't say what I wanted to say
coz my mind went blank and I just spoke shite, which you
already know, of course. I wanted to say you've kept me going
this holiday and you're the funniest person I've ever met (and
I've met loads), and you're dead fit, too. There, said it now, piss
yourself. I know you won't believe me. You're always putting
yourself down, but it's true. When I get back I am so taking
you out somewhere nice. Don't know where, don't know how,
but I will and that's a promise. So get your thinking cap on
and decide where you wanna go and I'll take you. Within
reason. Deal?

Mum has put Abba on the car/motor home stereo. It's that
slow song where they keep going, 'I believe in angels.' I feel
like banging my head against the glass window and cutting it
in two just to get OUT OF HERE.

Save me, Jodie. Save me.

Gxx

P.S. All this Abba – Your Joey's perfect holiday . . .

He called me the Angel of Liverpool. Oh God. He really had
forgotten what I looked like. Maybe I should be encouraging
him to stay away for ever so that he never goes off me? Absence
doesn't make the heart grow fonder, it makes the memory go
all rose-tinted. Oh well.

Letter number ten:

Well, I thought we were going to Inverness, but we're actually
in a place called Fort William, which is just *near* Inverness.
As you know, the plan is to stop here for a few days because
Mum has family here and she wants to see them. I have to say,

it's pretty impressive. I've never seen countryside like it. I now understand why people like hiking and rambling and walking, everywhere you look you're just . . . I dunno . . . shocked by how stunning everything is. Better than any photo. Better than any movie. I'm gonna bring you here one day. It literally takes your breath away. And it's in our own country (United Kingdom. I know we're not Scottish).

When I was little we used to go to church and sing that hymn about the purple-headed mountain with the river running by. We used to have jokes about it coz Teresa-May said cocks had purple heads – mine's green by the way; all will be revealed at a later date – and I thought it was a bit mad because everyone knows mountains are green, or white if they've got a bit of snow on them, but here they actually are purple. They're every colour under the sun, and they seem to change colour at different times of the day. Madness. But nice madness. I feel so small. Part of something massive. I've taken loads of photos, but I know for a fact, Jodie, nothing will ever be as good as the real thing. I'm sounding like a mad born-again or something, aren't I? But d'you know what? You really do feel like God's here, you know. When you see something as amazing and perfect as this it makes you think. Someone else had a hand in this, I'm telling you. And it wasn't Tony Blair, I know that much.

Right, I'm going to stop going on about the scenery or else you'll think I've turned into a God botherer and you'll be dumping me and thinking I've gone all barmy on you.

Hey, something funny happened earlier. Mum wanted to go and see this local church, so she and dad went and said they'd only be half an hour, but they were gone for two hours and when they came back they told me this.

They went and sat in the church, at the back, taking it all

in. And these people came in, so they thought, OK, there's a service, let's stay. And the church started to fill up. Then all of a sudden the organ starts to play and everyone stands up and guess what? A coffin was brought in. So they couldn't leave coz they would have looked like arlarses, so they had to stay for a funeral of someone they didn't know. And it doesn't stop there. At the end someone got gabbing to them and, to cut a long story short, they ended up going to the drinks do afterwards and had to lie and said they only vaguely knew the dead fella. I must admit we did have a laugh when they told us about it when they got back. I was wondering where they'd got to.

Oh, OH! Good luck with the audition for *Acacia Avenue*. I haven't stopped going on about it. What a piece of luck, someone from the telly seeing you in *Say No to Date Rape* (I still say *Asking For It?* is better – never forget the question mark). I think you'll be brilliant as a newspaper girl. I am assuming that means she delivers newspapers. She can't work for a newspaper at thirteen, right? I will be keeping everything crossed for you tomorrow. I bet you'll be brilliant. And yeah, like you say, if you don't wear make-up you might look younger. And as for your comment about your boobs, I'm saying nothing. I am a gentleman! Everyone here wishes you good luck, too. Even all Mum's relatives – she's been showing off about you. Can't wait to hear how you get on.

Right, this is turning into some dead long book so I am going to sign off (phew says Jodie, bored rigid) and say I'll speak to you soon and see you soon, I hope.

Not long now. Seven more sleeps.

Good luck tomorrow, though you'll have done it all by the time this arrives.

Love Greg xx

PS If I haven't said it enough I'll say it again. Good luck x

Greg seemed to have every confidence in my acting. He really had forgotten what I was like, hadn't he? Oh God. It was all going to go tits up when he got back. For sure.

Letter number eleven

Dear Jodie,

I'm sorry about last night. I was a bit all over the place. I know you'll be worried about me now. Don't be. I'm OK really. Well, I will be. I didn't sleep much last night, no one did, and I kept playing what happened yesterday over and over again in my head. Even when I closed my eyes to try and sleep it's all I could see, all I could think about. I know I wasn't making much sense on the phone and I know you were dead shocked, but as you said, something's not been right on this holiday and now we know what it is. I couldn't stay long on the phone anyway coz Mum's cousin Morag's a bit tight and kept coming into the hall, tapping her watch and sighing, so sorry about that. Where do I begin?

It all started with a boiled egg – I know. A boiled egg. Mum had made us a packed lunch for this walk we were going on to see a castle called Inverlochy. We couldn't look round it as it's not a proper castle any more, it's actually a hotel that costs like a million pounds a night to stay there, so the plan was to walk up to it, go in and ask for a leaflet pretending we might want to stay there, then go and look round the grounds and have our packed lunch, hoping no one would see us. Everything went according to plan, though you could tell the fella in reception sussed us out straight away. As he gave Mum the leaflet he goes, 'Madam, I must warn you our room rates are quite pricey,' to which Mum goes, 'Well that's handy, coz I'm quite rich.' I couldn't help but laugh. When we were having our packed lunch in the grounds, hidden behind some trees on a bench that Mum reckoned was a trysting place where people went to cop off in the olden days, Teresa-May moaned that her hard-boiled egg was green inside. I looked and it was. Ish. It had green splodges on the white bit. Big deal. Dad told her to shut up and eat it. She goes, 'I won't.' He goes, 'You will.' Then she threw it in the lake. (We were by a lake. Well, it might have been a river. Water anyway. I should have mentioned the lake/river/water thing before.) So Dad starts kicking off, and I don't blame him, coz actually she hit this duck on the head and it like knocked him out for a few seconds, which TM thought was hilarious. So Dad starts ranting on about how most serial killers start their lives hurting animals for a laugh and Mum's telling him to calm down and TM's going, 'Oh what, so I'm Fred West now, am I?' And Dad's going, 'Your mum made that egg. Have some fucking manners.' And Mum's going, 'It's only an egg, Tony.' And Dad has this like breakdown thing and keeps saying, 'It's not just an egg. It's not just an egg. It's your egg.' And then he starts crying. REALLY crying. He sits back on the bench and puts his face in his hands and his shoulders are bouncing up and down and no one knows what to say. And that's when Teresa-May turns to me and says, 'Mum's got cancer.'

At that point someone from the hotel came out and told us that as visitors we were more than welcome to eat from their lunchtime menu and they could sort us out a table, but they couldn't really let us carry on eating our packed lunch on their premises. He obviously hadn't noticed Dad sitting there blubbing like a baby. But he soon did because Dad jumped up and started yelling at him that his wife was dying and he can fuck off and stuff like that. Well, God love the fella from the hotel, coz he was mortified and backed away and said, 'Take as long as you want,' and five minutes later they sent a tray of tea and cakes out for us free of charge. The cakes looked really nice, but Dad said it was time to go home, so we all had to get up and start walking home. TM stuffed as many cakes as she could in her pockets.

Mum put her arm round me as we were walking along the river (it was a river, I've remembered now). I asked her if it was true. She said yes. I asked her if she was really dying and she said we all die sometime. But the doctors have said it could be anything between six weeks and six months. She said she was sorry it had come out the way it had, but she had meant to tell me tomorrow on the last night of the holiday. This is why they changed their plans and stayed in England, she's not well enough to fly and she wanted to see a load of places she'd never seen before she died. I just couldn't believe what I was hearing, what she was saying. It just didn't make any sense. Apparently they have caught the cancer too late and she can't have treatment and . . . Oh, I don't know, Jodie, it's all just so MAD. I can't really take it all in.

And now I feel lost. All I've done this holiday is moan about how crap it is, and all the time it was making Mum's dreams come true and stuff like that and I went and ruined it. I can't even say sorry to her coz I can't speak. It's like I've thought too many things last night and this morning, and the words those thoughts used were sucked up into my brain from the back of my throat and I've got no words left to say out loud. That's the way I look at it anyway.

Six weeks is nothing. Six months is better. But they might have got it wrong. You hear about it all the time, don't you? People getting better with miracle cures or just stuff to do with praying and God and shit like that. TM says she heard about a woman at their work who cured herself from cancer by eating nothing but carrots or something. Mum likes carrots but says its all gobbledegook.

I don't know what else to say, Jodie. I'm gutted. I know people say that a lot about silly things, but on this one I really do feel like my guts have been wrenched out. I hate it. You'd better be good at hugging for when I'm home, baby girl.

And even though I called you last night I never even asked how your audition went. How crap am I? Think you'll forgive me though (hope so). Well, I'm sure I'll hear about it soon enough.

I wish I could turn the clock back and we could do this holiday all over again so I could at least pretend to be interested in staring at ponies in the New Forest all day long. Wish I'd taken more pictures now as well. At least I liked Scotland. Scotland's boss. I wish they'da told me before we came away and then I would've understood why we was doing it. Now I just feel like an arlarse. And then I wish they'd never told me at all coz I hate knowing coz I can't think of anything else and it makes me feel weird.

I'm gonna sign off now. Depressing myself too much, but I just wanted to explain.

Greg x

Shit. SHIT. And a bit more shit. Well, a lot. Oh GOD. Letter number twelve:

Hiya,

Don't be so daft, it's fine. We've all got our problems and it's good for me to hear about things in the real world – I feel like I've been in a bubble these last few weeks – so honestly, forget about it. You had no idea what was going on when you wrote that letter, so quit worrying, bitch!

Listen. *Acacia Avenue*'s a shit show anyway. You don't wanna be on that, you're too good for them. And who wants to play a newspaper girl anyway? I'm gutted for you obviously coz I know how much you wanted it, but I swear, Jodie, everything happens for a reason and there's plenty more fish in the sea. Of course you forgot all your lines when you went in to meet them – nerves get the better of all of us every now and then. Like when we had that mock French oral test and Mrs Byrne asked us how often I played football and I couldn't remember the word for week (*semaine*), so I told her I played every saucepan. WHAT A KNOBHEAD. And you never forgot your lines in *Say No to Date Rape*, did you? And even if you had to make them up as you went along you never let anyone down, like. In fact, you were so good it got you an audition for *Acacia Avenue*, which is shit as we all know, but it was a proper audition for a proper job and you're only fifteen. Sixteen soon, though, and you know what's legal then? CAN'T BELIEVE I SAID THAT! SHIT! And as for that rude fucker who you said kept looking at his watch while you were trying to remember your lines, tell me who he is and I'll get the lads from St Eddie's round to set fire to his house. He's a piss poor excuse for a man and has no manners. And so what if you took a swig of water from your bottle and spilt it down yourself coz you were shaking so much with nerves. We've all done it. And at least you made them laugh by saying, 'Get me with my drink problem.' See? That's a boss thing to say. I'da never thought of that. You're dead funny. And they did laugh. And I don't reckon you're right. I don't reckon they were laughing coz they were mortified. They were just laughing because you're a funny girl, Jodie. Trust me. I've seen Michael Barrymore live and you're a million times funnier than him. And a million times fitter, too. You, me and Barrymore on a desert island? I know who I'd go for HAHAHAHA.

I'm glad you've made your mind up about where you

wanna go on our date and I think it sounds boss. Fish and chips in Southport and a ride on the Traumatizer (sponsored by Tizer no less) it is. Can't wait. We can go Saturday. Bring nothing but your good self.

I tell you what, babe, as soon as this motor home pulls up in our yard I am getting on my BMX and coming right over to see you. So get your laughing gear ready for some lip-locking action. We're stopping at Gretna Green tonight, so jump on a coach and we can be married by morning. Joking (or am I?). Mum says we need to talk more about death (help!). She says in the olden days when Queen Victoria was on the throne (that was a long bloody dump by anyone's calculations) people were dead into death and funerals and they used to make a big deal out of it. Horse-drawn carriages, big statues by the graves and stuff. But then there was the First World War and people were dying left, right and centre and it was mostly young fellas like just a bit older than me and people got sick of death and it became more upsetting, so people stopped talking about it (God knows where she got this from, I've no idea) because it was so senseless. And she reckons we never really got over that, but we need to start celebrating death and life again, and talk about it and not be scared of it.

Fat chance.

Anyway. See you before you get this probably.

Your Greg xxxxxxxxx

We didn't wait till my sixteenth birthday, we threw caution to the wind, broke the law and consummated our relationship on Derek and Eileen's bathroom floor with the door locked on the night of Greg's mum's funeral a month or two later.

It was a lovely send-off and there wasn't a dry eye in the house when they played that Abba song about the angels. Greg said he needed to do it to feel alive and I wasn't complaining. We made the bathroom dead nice, turning off the lights and lighting some candles. The earth didn't move, but the toilet seat did. The earth did move the second time, in Derek and Eileen's potting shed, and it continued to move from that day onwards. We became inseparable. Our names were rarely said alone. It was Jodie and Greg. Greg and Jodie. Loved up didn't even touch the sides.

SIX

2004

'Excuse me, love. Can you tell me where you keep your Tena Lady?'

The woman staring down at me had lipstick stains on her teeth and weird dyed orange hair. It's one thing being born with it, but to have it by choice . . .

'Er, sorry?'

'Your Tena Lady love. Where d'you keep them?'

'I'm not sure.'

There was a distinct tapping of foot now.

'You mean you don't know?'

God I hated working in this bloody supermarket sometimes. Especially in the run-up to Christmas when they expected you to wear a Santa hat as well as your badge saying, 'Hi, I'm Jodie. I'm here to help.' I wasn't here to help, I was here to stack shelves.

'Well . . .'

'So. Let me get this straight . . .'

'Aha?' I said, jumping up acrobatically from a kneeling position.

'You work here?'

'I do.'

'But you don't know where you keep your Tena Lady?'

'That's right,' I said facetiously. 'I work here and I have absolutely no idea where the Tena Ladies live. Sorry, Madam.'

'This is outrageous. I'm gonna get you fired.'

And she turned on her heel and went in the direction of the Home Bake aisle. She certainly wasn't going to find them there. Debs hurried over, reloading her special offer pricing gun.

'What's her problem?'

'Weak fanny, silly arl boot,' I said and we both giggled. As if by magic, Hayls was on us like a ton of bricks from her section, pretending to reload her special offer pricing gun in case Kim the manager was watching from her bird's-eye office high above the shop floor.

'What did she want? Her with the red hair?'

'Nothing,' I said dramatically, 'She was just really giving me bad attitude and all that.'

'You're joking! Go'way! Was it really messing with your head?'

'Big time,' I said with a dramatic tremble.

'God, it's messing with mine and I wasn't even here,' said Hayls. Debs put her arm round me. Hayls carried on, 'Did you see the state of her head? She looked like Googie the Liverpool Duck.'

Neither me nor Debs had a clue who Googie the Liverpool Duck was, but it was a phrase Hayls used often, usually to describe someone with bad hair, bad teeth, or a bad face. Or all three.

'I know,' I said. 'I hate working here.'

'I know, it's well cuntified,' said Debs, and she took her gun and wiped it on my forehead, leaving me with a special offer sticker for £1.99. We all smiled.

'D'you wanna go for a ciggie in the stock lift? Might help?' she said, ripping the sticker off and sticking it on her left breast.

I nodded. 'Don't let Kim see.'

So we snuck behind a cage of toilet rolls and wheeled it towards the stock lift, looking to all the world – and Kim if she was watching – like the three of us were hard at work.

The two good things about my life at the moment were that me, Debs and Hayls were all working together. The other good thing was that me and my Greg were still an item.

The really great thing about the stock lift at the supermarket was that there was a STOP button, and if you pressed it the lift stopped, amazingly, and didn't start again till someone else called for it on another floor. It was a great time killer in the middle of a boring shift, and it was a great place to smoke and chew the cud with your best mates.

'So,' said Debs, handing round the Black Cats as Hayls struck her lighter up, I pressed the STOP button and we juddered to a halt. A toilet roll landed on my head and bounced onto the floor of the lift. I didn't even like smoking, but I'd do anything to avoid stacking more shelves and having run-ins with the likes of Googie the Liverpool Duck. 'Your Greg's twenty-first tonight.'

'I know.'

'I can't wait,' said Hayls. 'I've got this gorgeous new boob tube from Miss Selfridge, lime green, wait till you see it, yous'll have a spaz.'

'Oh God, I can't wait,' said Debs.

'I know.'

We said this a lot, me and the girls. I know. Our Joey said it, too. It didn't really mean anything. We may as well have just made a noise. Sometimes I thought we just said words for something to say, with scant attention to their meaning. Debs looked at me.

'Are yer excited?'

I nodded. 'God, yeah. Me bottle's well gone.'

'Why?!' gasped Hayls, sensing gossip.

'Haven't you heard?' gasped Debs.

'No, what?! Tell me!'

Debs looked at me. 'You tell her. It's your gossip.'

'It's not really gossip,' I protested, 'but . . .'

Debs and Hayls looked at me, smoking in unison. I'm not sure they'd noticed I wasn't really dragging on my ciggie.

'Greg phoned last night and said he was making a very big announcement tonight at the party.'

'Go'way, you're joking!'

'I know,' I said.

'Well, you know what that means,' said Debs. 'I mean, it can only mean one thing, d'you know what I mean? Tell her, Hayls!'

Hayls nodded. 'He's so proposing to you.'

'I know,' said Debs. 'Can you believe that?'

'I know,' said Hayls, 'I can't get over that.'

'I can't,' agreed Debs.

'I don't know for sure, like,' I said with a shrug.

'Bollocks, Jode, yous've been going together for ages. Since . . .'

'Year ten.'

'Year ten! That's, like . . . a lifetime. It's about time he made an honest woman of you.'

'Yeah, but for all I know he's gonna announce . . . I dunno . . . something else.'

'Like what? He's pregnant?' said Debs incredulously, one eyebrow arched.

'Or, like, he's gonna vote Tory?' said Hayls with a similarly arched brow. She was like that sometimes, Hayls, she could be dead political.

'Oh God, you have to drag politics into everything,' said Debs.

'Can't help it, Debs. I'm what you call a political animal. God this ciggie's gorgeous. I'm totally loving it off.'

'I know. I love smoking, me.'

'I know. I do an'all.' And this time I really did take a drag, and immediately regretted it. It was vile.

I was so excited about that night. I had a feeling the girls were right. Greg kept asking what I was wearing to the party, which was unheard of for him. And he'd even given me a tenner to go and get my hair done, so I knew something was up. He hadn't gone so far as to measure the circumference of the fourth finger on my left hand, but it felt like he'd done everything but. Every time I thought about the party I got butterflies in my stomach and my head went a bit dizzy, so I was either excited or pregnant. And as I was on the Pill and kept doing an inner squeal anytime anyone mentioned the do, I guessed it was the former.

'Where you getting your hair done, Jodes?' Hayls asked.

'Panache in the Precinct.'

The girls nodded, impressed. Panache was a big deal. There was a woman who worked there who'd cut Sporty Spice's hair before she was famous. Even though her hair was always a show before she was famous.

'And I might even go and get a fake tan as well, if there's time.'

'There's always time,' said Debs, flicking her hair extensions back. A lot of people thought Debs was Asian, she was so fond of the spray gun.

'Where will you go?' asked Hayls.

'Now is the Winter of Our Discount Tans? On Everley Crescent?'

'Oh don't go there,' insisted Debs. 'The woman what runs it's half blind. She sprays half the gunk up the wall. Go to Fake N Bake on Stan Boardman Walk and say I sent you. Gotta look your best if you're gonna be proposed to.'

'I know,' said Hayls with an air of sadness. Debs looked at her.

'You'll get a fella one day, Hayls. And he'll be just as gorgeous as Jode's Greg and my Alex. More gorgeous in fact.'

Hayls didn't look so sure. No matter how many times me and Debs told her she was pretty, she was always convinced she looked like a knackered sow (her words not mine). She once said that me, her and Debs were on parallel conveyor belts heading for a door called marriage. Mine was going like the clappers, so much so I could feel the G Force, and Debs wasn't far behind me. But she claimed hers had broken down and she was sitting there in a puddle of her own failure, calling out for help but none was coming.

Greg's family were from the same estate as us, but because his dad had made a bit of money with his skip-hire business they had recently moved a mile or two down the road to a farmhouse on the leafy lanes of Cheshire. As a result, it had been decided that his twenty-first birthday would take the form of a barn dance. Me, Debs and Hayls had never been to a barn dance before and just assumed it was like any old dance, or disco, only set in a barn. So imagine our surprise when me and the girls got out of our taxi at the farmhouse several hours later, tottering in high heels and with skirts so short you could see what we'd had for breakfast, only to look around us and see that everyone else arriving seemed to be in cowboy boots, checked shirts and straw hats.

'Oh my God, it's like going to a Wurzels gig,' said Hayls.

Hayls' reference points could be very old-fashioned. Me and

Debs put it down to her being the youngest of ten and often re-quoting her elder brothers and sisters.

'What's going on?' continued Debs. 'Did everyone else phone each other up before they come out and go, 'Hey, let's all choose the shittest clothes we've got and put them on?''

'I know,' said Hayls. 'I feel ashamed for them.'

'Jesus, what've you three come as? The Good, the Bad and the Ugly?'

We looked round. Greg's dad was walking towards us in a – yes, you guessed it! – checked shirt and – oh my God – flared jeans. He had straw sticking out from the collar of his shirt, too, God alone knew why. And yet he had the *cheek* to criticize *our* clothes? We looked pretty amazing, I'll have you know. I was wearing a stunning white blazer – back to front – with matching white trilby and white micro skirt. Rather daringly I was wearing nothing under the blazer, so there was a flash of fake-tanned bare back (no bra). It was a look I'd copied off Celine Dion's outfit for the Oscars years earlier, which I'd seen in a magazine. Debs and Hayls said I looked amazing. They stood either side of me, Debs in a burgundy rubber minidress and Hayls in spangly lime-green leggings and matching boob tube. We thought we looked fierce as we scowled as one at Greg's dad.

'And what've you come as, Mr Valentine? Worzel Gummidge?' said Debs. Me and Hayls nodded, Go Debs!

He laughed and headed into their barn, calling, 'C'mon! Let's get this party star-ted!' in a shite American accent.

I hated that phrase. I loathed it, in fact. It was the sort of thing wannabe trendy types said in American movies at a frat party when they'd sneaked in some contraband cider. Other phrases I hated were, 'I'm MAD like that!' – usually following a very mundane revelation (I just ate two Curly Wurlies. I'm

MAD like that). Oh and, 'She's more like a best friend than a mum.' Which roughly translated means, 'My mum hates my dad, and in the absence of having anyone to talk to she tells me all her boring shite. Plus she dresses too young for her age and ergo looks like a big slut.'

'God!' said Debs. 'I feel ashamed for him.'

'I know. The *shame* of it,' agreed Hayls. And then I saw something that made my heart sink.

My Greg. My lovely Greg was coming out of his house – the *farm*house no less, complete with thatched roof, thank you very much – dressed just like everyone else at the party, his dad included, except Greg was wearing . . . oh my God, I can hardly say it . . .

A pair of dungarees.

Denim dungarees.

No. This wasn't happening. This was meant to be the most perfect of nights. I was looking stunning and he was meant to look stunning. A guy with a face and a body like his needed little help to make himself look stunning. (Me? It took me about forty-eight weeks, and that was just to cover up all my zits.) He was meant to look divine as he stood in the spotlight and uttered those magical words. 'Jodie, will you . . . marry me?' But instead he was going to look like an Eighties lesbian, or worse still, a kids' TV presenter.

'Jesus, Jodie, what are you wearing?'

The girls tutted in unison.

'That's what your dad said,' went Debs.

'It's dead misogynistical,' said Hayls, political as ever.

'What are *you* wearing more like! You look like Sandi Toksvig!'

'It's a bleedin' barn dance. A hoedown.'

'Who are you calling a ho?' Debs was *fuming*.

'Country and Western, all that shite, yeah?' explained Greg.
'Oh,' I said. 'What? Like . . . line dancing?' I asked.

I hated line dancing. Mum had started taking classes and we never heard the end of it. She was forever tucking her thumbs in her belt and sidestepping her way across the through lounge to Dolly Parton. Blimey, she'd have been in her element here tonight, but unfortunately she and Dad had been double-booked and had tickets to go and see a psychic playing the Pavilion in Southport.

Greg nodded. Yep, indeed and a big fat yee-haw! Line dancing seemed very much the order of the night. And as if to prove the point, we suddenly heard a scratchy violin screeching out from the barn and someone on a PA system telling everyone to 'take your partners'. Greg flicked his head in the direction of the barn and said, 'You coming, Jode?'

'No, it's just the way she's standing!' laughed Debs, and Hayls roared her approval. This was number two in my Top Ten Detestable Quips. Number one was, 'D'you want sugar in your tea?' 'No thanks, I'm sweet enough!' followed by chortles of mirth, as if that joke had never been said before.

I rolled my eyes. 'Yeah,' I said with some trepidation as I linked arms with his and we headed towards the barn, Debs and Hayls traipsing behind. It wasn't easy to negotiate the farmyard cobbles on the ground and I nearly went arse over tit a couple of times, but he held on tight. Greg always held on tight. He was good like that. He was, to quote Mary Poppins, practically perfect in every way.

SEVEN

'Partners to your places like the horses to their traces and a-ladies bow and a-gents know how!'

The caller in the barn was a short fat squidgy thing in a straw boater, black shirt and red dickie bow with matching waistcoat. A bit like the Pillsbury Doughboy at a fancy dress party. He was wearing black jeans that were far too big for him, and the way they were jammed into the tops of his cowboy boots made him look more like a Cossack dancer than the MC of a high-kickin' hoedown. The band alongside him were called Veejay and the Bull, for reasons best known to themselves, and though they were teetering on the geriatric and looked like they might at any moment need oxygen and a defibrillator, they strummed, twanged and scratched their strings with gusto. Veejay, who was a bit younger than his cohorts – if a bit equals thirty years – emitted the occasional, 'Yee-haw!' as he played the violin, which sounded odd with his Ahmedabad accent.

'And a right-hand turn and a left-hand turn and whoop that fiddle, boy, whoop!'

And Veejay did indeed whoop. I was a bit sick of do-si-do-ing in high heels by now and a tad dizzy from being spun round like a top, so I slunk away to the back of the barn, pushing my way through stray balloons and exploding party poppers as I went. I was just helping myself to a battered prawn off the monolith of a buffet table when one of Greg's aunties, elbow deep in trifle, nudged me and said, 'God, girl. You look hilarious!' And then laughed as if she'd heard the funniest joke in her life. I readjusted my trilby and tried to ignore her, though when I looked back she was clutching the table as if she might collapse with the hilarity of it all. Through an open door I could see Teresa-May sticking candles in a cake and I realized that some sort of presentation and announcement might be imminent. I needed the loo but decided to hold it all in. Nothing worse than Greg proposing and me not even being there. Embarrassing! I looked around the room and tried to steady my nerves. Another glass of punch might help. I pushed my way over to the bar, where a woman I recognized from Mum's work was serving drinks in a ten-gallon hat and calling everyone 'Y'all'.

'What d'you want, y'all?'

'Glass of punch, please.'

'OK, y'all.'

And all that without even attempting an American accent. I didn't care, though. In a few moments I was going to be the centre of attention. Up until then I was just the girl in the stunning white outfit, Greg's girlfriend with the mismatching eyes, but five minutes from now I would be as famous to them as the late Lady Di. I would stand proudly at Greg's side, just as she did on her engagement day. The only slight difference being my Greg wasn't knobbing some ugly old boot called Camilla at the same time.

I watched the dancing, trying to work out where Greg was. I'd not seen him for ten minutes since he'd said he was nipping outside for a ciggie. I could see Hayls trying to do-si-do with some guy in a motorized wheelchair who'd been after her all night. At the beginning of the evening she'd sworn she'd 'never be seen dead with no spazzy on her arm', but she seemed to be warming to the idea, and him, as the hours went by and the punch went down. As I watched, she sank onto his lap and he took her for a spin in his wheelchair, doing a figure of eight round the barn. They only bumped into two people, and their injuries were minor: laddered tights and a scuffed shinbone.

Our Joey was here. He'd been working for Skippy Skips every Saturday answering the phones in the office (which Greg's mum used to do before she died) for the past few months now. In fact, Greg's dad liked to joke that Our Joey's voice was so girly most customers thought Greg's mum was still working there. Our Joey was sat in a corner with what was commonly known as 'a gob on him'. That is, he looked like he was in a foul mood. Oh dear, maybe his hot date wasn't going well. Our Joey had brought this lad he'd met in some club in town the week before, a club called Sadie's Bar Royal, and the lad was sitting there next to him, also in a bad mood. I was the only person in the room – well, barn – who knew they were on a date – apart from Our Joey and the lad, of course, who was called Mooey – because I was the only person who knew he was gay. He'd not told Mum and Dad yet; he said he was biding his time till he was eighteen, and until then he'd just go to clubs in town and not explain which ones he was going to. Everyone at the barn dance assumed Our Joey had just turned up with a mate.

Debs sidled up to me wiping some Marie Rose sauce off her rubber dress with a serviette.

'I feel a cunt for Hayls, Jode.'

'I know,' I echoed, though I didn't at all.

'Are your nerves gone? Are they jangling?'

I nodded. 'I think it's gonna be soon. I just saw Teresa-May putting candles in a cake.'

'Have you given him your present yet?'

'No, he said he'd get it later, when everyone else has gone.'

'What was it again?'

'Signet ring and *Meet the Fockers* on DVD.'

Debs nodded, impressed. Just then I saw Mooey pushing his way across the dance floor and putting his coat on, like he was leaving.

'Mooey! Mooey! Where you going?' I started following him out and he spun round.

'As far away from your brother as possible,' he said, and you could hear the tears rising in his voice.

'What Mooey? What's happened?'

'I can't say it. It's too hurtful.'

'Has he dumped you?'

'Dumped me? I've only known him five minutes.'

I looked round. Our Joey was still stewing in the corner and looked away as I looked over at him.

'OK, Jodie. D'you wanna know why I'm getting off?'

'Er, yeah.' I was starting to find the slight edge of hysteria in this fella's voice quite unnerving. If he wanted to go, fine. The last thing we needed was someone ruining my proposal with a hissy fit.

'Coz your "brother"' – he actually mimed the inverted commas. No, this fella had to go – 'Your "brother" . . . had the cheek to say to me . . . to say to me . . .'

I had this image in my head of one of those Airplane movies and the camera cutting back to see me putting a noose around my neck. Jeez he was dragging this out.

'He said . . .'

And I hang myself . . .

'He said that your Greg was better looking than me.'

I let out an involuntary chuckle. Was that all? Mooey gasped, as if I'd agreed with an argument that all children under the age of five should be slaughtered to a backing track of The Smiths' 'Reel Around The Fountain'. I realized I'd done a bad thing.

'You heartless . . . bitch!'

With that, he seemed to clutch some imaginary pearls, spin round on his cowboy boots and speed away from the barn.

What a bizarre thing to be upset about. It was as clear as the nose on anyone's face. Mooey was no way better looking than Greg, and if he couldn't cope with Our Joey being honest then he needed to get over it. Of course Our Joey had said Greg was better looking. Greg was the best-looking fella in Merseyside. And he was about to propose to me!

I felt faint every time those words entered my head, but that might have been because I'd only eaten two battered prawns all night and drunk gallons of punch – I didn't want a fat stomach in case people thought I'd only put my jacket on back to front to hide it. The enormity of the situation hit me like a brick on the back of my head. All the roads I'd travelled in the last five years had been leading towards tonight. We'd joked so many times about getting engaged and getting married. Greg knew exactly what sort of big day I had planned; it was just a matter of when he would surprise me with the big proposal. And that time was now. We were soulmates, he'd shown me that. I'd been there for him when his Mum had died; we'd been for weekends away together to the highlands of Scotland (he was right, the mountains were pretty big); our families had met and got on like a house on fire (I'm sure Mum actually flirted with Greg's dad, who she remembered as being 'a bit of a catch in his day'); we'd even decided on baby names we liked (Connor for a boy, Edie for a girl). I stayed over at his place; he'd stayed over at mine (admittedly when Mum and Dad had gone to Beddgelert for the weekend). I'd even started a wedding plan in my Hello Kitty jotter, which Greg had made suggestions for:

WEDDING PLAN

Location: St Hilda's C of E Church, Hunt's Cross. Must start going. How late can I leave that?

Bride: Jodie Paula McGee

Groom: Gregory Adam Valentine

Bridesmaids: Deborah Rawcliffe, Hayley Johnson, Amelia Melrose (Greg's cousin's little girl. Adorable in photos if that rash clears up), the little girl off the Andrex ads (Our Joey's idea. Not sure practical).

Presents for bridesmaids (think that's what you have to do): charm bracelet with two charms on: J for Jodie and G for Greg.

Page Boy: Joseph McGee (though he wants to be a bridesmaid)

Best Man: Kelvin Fitzpatrick (Greg's best mate)

Transport: Greg wants me to arrive at the church in a low loader skip carrier, pleasantly decorated for the occasion – I am a person not a house clearance. (I would prefer a red London bus.) My dad the postman is insisting on GPO vans driving everyone (must price up mattresses for back).

Music: Enter church to 'Here Comes The Sun' by The Beatles (Greg's idea. Like it. Unusual). Hymns: 'I Vow To Thee My Country' (as used in Princess Di's wedding. Mum is insisting) and 'Oh Jesus I Have Promised' (the catchy version). During the signing of the register: special song composed and sung by Hayley Johnson (working title: 'One Sausage Roll, Two Lonely Souls'). Leaving the church: 'Perfect Moment' by Martine McCutcheon. (Greg not happy about this. Wants 'Praise You' by Fat Boy Slim.)

Poetry Reading: by Joseph McGee. He wants to write a poem

(hope it's not rude or that one he read at his sixteenth: 'There once was a bishop from Birmingham, who buggered the boys whilst confirming them.' It gets worse. I can't actually write some of the words down).

Groom's outfit: White suit; white shirt; turquoise tie; white shoes; turquoise carnation; white trilby.

Bride's dress: Self-designed strapless white, tight-fitting, with inlaid butterfly motif, which Mum's mate Maureen is going to make; white trilby and veil; lacy fingerless gloves; 20-foot removable train.

Wedding breakfast location: Greg's dad's barn.

The meal: Prawn cocktail starter. Chicken Kievs with mixed vegetables main. Tiramisu pudding.

Wedding cake: a wedding cake (must look up options – would really like Death By Chocolate, but worried about staining dress).

DJ at wedding party: Joseph McGee.

First dance: 'The Power Of Love' by Jennifer Rush (Greg's mum's favourite song – remembering the dead etc.).

Honeymoon: The Maldives (must find out where they are, cost etc.).

Divorce: Not a moment too soon! (Greg wrote this. Greg is a bastard).

Wedding Invites: Tasteful, understated. Possibly using that photo of the pair of us done up in Wild West gear from when we had that weekend in Blackpool. Though not too happy about this coz makes me look a bit gozzy. Alternatively go to one of those makeover places that make ugly people look like Brad Pitt and Jennifer Aniston. If they can make Fat Brenda from Now is the Winter of Our Discount Tans look half decent, imagine what they can do for us. (Phone Brenda and ask her where she got it done, cost etc., without being rude about her looks/figure/having her jaws wired not working coz she kept pureeing chips and drinking them through a straw.)

Flowers: Turquoise roses (check if these exist or if we'll have to put white ones in jug of water and food colouring, like in primary school experiment)

Make-up: Subtle, understated, heavy on the fake tan.

Something old: Necklace from Nana.

Something borrowed: Necklace from Nana (I never asked if I could have it and then she died. Oh well, it's what she would have wanted).

Something blue: Turquoise flowers (check if turquoise can be described as blue. If not, navy blue knickers – but make sure they don't show through the dress).

Vows: Write our own. Not arsed either way about obeying coz want the wedding to be traditional, but with a twist.

Ideas don't like: The Bo Peep theme as suggested by Our Joey. The Madonna theme as suggested by Our Joey. Roller Disco in Barn as suggested by Our Joey.

Date: Watch this space!

As Veejay and the Bull reached the end of their current number, Pillsbury Doughboy took to the mic and said, 'Ladies and a-gentlemen. If you could please be upstanding . . .' to which Hayls could be heard yelling, 'That's unfair! That's unfair! What if you're in a wheelie?!' and the bloke in the wheelchair looked dead proud of her and slapped her on the arse.

'. . . and if I could invite the birthday boy to the stage, please!'

A round of applause went round the barn as Greg appeared out of the crowd and clambered onto the stage, which was admittedly a very grand term for what appeared to be a row of upturned pallets. Someone dimmed the lights and Teresa-May walked through gingerly with the cake, her face looking waxy in the flicker of the candles. The band started to play 'Happy Birthday' and we all began to sing. I followed the cake through the parting crowd so I could get a prime position nearer the stage, ready for the imminent proposal. I didn't want to stand too close, though, in case it all looked pre-planned. I had to remember to act surprised – possibly falling short of fainting – so I positioned myself three people back from the front. Just close enough, but not desperation close. I realized I was shaking, more out of excitement than anxiety. Greg found me in the crowd and winked at me, I winked back like I was in on the secret plan, and as the song drew to a close I felt Debs slip beside me. She squeezed my hand tightly and mouthed, 'Good Luck,' as Greg blew out all the candles with one headbanging blow. This got another round of applause and the lights came back up again. Damn! I wished he wasn't wearing those hideous dungarees. He took the microphone from Pillsbury Features and tapped it like they did at soundchecks for big gigs. It sent a ricochet of feedback around the barn and Pillsbury barked at him, 'It's on, you meff!' I wanted to punch him. I realized I was getting very overexcited. I was shifting my balance from one foot to the other and slapping the sides of my thighs with my fingers. Greg's dad hopped onstage at this point (which was odd, what did he have to do with the proposal of the year?). My excitement just kept bubbling up and up and up, like an overfilled kettle coming to the boil. It was only a matter of time before I was going to start squealing with orgasmic joy!

But Greg was speaking. So I tried to keep a lid on it.

'Er, I just wanna say a few words, coz I've got a bit of an announcement to make.'

I nearly swooned. I did. My legs buckled and I did a

backwards headbutt on some bloke behind me, who shoved me back upright and said, 'Are you all right, love?' to which I snapped, 'Fine! Shut up he's talking!' Then I shot him a quick smile coz I sounded dead bitchy. God, I was all over the place.

But actually he wasn't talking. He seemed to be struggling to speak, poor love. Well, it was a big deal, proposing to your beloved in front of eighty people in denim and check. Oh, but now he was talking. Finally!

'Erm. Before my mum died . . .'

'God rest her soul!' a drunken aunty called out.

'God love her!' agreed someone else.

'God love the BONES of her!' someone else outdid them.

'We went on holiday. In a motor home. To see all the places she'd ever wanted to see.'

I noticed Teresa-May was fighting back tears. I wanted to scream out, 'Cheer up, love, this is gonna have a happy ending!' but I kept my lips firmly shut.

'And she sat me down and we had this chat and she said she wanted me to be happy.'

And at this point he started to struggle again.

'Anyway. I . . . talking of happiness . . . there's something I want to say tonight. And . . . that . . . is . . .'

And then he stopped. God, he had the audience on the edge of their seats/cowboy boots. He closed his eyes like he was finding it really hard. Bloody hell, time to put the poor guy out of his misery. So I did it. I couldn't help myself. I screeched at the top of my voice, 'YES!'

His eyes flickered up and over to me. He looked bewildered. People turned to look at me. I felt I had to explain, so I screeched again.

'YES, I WILL MARRY YOU!'

Still, he looked dazed.

'WELL THAT'S WHAT YOU WERE GOING TO SAY, ISN'T IT? AND THE ANSWER'S YES! I WILL MARRY YOU!'

Silence. People were looking at me like I was mad. There were a few nervous giggles from the back of the barn. I couldn't work out why Greg was looking so shell-shocked. I'd done him a huge favour and helped him out. What was his problem?

At this point his dad took the mic off him and spoke: 'What Greg was going to say was – and this is our special announcement tonight – that on this the occasion of his twenty first birthday . . .'

I heard someone behind me say, 'She's pissed.'

And someone else agree, 'I know, she's got her coat on back to front.'

'We are delighted to announce that Greg is going to step up to the plate and become . . .'

Say it. MARRIED!

'A fifty per cent partner in Skippy Skips! Way hey!'

Way hey? Way bloody hey? A cheer went up around me and my head began to spin. I looked at Greg, who was staring at me like he was very, very scared.

Oh God. I'd got it wrong. I'd got it wrong on so many levels. I looked at Debs, who had frozen mid-gurn, possibly at the point when she'd realized I was making a holy show of myself. I felt my knees buckle once more and I backwards headbutted the bloke behind me again. He levelled me and I heard some more mutterings about the state of my inebriation.

I had never been so completely and utterly mortified in my whole life. I turned quickly and ran from the room, sweat pouring off me. Or at least I attempted to run. There were so many bloody people in my way it took me about five minutes to get out of the place, and people were looking at me either with disdain, amusement or fear. Make way for the mad woman, their eyes seemed to say.

And who could blame them? I was. I was completely mad. I had to be. How else could I have got it so wrong?

I eventually pushed myself out of the barn and staggered into the moonlit yard. I stood there, catatonic with shame, and burst out crying.

'Jodie! JODIE!'

I could hear Greg shouting behind me as I trampled across the field behind his farmhouse. I had no idea where I was going, but I was definitely walking with purpose. The purpose being to get as far away from the Barn of Shame as possible.

'Jodie, where you going y'knob?!'

I didn't answer him. I didn't even turn round, I was that embarrassed. Especially as I hadn't bargained on how muddy the field would be and had splattered my boots, legs and skirt with what was probably manure. As if I wasn't humiliated enough, I couldn't let him see me looking like this.

'Jodie! Come back!'

'I'm fine!' I shouted. 'I'm just looking for a taxi!'

'In the middle of a bloody field?!'

'I'm absolutely fine!' I said, and with that I felt the ground disappear from under me. The next thing I knew I was tumbling face down into a ditch.

'ARGH!' That was the sound of the tiny bit of dignity I had left vanishing into the ether. I'd scrunched up my eyes, as if that would break my fall, and when I opened them I saw a velvet black sky and a full moon. Jeez it was bright. For some reason I'd thought the field was floodlit, but now I realized it was moonlit. Advancing squelching noises told me Greg was running over. I saw his face peer into view, blocking out the moon like a doctor in a horror movie, his eclipsing curls singed with moonlight.

'Jodie!'

'Leave me alone, Greg. I'm not in a good place right now.'

He nodded. 'I know. You've gone arse over tit into a ditch, you dozy melt.'

He held out a hand, took mine, then pulled me up like he was yanking an onion from the earth. I popped out with about as much grace. My beautiful white boots were brown with mud, and my skirt, too. I didn't even dare look at my state-of-the-art back-to-front blazer. Greg turned, not letting go of my hand, his face snapping from black to white as the moonlight hit him. God, even through a veil of vexation his beauty had the power to take my breath away.

'What was that all about?'

'Greg, you know what it was all about. Please. Don't rub it in.'

I tried to pull my hand from his grasp, but he wasn't letting go. I was hating this. I just wanted to run. Far, far away. As far away from this God-awful mess as was humanly possible.

'You thought I was going to propose to you?'

'Well, you told me you had a big announcement to make. Me and the girls just assumed . . .'

'It was about Skippy Skips.'

'I know that now.'

'What made you think . . .'

'You gave me money to get me hair done. You kept asking me what I was wearing. You never ask me things like that. So I thought . . .'

'I kept asking you coz you say I never take an interest in all your plans for how you look an' all that.'

'I'm so embarrassed. I can never look your family in the eye again.'

'Don't be daft.'

'I ruined your night.'

'You never.'

'I ruined my night. Actually scrap that, I ruined my LIFE.'

And he started to chuckle.

'God, drama queen Jodie!'

'Everyone thought I was pissed. I'm not. Well, I'm a little bit titsy.'

'Tipsy.'

'Don't you start.'

'Well, you did put your coat on back to front.'

'Two words, Greg. Celine Dion!'

'Jodie, can we go back in? It's freezing out here. And Hayls is practically going down on my cousin.'

'In the wheelie?'

Greg nodded.

'I can't go back in looking like this, Greg. I look like I've been shooting a pervy mud-wrestling video.'

'I'll lend you me dungarees.'

'I'd rather go home.'

He brushed some hair out of my face. I think it was mine.

'Jodie, I do want to marry you. But when I propose to you, it's not gonna be in front of a room full of people I either half know or can't stand. D'you know what I'm saying?'

I nodded. I kind of did. It didn't lessen the embarrassment, but it did lessen the pain.

'Coz when I propose to you, it's just gonna be . . .' He looked around, like he was searching for the words. He smiled, then looked back at me smugly. '. . . in front of a sky full of stars.'

He raised his eyes and I followed them. There was a small smattering of stars now. The moon was paler and clouds wrapped round it like cotton wool. I felt Greg slump to the floor. I panicked.

'Jeez, Greg, you all right?'

He looked up at me and nodded.

'I just want it to be intimate. You. Me. And a shitload of stars. Jodie Paula McGee?'

'What?'

'Will you, like, marry me and that?'

Oh God. Oh God. He had actually said it. He had actually proposed. The outfit and outburst were worth it! Again, I felt faint and my knees buckled underneath me. I slumped down to meet him, my classy white jacket rubbing against his vile lezzie dungarees. I threw my arms round him.

'Oh God, Greg, I love you so much!'

I was squeezing him so hard I was actually hurting him. He wriggled free and looked at me.

'You never answered the question.'

I nodded. 'Yeah. Yeah, I will.'

He hugged me and whispered, 'Not too hard, yeah?'

I nodded and hugged him back gently. He then pulled away, realizing something.

'I haven't got you a ring.'

'S'OK. Haven't got you one, either.'

'No, I'm the bloke. The bloke always has to get the bird a ring.'

'Tweet tweet to you an'all, knob.' I hated being called a bird. Hayls reckoned it made me a feminist.

'Hang on.' He went into the front pocket of his dungarees and pulled out a bunch of keys. He spent a minute or so prising the keys off the keyring, then slipped it onto the third finger of my left hand. Dangling off it was a plastic fob housing the logo Skippy Skips and their phone and fax numbers.

'How does it feel?'

'It's a perfect fit.' It was, of course, about ten times bigger than my finger. 'And I love the logo. Everyone's wearing Skippy Skips in Paris. You can't move for them on the catwalks.'

'Come 'ed then.' He stood and dragged me to my feet.

'What? Where we going?'

He nodded towards the other end of the field.

'Back to the barn. We've got some celebrating to do.'

We held hands and walked through the field. I didn't care that he was wearing dungarees now. And I didn't give two hoots that I looked like I'd taken a shower in manure. I was going to walk back into that barn with my head held high. Love was blind, love was great, and I was engaged to be bleedin' married!

EIGHT

I lay in my bed the next morning feeling a mixture of excitement and shame. And that's a heady mix. I'd rather have been lying in Greg's bed, tangled up in his arms and legs, obviously, but despite me being twenty, Mum and Dad still didn't think it was becoming for me to sleep over with him too often. And if there was any chance of getting me home then they insisted on it. I'd tried to wangle a stopover the night before, but the fact that our Joey would be getting a taxi back from the barn dance and therefore I could share with him meant it was a done deal. Sunlight was blazing in through my too-thin powder-pink curtains, and as I looked at my walls, adorned with black-and-white posters that I thought were arty and tasteful – a naked man holding a baby, Audrey Hepburn with a cigarette holder – I felt excitement that my plan was finally coming together. We were now engaged. The shame of squealing like a stuck pig in front of the gathered guests still made me go pink-faced – I could feel it – but as Hayls always said: the ends justified the means. I was just a bit worried that I'd bullied Greg into proposing. I comforted myself in my confusion by reminding myself of my wedding book, and how Greg had known about it and contributed to it. So if a wedding had always been on the cards, all I'd done was speed things up a little, I thought. No, I knew. Oh God. I wished I was more decisive.

Our Joey and I had rolled in at just after two in the morning with a bottle of fizzy wine and streamers dragging from our ankles, and I'd run upstairs, burst into Mum and Dad's room, snapped on the lights and shouted, 'Mama's getting married!' in a corny American accent. Cue groans and screwed-up eyes as Mum and Dad sat up, dazed and confused by the sudden interruption to their dreams.

'Jesus, Jodie, what happened to you? Are you all right?' asked Mum.

'Have you been mugged?' added Dad. I'd forgotten I was covered in mud.

'No, I fell over. Shortly before Greg proposed to me!'

'Where did you fall, love? In a frigging sewage farm?' Dad was bewildered.

'GOD! You just don't get it, do you? I'm ENGAGED!'

Mum reached out to the bedside cabinet and put her reading glasses on. Maybe now she'd read the situation better she'd be thrilled. No such luck, her face fell.

'Your coat's on back to front. Has something happened, Jodie?'

'It's not a coat, it's a jacket.'

'It's a blazer,' Our Joey said. I'd not heard him slink in behind me.

'And it's meant to be back to front, it's stylish.'

I could hear Our Joey tittering. That wasn't helpful.

'We'll talk about this in the morning,' Mum said sternly.

'How was the psychic?' asked Our Joey.

'Shite,' said Dad.

'Malcolm!'

'Well she was. Telling you your mother died in a car crash. She died on the toilet. All the way to Southport for that?'

'There's still no need to swear.' Mum looked back at me and Our Joey. 'Jodie, it's two o'clock in the morning. Get some sleep and we'll discuss this in the morning.'

Me and Our Joey retreated downstairs, cracked open the fizzy wine and danced round the through lounge to the sound-track to *Muriel's Wedding*. Five minutes later there was a bang on the ceiling and Dad hollered to 'turn that shite down', followed by Mum hollering, 'Malcolm!' We turned it down and, deciding the fizzy wine tasted like cat's pee that had gone through a Soda Stream, reckoned it was time for bed.

The next morning, I woke to hear noises downstairs and decided it was time to face the music. I sat up, rubbed my eyes, yawned, decided I didn't feel too bad considering the amount of punch I'd drunk the night before, and the tiny amount of food I'd lined my stomach with, and pulled my dressing gown on.

'Where's your ring?' Mum said five minutes later over break-fast. I was having toast, she was having a ciggie out of the back door and we both had a cup of tea on the go.

'He's saving up for one,' I said. She pulled a face.

'What, he proposed to you and he hadn't bought a ring?'

'It's the thought that counts. I'm not materialistic like that.'

'He's tight, you mean?'

'No. Anyway, it was all a bit . . . spur of the moment.'

'D'you not think you're a bit young, love?'

'Why?'

'Well . . . on account of your age.'

'No, I mean . . . Why can't you be happy for me? Everyone

else is made up for me. So why do you have to be the moany one?'

'Coz she's your mother and she loves you, you dozy mare,' said Dad, coming in with the paper he'd bought while walking the dog. He hung about Mum as she stubbed out her ciggie, shut the back door and went about finishing off a cup of tea for him. This happened every morning.

'Your dad's right. And we love you more than anyone else does.'

'Except Greg,' I countered.

'*Including* Greg.'

'Well, if you did love me that much, you'd be happy for me.'

'I am happy for you, love. We both are. As long as you know what you're doing.'

'And all your mum's saying is, you might be a bit young to go rushing into decisions like that,' Dad chipped in. They're good at doing that, dads: chip city.

'I'm not rushing into anything. Five years I've known him.'

'I know, love.'

'And anyway, I'm not too young. I'm twenty! Most girls round here are grandmas by now.'

'I know, love,' concurred Mum. Dad rolled up his paper, then she handed him his tea. This meant he was about to go and spend about half an hour on the toilet. If any of us needed a wee in the meantime, we had to go in the back garden. Mum came and sat at the kitchen table with me.

'Don't pick my nice lino tablecloth, love.'

So I stopped. I looked at her face. She was smiling, but it was a sad smile. Eskimos might have a million different words for snow, but my Mum had a million different smiles, and this was the sort that made my heart sink.

'I don't see what your problem with Greg is.'

'Jodie, I don't have a problem with Greg. He's a nice boy, he's got manners and he's going places. I just . . . worry about you.'

'Well don't.'

'Well I do.'

'Well don't. At least he's not some smack-head or wife-beater or mass murderer. I'd understand why you were banging on if he was.'

'Jodie, I know you think marriage is the be all and end all, but it's not.'

'Well you're happy, aren't you?'

She hesitated, then shrugged. 'Of course.'

'You don't sound so sure. If you're not happy with your relationship then don't take it out on me.'

She narrowed her eyes, which was commonly known as 'giving me a look'. It usually meant I was on rocky ground, and clearly in this case I was. Her smile had gone now, but the lines around her mouth remained in place. Years of smoking had caught up with her and she would always have three little dents on either side of her mouth. Dad said they made her beautiful. He reckoned they looked like footsteps left by tiny sparrows. Beauty is definitely in the eye of the beholder.

'It just seems like, since you left school, all you've been bothered about is Greg.'

'And what's wrong with that?'

'Nothing. But what do you want from life, Jodie?'

'How d'you mean?'

'It's different for girls your age now. You don't have to just settle for marriage to make you happy. You can do whatever you want with your life.'

'That's what I'm doing. I'm marrying the man I want to spend the rest of my life with.'

'Doing what? His cooking and cleaning? Raising his kids? Is that what women burned their bras for?'

I couldn't believe she was saying this. It's hardly like she was on the frontline at Greenham.

'I don't know why you're so down on marriage all of a sudden.'

'I'm not. It's just you're twenty years of age. I don't want you to give up on all your dreams just coz of some fella.'

'My dream is being with Greg. My dream's coming true. You should be happy for me.'

She started playing with the sugar bowl, grinding the granules with a teaspoon. She was clearly leading up to something. I chewed on my toast and waited.

'You . . . you used to wanna be an actress. On *Acacia Avenue*.'

'Yeah, well I had my chance and I blew it.'

'That was years ago, Jodie!'

'So?'

'So are you really the sort of person who gives up at the first sign of failure?'

'Oh, so I'm a failure now, am I?'

'I didn't say that. It's just you're good at it, Jodie. Everyone says. Mrs Mendelson used to sing your praises. You've got a gift.'

'There's loads of actresses out there. I'd never make it.'

Mum shook her head. Her dyed blonde hair fell across her face and she scraped it out of the way. She looked less like Princess Di these days. Princess Di never had inch-long roots.

'Look, if you want to get married to Greg then fine. I just want you to think long and hard about what you want from life.'

'I have.'

'Have you?' She, of course, didn't look so sure.

'Yeah.'

'Right. Well then, that's OK.'

Then she smiled again, and to any casual onlooker it would have looked like she'd given in and everything was fine, but I knew it was forced, though it didn't make me any less grateful for it. Maybe now she'd stop giving me a hard time.

I could hear Our Joey in the living room. He flicked the telly on and suddenly the Welsh burr of Bronwen from *Brunch With Bronwen* played as a backdrop to my none-too-comfortable tête à tête with Mum. If I'd thought it was over I was wrong. Our Joey's close proximity seemed to kick start another angle of attack for Mum.

'Our Joey knows what he wants from life.'

'Bully for him.'

'He wants to be a DJ.'

'I know.' I felt like adding, in the gay clubs, but there was no point dobbing him in now.

'He's really focused about it. Buying all the latest records, making tapes, saving up for new decks.'

'I know.'

'He's not taking his eye off the prize. He's not even allowed himself a girlfriend.'

I looked into the living room and saw Our Joey staring at me with a look of alarm. I looked back at Mum.

'I know. He's such a martyr.'

'No, Jodie. He's got his priorities right. There's no need to be sarcastic.'

'Well maybe he can DJ at the wedding.'

'He knows. Career first, girls later.'

I felt like saying, 'Yeah, much later, like, after he's dead.' But I didn't. Our Joey ambled into the kitchen, clearly wanting to change the course of the conversation, but covering it with a pretence of nosiness.

'What yous two jangling about?'

'What do you think about me getting married?' I said to Our Joey accusatorily, convinced he'd back me up. After all, he'd danced round the through lounge with me to 'Sugar Baby Love' in celebration, hadn't he?

'None o' my business,' he replied, and he scratched his bum and yawned as he flicked the kettle on. His words were like a dagger through the heart. After everything I'd done for him – covering for him, lying for him to Mum and Dad – it really hurt. Why the sudden change of heart?

'What's the matter, Joey?' I said. 'Got splinters in your arse from sitting on the fence?'

'Jodie!' Mum was aghast.

'People say arse, Mother, whether you like it or not.'

'And is that what Greg's attracted to, is it? Your sewer of a mouth?'

'Clearly! I mean, he couldn't possibly think I was pretty, or funny, or a nice person. He's just marrying me coz I know a few dirty words.'

'Very defensive all of a sudden . . .'

'It's human nature, Mum. Especially when you're under attack.'

I did my best impersonation of a flounce into the living room and stared at *Brunch With Bronwen*. In the kitchen I heard Our Joey sucking up to Mum.

'Mum? D'you want me to sort out your roots tonight?'

'Oh, would you, Angel?'

Well that was it then. He was obviously an angel, and I was the devil incarnate. At the other end of the bungalow I heard the toilet flush and the hiss of air freshener. I took myself off to my bedroom and began doodling in my wedding planning book.

I couldn't shake off the feeling that me and Our Joey were growing apart. On one level I guessed it was inevitable. We'd grown up cocooned in Sandalan with each other for company, us two against the world. We'd played together, dreamed together, put on dance displays in our through lounge together, charging ten pence admission to our parents and claiming the money was going to charity – T.P.O.J.A.J., we said, 'the pockets of Jodie and Joey' – but we weren't kids any more, and as we got older our relationship began to consist of snatched time in the evenings, gossiping about what we'd got up to and who with. Admittedly, most of this was what I'd got up to, as Our Joey found it hard to make friends. Not that he was a social nightmare or anything, it's just that he was a bit girly and camp, and lads his own age were suspicious of this, though he had no end of girlfriends – all platonic, of course. Then I'd left school and got my job at the supermarket with Debs and Hayls, who were my best mates from school. I felt a bit sorry for Our Joey during the two years he'd had at school without me there. He didn't have that many allies, but he seemed to cope OK, possibly because he'd started going out on the gay scene in Liverpool a few nights a week. At least it made our catch-up sessions a bit more interesting and scandalous when we did see each other, with his tales of topless men, drag queens and amyl nitrate. But then when he'd left school at sixteen with a clutch of GCSEs he'd started working for Greg's dad's company and we naturally ended up spending more time together again, as he was in my 'in-laws' orbit, too. Every time I popped round to Greg's house, Our Joey was beavering away in the barn they'd converted into an office, wearing a headset phone, typing really fast and drinking tea from a mug that said, 'You don't have to be mad to work here but it helps'. He claimed it was ironic. He seemed to fit in perfectly and Greg's dad thought the world of him because he was keen, polite with the customers on the phone and kept the office immaculate. The only time they had a disagreement, as far as I'm aware, was when Our Joey changed the music on the phone's call-waiting system from 'Greensleeves' to 'Believe' by Cher ('Coz I love what she does with her voice on it'). Our Joey really couldn't see what the issue was. I must say, that did tickle me.

There was a knock at the door and Our Joey came in looking a little shame-faced.

'Sorry about that,' he said.

'So you should be. You've got more faces than the town hall clock.'

'The town hall's only got one clock.'

'Yeah, and you've got more faces than it, coz you've got two,' I countered, desperately trying to make my analogy work. He came and sat on my bed. I moved my feet reluctantly so he could squeeze on.

'It's just . . . Mum was getting a bit too close to the bone.'

'About me?'

'About me. I'm sure she knows, you know.'

'She doesn't.'

'So why does she keep going on about girlfriends?'

'Coz she thinks you're bloody brilliant, putting your career ahead of them.'

He stared at the carpet.

'I hate this,' he said after a while.

'Lying?'

He nodded.

'Then tell them.'

He looked at me like I was crazy. 'They'll kick off. They'll kick me out. They'll think it's not . . .'

'Becoming?' I suggested. He grinned and nodded, relieved

that someone else on this planet understood our parents as well as he did.

'I will tell them. One day.'

I ducked. He looked confused. I winked. 'Just ducking them pigs flying across the sky.'

He slapped my ankles. 'I will. I'll tell 'em. You watch.'

As it turned out, he didn't have to. The police told them.

NINE

Greg's cousin, who Hayls copped off with at the barn dance, was called Lotan O'Grady. He'd claimed to have ended up in a wheelchair after playing on the railway lines as a kid and getting himself electrocuted. Whereas most of us thought that made him a bit of a knob, Hayls thought he was some kind of war hero, or the victim of a huge miscarriage of justice. After a few Lambrinis she had even been known to moot the idea of a conspiracy theory about the railway bosses using him to make an example of what happens when children break the rules and go against the state. God love Hayls, ever the political animal, if a slightly misguided one.

Then one day his mum had told Hayls that Lotan had always been in a wheelchair, so she dumped him because he'd lied to her.

'He can't always have been in a wheelchair,' I said, while Hayls cried on my shoulder in the stock lift.

'He has. His Ma said,' she spluttered between breaks in the tears.

'Well, he can't have come out of the womb in one,' I pointed out, which mollified her.

'But why did he lie to me?' she asked.

'I dunno,' I said with a shrug.

'Maybe,' said Debs, 'he was just trying to sound more interesting.'

'Oh yes.' I ran with this. 'Like that time you told everyone your aunty was Wincey Willis.'

Hayls blushed, though it was hard to tell under all that fake tan.

A week later they were back together. Hayls was very quick to inform everyone that Lotan hadn't lied through choice, but that society had forced him to lie. None of us minded as Lotan was basically a decent guy.

Hayls thought he was the bee's knees and fussed over him like he was a precious newborn baby, treating the wheelchair like an oversized pram. She was forever lifting him out of it onto your couch, then folding it up with two sharp slaps and a kick and moaning about the lack of wheelchair access – even at Sandalan. Honestly, she couldn't even pop round for a coffee without answering the first 'How are you?' with 'Well, Jodie. I'm fine. But what I'm thinking about is . . . how would Lotan have made it up them stairs?' It was enough to drive you mad. We lived in a dormer bungalow, for God's sake! There was *one* step up from the drive to the front door, and she made it sound like we lived at the top of the Thirty-Nine Steps. (Even mentioning that film could send her into flights of apoplexy. 'All them stairs?! All them stairs?! What about the poor kids in wheelies?!') It had to be said, Hayls seemed more obsessed with Lotan's disability than he was. He seemed to forget he was in a chair most of the time, whereas it was constantly at the forefront of Hayls's mind, which seemed to embarrass her beloved. She was up on all the disabled jargon, too. God help you if you dared describe Lotan as 'confined to a wheelchair', she'd be down on you like a ton of politically correct bricks. 'Wheelchairs are liberating, Jodie, not confining! GOD!'

Everything came to a head for Our Joey on the night of Lotan's twenty-first. We were all meeting in a pub called the Baby Elephant in Woolton Village, whose wheelchair access, Hayls claimed, was second to none. The Baby Elephant had always been our watering hole of choice, ever since school. There were two pubs next door to each other on the high street in Woolton, a big one called the Elephant, which was full of old crumblies banging on about the war, and a smaller more modern one next door called the Baby Elephant. Now I'm not saying they encouraged underage drinking, but the fact that its nickname was Schoolies Corner will give you some idea of its clientele. We knew we should have outgrown the place by now, but Hayls couldn't get enough of their ramps and low-slung bars. Plus they had a disabled toilet, which Hayls had been known to police, practically glassing anyone with fully working legs who ran the gauntlet of trying to sneak in when she wasn't looking.

Debs had been seeing a guy called Alex for ages. He was a bit of a prick, but he was harmless enough, despite being a soldier and thus, as Debs always said salaciously, 'a trained killer.' Fortunately, because he was in the army he was hardly ever round, which suited me just fine. I wasn't a big fan of blokes coming between me, Hayls and Debs, and I'd tried very hard not to overlook the girls in the pursuit of my full-blown love affair with the sex god otherwise known as Greg. Debs was good at keeping our friendship going, mostly because Alex was away a lot 'on manoeuvres' or 'down the NAAFI', but Hayls was more than happy to drop us in favour of her new cause – sorry, flame – Lotan. In fact, when we did meet up with Hayls she would either bring him with her or, if he was busy, she would come alone and talk about nothing but him. She'd say provocative things like, 'It wasn't till I met a paraplegic that I really understood what true love-making means.' And then be disappointed when Debs and I ignored her and talked about the latest episode of *Acacia Avenue*. Mind you, she hated *Acacia Avenue*. 'Where's our visibility?' she'd say. I really think she thought she was disabled, too.

A small gang of us had gathered at the pub before Hayls and Lotan arrived. I only knew Debs and Alex, but I smiled overenthusiastically at anyone who looked my way as we were all going to be spending a few hours together and I didn't want anyone thinking I was 'that moody boot in the corner'. I glanced at my watch as Debs came back with our drinks.

'What time's your Greg getting here, Jode?'

'He should be here by now, but he was waiting on a lift from one of the guys from work.'

The pub door swung open and I instinctively looked to see if it was Gorgeous Greg. Instead I saw Lotan approaching and a small cheer went up from our crowd. The door swung shut behind him – no sign of Hayls.

'Where's Hayls, Lotan?' Debs shouted out.

'She's just coming,' he said.

'Yeah, I heard it took her ages!' giggled Debs, just within earshot of me and Alex, who guffawed into his pint.

'She's just got a bit stuck on the ramp,' explained Lotan, though none of us knew what he meant. As Lotan wheeled himself over we saw the door open again and another wheelchair came in – with Hayls in it. She was dolled up to the nines and looked slightly out of breath. Mine and Debs' mouths dropped open.

'What are you looking at?' she said fiercely. 'Never seen a girl in a wheelie before?'

She pushed herself over to our table.

'But you're not—' Debs stopped herself from saying something offensive as Hayls glared. 'You're not disabled.'

Hayls shook her head, sickened. 'Can't you see what I'm doing, Debs?'

Debs shrugged. 'Making a holy show of yourself?'

Hayls fixed her with a look. 'I'm challenging society's preconceptions about disability. Get me a lager and black.'

'Get it yourself,' Alex butted in. Hayls turned a steely glare on him.

'I'm in a fucking wheelchair.'

At this point in the evening I really did think the world had stopped making sense. And it didn't get any easier to fathom from then on in.

'Look,' I said, ever the peacemaker, 'I'll get her a drink. Lager and black you say?'

'Nothing wrong with your hearing is there? Unlike me,' said Hayls. 'I've just found out I'm deaf.'

'So how did you hear what she said?' asked Alex. It seemed like a completely reasonable question.

'Sorry, can you speak up? And move your lips more?'

'So what, you're deaf now?' I said. Hayls nodded her head.

'Deaf and thirsty.'

I headed to the bar. It took me ages to get served and eventually Debs came and joined me, ostensibly to give me a hand, but really to bitch about Hayls.

'She's off her head,' she said.

'I know. I think she's actually mentally ill or something.'

'Apparently she had a hearing test today. God knows why. And the doctor said she only had ninety-five per cent hearing in her left ear.'

I rolled my eyes. 'She'll be parking in disabled bays next.'

Just then Greg arrived, looking panicky. I wanted to throw my arms around him because a) he was so bloody lovely and b) it showed all the lay-dees in the pub that he was taken.

But I didn't because he was all on edge. He didn't bother with pleasantries and dove straight in.

'Have you heard about Your Joey?'

'What about him?'

'I phoned yours to see if you wanted a lift, but you'd already left and your ma was having an eppy.'

'Why?'

'Your Joey's been arrested.'

I felt my innards lurch downwards. 'What for?'

'Getting up to all sorts on Otterspool Prom.'

'All sorts?' chipped in Debs. 'What does all sorts mean?'

I had a horrible feeling I knew exactly what it meant. I paid for the drinks, made my apologies to Lotan and Hayls – who hissed that I was leaving because I was uncomfortable around cripples or something – and went outside, where we jumped into Greg's car and sped away. We sat in silence on the journey home. I was dreading what I would find when I got to Sandalan. I knew that most people went to Otterspool Prom for a nice brisk walk, or to sit in its various gardens and watch the brown Mersey floating past, but Our Joey had also told me that some gay men nipped through a hole in the fence that led to the railway lines and got up to . . . well, all sorts.

When I walked through the front door it felt like stepping into a heavy-going *Play for Today* from the Seventies. The whole atmosphere of the bungalow had changed. It was as if it had suddenly turned black and white. As I walked in I could tell that Mum was in the through lounge, Dad was in the kitchen and Our Joey was in his room. They might not have been saying anything to each other, but through the silence they were screaming. I could hear Our Joey pacing in his room, I could hear Dad rummaging through drawers in the kitchen and Mum was sitting, catatonic, in the through lounge.

Greg leaned in to me. 'I'll go and check Joey's all right.'

I nodded – God love him – and he disappeared into the hall.

Mum didn't acknowledge my arrival, she just kept staring straight ahead, her eyes on the blank TV.

'I suppose you knew.' There was so much vitriol in her tone of voice. Like I'd made him gay just to spite them. Like I'd been laughing behind her back all this time.

'Mum?' I was acting dumb. Something I was very convincing at as I'd had a lot of experience doing it for real.

'I suppose you knew Our Joey is a freak.'

'He's not a freak.'

Dad came bombasting in from the kitchen now.

'Oh, and I suppose you think it's normal to go shagging blokes in the great outdoors?'

Things must have been bad as Mum didn't tell him off for saying 'shagging'. Though she did shiver like someone had rubbed a piece of ice down her back.

'Well, no I don't,' I agreed.

'Otterspool Prom!' cried Mum. 'We used to take you there for picnics.' He'd clearly sullied her memory of it for ever.

'What was he actually arrested for?'

'Gross indecency in a public place,' said Dad, and each syllable was punctuated with his disgust.

'He wasn't arrested; he was just cautioned. Coz of his age.'

'I mean, Jeez, it's one thing being a gay; it's another thing doing it in a frigging park.' Dad shook his head.

'Malcolm!' Oh, so she was getting her mojo back. 'And it's not a park, is it? It's a beauty spot!'

'A beauty spot?!' I laughed involuntarily and she gave me one of her looks. It brought me up short. Time to back-pedal. 'Well, yes, it is a thing of beauty in . . . spot form.' God, must do better! Mum sighed.

'Oh well,' I said, trying to lighten the load, 'now we know why he's put his career ahead of girlfriends!'

Mum rolled her eyes. 'Don't make this about you, Jodie.'

Why shouldn't I? Just for one moment. Surely she could see that I was fighting Our Joey for the crown of golden child. Surely I'd be allowed some Brownie points now for being . . . well . . . normal!

'The shame of it, Jodie. We had to go to the police station to get him. And he's completely unapologetic.'

'He did say sorry, Sandra.'

'Well, I didn't hear him.'

'I mean, he did sound a bit sarky when he said it, like.'

'Poor Joey,' I said. Whoops, bad move. Mum jolted in her seat like she was in the electric chair.

'Poor Joey? Poor Joey? What about poor us, having to go to the cop shop to fetch him?!' Mum had been watching too many soaps and had picked up most of her phrases from them. She'd start calling me Treacle or Princess next, like Dirty Den. 'The shame of it, Jodie. The utter shame. The way they were looking at us. Judging us.' And she dissolved into tears, pulling a paper hankie from the sleeve of her cardigan and burying her face in it. Dad rubbed her shoulder. It was hardly the most affectionate of moves: he looked like he was rubbing something off a car-seat cover. Just then we heard footsteps coming across the carpet, and suddenly Our Joey was stood in the doorway with a bag over his shoulder. Greg followed behind him.

'Don't be a knob, Joe,' Greg was saying. Joe? He called him Joe? I'd not heard that before.

'Where d'you think you're going?' said Mum, sounding like all the things she hated: common, unbecoming and fishwife-esque.

'As far away from here as possible!' gasped Our Joey. He sounded like he was in an episode of *Dynasty*.

'You've got nowhere to go,' I pointed out.

'Haven't I?' said Our Joey.

'You've brought shame on this family, lad,' Dad said, pointing at him. It didn't look like a convincing move. In fact it made him look quite wimpy, even though the conviction of his words was definitely at the vehement end of the scale.

'I can't help who I am.'

'OTTERSPOOL PROM!' Mum suddenly shrieked, then cried into her hankie again. Dad rushed to rub her shoulder.

'This is killing your mother.'

'Then I have no choice but to go,' said Our Joey. Gosh, from *Dynasty* to a costume drama in one fell swoop. I could tell Mum didn't want him to go. Mind you, she didn't want him to stay either.

'It's the tackiness that gets me, Joey,' she said. 'In a beauty spot. With a complete stranger.'

'A beauty spot?' said Our Joey.

'What happened to the other fella? Was he arrested as well?' I asked.

Joey shook his head. 'He got off. He legged it quicker than me.'

Suddenly, from nowhere, Mum said, 'Greg would you mind taking your trainers off, please? I've only just had this carpet cleaned.'

I knew for a fact she'd not had it cleaned, but when I checked out Greg's trainees (for the first time that evening) I saw Mum's point. They were caked in mud, like he'd been walking through a bog. He must have come straight from work and not got changed.

'Sorry, Mrs McGee,' he said as he bent down to slip them off. Our Joey sighed and rolled his eyes.

'So anyway, like I said, I'm going. So . . . don't try and stop me.'

They didn't. Not because they wanted him to go, but because they just didn't know what to say. Our Joey scowled, pulled his bag closer to him, then walked out. As the front door slammed, Mum broke down again, gasping to Dad, 'I've lost my baby. I've lost my baby boy. I don't recognize him any more. Who is he, Malcolm? Who is he?'

'Mum!' I said, losing patience. 'He's still your baby boy. He's still Our Joey. Nothing's changed.'

'Everything's changed! I'll never have grandkids now!'

'Mum! I'm still here. I'm gonna have about a million kids, so that's not strictly true, is it?'

'It's just such a shock.'

I sighed. 'Is it? Is it really? He's always been more girly than most lads. He's obsessed with the Eurovision Song Contest. He's never had a girlfriend. He does your roots, for God's sake! And what did he ask for for his fifth birthday?'

'I forget,' she said dismissively. She hadn't forgotten. She knew full well.

'A pair of ruby slippers, like Dorothy in *The Wizard of Oz*. Mum, this was a done deal years ago.'

Mum visibly smarted. 'Oh, so are you trying to say I'm stupid?'

'No. No, I'm not. But just because he's gay, it doesn't make him a bad person.'

'No,' she seemed to agree. 'But gross indecency in a public place might.'

'Well, maybe he went to Otterspool Prom because there was nowhere else to go. Have you ever thought of that?'

Mum looked to Dad and muttered, 'There's no talking to her, Malcolm.'

Greg put his arm round me and said softly, 'Shall we go and find Joey?'

I nodded. Mum looked at Dad. 'Malcolm, fetch me a gin.'

We found Our Joey sat at the bus stop with his bag on his knees. I was right, he had nowhere to go, so Greg suggested we all go back to his and he could stay the night there. I phoned Mum from a phone box and told her, informing her that I'd be staying the night as well. Usually she'd kick up a fuss about me sleeping over with Greg, but the fight had gone out of her today. She was probably relieved that I wasn't having some lezzie bunk-up with Teresa-May, so she let it go.

We returned home the next day, me and Our Joey, and as is the tradition of the great British family, nobody said anything about the police caution, Our Joey's departure, or indeed his sexuality. It was a white elephant in the dormer bungalow. The elephant grew bigger each day till its trunk was practically cracking the roof. It was then that Our Joey burst out over tea one night, 'I promise I'll never go to Otterspool Prom again. I'll never get into trouble. I'll meet a nice fella and you'll be proud of me!'

I looked from Mum to Dad, panicked slightly by their alarmed expressions. Mum considered him for a second, before saying, 'Malcolm? Pass the Daddies.'

And Dad passed her the brown sauce.

Over the coming months, the incident wasn't mentioned again. None of the neighbours found out, the only people who knew about it apart from immediate family were Debs, Hayls and Greg, and they knew better than to blab. Mum's way of coping with it was to pretend it never happened. Her one concession to Our Joey being gay was that every now and again, when a handsome fella was on the telly, she'd go, 'Oh he's dishy.' And she'd look to Our Joey and Our Joey would nod, even if it was Eamonn Holmes or Richard Madeley or someone. And then something brilliant happened. Mum's friend Maureen from work started bragging that her daughter had just come out as a lesbian. It was all she'd bang on about at the factory, and the women in their section seemed to be jealous that she had such an exotic child. So Mum outdid her by announcing that Our Joey had been gay for years and she was really cool with it and practically let him have orgies in the through lounge every weekend while she cracked open a tube of Pringles and played a selection of disco classics on the accordion. After that she started to be irritatingly down with the gays. Whenever she mentioned him in conversation she'd say, 'My lovely gay son Joey,' almost daring people to disagree. She encouraged him to write to anyone she thought was slightly camp on the telly, asking them out on a date (he didn't). Never did keeping up with the Joneses play so much in Our Joey's favour.

And, eventually, mine. Her new found laissez-faire attitude altered her opinion of my engagement. Although me and Greg hadn't set a date for the big day, she returned home one night and placed a book on the kitchen table in front of me.

Plan Your Wedding: With Idaho Manchester.

'Mum!' I gasped, tears pricking my eyes, 'You shouldn't have! Let me . . . let me give you the money!'

She shook her head.

'You're all right, love.' God, she could be so *nice*. 'It's from the library.'

Still, it was the thought that counted.

TEN

Hello, I'm Idaho Manchester. I've been co-ordinating weddings for over twenty years. Yes! Twenty years! I know, I don't look old enough. But can I let you in on a little secret? It's not the surgeon's knife that has kept me so fresh – it's my hands-on work with loving couples and their families as they plan the most important day of their lives. I feel truly blessed by God to have found such a wonderful, life-affirming vocation. I design weddings with a personal touch and creative eye, and guide my brides and grooms graciously throughout the planning process, from innovative concept to flawless execution. Here, in this purse-sized book, you can benefit from my decades of expertise for a fraction of my usual fee! Everybody is unique. You're unique. Let's see if I can help you design the perfect wedding that is as individual as you are . . .

'Can I just say?' said Hayls, squatting on the end of my bed, looking at a photo on the back cover of the book. 'Idaho Manchester is a SHOW!'

'I know,' added Debs, kneeling on the floor next to Hayls, 'she looks like she's taken that perm off, given it a few minutes in the frying pan, then chucked it back on her head!'

We were having a *Grease*-style slumber party. Us girls had Carmen rollers in our hair and Our Joey was wearing a face pack while we drank white wine spritzers and listened to CDs.

'She's definitely had surgery round her eyes,' Our Joey joined in as he backcombed the hair on an old gonk of mine. 'It's just a shame they didn't manage to correct her squint at the same time.'

'Stop being so bitchy you lot!' I moaned. 'That book's gonna make my wedding go without a hitch.'

It was true, though, Idaho Manchester wasn't the prettiest lady in the world. Her photo showed her leaning on the back of a couch, her head resting on a lacy gloved hand, and it was taken with so much soft focus that whenever I looked at it I thought I needed an eye test. But for me, right now, she was Saint Idado, who was going to sort out all my problems.

'She sounds like a fucking drag queen,' murmured Our Joey.

'And listen to this!' screeched Hayls, reading from the inside cover, 'Idaho lives in The Hamptons with a menagerie of cats and parakeets!'

'The bitch isn't even married?!' That was Debs.

'No wonder she's wearing gloves, she's covering up the fact that she's not got so much as an engagement ring, never mind a wedding band!'

'Stop picking on her!' That was me. I'd read the book so many times I felt Idaho was my friend. I'd even toyed with inviting her to the wedding, so helpful was the book, with its handy hints not to drink caffeine or alcohol before the service in case you needed to go for a wee during the vows.

'She's weird,' Hayls continued. 'Obsessed with weddings coz no man'd go near her.'

'You're so cruel!' I said, incredulous. Though thinking about it, maybe they had a point.

'Show us your ring again, Jode?' said Debs, and I waggled my beautiful engagement ring aloft while they all cooed.

'Oh tell us the story again. It's so romantic!' said Debs.

I saw Our Joey roll his eyes. 'Romantic?'

'I think it's dead romantic, yeah,' said Hayls all dreamy-eyed, toying with the hearing aid we all knew she didn't really need.

So I told it anyway.

Greg and I had traipsed round all the jewellery shops in the centre of Liverpool and he was starting to think I was very high maintenance because I couldn't decide on a ring I liked. I wanted something classic, but with a twist. I just couldn't really say what that twist might be. I liked the look of the diamondy ones, but of course they were vastly expensive, then some days I fancied a ruby, or an amethysty one, or even a sapphirey type. Our trips round Liverpool always ended with disappointment, though on the upside, we found a café that served something called rocky road pie, which we both discovered we loved. In fact, we adored it, and on some trips to the city centre we couldn't be bothered hauling our tired arses round the shops, so we headed straight for the café instead. One day I decided to put Greg out of his misery. It was a Tuesday, it was raining and it felt like the end of the world because not only had we not brought an umbrella with us – I'm so crap at being a girl sometimes. Proper girls carry microscopic emergency umbrellas with them at all times. Even in the desert – so we were soaked to the skin, but when we got to our café of choice the blousy server told us the rocky road pie was off. I burst out crying – I was pre-menstrual, you know how it goes – and Greg delivered a tirade of abuse to the not-so-blousy-but-actually-looking-a-bit-scared server who had ruined our day. He said something about 'this country going to the dogs', which sounded more like his dad than him, but he was only trying to defend my honour – or my desire for chocolate-based confectionery anyway. She tried to placate us with banoffee pie, which Greg took as a huge insult – 'How can you even compare the two? They're not like for like. Rocky road is the king of pies' – which I thought was going a bit far as the banoffee looked lovely, and with that he walked out of the café. Through my tears I gave an apologetic smile to the unimpressed server and followed him out. On the bus home Greg was tense and irritable, a junkie who'd not been able to get his fix. I came up with what I thought was the perfect solution. I told him that because this engagement-ring-finding business was turning into a nightmare/joke, maybe we needed to rethink. Neither of us wanted our wedding to be too conventional, so what if we did away with the whole notion of even having an engagement ring? We knew we were engaged. The whole world knew we were engaged. Why did we need a ring to prove it? Clever, huh? Greg considered it for a while, then said, 'Before Mum died she made me promise that if I ever got a girlfriend I'd treat her right and do the right thing. You're having an engagement ring.' His tone added 'whether you like it or not'. We continued our journey in silence.

That weekend Greg invited me to his house for a candlelit dinner for two. His dad was out and their Teresa-May had gone to an Ann Summers party in Poulton-le-Fylde, so we had the place to ourselves. Greg cooked a three-course meal and served wine in proper big glasses. It was magical. For a starter he'd made carrot and coriander soup – I say made; he'd opened the carton and heated it up. Still, it was lovely. For our main course we had sausage, egg and chips – again, a triumph – and then came the pièce de résistance. I had no idea what pudding was going to be, but when he opened the fridge he brought out the most amazing rocky road pie. It was huge and it was ours, and he'd made it all himself from scratch! How amazing was that? He spent a while turning the pie round on its plate. I wasn't quite sure what he was doing but it felt quite self-indulgent, so I urged him to get a move on (swearing may have been involved). Eventually he cut me a slice of pie, decanted it onto a smaller plate, then handed it to me with a fork, like it was the most precious thing on God's earth. After he cut himself a slice we tucked in. And IT. WAS. HEAVENLY. It was like eating an orgasm. We both sat there groaning. And in that moment I decided that this was the sort of cake we should have at our wedding reception. And that Greg should make it. He was practically a Michelin-starred chef in my eyes by now! But when I took my third bite, something went wrong. I have a tendency to be gluttonous, and if I like the taste of something I'll often shovel it in and swallow without even chewing or tasting it. Which is what I did with the third mouthful. And instantly regretted it.

I tasted something very un-rocky road pie-like passing through my throat, something metallic, and instantly started to choke. Greg looked alarmed.

'Ah bollocks!'

I wanted to say 'What?!' but couldn't speak. Instead I swallowed.

'I hid your engagement ring in the pie. I thought you'd find it.'

Too bloody right I found it. I found it passing down my pigging intestines.

'Quick!' Greg said, getting up. 'Make yourself sick!'

We ran to the bathroom, where I shoved my fingers down my throat, but no matter how much I tried I only managed to dry retch. And all the while I could feel the ring slipping further and further down inside me. It seemed to be skipping around in there, going this way and that; it just felt weird. The further down it went, the more able I was to speak, though I was shaking with a panic attack as I called Greg all the names under the sun.

'I wasn't trying to kill you!' 'I'm really sorry!' 'I just thought you'd cut into it and see it and . . .' 'It was meant to be romantic!' 'I thought the worst thing that could happen was you'd bend your fork,' he kept on saying. He dived for the phone and called 999.

Again, there may have been swearing on my part.

'Hello, yes, my fiancée's swallowed her engagement ring. I'd baked it in a rocky road pie you see and . . . Sorry? Oh yeah. No, she's a bit shaky. No, it hasn't got any jaggedy bits on it, it's quite smooth, it's like a band with a jewel inside it. Diamond actually. Sorry? Er . . . no, I've had three glasses of wine, I don't think I can.'

As he gave them the address of the farm I realized an ambulance was being sent out for me. I convinced myself I was going to die. I could just see the headlines now: GIRL KILLED BY ENGAGEMENT RING. God, the mortification.

When the paramedic arrived she said I wasn't going to die. It took her about five minutes as she had a stutter.

At the hospital they took an X-ray. My first view of my engagement ring was as a white highlight next to my white bony spine (good job it was bony, if it hadn't been I'd've got a shock). I was dreading the doctors having to open me up to get it out, but a nice friendly fat guy in very tight blue overalls, which I took to mean he was a doctor, he seemed very knowledgeable if not, told me with a chuckle that there was no need for surgery. I'd have to 'poop' it out instead.

Yes, he actually said 'poop'.

They sent me home with instructions to eat lots of prunes

and fibre and wait for nature to take its course. Which it did. I shall spare you the details in case you have a queasy stomach. Needless to say, I never intend to swallow any type of jewellery again, though I will say this. I don't think I've ever bought so much Dettol in my life.

The engagement ring was beautiful. It was Greg's mum's engagement ring, and even though Debs and Hayls had him down as a tight-arse cheapskate for giving me something that hadn't cost him anything, I was incredibly touched. He loved his mum. His dad loved his mum. So for them to let me have her ring showed just how much they thought of me. Just looking at it could make me weep. Not in a sad way, but in a 'God I can't believe my luck!' kind of way. I really was the luckiest girl on the planet.

After telling the story Our Joey led the girls in an impromptu rendition of 'Brown Girl In The Ring', changing the line 'show me emotion' to 'show me a motion' – a gag I thought had gone out with the ark, and I told them so. God they were childish.

Greg and I had set a date for 15 August that year, his mum's birthday, and with only a few months to go our preparations were gathering momentum. Well I say 'our', it was really 'my' – I'd taken control of everything and Greg seemed to like it that way. Idaho Manchester became my best friend. I had reborrowed the book from the library about eighty times and whenever I was convinced there was something I'd forgotten I'd quickly thumb through her tome and she would quickly put my mind at rest. If I'm honest, I'd already covered most things in my Hello Kitty wedding jotter, but just knowing an expert was on hand in case there were finer details I'd forgotten – like whether or not to invite people's pets to the wedding. I don't know where she got that idea from?! – was terribly reassuring.

The best thing about the book was that it had a chapter

called 'Checklist for Problems on the Day'. I jotted down her headlines, thought of a few of my own and wrote up my solutions in the jotter:

Caterers Do a No Show – Not gonna happen. Greg making the cake. Mum's mate Maureen's daughter Lesley is doing the food through her catering company Lesley Spreads – Mum thought it was called Lezzy Spreads for a while, what with her being a big lezzer – and if they don't turn up Mum'll kill them.

Car Won't Start – No problem. Get a bus/taxi, or walk. Church only two streets away.

Breath Stinks – Strong mints in chief bridesmaid's purse. I think purse is American for handbag. Now wondering whether each bridesmaid should have a nice big handbag to match their dresses, but don't really see the point of expense. Our Joey suggested combining the handbag with the flowers, so we each carry a handbag with flowers cascading out of it, but I think this might be too much. Will think on. (See Emergency Kit below for mints thing.)

Bad Weather – Am having parasol as part of my look anyway, but rain shouldn't be a problem as middle of August. Greg says we should get a load of umbrellas and keep them at the back of the church, then take them to the barn. Good thinking, Batman.

Emergency Kit – Idaho suggests having an emergency kit to cover all eventualities. Genius idea, Idaho! This will include:
- Clear nail varnish – In case tights get laddered.
- Spare tights – In case tights get seriously frigged.
- Tampon – In case come on my blob. Might put one in anyway?
- Spare false nails.

- Rescue remedy – In case have a whitey.
- Spare make-up – This bag's gonna be *huge!* Better give it to Mum to mind.
- Hairspray – In case of hair emergencies or rain affecting hair if parasol blows away in force-ten gale.
- Make-up-remover pads – In case cry so much look like panda.
- Antihistamine tablets – In case allergic to flowers.
- Brandy miniature – In case nerves get the better of me or get overexcited or just fancy a drink.
- Paracetamol – In case get headache with stress etc.
- Needle and thread – In case dress gets ripped. (Make sure thread matches dress. Would look a holy show if ivory dress had black thread on it like some big meff's dress. Yuk!)
- Stain removal kit – In case some bastard spills red wine on frock. Maybe no red wine? Mind you, beer will look just as bad. Maybe dry wedding? Greg says no. Stain removal kit it is. Though might be too pissed to care . . .

Best Man Forgets Speech – Greg is going to print all speeches off on computer so there is always back-up.

Official Photographer Doesn't Show – Subtly encourage relatives to invest in new cameras in run-up to wedding so lots of professional equipment to fall back on. Must start slagging off people's cameras *soon*.

DJ Doesn't Show – it's Our Joey. Not gonna happen.

Some nights I'd dream that everything on the list had gone wrong and the back-up handbag wasn't handy. I'd wake in a cold sweat and have to switch the light on to convince myself it had only been a dream.

*

A few weeks before the wedding, Our Joey came home from work and announced that he and Greg were going to Torquay for the weekend. My face must have looked a picture because he laughed and said, 'Duh! Representing Skippy Skips at the National Waste Management Convention?' As the office secretary he had booked them into a nearby hotel which, instead of having rooms that had numbers, had rooms that were named after famous West End musicals. He was going to be staying in *Mame* and Greg was to be staying in *Me And My Girl*. He'd found the hotel in the back pages of *Gay Times*, which Mum had enjoyed displaying on the coffee table over the last few months in a fan formation, as she felt it impressed anyone who dropped by. He seemed to think it was hilarious that my lovely Greg was going to be surrounded by screaming queens every evening after the conference. Greg asked if I wanted to join him, but biting my tongue to stop retorting, 'Only if we stay in *West Side Story*', I informed him I couldn't. That particular weekend I had the final bridesmaids dress fittings, which I needed to be at as Debs had been threatening to make her dress 'really slutty' as she and Alex had recently split up and 'weddings are brilliant places to pull'. I wasn't keen; I wanted my bridesmaids to look tasteful and demure. I asked Greg if he realized what sort of place he was going to be staying in and he laughed and said, 'Well, at least you know I'm not going to be playing away.' Actually, it was a reassuring thought. Not that I ever felt Greg would be unfaithful to me. The kind of guy who made rocky road pie and gave you his mother's engagement ring surely wasn't going to go eating from a different tray of muffins, if you follow my cake-based analogy.

Our Joey was really looking forward to the Waste Management Convention. But something told me he was looking forward to staying in the gay guest house more. He kept reading things out from the brochure – 'If you're stuck for something to do, ask our resident drag queen, Tequila Mockingbird, she knows all the local attractions' – and he went out and bought three new outfits and loads of new underwear. Clearly he was intending to pull. I had to have a word with him: 'Joey, you're going away on business. Not funny business.'

He tutted and scowled.

Mum intervened: 'Don't deny him the right to express his sexuality in a positive way, Jodie.'

Our Joey gave a victorious grin, then went to pack his two matching pull-along knock-off Louis Vuitton suitcases, which he'd got from Brenda the Fence especially for the occasion.

Well, God alone only knows what Our Joey got up to in Torquay, but he came back from the weekend, which had been successful for me – I'd convinced Debs to go with a nice floor-length number; I'd practically got her in a burka – and announced that he'd decided waste management wasn't for him and he was handing in his notice at Skippy Skips. On further questioning he just said he'd been bored rigid at the conference and that skips now 'did his swede in'. When he left the room, Mum leaned over me and proffered the conspiracy theory that what had actually happened in Torquay was that an internationally famous gay man had been staying at the guest house, had met Our Joey, fallen head over heels in love with him and Our Joey was planning on running away with him to Hollywood. When I asked which celebrity she was thinking of she shrugged and said, 'Graham Norton or Tom Cruise.'

Dad looked up from his paper. 'He's not a fruit, is he?' he asked, incredulous.

Mum tutted. 'Graham Norton? Oh Malcolm. You need to get with the flaming times, love!'

Dad whistled through his teeth and shook his head, as if to say, 'Would you believe it?'

I was more shocked that Mum had used the word 'flaming'.

When I saw Greg that night over cocktails in the Blue Lagoon he seemed to despair of Our Joey's sudden turnabout, but he couldn't really throw any light on his reasons for wanting to leave Skippy Skips. He said Our Joey was up late in the hotel bar both nights, singing show tunes with Tequila Mockingbird, and had subsequently yawned his way through the majority of the conference, something I said was unprofessional. Greg just shrugged and admitted, 'Well, it was deathly dull.' When I asked him how he'd got on at the hotel he just smiled and said, 'Well, I won't be rushing back.'

I looked at him and could just imagine the thrill the blokes at the hotel must have got when he'd first walked in. Whenever he walked in, in fact. I bet tea was spilt on tablecloths when he was ordering his kippers for breakfast. The hottie with the blond curls sitting with that campy one with the snub nose and freckles. I bet they thought Our Joey was punching above his weight and they'd give it three weeks. The idea made me smile.

'You're so gorgeous when you smile,' he said (he might have sworn as well) and I melted. Even now his good looks had the power to shrivel my insides. The thick lips, the plaintive eyes like brown planets floating in white skies. I even thought the little mole on his neck was cute, though Mum had commented that he might be prone to melanoma later in life. God, she could put a dampener on things. In two weeks from now I was going to be his wife. I really was the luckiest girl on the planet.

Greg started telling me about everything he'd learned at the convention. How he'd always told his dad that websites were the way forward and how he'd insisted the company would have to invest in a graphic designer to rebrand them, but that his dad was dead set against it. He said the technical revolution had come, and they needed to grab hold of it or kiss goodbye to the business. As I yawned, I considered his first response to the convention was correct: it was deathly dull. And what was even more clear to me was that our Joey had made a wise move by getting out.

The Saturday before the wedding was a big night. I was having my hen party and Greg was having his stag do. Me and the girls were going on a pub crawl down Wavertree High Street and Greg and co were doing something similar in town. Hayls and Debs were in charge of my hen night and they'd decided it would be hilarious if we all dressed as St Trinian's Girls. I thought this an amusing choice: a load of ex-comprehensive schoolers going out dressed as posh public-school types, and wondered if some ex-Roedean girls might be going out on a hen night dressed as the cast of *Grange Hill*.

On the Saturday afternoon me and Hayls had popped down to Allerton Road to shop for pleated miniskirts, fishnets, white shirts and straw boaters. We were just coming out of a school uniform shop (that amazingly didn't sell fishnet stockings, can't think why . . .) when I bumped into a familiar face. Well, obviously it wasn't just a face, that would have just been plain weird, it was Mrs Mendelson. I was a bit embarrassed to see her and tried to hurry past, hoping she'd not clocked me, but I heard her familiar klaxon of a voice bellowing out, 'Jodie? Jodie McGee? Is it you? Of course it's you!'

So I swung round and gave a very convincing performance of someone going, 'Who's that calling me?' – looks around pavement, clocks fat old bird in nylon flower-print kaftan – 'Oh why, it's my old drama teacher, Mrs Mendelson!'

'Mrs Mendelson!' I said and leaned forward to hug her. She smelt of lily of the valley and Pernod. She clutched my hand as

I stepped back. She looked a bit misty-eyed as she said, 'What happened to you, Jodie?'

'Er . . .' I pretended I didn't know what she meant, though I understood completely.

'You just disappeared. There one week, gone the next. You had so much promise, Jodie, handbags of potential. You really could have gone professional.'

I blustered a bit.

'One knock and you were down,' she said, no doubt referring to my dreadful *Acacia Avenue* audition and my subsequent non-attendance at her classes. Truth be told I'd been too mortified to show my face. 'I really had more faith in you than that. Didn't have you down as a bolter.'

'I'm sorry, Mrs Mendelson,' I heard myself saying. There was a slight pause, so I tried to be bright and breezy and started telling her how I was getting married the following week and that this was my friend Hayls, and she'd better speak up as Hayls was a bit hard of hearing – Hayls was thrilled when I said that. But Mrs Mendelson didn't appear to be listening. She just interrupted and said, 'Never give up, Jodie. Come back to it one day. You'll have to. You're too good not to. You'll need to.'

You'll need to? It was like she was seeing my future and I didn't like it.

With that she steadied herself on her walking stick, then turned and walked away. I felt terribly sad all of a sudden. She was right, I had bolted at the first sign of failure and it was a regret of mine. Acting at her drama classes had made me so happy, so alive. At first I had missed the fulfilment it gave me, but then I'd found fulfilment of a different sort going out with Greg. And surely that was a more practical, more real kind of happiness than pretending to be other people in a room above a betting shop on Allerton Road. Of course that made me happy, but it didn't mean anything. It's one thing being a big fish in a small pond and being good for Mrs Mendelson, but it was another actually going out there in the real world of showbiz and making a name for yourself. That was never going to happen, not to someone like me. So the happiness I'd found – in the real world of being me and not someone else – was surely the better kind of happiness to have. Wasn't it?

Yet she'd seemed so sure. As if she knew. Like when I saw the gypsy who told me I'd win an Oscar. Maybe I would go back to acting. I'd have to if I was going to win an Academy Award. I wasn't going to win one stacking shelves in the local super-market.

There was something about my crossing paths with Myrtle Mendelson that unnerved me for the rest of that day. It was an odd feeling I couldn't shake off. And although I went through the motions of the hen night and drank enough alcohol to sink Venice, it didn't even touch the sides. At the end of the night I felt stone cold sober. I even got my key in the door on the first attempt. That was unheard of for me after so much Tia Maria. My legs were weary from being on my feet all night in high heels (and fishnets) and I kicked off my stilettos as I came into the through lounge. I got a bit of a shock when I saw Our Joey sat on the corner settee staring into space. He didn't even have the lights on. I flicked them on and he jumped a bit, a startled deer in the headlights.

'Joey, what's wrong?' I asked. I knew him well enough to know something was up. I went and sat next to him, rubbing my ankles through the fishnets. He looked at me oddly.

'What?' I said.

'It's hard to take you seriously with pretend freckles painted on your face and your hair in bunches.'

'Answer the question, knobhead.' But I said it nicely, the way you can when it's your favourite/only brother.

'Are you sure you're doing the right thing?' There was an element of restrained alarm in his voice, which unnerved me in the same way as Mrs Mendelson had.

'Doing what?'

'Marrying Greg.'

That completely took the wind out of my sails. It was one thing Mum questioning me all those months ago, but even she'd warmed to the idea by now. But Our Joey? No. This wasn't happening. Our Joey knew me better than anyone on earth. Probably better even than Greg did. We'd shared so much. I would never have said something like that to him if the boot had been on the other foot. It hurt. It really hurt.

'Why d'you say that?' I asked, worried now about what the answer might be. Had Greg done something bad on the stag do? Had he kissed a stripper? What?

Our Joey shrugged. 'Dunno. Just wanted to check you were OK really. You've been so excited about it all, but it's been like you were excited about getting married and . . . well, not much else.'

'I'm excited about getting married to Greg,' I said defiantly.

'But . . . but . . .' He was clutching at straws here, I could tell. 'But you said you wanted to go to the Maldives on your honeymoon. And you're going to North Wales.'

'Joey, I could go to Bootle and still be happy, as long as I was with my Greg. And anyway, d'you know where the Maldives is? It's fucking miles away. I looked on the map.'

'And you've gotta move in with his dad.'

'So?'

'So you should wait till yous can afford a place of your own.'

'We're moving into his granny flat.'

158

'His poor arl granny. Where's she gonna go?'

'He hasn't got a granny, and well you know it. And anyway, we won't be on top of each other. We'll hardly ever see his dad.'

'So you're happy?'

I nodded. 'Like you need to ask.'

'I do. You're me sister.'

I sighed. 'Joey. Will you stop worrying about me? I'm dead happy.'

This appeared to appease him and he visibly relaxed. 'Well, that's boss then. Nightcap?'

'I don't suit them.' This was a running gag of ours. 'Oh, you mean a drink?'

He winked, got up and headed to the kitchen. I knew there was something he wasn't saying, though. I got up and followed him to the fridge, where he pulled out two cans of lager.

'Joey. Did . . . did Greg do something tonight?'

'Like what?' he cracked open the cans.

'You tell me. You were on his stag do.'

'What, like rim the stripper?'

'So there was a stripper?'

He nodded. 'There was a stripper.'

My heart sank to my aching feet. He had. He'd snogged her. He was probably with her now, having one last fling. Our Joey could see the panic on my face.

'He didn't do nothing.'

'That's a double negative. That means he did.'

'Get that down your screech and relax,' he said, handing me one of the lagers. 'Greg Valentine's never so much as glanced sideways at another woman in all the time he's known you.'

Bless him. Our Joey knew just the right thing to say sometimes.

ELEVEN

'There's nothing worse than lack of sleep through excitement. A face full of slap can hide black rings under your eyes, but your nerves'll be shot to bits.' Mum said the night before the wedding, as her mate Maureen slid a foil strip out of the inside pocket of her swing coat and popped a few pills out of it onto the kitchen counter.

I'd always wondered why Maureen had such a glazed look in her eye, now I knew. Mum took the breadknife and sliced one of the pills in two, like a seasoned pro. She slipped me half and necked a whole one herself.

I looked at it anxiously.

'What would Idaho Manchester say?'

'She's got a face like a smacked kipper,' said Mum, being uncharacteristically ungenerous. 'You're not telling me she doesn't need Idaho's Little Helper to see her through the day?'

We washed them down with shot glasses of neat vodka.

'Jesus,' I said as I felt the hot hit of vodka slipping down, 'when did I move into the Valley of the Dolls?'

Mum tucked the remaining half into her cardigan pocket, and when she saw me looking amazed she shrugged: 'Your father snores something terrible. Now, Night Nurse chaser.'

Maureen rubbed her hands as Mum poured a shot glass of the bright green liquid.

'No, it's for our Jodie,' she said. 'You've got to drive, Maureen. You don't want a repeat of last Easter.'

Maureen had driven her moped into a bus stop at two in the morning while returning home from an all-night chemist, claiming her Tony was ill in bed with a fever and she'd needed emergency Lemsips. It was one of those things that people rarely mentioned, like Our Joey's police caution or the time her from number eight was caught with a frozen turkey under her rain mac a week before Christmas. And chilblains no doubt. I swallowed the green gunk and started to feel woozy almost instantly.

The next thing I knew I was waking up in my own bed, in my nightie, feeling incredibly calm and refreshed as daylight streamed in through the curtains. I lay there for a moment, warm, cosy and content. It was the day of my wedding. Anything life could throw at me now I was ready for, I would be unfazed, I would be calm, collected, centred. The tiny bit of tranquilliser no doubt still floating around my system threw any sort of anxiety out of the window and allowed me to get on with the job in hand. The job of getting married. If I could ever be bothered to actually get up that is.

The first face I saw was Our Joey's. He tapped on my bedroom door and crept in singing a gentle rendition of 'I'm Getting Married In The Morning', like Eva Cassidy with tonsillitis. He was carrying a tray holding my wedding day breakfast: two poached eggs on toast with Marmite – my absolute favourite. I knew that he'd made it, because he was much better at poached eggs than Mum, and these were perfect. The tray looked lovely, and even the cutlery matched, which was unusual for our house. And beside it on the tray was a mug of builder's tea. Fantastic. I sat up and he slipped it onto my lap with a wink.

'Get that down your screech, girl.'

I was ravenous and wolfed the lot in minutes.

Chaos ricocheted around me all morning as everyone else went into meltdown about the clock ticking and how much there was to be done. I was the eye of the storm. An outsider might have said I was a smug bastard, smirking quietly to myself and not exhibiting any emotion. It was like the veil was on already, a cloud of calm had descended. But then again, I had organized the day to within an inch of its nuptial life. I knew what had to happen and when it had to happen and nothing had been left to chance. My Hello Kitty jotter was always close to hand. Even when Mum spilt some courage-bolstering Baileys on it, I didn't mind. As the pale brown liquid smudged my handwriting she burst out crying.

'What did it say? WHAT DID IT SAY?!' she yelped as the words disappeared. But I put a finger to my lips to silence her. I knew every word I'd written in that book by heart. All was fine.

'It said, "This is the page for Mum to spill her drink on."'

'No!'

'No. It was a reminder for me to hide the bridesmaid's presents in the boiler room next to the barn.'

'Oh.' She seemed almost disappointed.

'They're in the holdall under the stairs. Can you take them in your car so the girls don't see?'

Mum nodded and repeated to herself, 'Holdall. Stairs. Car. Girls no see.'

'Boiler room.'

'Boiler room!'

I saw that her hand was shaking. I was surprised she wasn't licking the inside of the Baileys glass. Poor Mum, I was beginning to realize that this day was as important for her as it was for me. She was losing a daughter, gaining a son-in-law and attending the only wedding one of her kids was ever likely to have. No wonder she wanted it to go well.

'Everything's gonna be fine, Mum. I promise you,' I said and held her hand.

She nodded and bit her bottom lip. She sighed and then shook her head.

'I'll never forget marrying your dad. Coming out of the church we had a long walk to the reception. There we were, walking through town, me in my bridal gown, your dad in his suit, heading for Reece's Cafe in town.'

I had heard this story several thousand times before. Usually it would irritate me to have sit through it again, but today I lapped it up.

'Your Dad walked a few yards in front of me and I kept trying to catch him up. But every time I got nearer he'd walk a bit quicker. Eventually he said,' at this point she gulped, 'I'm not with you.'

I nodded. I knew this.

'He was just mortified to be seen out in public with me.'

Up until then, whenever my Mum had told this anecdote, she had always made it seem funny. Many's the time I'd seen her howling with laughter with her mates from work, sprawled over our couch, a Doris Day movie on the telly, several bottles of wine already drunk, tears pouring down her face. But today it felt tragic. She looked at me.

'Thank God you're not marrying someone like your dad.'

I froze. I wanted to nod, but felt that would make me complicit in slagging him off.

'But . . . you love Dad,' I said. 'Don't you?'

At which she gave an airy laugh, leaned in and kissed me.

Then she hurried out of the room and I continued to get myself ready.

After that, everything went like clockwork. The dresses fitted. The hairdresser was punctual. The make-up artist was a genius. The cars were early. The flowers were perky. Our Joey looked really handsome in his page boy's outfit – a suit basically. Hayls, Debs and Greg's cousin's little girl Amelia looked adorable in their turquoise Bo Peep-style gowns. The day was bright. When I finally stepped out of my bedroom to walk the length of the bungalow hallway I saw Mum and Dad standing by the front door. As I neared them I realized Mum had tears in her eyes.

'I don't look that bad, do I?' I joked.

She shook her head, unable to speak. She was proud. Finally. So this is what it took!

'Jodie,' gasped Dad, 'you look like a fucking princess.'

And Mum nodded, backing him up. And then she slapped him when she realized, with delayed reaction, that he'd sworn. Dad lifted up his camera and took a photo. Mum stepped forward and put her hand on my shoulder.

'Jodie, look.' She turned me so I faced the full-length mirror in the hall. 'You're beautiful.'

I didn't really recognize the woman looking back at me. All my life I'd felt like a girl. And yet here I was, a woman. A woman who was about to be centre stage again.

'She looks like a bloody movie star!' added Maureen, who'd come round to go in the car with Mum and Dad.

I was just about to agree with them – in my head; I'd never have said it out loud because it would have sounded arrogant – when Mum said, 'Ellie from number three did her make-up. She covers a multitude of sins.' Which kind of took the wind out of my sails, obviously.

'True,' agreed Maureen. 'Coz she's not got the best complexion in the world.'

Jees, my skin's not that bad!

'And the way she's done her blusher, it actually gives the impression she's got something approaching cheekbones,' Maureen went on.

OK, so I was a spotty fat heifer with a face like a beachball.

'And the fullness of the skirt hides her ginormous arse.'

Debs said that, but I knew she was only taking the piss.

'What did you say?' asked Hayls, and in the mirror I saw Debs turn to her and mouth the words while Hayls collapsed laughing. Our Joey was just coming out of the bedroom then, holding hands with five-year-old Amelia, the mini-bridesmaid. He smiled and said calmly, 'He's a very lucky man.' Then he smiled sadly and looked like he was going to cry.

'My thong keeps riding up my arse crack, does yours?' Hayls asked Debs.

'It's like a bloody cheese grater.' Debs nodded.

'Mine, too,' said Mum.

'And mine,' added Maureen.

I blocked it all out. I didn't care. I took a final look in the mirror and smiled. They say a bride never looks as good as she does on her wedding day. And if I never looked this good again it was of no consequence. I had scrubbed up well. I was going to make my Greg proud, and that was all that mattered. I turned to face the front door, which Dad had now opened.

'That dress looks familiar,' I heard Maureen say as Debs handed out the bouquets of flowers, fresh from the fridge.

'It's a replica of Princess Diana's,' said Mum.

I rolled my eyes. 'Mum it's not, it's just got a slightly full skirt, and anyway, she had a twenty-foot train. Jeez.'

Mum widened her eyes to Maureen as if disagreeing with

me. And Maureen nodded as if to say, Don't worry, Sandra. Any fool can see she's the double of Di.

I had designed the dress myself. It had a full skirt, nipped-in waist, sweetheart neck and leg-of-mutton sleeves. Which, OK, does sound a bit like Lady Di's. But did Lady Di have a butter-fly motif inlaid up the bodice? No. Plus she never had a twirly parasol. Or gypsophila in her hair, which I thought was more of a statement than a predictable veil.

'Mind you,' Dad commented under his breath as I made my way to the front door, 'her dandruff's shocking.'

'It's *gypsophila*!' I grunted through gritted teeth as I stood on the front doorstep. It felt like I was standing on the threshold of a new life, and in that moment I saw clearly a fast-forward movie of the rest of my days. The wedding. The honeymoon (a week in Portmeirion). Me and Greg living together in the granny flat at the farmhouse till we got together the cash to buy somewhere nice. Kids. Dogs. Grandkids. Happiness. The film got quicker and quicker, but its running theme was one of pure, unabated joy. Like the pantyliner advert where the girl rollerskates along the beach in the sunshine with a shaggy dog. It ground abruptly to a halt when I felt a dig in the kidneys and Dad going, 'Come on, love. Don't wanna be late. Greg'll think you've stood him up.'

I stepped down onto the path. My two eldest bridesmaids fussed around me as I moved from the bungalow to the waiting car – Dad had booked a fleet of Post Office vans to take us to the church. A load of neighbours had gathered round the gar-den gate and gave a round of applause as I walked as daintily as I could down the path. I thought Amelia, Hayls and Debs looked pretty in turquoise, though I did hear one (quite rude) old neighbour muttering, 'Jesus, I'll need bleeding sunglasses if I go to the church.' Jealous I reckon. And then when Mum and Dad followed us out I heard the same woman saying, 'Jesus Christ, it's Old Mother Riley.' Which I didn't understand. I have to say Mum did look lovely in her crocheted pashmina and long silk skirt. She'd wanted to 'wear long' ever since she'd seen a documentary about a New York Jewish wedding where all the women wore evening wear. She thought it looked chic. I thought she looked like she was going to the annual dinner dance up the fag factory.

I put down my parasol and got in the first red van with Dad. They'd put a mattress in the back and we sort of lolled alongside each other as his workmate Mad Georgie drove us sedately to the church. Although I couldn't help but keep singing the theme song from *Postman Pat* to myself as we glided along.

'This must be what it's like going to your own funeral,' Dad commented, which I didn't think was very positive on my wedding day. I overlooked it and tried not to crush my flowers whenever Georgie took a corner.

From then on the day felt like an out-of-body experience, as if it was happening to someone else. It all seems to have faded into a bit of a blur now, and one day I may watch the wedding video to see what actually happened and in which order, though I do remember several things:

1 Catching sight of Greg as I walked down the aisle to 'Here Comes The Sun'. He looked so handsome as the light from the stained-glass windows hit his blond curls. The smile he gave me then told me we were going to be together for ever.

2 The vicar had a very long hair protruding from his nose that tickled his top lip every time he spoke.

3 Hayls' specially composed song was brilliant as we signed the register. She introduced it by saying, 'Even though I'm deaf, I feel music.' The song went like this:

In a canteen far away, I remember my friend did say
'He is well fit, he's a sure hit
I will make him mine some day.'
There were burgers, doughnuts with holes,
There were eighteen sausage rolls.
And my friend said 'I will make him mine some day.'

It was accompanied by a tape recording of a tin whistle and a Spanish guitar. She told me it was a Spanish guitar, but I don't know how she knew, or what the difference is between a normal guitar and a Spanish guitar. Except one must come from Spain.

4 Our Joey's poem, when he read it, was a bit maudlin. It was about losing a friend. A lot of people said it was like something from a funeral. There were lots of references to 'kissing you goodbye at the bus stop' and 'never seeing you again', which I found a bit over the top, frankly. I was his sister. He would see me all the time, knobhead! It seemed to embarrass and annoy Greg, too, as he kept fidgeting in his seat, staring at the floor and sighing.

5 Amelia, the youngest bridesmaid, had to be taken to the toilet during the address by the vicar. Very loudly from the back of the church we heard her voice coming through an air vent, saying, 'I can't poo,' which made everyone laugh. Apart from Hayls, who could be heard whispering, 'What are yous all laughing at? What's going on?'

6 Mum attempting an operatic style descant in 'I Vow To Thee My Country'.

7 Dad elbowing Mum in the ribs during said descant, telling her to shut it coz she was 'making a show of herself'.

8 Mum elbowing him back and saying, 'Shut it, Malcolm. I just want you to know you've ruined my life.' I think she'd had too much Baileys.

9 Greg's sister sobbing through most of the hymns in a 'I wish Mum was here to see this only she copped it with cancer a couple of years back' sort of way.

10 When the vicar said to Greg, 'You may kiss the bride,' he grabbed me and gave me a big tongue sandwich with such force that I bent backwards like I was trying to do the crab and the congregation burst into spontaneous applause.

11 What was at first endearing became slightly attention-seeking when Teresa-May continued to cry throughout the service. She was practically caterwauling by the time we left the church and people were giving her 'God, will you shut up, love?' looks, myself included. It was bad of me, however, to try and poke her with my parasol as I headed back up the aisle.

12 As we posed for pictures in the grounds of St Hilda's I twirled my parasol and a seagull crapped on it. The spin made the droppings splatter all over Mum's pashmina and Maureen's crocheted coat. Fortunately there were Wet Wipes in the emergency holdall for this eventuality and everything was sorted within minutes.

13 Teresa-May sobbed hysterically through all the pictures and had to be given some Rescue Remedy from the emergency holdall. This seemed to do the trick, but within minutes she was interfering with all the poses the photographer wanted. She kept repeating everything he said in a very bossy way, so if he said, 'Bride's family!' She'd go, 'BRIDE'S FAMILY! COME ON GUYS! CHOP CHOP!' Again, deeply irritating. Debs actually wondered whether someone had laced the Rescue Remedy with

amphetamines as she seemed to go off on one. She was the same when we were getting into the Post Office vans to go to the reception. Shouting, 'BRIDE AND GROOM IN CAR ONE, PLEASE!' Even though she was standing right next us at the time.

14 Greg snogged me in the back of the GPO van all the way from the church to the farm for the reception. I thought he was going to try and shag me and I was a bit mortified coz Mad Georgie was copping a look through the rear-view mirror. In the end I slapped Greg off me and told him to wait till later.

Now that I'd had my frock on for several hours it was beginning to weigh me down. I just wasn't used to carrying that much excess material around with me, I realized as I snaked from table to table through the barn, saying hello to the various revellers in their differing states of intoxication. Our Joey had once told me that when the feuding actresses Bette Davis and Joan Crawford had been filming *What Ever Happened to Baby Jane?* Crawford had weights sewn into her dress before a scene in which Davis had to drag her across the floor. I was beginning to wonder whether my dressmaker had it in for me and had done something similar.

'Boss do, Jodes!' cried a distant cousin, raising a pint of snakebite in my general direction and sloshing some over the table, 'Food was gorge!'

'Ah, glad you liked it!'

'What was the name of that cake?'

'Rocky road pie. Greg made it.'

'You're joking! Is he as good in the bedroom as he is in the kitchen?'

'Better,' I said with a wink, then moved on to the next table, where an aunty of Greg's grabbed my skirt and commented, 'Well that's not bri-nylon, is it?' I shook my head.

'Third Finger, Left Hand' was booming out from the DJ's table and the dance floor was heaving. I could see Mum, Maureen and a few other women doing the Wigan Slosh – two steps to the right, clap; two steps to the left, clap; two steps to the right, clap; under the legs and change direction – practically taking over the whole dance floor as more and more aunties and cousins fell in alongside them and joined in. Dad and Greg's dad were propping up the bar in the corner with a few other uncles and male cousins, mostly red of nose and with their top buttons undone, ties slackened like schoolboys embarrassed to be seen in uniform. Hayls was sitting on Lotan's lap, snogging the face off him, and Debs was by the DJ's desk, laughing and joking with Our Joey's mate Mooey, who was helping him spin the decks. From the way she was throwing her head back and laughing, and the inane grin on his face, I could see that she fancied him like mad and was following our 'early stages of flirting rules': laugh your head off at his jokes and be ever so suggestive with an open mouth. I wasn't quite sure where Our Joey was; out the back having a ciggie maybe.

Teresa-May was advancing towards me between two nearby tables, waving to get my attention. She'd seen me clock her, so I couldn't run in the opposite direction – I couldn't run anywhere, my dress weighed a *ton* – so I scooped my skirt up in my hands to try and lighten the load and waddled obediently but reluctantly towards her.

'Jodie, have you seen our Greg?'

I looked around and realized I'd not seen him for five or ten minutes. I was just about to say maybe he'd nipped out for a crafty Cuban cigar with his uncle Derek, who'd been bandying them about like he was the Big I Am, when Teresa-May cut in.

'Only I think it's time to hand out the prezzies.'

In a break with tradition, Greg and I had decided to do the presentation of gifts to everyone who'd helped a long while after the dinner, just to be different.

'Er, OK,' I replied, though frankly I didn't see what the hurry was. I think I preferred the sobbing version of TM, not this new-fangled, uber-organized, interfering busybody. But as Greg had said earlier, 'I think she's just trying to make up for the fact that me ma's not here.'

'Now, I've got the flowers out for your mum and that, but what I can't find are the bridesmaids' presents.'

'Oh, they're in the boiler room, I'll go and get them.'

'No, Jodie. I'll get them.'

'No, Teresa. I can—'

'Jodie, it's your wedding day, I'm only trying to—'

'NO, TERESA!' I almost bit her head off. Her bottom lip trembled, so I back-pedalled. 'I know where they are.'

She nodded. 'Well, I'll come with you then, give you an 'and.'

'You're all right, Teresa. You go and find Greg, tell him we're ready to do the presentations.'

She perked up when I said that. She had a new job to do. I thought she was going to say, 'Synchronize watches,' but instead she legged it across the barn. Well, that had got rid of her anyway. I'd go and get the presents in a bit. Especially as 'YMCA' had just come on the turntable and everyone was rushing towards the dance floor. I got caught up in the general scrum and found myself forming the titular letters with my arms alongside Lotan. Hayls was scowling from the sidelines, so I gave her a wink, encouraging her to cheer the fuck up. She shrugged and walked off, so I gave Lotan a look, as if to say, 'What's her problem?'

172

He shouted to me, 'She's just fuming coz this song excludes people with no arms.'

I had just about heard it all now. I was about to say as much when I felt a dig in my kidneys. I swung round to see Teresa-May standing before me, arms folded and tapping her foot.

'That's not how you do the "YMCA"!' I laughed, but she was having none of it.

'Er . . . prezzies, Jodes?'

Usually when people called me Jodes I like it. It's a term of endearment. But on the wrong lips, i.e., Teresa-May's, it sounded patronizing and insulting. I was about to tell her this, but then realized a) I couldn't be arsed and b) it would only set her off crying again, so I nodded submissively, picked up my skirt and headed for the exit.

I half expected it to be dark when I got outside as it had been a long day, but of course it was only about five in the afternoon and the sun was still high in the sky. The courtyard was quite busy with people who'd come out to smoke cigars/take the air/throw up, and I looked around to see if I could spot Greg amongst them, but couldn't. Maybe Teresa-May already had him in hand and was guiding him to the microphone, ready to do the presentations. It took about five minutes to walk the twenty yards to the boiler room, as I was grabbed at every step by well-wishers and dress admirers. Maybe I should have asked Teresa-May to get the presents after all.

Greg's Uncle Derek, a round man with a drinker's nose and smoker's teeth, was chewing on a cigar the size of a draught excluder, holding court with some admiring younger relatives about the time he'd pinched Barbara Windsor's arse at a party in the Sixties. His wife maintained he'd done no such thing and that he'd never even met Barbara Windsor, just a cockney sparrah with blonde hair at some party in the East End, but the way he went on about it you'd think he'd personally scalped hard bastards for the Krays.

I bypassed him and his gang and let myself into the utility block, hoping to God that Mum had followed my orders and hidden the gifts where they were meant to be. I stood in the narrow white tiled corridor and it felt nicely cool. I stopped and leaned back against the wall, realizing this was the first time I'd been on my own since I'd woken up in my bed that morning. I savoured the stillness, the peace and quiet, the noises from the crowd outside feeling further away than they really were. I also realized that since the meal I'd been so busy hobnobbing with the guests that I'd not had a single drink. I decided that as soon as I got back to the barn I'd get myself a nice cold glass of champagne, and after the presentations, maybe I'd sneak Greg away for a bit of sexy time in our new bedroom. I looked at my left hand and the slim gold band that said I was a proper married woman. A wife. I twisted it this way and that; it was a lovely fit, just like me and Greg. I felt a sudden rush of excitement as I said the words to myself in my head. I was Greg's wife.

Greg's wife.

Greg's—

But then something startled me. A grunting and someone moaning like they were in pain. It seemed to be coming from the boiler room. I lifted up my skirt and practically skidded down the tiled floor to the boiler room door. I stopped and listened again. Silence. Maybe I'd been imagining things, but no, there it was again. Another grunt. Someone was in pain. Someone was locked in the boiler room. Without further ado I grabbed the handle and pushed the door open, fearful I'd see someone tied up and gagged. Blindfolded maybe. Kidnapped. A ransom demand nearby.

But the sight that greeted me was far, far worse than that.

Bright light was streaming in through a skylight, so there was no mistaking what I saw. I couldn't misconstrue it with the excuse of a darkened room.

Leaning against the boiler was Greg. And kneeling before him was Our Joey.

At first I wondered what was going on. Why was Our Joey kneeling down? Had he dropped a contact lens? But he didn't wear contact lenses . . .

Greg's eyes were shut and he was groaning.

And then I realized. My brother was giving my husband a blowjob.

Greg's eyes opened and immediately widened in panic. My mouth dropped open and I went to scream, but nothing came out. Greg started pushing Our Joey away, but he wasn't letting go. He kneed him away and Our Joey fell backwards onto the hard tiled floor. As he did his head spun round and he saw me frozen.

'Jodie!' gasped Greg.

I didn't freeze for long. I grabbed my skirt and ran back down the corridor and out into the courtyard. Suddenly my dress wasn't heavy any more as, with superhuman strength and agility, I ducked through the clumps of guests outside. I headed for the gate that led to the lane and I kept on running. I could hear Greg giving chase, calling my name, but I just kept on going. I had no idea where I was going, but I didn't look back.

PART TWO

PART TWO

TWELVE

2005–2007

After the gruesome debacle of my wedding I locked myself away from the world as I contemplated what had happened and what I was now going to do with my life. Locking myself away involved lying on my bed, staring at my posters and saying very little to Mum and Dad apart from, 'I don't want to talk about it,' and, 'I'm still not hungry.' For once they saw sense and sided with me, suggesting to Our Joey that he move out on a temporary basis, and I believe he went and stayed with his mate Mooey, though I couldn't really be sure. He was gone. That was all I cared about. We were no longer breathing the same air.

I couldn't face going to work as I thought that everyone was going to laugh at me. I couldn't even face Hayls and Debs. They came round a few times and sat on my bed with such scary looks of pity that in the end I told Mum not to let them in when they came knocking. I didn't feel I could leave the house, I just knew that the gawping neighbours who'd stood at the gate wishing me well on my way to the church would now be twitching at their net curtains, laughing at my misfortune. There she goes. The one with the gay husband. What did she do wrong that he ran to the arms/groin of her brother? It didn't bear thinking about.

Greg bombarded the house with phone calls, but I told Mum I didn't want to speak to him. What could he say? What could he possibly say that would excuse or explain what had happened? I'm sorry. It was a moment of madness. I don't know what came over me. Whatever he had to say, I didn't want to hear it.

I lay on my bed and pieced together all the clues. Greg had always been Our Joey's defender. He had walked him home from school most nights, stuck up for him when others picked on him. He'd been the first to know when Our Joey was arrested at Otterspool Prom. I realized now that maybe Greg was the guy he'd been caught in the bushes with. They'd gone away to that gay guest house together and come back not speaking – maybe their first row? Our Joey had been dead set against me marrying him the night before the wedding. And then there was the poem he'd read out at our wedding and Greg's obvious discomfort during it. I became obsessed with thinking about these things, over and over again, almost gaining comfort from my Jessica Fletcher-style detective work. But as with any obsession, it wasn't a healthy place to be, and I was left exhausted by constantly replaying every moment of the relationship, with Our Joey never far behind.

I knew that Mum and Dad were worried about me. Who wouldn't be? But I knew I was going to be OK. Despite the despair I was feeling, part of me knew that this was a process I had to go through. Call it survivor instinct, whatever, I knew I needed to think about all the bad things before I could face the rest of my life. And I sort of knew that my period of bed rest would last approximately as long as the honeymoon would have. I'm not sure if this was instinct or a decision I made, but one thing I did know was, I wasn't going to stay in my bedroom for ever. After about ten days of concentrating on the past, I started to contemplate my future, and I came to the decision that I had to get away from home. In fact, I had to get away from Liverpool. I didn't want to run the risk of bumping into Our Joey, or Greg, or anyone who was at the wedding, ever again. But where would I go? That was one thing I was unclear about. I had to get out, but to where?

Then one day my fairy godmother came to visit and everything became clear.

Mrs Mendelson sat on the chair in the corner of my bedroom, dutifully sipping weak tea from Mum's best china cup and saucer. Her kaftan was so big and billowy that it completely hid her chair and made her look like she was squatting there acrobatically as she sipped away. She didn't mention Greg once, but I guessed she must have heard about it or else why would she have been here? My hunch was that Mum had phoned her. I could tell she wasn't enjoying the tea – not enough vodka in it, no doubt – but she didn't scuttle off to the toilet to top it up from a secret hip flask; instead she gave me her undivided attention.

'What you are lacking, Jodie, is a purpose.'

I nodded.

'And I think you were put on this planet to act. To move people. To touch them. To lift a mirror to their own foibles and inadequacies, their joy, their pain, and reflect it back at them so that they can learn.'

OK.

'You have talent. You have promise. But what you don't have is a process.'

Er . . .

'In order to learn your process you need to study. You need to train. I suggest you go to drama school.'

Immediately images of the TV show *Fame* crackled in my brain. Legwarmers, cellos, bowler hats and flouncy skirts – 'Fame costs . . . and here's where you start paying . . . in sweat!'

'Why, you may ask yourself, would you want to work in a profession where 90 per cent of actors are, on the whole and for most of the time, unemployed? Well, my answer to that is simple. I am of the belief that you are employable. You have something. A certain *je ne c'est quoi*.'

Oh God, I wished I'd concentrated more in French at school.

'But before throwing you to the lions in the business proper, we need to get you a head start on the others. That head start should be drama school.'

OK. Simple. I would go to drama school. Now, if needs be. Quick while I sort my hair out.

'However, you are not ready for drama school.'

Damn! Put that scrunchy back in!

'But I can prepare you. The journey usually takes about a year. It's August now and most courses begin in September, October. But I have spoken to my dear friend Rupert at L.A.D.S. – the London Academy of Dramatic Sciences – and he has a vacancy for the three-year acting course beginning in October.'

Gulp. This was all happening a bit fast.

'One of his prospective students has had to pull out because she's landed in the family way. Usually he would source a replacement from the people he's already auditioned, but I have asked him to hold fire until he's seen you, and he has agreed. He respects my taste. He will audition you in ten days' time. You must prepare one Shakespeare piece and one modern. I will prepare you. We will train in your lounge every day from ten till six and then you will go and meet Rupert. You will not let me down.'

It looked like I had no say in the matter. Oh well, it looked like I'd found a purpose.

'It's actually a through lounge,' I pointed out. She nodded.

'Now. Do you think you might help me get out of this chair?' I climbed off the bed.

First impressions counted. I knew that. And I knew I had to impress this Rupert fella when I met him. Thinking back to when I met Nona Newman from *Acacia Avenue*, I knew that acting was a very glamorous profession, so I decided to dress to impress by wearing what I assumed most actresses might wear for the average rehearsal day. I wore brand-new silver tap shoes, white leggings, silver legwarmers, a chainmail tunic with a white fur trim and huge silver hooped earrings. Mum, Dad and Maureen agreed I looked sensational and excitingly futuristic. Maureen's friend Patsy came over and styled my hair – I said I wanted it so big I'd struggle to get through the door – and as Mum, Maureen and I stepped sideways onto the train to London I thought I looked like Jane Fonda in *Barbarella*. But with bigger hair.

The London Academy of Dramatic Sciences was housed in an old red brick Victorian school, complete with railed playground on the roof, in a part of London called the Oval. We went up some steps and in through the main door, where Mum announced to the receptionist that we were here to meet Rupert Dale, at which she rolled her eyes, pointed to a door and muttered, 'You and a million others.' We headed through the door and found ourselves in a canteen, where about twenty-odd student types – all dressed in black – were milling around. Some were stretching, some were singing, some were sitting at tables with their eyes shut, mouthing words. My heart sank, because:

1 I was completely overdressed.
2 I was wearing more make-up than the rest of them put together.
3 I was the only one accompanied by their mum and their mum's best friend.
4 I was the only one whose mum was producing sandwiches from her holdall and offering them round to my competitors.
5 Mrs Mendelson had given me the impression that I was the only person Rupert was auditioning.
6 I was screwed, basically.

We arrived at 2.15p.m. and I didn't go in to meet Rupert till half past five.

Rupert Dale was a crumple-faced guy with hair like Rod Stewart and the longest legs I'd ever seen on a human being. Despite the preconceptions I had about his name – he'd be posh, camp, irritating – he was in fact a gruff northerner, which put me immediately at ease. He wore bell-bottomed jeans, which I found inexcusable, and a tank top – nothing else. He laid back in his chair with his arms behind his head, displaying greying tufts of armpit hair and matching mini tufts on his toes. An unlit roll-up hung from his lips and he grinned through my prepared pieces: a speech from *The Comedy of Errors* and then a monologue from a play called *The Fall and Rise of Little Voice*, in which I was playing a middle-aged tarty piece that really made Rupert smile. His roll-up fell out of his mouth, and he didn't even bother to pick it up and stick it back in till I'd finished.

I stood there, waiting for him to tell me how brilliant I was.

Instead he leaned over, elbows on knees, and stared at me. I stared back. He kept on staring. So I held his stare. Eventually he said, 'Why do you wear so much make-up, Jodie?'

Oh Gosh.

'Never go anywhere without my war paint!' I quipped.

'Ah, so life is a battle?'

'I just wanted to make a good impression,' I countered.

'If you come here, I will strip all that away from you. Find the real Jodie. Are you prepared for that?' He spoke with a coarse Northern accent, yet placed his words warily, as if English was his second language.

'Yes,' I lied. I actually wanted to go to drama school so I could spend three years being anyone other than me. Isn't that what actors did? Pretended to be other people?

'You are young. You have never lived away from home before. London is a big place.'

I shrugged like it was nothing. 'Liverpool's a big place. I'm from the school of hard knocks.'

Blimey, I sounded like a cliché. My Liverpool accent had become ten times stronger as I'd felt backed into a corner, and my main purpose became to defy him. Next I'd be telling him to 'shove his drama school up his Yorkshire arse, love', but I kept my cool. Ish. I also wasn't sure if he was from Yorkshire or Lancashire, so . . .

'You seem to carry pain with you. Outwardly you give the impression of being cocky, confident, and with a zany sense of humour.'

Did I? I'd not cracked that many jokes. Oh heck, I hope he wasn't referring to my clothes.

'But underneath there's a well of loneliness I'd like to tap into.'

I shrugged. I wasn't sure what to say to that. Me? Lonely? I had loads of mates. OK, so I'd chosen not to see any of them since I'd found my brother sucking off my husband on our wedding day but . . . Just then the door at the back of the audition room opened and Mum walked in. Rupert looked round.

'Yes?'

'Sorry, love. I'm Jodie's Mum. You Rupert?'

'I am.'

She stepped forward and shook his hand.

'Hiya, love. I'm sorry but we're gonna have to go. I've booked us onto a train in an hour and we can't miss it or we'll have to buy another ticket. You have kept us waiting an awful long time.'

Rupert looked rather bewildered, then he looked at me and said, 'I'll be in touch.'

I curtsied. CURTSIED! And then left the room.

Why did I curtsy? WHY?

We returned to Liverpool, me, Mum and Maureen, and I expected never to hear from Rupert again.

The next day he phoned the bungalow. I heard Mum answering it.

'Hello? Oh hiya, Rupert love, how's you?'

I heard the scratch of a cigarette lighter and I could just picture her settling down for a long gab with him, so I hurried into the hall and snatched the receiver off her.

'Hiya, Rupert, it's me, Jodie.'

He sighed at the other end of the line.

'I would like to offer you a place at L.A.D.S. On one condition . . .'

My heart practically somersaulted out of my mouth, hit the ceiling and then plunged back in again.

'What's that?'

'That you never turn up for classes in make-up.'

Oh. Was that possible? Three years with NO MAKE-UP?

I contemplated a future here in Liverpool, bumping into Greg and Our Joey at the Asda as they picked out matchpots to paint their spare room. That was the alternative. Oh, God. I straightened my back. Head up, eye on the prize, as Mrs Mendelson used to say.

'Rupert, it's a deal.'

The night before moving to London I went for drinks with Hayls and Debs at the Blue Lagoon. It was a sombre affair, mostly dominated by Hayls claiming she was worried she was going blind, but Debs reckoned it was just the subtle new lighting in the bar. Debs had heard a rumour that Our Joey had moved in with Greg to an apartment down by the docks, like the posh people used to do in *Brookside*, but I told her I wasn't interested. Hayls said she'd heard Greg was making gay porno movies for the foreign market, and again I shrugged and shook it off. Admittedly they both said they'd also heard that Greg and Our Joey were no longer speaking, but it was enough for me to realize that they were a source of gossip and that therefore I was, too. If I'd been having any second thoughts about moving away, this was enough to confirm I was doing the right thing. We bid each other a low-key goodbye outside the chip shop, promising to phone and write every week. The girls said they were looking forward to coming and staying with me and painting 'that London' red. But as I hugged them goodbye I had a hideous, overwhelming desire to push them both away. They reminded me too much of that day, those months, those years. Unreasonable as it seemed, I wanted to discard them to the wastepaper basket of history, along with Greg and Our Joey, allowing me to make believe it had never really happened.

I returned to Sandalan and sat in the kitchen with the lights off. In the lounge my bags sat, packed, ready for the off the next day. As the moonlight hit them, on the mantelpiece behind them I could see a school photo of me and Our Joey. I looked away, sharply reminded that if I stayed here there would always be something to spoil the view.

The main feeling I had through my first year at L.A.D.S. was one of bewilderment. Rupert had been right, London was a big place, and if I got lost on that underground once, I got lost a million times. I was overwhelmed by the pace of life, the passive aggressiveness of strangers, the noise. And then there was the college itself. If I'd not understood the meaning of the phrase 'fish out of water' before, I soon did. Everyone seemed posher than me, more confident than me, more knowledgeable about everything that we were asked to do, or the things we discussed. What's more, they all seemed more talented than me. It had been one thing being good in Mrs Mendelson's classes, and shining gloriously in *Say No to Date Rape* (an improvised piece), but these guys commanded your attention like seasoned pros.

On my first day I found a girl crying in the girls toilets, her badly henna'd hair punctuated by an Alice band. I asked her what was wrong. She looked at me and attempted a smile, saying, 'I miss my horse.'

'Horse is . . . your boyfriend?' Wow! I knew what that nickname implied. Lucky girl. But she looked at me like I was mad.

'No he's my . . . horse.'

At that point I realized I wasn't in Liverpool any more. And that in itself was bewildering. She fell into my arms and sobbed on my shoulder as I stroked her hair.

'I'm Moth,' she sobbed.

'You're what?'

'Moth.'

Oh well. I was used to strange names. I'd knocked about with a guy in a wheelchair called Lotan. I shrugged it off as a part of London life I could deal with and replied, 'I'm Jodie.'

She stepped back, beaming: 'Jodie?!'

I nodded.

'I had an imaginary friend called Jodie!'

Oh God, she was a complete loon. Her face clouded over.

'She was a bit of a bitch.' Then she smiled again. 'But you seem really nice.'

Ah! She might have been a complete loon, but she was a good judge of character. Result!

In one of our first acting lessons, Rupert made the group imagine a good taste or a bad taste. I chose rocky road pie. We then had to stand there as he walked around the room, watching us pretending to eat whatever the good or bad taste was. I caught Moth looking at me like this was plain weird, so I winked at her and mimed putting something in my mouth and then nodding as I enjoyed 'eating' it. She winked back and followed suit, rubbing her tummy for good measure. Some of the others were getting really into it. One girl, Amanda, started screaming, 'Oh God I can't eat it, it's vile! It tastes so disgusting, I can't! I'm sorry! Where's the bin?' And then she started dry retching all over the room, staggering round like she was drunk. *What* a drama queen.

I'd known the minute I clapped eyes on Amanda that I wouldn't be able to stick her. She had a perfectly pretty heart-shaped face, but because she wore her precision-cut blonde hair in a ponytail that bobbed every time she moved, she put me in mind of a prancing pony. Oh well, maybe it might make Moth miss her beloved horse less with her in the group.

As Amanda bent over a bin in the corner of the room, daring some bile to shoot from her mouth, I saw several of the lads in our class craning their necks to get a look at her backside. One of them, Oliver, all angular cheekbones and gelled-back black hair, murmured something to the guy next to him and they shared a laugh. I decided I'd have to watch him. Amanda's OTT performance triggered several other members of the group to crank up the volume of their performance in a never-ending Mexican wave of perforgasm. The whole thing, appropriately enough, left a bad taste in my mouth. I sat on the floor and quietly continued to pretend to eat rocky road pie, unsure what this was all about.

Amanda explained in the canteen at lunchbreak.

'I think Rupert wants us to learn how to use our imaginations and stuff?'

Amanda seemed to end every sentence like it was a question.

'To really play, use all our resources? Our past, our senses, so we can be truly alive on stage?'

Moth and I nodded eagerly, knowingly, as if this was old news. A bit of Moth's strawberry yoghurt was dribbling down her chin. It endeared her to me even more. Amanda continued, 'It's Stanislavski and method acting, kind of all rolled into one?'

'That's what I thought,' I said. Another complete bare-faced lie. I felt myself blush, not because of the lie, but because Amanda was really studying my face. I wondered if I, too, had strawberry yoghurt dribbling down my chin. Which would have been odd, as I was eating a pork pie. She saw my discomfort.

'Sorry!' she said, without even a hint of embarrassment. 'I just think you have a great face.'

Oh well.

'Really interesting. The camera will love it. Really kooky, really . . . characterful?'

Hmm, were the great beauties of world kooky? Characterful? I feared not.

'It's like . . . whatever the complete opposite of aristocratic is?'

I knew what the opposite of that was. Peasant-like. I was about to be offended when she added, 'I think you stand a really good chance of getting work when we leave?' Which placated me because, much as I'd enjoyed it at the time, I didn't particularly want to go back to stacking shelves after three years of drama school.

'You're, like, the only truly working-class girl on our course and stuff?' she continued.

I was rather taken aback by this. There seemed to be a received wisdom that everyone with a Liverpool accent, even a soft Liverpool accent, was working class. Everyone from Liverpool knows that wherever they go in the country they only have to open their mouths and judgements are made. Usually the sort that make women reach for their handbags and men check out of the window to make sure their car's still there. Amanda's assumption that I was working class didn't exactly offend me. I probably was, but it did make me think of Mum. And how angry she would have been on my behalf.

Yes, we lived in a tiny bungalow on a council estate. Yes, my dad was a postman and my mum worked in a cigarette factory. Yes, I got a full grant. But Mum, despite all this, had always insisted we were lower middle class. With her obsession with things being 'becoming' or not, or 'common' or not, she really did think she was a cut above everyone else on our street. I'd read a book when I was a kid called *Twopence to Cross the Mersey*. Mum had cried her eyes out reading it, as had her mate Maureen and every woman in our street, so I'd had a crack at it, believing it would make me look ladylike and grown up. It was set in the olden days and in it a posh family on the Wirral, who had staff and a drawing room, fell on hard times and had to move to a slum in Toxteth. Despite living in poverty and being surrounded by riff-raff, the mum in it never forgot where she came from, and always tried to behave like a lady – even if she was making one potato feed a family of eight for a fortnight. She kept her airs and graces, and her nose firmly in the air. Reading it – I sobbed, too. At one point Our Joey had to slap me round the face to sober me up from my heaving hysterics – I got it into my head that my mum was landed gentry fallen on hard times. Complete nonsense, of course, but it just seemed to fit her for some reason.

Looking at Amanda now as she tucked into the sashimi she'd brought in a Tupperware container, I thought that if Mum had been sat with us now, she would have dismissed Amanda's assumptions – no matter how correct or incorrect they were – as irrefutably common.

It seemed Rupert was of that opinion, too. He informed me that as I'd probably have a long career playing 'the maid' or 'the cheeky secretary' – I was thrilled, a long career playing anything would do me just fine – then the job of drama school was to stretch me and make me take on roles that took me out of my comfort zone. Basically this meant that whenever we did scenes from plays, or put on productions, I would be cast as the lady of the house, whereas Moth would be the maid, forever doffing her cap to me and calling me 'Ma'am'. When I told Mum on my thrice-weekly phone calls home from the phone box over the road from my lodgings, she was over the moon. She saw it as a personal affirmation that the McGee family had inherent class in everything they did. I didn't want to spoil it by explaining the rationale behind Rupert's casting.

Another reason the likes of Amanda had me down as the drama school equivalent of a free-school-dinners kid was that, because of my late admission to the course, I'd had less time to find somewhere to live in the Big Smoke than the others. And as such I was invited to board with one of the patrons of L.A.D.S., a septuagenarian semi-retired actor (usually, in his case, pronounced ac-TOR!) called Bernard Bennett (pronounced Bennay).

Bernard lived in a tiny flat a stone's throw from L.A.D.S. One side of the flat looked over Kennington Park and the other was overshadowed by the stadium walls of the Oval cricket ground. Every time I went inside it was like stepping onto the set of one of those claustrophobic submarine movies. I felt I had to physically shrink to get in. Everything about the flat was long and narrow, from the galley-style kitchen to Bernard's uber-aggressive cat Freckles, who looked like the feline equivalent of a sausage dog, and who I assumed had evolved in a very stretchy way to adapt to his surroundings. The flat had but one bedroom, which Bernard had kindly given over to me, while he slept on a sofa bed in the living room. This wasn't as good an arrangement as it first sounded. My bedroom was predictably tight on space, featuring a single bunk bed with a desk underneath it. And because Bernard slept in the living room, through which I needed to walk to access the kitchen, if he wasn't awake when I got up in the morning, I had to go to college without so much as a glass of water inside me. Eventually I got wise to this, moving a kettle and toaster into my bedroom, which was great for my general levels of health and hydration, but meant there was even less space for me to move about in.

Twice a week Bernard was up with the lark, practising star jumps in the living room. Who needed an alarm clock when you were juddered awake by a bouncing thespian? The reason he was up early these mornings was because he was a part-time voice coach at the college. We had to be trained in case we ever got a theatre job and needed to project our voices so everyone in the auditorium could hear, and to do it in such a way that we could keep on doing it every night for as many months as possible without getting a sore throat and sounding like Johnny Vegas after a night on the fags. Everyone else hated their lessons with Bernard, because instead of teaching us anything he would sit at the front of the class and regale us with anecdotes from his career, mostly invented. Like the time he told Dustin Hoffman to reign it in on *Marathon Man*, or how he cured Julie Andrews' lisp on *The Tamarind Seed*. He became a bit of a laughing stock with the others, and they saw my defence of him as solely down to the fact that he was my landlord. But it wasn't like that for me. I loved his stories; Moth did, too, and we sat chuckling throughout, lapping them up. People like Amanda complained about him to Rupert, saying he wasn't value for money and that she was fearful her intended career at either the National Theatre or the RSC was in jeopardy because of his ineptitude. Rupert would just smile and say, cryptically, 'Slowly slowly, catchy monkey.'

Which sounded even odder than you might think in a Yorkshire/Lancashire accent.

One day, towards the end of my first year, I came in to college to find a letter in my pigeon hole. I recognized the handwriting immediately, and it made my blood run cold. I saw the words shake before me and realized my hand was trembling.

'Jodie? Are you OK?' I heard Moth say beside me. I turned to her and smiled, nodding as I shoved the envelope into my bag.

'Fine, Moth. Come on, we'll be late for Rupert.' And I hurried off down the corridor.

All morning I felt the letter burning a hole in the bottom of my bag. I couldn't concentrate on my classes and stumbled through them as if sleep walking. Rupert mistook it for pure concentration and singled me out for praise. At lunchtime I had no appetite, so I slipped away while no one was looking, crossed the road and went and sat on a bench in the park. Every fibre of my being was telling me to read the letter, but the brave part of me was daring me to take the envelope out, rip it up and let it float away on the breeze. Except there was no breeze. And sometimes I was a coward. And too nosey for my own good. And besides, I missed him.

Deep breath, eye on the prize.

> 25 Marigold Court
> 17 Hancock Close
> Rusholme
> Manchester M14 5UW
> 1 June 2002

Dear Jodie,

First off, can I say please, please, please, keep reading. Don't rip this up and chuck it in the bin. I know you'll want to do that. I can't say as I'd blame you if you did, but I really hope you won't.

The first thing I want to say is I'm sorry. I'm sorry to have caused you so much pain and I'm sorry I ruined your wedding day, and your marriage. I know how happy you were with Greg and my behaviour was inexcusable. I know you don't want to know the ins and outs of it, and I don't want to hurt you any more than you are already.

I have had a lot of time to reflect on my actions and what

I did and what I let happen, and I now feel so bad and so foolish and completely hate myself for the mess I created.

As well as doing a lot of thinking in the past year I have also done a lot of growing up, and I now understand that the shitty things I did to you were the shitty things a kid would do. And I don't think I'm a kid any more.

I'd had a major crush on Greg ever since he stuck up for me at school when I was getting picked on. I never in a million years thought anything would happen coz I knew – well, I thought – he was 100 per cent straight. I tried it on with him, not the other way around. I was pissed and would never have dared do anything of the sort if I'd been sober. I'm not saying I've got a drink problem, but it was certainly a factor. So you could have blown me down with a feather when he reciprocated.

Then, of course, there was the next morning and the guilt and feeling an arlarse about you. Greg said it would never happen again and that he loved you. He was always adamant about that. I know it'll sound weird and nonsensical, but it's true. But of course it did happen again, and then I just couldn't stop worrying. I knew he wasn't husband material. What husband goes round shagging their brother-in-law? But I just didn't know how to tell you.

And then there was the wedding day. I was really pissed. He initiated it that day, even though I'd sworn to myself after our chat a week or so before that I wouldn't ever go near him with a barge pole. Which of course I did, as you know only too well.

I just want you to know that I haven't seen Greg since the wedding. Nor do I want to. We had a major row after you ran away from the do, which ended with him punching me coz I called him a c**t. But really, we were both c**ts, I guess. I just didn't want you to think we were living together or something, happily ever after. I never want to see him again as long as I live. It's too messy. It's made too many people sad.

I might not want to see Greg again, Jodie, but I would give anything to see you. I really miss you and the laughs we always had together. Nobody on this planet understands me better than you, which is why my betrayal of you is all the worse.

Mum has told me all about your move to London and that you are going to acting school, and I really think that's boss and I'm not surprised. I hope that if anything positive has come out of what happened, it is that you finally know what you want from life and that you can now go out and get it.

I have moved to Manchester, where I am living with a lovely guy called Pete. He has the nicest smile. I am working at Next in menswear, but I'm getting more and more DJing gigs. I spend every penny I can on records. It's mostly weddings (sorry) and birthday parties and shit like that, but I'm getting my face known round the gay scene and starting to get the odd set in some of the skankier clubs, so you never know.

Jodie, I am so sorry I hurt you. Please find it somewhere in your heart to forgive me. I love you very much, and I'm sorry for being such a huge twat. I would really love to see you again and would be more than happy to come to London to say hello. Or I could come to Liverpool next time you're home. I will leave the ball in your court, as they say.

Hoping this didn't end up in the bin.

I do love you, you know.

Joey xxx

P.S. Nightcap?

I re-read the bit about me finally knowing what I wanted from life and going out and getting it, then I ripped the letter up and put it in the nearest bin.

That night I went out and got hideously drunk. I woke the next morning on a patch of grass, clutching an empty bottle of gin, with no idea where my shoes were. I took the bus home and staggered all the way along Clapham Road, barefoot. Fortunately, no one from college saw me. Thus far, I had never let my hair down in front of them. And I didn't intend to start now.

THIRTEEN

I pulled back the cheesecloth curtain in the bedroom of my basement flat and looked out onto the grey pavements of Clapham Road. The speckled black tarmac of the road. The terracotta bus lane. There was a light breeze outside and an empty Doritos packet floated past, landing, then taking flight again, a bird trying to soar for the first time and not quite making it. Stilettoed feet hurried by. The shiny shoes of businessmen. Another day was dawning in old London town, and in my new flat.

After a quick shower and a breakfast of black coffee and a piece of toast, I threw on my usual uniform for college, black leggings, black pumps and a baggy black jumper, scraped my hair back into a topknot with some clean, red polka-dot knickers, hastily drew black circles round my eyes with kohl and headed out.

In the hallway I found Moth crying. I was now Moth's flat-mate. In fact, her parents had bought this flat for her and only charged me a peppercorn rent. Poor Moth always seemed to be crying. She stood there in a similar black outfit to mine, leaning against the wall as if there was an earthquake rumbling and she was seeking sanctuary.

'Moth, what is it? What's the matter?!'

'Oh, Jodie. Jodie!' she was crying so hard her stomach was making involuntary contractions. This didn't look good, the enormity of her pain instantly suggested to me that she had lost a close relative or vital organ. As she seemed to be in one piece, albeit quite a juddery one, I plumped for the bereavement.

'Babe?'

'I've got my private moment this morning. And I'm really scared!'

And with that she launched herself at me, threw her arms round me and sobbed into my shoulder.

Moth and I were now in our second year. As part of our course we had to do something called 'private moments'. This meant you had to get up in front of your class and do something you would only usually ever do in private. One boy in our year had shaved all his pubic hair off and then studied himself in a full-length mirror. Another had danced with abandon to a song on his Walkman that none of us could hear. I'd recreated my bedroom from the flat and gone about tidying it and making the bed, dressed in my pyjamas.

'What are you going to do, Moth?'

She stepped back and wiped the tears from her eyes, smudging her kohl to create two warpaint stripes across her cheeks. She took a deep, staggered, breath, her tummy still contracting wildly, and said, 'I'm going to cut my toenails.' Then she burst out crying again and launched herself back at me.

I stroked her hair as I felt my shoulder become wet and cooed, 'Oh, Moth. Moth, babe, that's so brave. So brave.'

Of course, I'd not told anyone at college about my three-hour marriage, not even Moth. As far as my fellow students were concerned I was just some girl from the sticks with no baggage or past, who was focused on her studies and gave the boys a wide berth. Such a wide berth, in fact, that they called me Jodie the Fridge behind my back. Amanda kindly told me, but I didn't particularly care – let them think what they liked. I didn't even tell Moth when my decree nisi came through – my dad had applied for it on my behalf and Greg hadn't contested the divorce – I just put the form in the bottom of my knicker drawer and carried on as normal. I didn't feel jubilant, I didn't feel sad, I just felt a bit numb.

'People do like you,' Amanda informed me one day as she ate sushi and I chomped on a bag of Monster Munch in the canteen.

'Do they?'

'Yeah.'

'Even though they call me the Fridge?'

'That's just the boys, take no notice of them.'

'Maybe they're jealous of my talent,' I said, then laughed to show I was joking.

Amanda laughed a bit too loudly for my liking, then shifted uncomfortably in her seat and pulled a face.

'Are you OK,' I asked.

She rolled her eyes. 'Oliver's really into anal.'

My mouth dropped open. 'I didn't even know you were going out!'

She looked horrified. 'We're not. No WAY. God, I couldn't think of anything worse and stuff?'

Then she started talking about Stanislavski, as if we'd just discussed the weather.

And I thought I was unshockable. I ran and told Moth the next time I saw her.

'Ollie and Amanda did anal last night!'

Moth looked bewildered.

'Is that by Steven Berkoff?'

I was even more shocked. Was no one else on my course normal, like me?

There is a perceived wisdom that all students are feckless and fancy free, displaying the morals of a pack of particularly slutty alley cats. Now if I bucked the trend, the rest of my class were like Amanda, and certainly didn't. At one point it appeared that everyone, save me, had either Chlamydia or some other form of venereal disease. It felt like if one of us got a cold, pretty soon the whole group were sniffing. I suppose at least I had a few things to be thankful to Greg for.

I went on a few dates during my time at college, though admittedly I never realized they were dates till I got there. We were encouraged to go and see as many shows as possible, but it was hard for me as tickets were always so expensive. Our year broke down into two socio-economic groups: the haves and the have-nots. I came in the latter category. The have-nots spent every Easter, summer and Christmas break working their veritable bollocks off in pubs and shops, trying to earn enough money to buy food and books during term time. We would return to each new term completely exhausted, the stench of stale booze or half-price batwing jumpers still stinging our nostrils. The haves returned suntanned with heady tales of backpacking in Thailand or trekking in Nepal, shaking sand from their espadrilles and forever pulling out Euros in the pub and saying, 'God, I meant to change them and stuff?' really loudly, which got on my tits.

More often than not, I'd only go to the theatre if I knew another student who was ushering there, who could sneak me in on the sly, or if one of the haves invited me to go with them and they were paying. Oliver sometimes asked me to go with him, usually to see something classical or obscure at the

National Theatre so he could enjoy patronizing me afterwards by explaining what had gone on on stage. I always pretended I'd completely 'got it', but most of the time his discourses were welcome. The first time I agreed to go with him he arrived with a single red rose, which he handed to me. My sphincter clenched. Mortified, I gave it to a homeless person on the way home – he rolled his eyes and said the most sarcastic thank you I'd ever heard. Oliver asked after the rose for days afterwards and I reported back on its imaginary lifespan, before Moth told Amanda what I'd really done with it and Amanda told Oliver and he stopped speaking to me for a whole term.

It was weird going on quasi-dates with boys from college. They were so different from nights out with the boys from home. The student actors discussed their feelings, their knowledge of theatre, they shared and at least pretended to listen when I attempted to join in. Most lads back home took you to the pub and pretended not to be gutted when you couldn't name the line-up at the latest Liverpool game. Obviously Greg had been a bit different to that, but probably only because he was 'a big fat gayer', as Hayls and Debs so succinctly put it.

I was, of course, having less and less contact with the girls back home. Initially we'd phoned and written letters, as promised outside the Blue Lagoon. They'd come to stay with me a few times, when Bernard was away visiting his relatives in Neath. But as time drew on I think they thought I'd gone a bit weird. They were still working at the supermarket, whereas all my reference points for witty anecdotes or moments of gossip had changed drastically. I'm sure they thought my sole purpose in London was to arse around and spend my days watching other students cutting their toenails or shaving their pubes off. Which it was in a way. They were also distinctly unimpressed that someone as gorgeous as me – their words, not mine, I hasten to add – hadn't managed to bag myself a fella, getting over the tragedy of my mini-marriage to a confirmed homosexualist by jumping on some 'dirty big bastard' of a cockney. I saw them when I went home to Liverpool, but there was a distance between us now, and it wasn't just geographical. When I said anything they wouldn't just jump in and agree with me any more, there'd be a pause and I'd see a hesitant look dart between them, as if they were saying, 'See? She has changed. Her with her fancy London ways.' They'd eye my clothes suspiciously and ask if I'd bought them in 'that London', and when I moaned that I didn't have much money they reluctantly bought me drinks with the irritation of women who thought I'd intentionally gone out of my way to earn precisely nothing, daring as I had to turn my back on a life of shelf-stacking. Hayls was still seeing Lotan, though no date had been set for an engagement or wedding, and Debs had started seeing a scaffolder called Mick the Brick. Occasionally they tried to set me up with potential boyfriends, but as with them, I was beginning to feel we were poles apart.

One morning when I was back in London, at the beginning of our third and final year at college, I found Moth in the hallway studying the post. Amongst the free pizza delivery notices and offers for double glazing, she had found a postcard with a rather colourful scene of beach huts and sandcastles on the front.

'Ooh!' I said, feigning interest. 'Who's on holiday?'

Her parents were always going away somewhere fabulous: Mustique, Mauritius, Koh Samui. Places I could only dream of going.

Moth shrugged. 'It's been delivered to the wrong building.'

And with that she threw it on the floor. 'Come on, we'll be late.'

'But shouldn't we . . .?' I looked at the postcard on the carpet, thinking we should pass it on to its rightful owner en route to college, but Moth grabbed me and linked arms with a stern, 'There's no time, Jodes. I'll do it later,' before opening the front door. 'It's only a bloody postcard. It's not even from abroad, cheapskates.'

And off we went. When I got back that night I couldn't see the card anywhere, so I assumed Moth had done her duty and popped it through the correct letterbox.

About a week later I couldn't find the gas bill I was meant to be paying that week and turned the flat upside down looking for it as Moth watched, fingering a packet of Monster Munch and saying stuff like, 'It's just, like, a bill, Jodes,' and, 'God, yeah, get a life and stuff?' She had taken to speaking like Amanda recently and it got right on my tits. And stuff?

Eventually I found it. But I also found, in one of the kitchen drawers, the undelivered postcard. I rolled my eyes and Moth tutted.

'I meant to take it round.'

I gave her a look.

'It's only a postcard, Jodie. God!' Then she galumphed into her bedroom and started playing Tracey Chapman loudly. I turned the postcard over to check the address. It was meant for someone called Stuart Moses and he lived in a flat a few doors up. Oh well, I could just go and slip it through his letterbox. Moth was right, it was only a holiday postcard, it wasn't like someone had actually died.

And then I read it. I couldn't help myself. Well, people don't write anything too personal on postcards, do they?

Oh yes they did. I immediately felt awful and wished I'd not looked. It said:

Hi Stu,

I have come away for a few days with Ricky. I am seeing him now. Sorry to tell you like this, but maybe you shouldn't have been such a tit.

Have a nice life.

Karen.

P.S. Your Armani shirt that got burned on the iron? I done it on purpose.

Oh. My. God. It wasn't just a normal holiday postcard, it was a break-up card! This woman. No . . . this *bitch* Karen had dumped this Stuart guy by *postcard*. Something that anyone could read. It was hardly private. Wow! Some people could sink really low. I felt awful and sunk low myself, onto a kitchen chair, leaning on the table and taking in what had happened. I felt my right elbow slide a bit as I'd leaned in a small mess of marmalade, but I didn't care. I had bigger things to worry about.

A guy called Stuart, a few doors down, had been dumped by his girlfriend. And he had no idea! She had left him for another man and he was probably wondering where she'd got to. And yet the truth of the matter was that the . . . *skanky bitch* was sunning herself somewhere fabulous. Where was it again? I checked the front of the card. Sizewell Beach. She was in the stunning, uber-glamorous location of Sizewell with someone called Ricky. And poor Stuart had no idea. Oh Gosh, this was awful. I re-read the message and my heart plummeted to my boots. Well, slippers. And to top it all she'd been sabotaging his designer labels. It didn't bear thinking about!

But then, hang on. This Karen was making out her behaviour was justified because Stuart had been 'a tit'. Tit was mild. She could have used several much stronger words, any fool knew that. Behaving like a tit suggested minor misdemeanours like . . . like . . . well, like turning up at a fancy dress party dressed as a piece of toast. I'd seen someone do that once. He wore a huge brown latex square thing with his arms poking out of either side. In fact, they were poking out at such an angle he couldn't actually pick up a drink, and everyone agreed he was a bit of a tit because his girlfriend had to spend the night holding his drink to his mouth for him to sip it.

Oh no! What if that had been Stuart? No, that was a ridiculous notion. That was back in Liverpool, several years earlier. What would be the likelihood of him living a few doors down from me now?

I knew what I had to do. I had to go round to his place and apologize, hand him the card and explain that I was convinced my flatmate had already delivered it. None of this was my fault, I could explain, I really thought she'd redirected it. Don't blame me, I would say, blame the Post Office. Some vacant type in blue shorts and trainers had idiotically shoved it through our letterbox by mistake.

Or maybe it was on purpose. Maybe he was in cahoots with Karen. Or this Ricky. Maybe he was Ricky's brother and didn't want Stuart to find out, for some reason – or reasons? – none of which were very clear to me right now. I certainly knew from my postman father that it was practically a hangable offence for a postman or woman to lose mail in any way, shape or form. Maybe I should report him? Send the bugger down! Lock the door and throw away the—

I was getting ahead of myself. I sighed, stood up and headed out.

It was only when I arrived at Stuart's house that I realized I had come out in my slippers. I was tempted to nip back and change, but this was too urgent. I had to let this poor fella know he was dumped, and the sooner the better. It was very nearly a matter of life and death.

Like our house, the front door was up a load of steps, where a veritable xylophone of doorbells hung off the side of the doorframe. I checked Stuart's flat number again and rang the bell. No reply. I'd not bargained for this. What should I do? Pop it through the communal letterbox or come back later? I have to admit I was torn. On the one hand it would have been very easy to post it through the letterbox, but on the other . . . well . . . I was intrigued. I wanted to put a face to the name and see what this Stuart was like. I felt I'd invested in him somehow. I thought we had lots in common. He'd been dumped by Karen, even though he didn't know it yet, and I'd been—

Just then a voice crackled over the intercom. 'What?'

It was quite a surly 'what' and it brought me up short.

'Erm. I was looking for Stuart Moses?'

'Who is it?'

'Just . . . a neighbour.'

'Hang on.'

The intercom went silent and I heard footsteps inside, thudding down the stairs. Oh God. He was going to hate me. Not only was I the bearer of bad news, but he would know I'd read his very personal postcard. The front door swung open and a – OK, I have to be honest here – very fit guy was standing before me. And when I say fit, I'm not talking bodybuilder 'I take too many steroids and have massive biceps and a tiny winkie' fit, I'm talking 'throw you across the room after too many snakebites' fit. There was something irrefutably masculine about him.

'Yeah?'

He was sweaty, but in a good way. The fact that he was wearing footy shorts and a grey hooded top made me think he'd just been for a run or I'd caught him doing press-ups. He had a towel in his hand and a tattoo on his thigh, just beneath the hemline. He saw me looking and readjusted his shorts. Jeez! I hope he didn't think I was checking out his package.

'Sorry, I . . . just wanted to give you this. Are you Stuart?'

He nodded and took the postcard off me.

'It was delivered to my place by mistake. I hope you don't mind, but I accidentally read it.'

God that sounded like complete and utter bollocks. How could you accidentally read something? You either choose to read something or you don't. When did you last hear anyone say, 'God I really enjoyed that book. I read it by accident.'

'Gosh, how does that work?'

'Well. The book flew at me, flapping its pages in my eyes, and I had no choice but to read its printed sentences. I hadn't meant to. I was trying to watch reruns of *Fantasy Island* at the time.'

I had never heard anyone say that. Nor was I likely to.

Stuart didn't look up. He was reading the card. He showed no emotion, but he did do a big sigh and then nodded.

'Thanks.'

His accent wasn't London. I couldn't place it, but he wasn't a cockney.

'I'm so sorry,' I said.

He shrugged, like it was nothing.

'It's been lying in our flat for ages. I thought my flatmate had dropped it round. She said she was going to. I just found it and . . . are you gutted?'

He re-read it, then looked at me. Now I could see a flash of

pain in his eyes, though possibly this was the pain of embarrassment and thinking I was a nosey parker. God his eyes were
piercing. Part Pierce Brosnan, part psychotic serial killer.

'S'her loss,' he grunted.

I nodded eagerly. And his hair. Cropped Action Man short,
drawing attention to his cobalt blue eyes.

'My thoughts exactly,' I agreed. 'She's a bitch. Fancy dumping
someone on a postcard. And that Ricky sounds like a complete
knob.'

He laughed. He actually laughed. He didn't throw his head
back or anything, but it was definitely a faint chuckle. His eyes
narrowed as he did it and his Adam's apple wobbled. OK, if I'm
honest it might just have been a giggle.

'Thanks, anyway.'

'I know how it feels.'

He nodded again, looking slightly alarmed as he noticed I
was wearing my slippers in broad daylight. He took hold of the
front door as if to close it.

'Like I said . . .'

He was about to say 'thanks' when I heard myself blurting
out, 'I found my brother sucking off my husband on our wedding day!'

I blurted it really loudly. In fact, it was more like, I FOUND-
MYBROTHERSUCKINGMYHUSBANDOFFONOUR-
WEDDINGDAY!

A passing businessman did a double take and I'm sure
I saw a net curtain twitch to my right. My subtext was, I'm
not mad, I'm your friend. But maybe my acting wasn't up to
much because he swallowed warily and said, 'See you,' before
shutting the door. My subtext had obviously come across as, I
am a complete nutter. We are both single. Marry me?

As the door shut in my face I was crestfallen. I knew full well I'd made a holy show of myself.

Still, I thought, London's a big place. OK, so he lives a few doors down from me, but what are the chances of bumping into him again? Moth was always moaning on about how she'd seen some majorly cute guy on the Tube or in the corner shop, and how she hoped in vain to see him again and it never ever happened. Apart from the pervy guy who always seemed to rub up against her on the night bus (though Amanda claimed she made this up to appear sexy and appealing). So I was never going to see Stuart Moses again. Ever. So that was OK. Phew. And relax!

I bumped into him that very same night.

Karaoke night at our local pub, the Lost Camel, was a very competitive affair. The participants took it surprisingly seriously, arriving immaculately groomed and with their mates videoing their efforts, so they could watch them back later and discuss in impromptu focus groups dotted around the bar. A gang of us from college went every Tuesday night, if we weren't rehearsing our latest show, and joined in the festivities. I was always a bit embarrassed about getting up and exposing my singing voice, so I'd usually plump for a comedy classic. Well, I say classic, it was often something like 'The Birdie Song' or 'Goldfinger', which I would do in a pseudo Shirley Bassey grouch. On this particular night I leafed through the laminated book of song choices while Amanda was emoting on the mic to 'Love On The Rocks' and found my perfect – and I thought hilarious – choice.

Halfway through murdering 'Psycho Killer (Qu'est-ce que c'est?)', with my fellow students doing some comedy head banging around their table, I caught a startled gaze in the corner of the room. Stuart Moses was supping a pint with a couple of other fellas and his eyes locked on me. He was wearing some kind of denim jacket and had sunglasses perched on his head, but the eyes were unmistakable. Before I finished I saw him mouth something to his mates, knock back his pint, then get up and leave. As he snaked his way through the pub I called out, 'I didn't recognize you with your clothes on!' And he was gone. He had had it confirmed that not only was his slightly stalkerish neighbour a nosey private postcard reader, she was also a pscyho killer (*Qu'est-ce que c'est?*).

Still. I'd probably never see him again, eh?

I saw him three weeks later.

Mum and Dad came to stay for a long weekend. It was so lovely to see them, and they even brought the dog. What was extra nice was that Rupert had gone away to Brighton to be presented with an honorary doctorate for his work in theatre and he offered me his house to look after for the weekend, which meant Mum and Dad could have their own room and the dog had the garden to play in. My only responsibility was to feed and water Rupert's pet rabbits, who lived in a pen in said garden. There were loads of them, so many I lost count.

So far so good.

Until the dog came running into the house with a soily dead rabbit in his gob. He dropped it on the kitchen floor, wagging his tail, as if to say, 'Look what I did! Aren't I clever? I killed one of Rupert's rabbits! Do I get a gold star?'

Convinced I was going to be kicked out of drama school for having my parents' dog murder one of Rupert's prize pets, Mum decided the best plan of action was to replace the rabbit with a lookalike from the local pet shop.

Amazingly, they had one reasonably similar. A snip at fifty pounds – don't worry, Dad paid. I was just joking to the assistant that I was replacing one I'd killed – 'I am indeed a bunny boiler' – when I caught someone staring at me from the other side of a rack of dog leads. Those eyes again. Stuart Moses hurried out.

About a month later Moth and I were window shopping in Covent Garden when we came across a string quartet busking in the piazza. Moth asked me if I had ever learned any instruments. I told her I'd had a few lessons on the violin at school before deciding it wasn't for me, and she nodded, not really listening. Spotting an opportunity for a gag I added loudly, just as the quartet finished their last note, so the whole piazza heard, 'I guess you could say I was a kiddy fiddler.'

A thousand faces turned and looked at me. Jeez, the mortification. And then I saw The Eyes. Followed by Stuart Moses scurrying away again. Moth giggled nervously and the quartet started to scratch out a Brandenburg Concerto.

Brilliant. So not only did my neighbour think I was a psycho killer and a bunny boiler, he now also thought I was a paedophile to boot. Not exactly what you'd call a catch.

I toyed with popping a note through his door explaining my actions, but like Moth said, What did it matter? So what if he thought I was loop the loop? I didn't want a man in my life. I was training seriously for a career. I was focusing on me, not men.

There was a postscript to the Rupert rabbit story. When he returned, newly mortar-boarded from Brighton, he went out into the garden to say hi to the rabbits while I made a fresh pot of coffee to welcome him home. He returned moments later looking confused.

'Everything OK, Rupert?' I asked.

'The rabbits,' he said.

'Oh, I know. Aren't they *great*?'

'They're too much.'

'Oh, I know. They're *hilarious*. God I've spent . . . so many hours . . . just . . . you know. Watching them . . . being all . . . rabbity.'

'No I mean . . . there are too many of them.'

'Sorry, Rupert?'

'I only had five. Now I have six.'

'Gosh. Erm . . .'

Now I was the one looking confused. What had I done?

'I used to have six, but one died. I buried him in the garden, but he appears to have disappeared. And an extra live one has appeared in the hutch.'

Oh bollocks!

FOURTEEN

2008

To celebrate Moth's birthday, a gang of us had piled down to a boat on the Thames that was a popular drinking hole for fully fledged 'proper' actors. There'd been a flurry of excitement in our party when we got there because someone from *EastEnders* was pissed at the bar and one of her tits kept popping out of her wrap-around cardi. The clocks were going forward that night and there was anticipation in the air that summer was on its way and the days were going to get longer. We were now in our final year of college and it felt like the future was full of possibilities, a journey into an exciting unknown that could only bring us good fortune.

As we sat in the starboard corner knocking back warm bottled lager, I looked around the boat and considered the other revellers. Because of the reputation of the place I guessed they were all proper actors, and yet I recognized none of them apart from the drunk one at the bar, who was now leaning on the plump black woman next to her and laughing her head off. Were they all out of work? Was I training to be part of a profession where, for eleven months of the year, I was going to be signing on and then, for the remaining month, feeling grateful to be in an unpaid play in a room above a pub? I tried to shake off the feeling of insecurity with a few glugs of lager and joined in with the laughter round our table. Moth was doing an impersonation of Rupert, which was pretty much spot on, and we howled with laughter, not just because it was particularly hilarious, but because it was her birthday and there was a general feeling of excitement in the air.

When 'Hi Ho Silver Lining' came on the jukebox, Moth jumped up and started dancing in the style of Rupert and we all got up and joined in. 'Rupert Dancing' is a bit like something I often used to do at parties, which I called 'Dad Dancing'. This mostly involves moving off the beat from side to side while making 'come hither' movements with my hands, as if beckoning others to join in the gleeless jig. Moth's twist on this, to make it more like the daddy of them all, Rupert, was to chuck in a few clog dance moves. Our movement teacher would have been proud.

After a few Cossack jump downs and some inappropriate sand dancing I decided it was time for another drink, so shimmied my way towards the bar. The actress from *EastEnders* saw my movement and shimmied in her seat, laughing her head off, which caused her to suddenly slip from her barstool and land in a heap on the floor. She grabbed hold of her neighbour as she plummeted, pulling at the woman's blouse. The woman slapped the actress and screeched, 'Oi, watch me fucking blouse, wanker!' I liked her instantly.

She had a really big arse and, unlike most of the women I knew, she made no attempt to hide it. In fact, she positively celebrated it, wearing leggings and a bolero jacket, both of which were a deep crimson. I had an irresistible desire to slap her on her backside and say, 'Go Sister!' but I held back, fearful of getting a reciprocal punch in the teeth.

I helped her lift the actress back onto her stool and she flashed me a grimace that said she wasn't impressed with her levels of drunkenness, then said, 'Please don't do any more dodgy dance moves. She'll just wanna imitate you. She's at that stage where it's all gestures and incoherence.'

'You're all right,' I said, desperate to impress this fabulous, fierce creature. 'All my other moves are boss.'

'You a Scouser? Oh my God!' she shrieked.

'Guilty as charged,' I conceded, and she laughed.

'That's what they all say!' And then her face turned serious. 'You an actress?'

I shrugged nonchalantly and said, 'Yes.' Then I stepped nearer the bar to grab the attention of the barman, who was currently pulling fluff out of his bellybutton. The fabulous creature leaned in and growled, 'I'll get this. What you having?'

'Er, a bottle of Becks, please.'

I was going to get several others, but I couldn't be that much of a cheapskate to get my new best friend (OK, slight exaggeration there) to fork out for my friends' drinks, too.

'Are you sure?' I added, and she nodded, like it was a stupid question. Then she snapped her fingers in the direction of the barman and growled.

'Oi! Tonto! If you could, like, pull down your T-shirt for two seconds and serve me?'

The barman waddled over and soon I had my beer.

'So,' she'd turned her back on *EastEnders* lady and gave me her undivided attention, 'who's your agent?'

Oh God. Now she was going to know I was lying. Now I'd have to come clean and say I wasn't really an actress, I was only training. My cover was blown, so I just shrugged and said, 'Haven't got one.'

She didn't seem to be listening, instead she was looking me

up and down, sizing me up. She didn't go so far as to lick her teeth and say, 'Tasty,' but I felt like a prize heifer on slaughter day and she was the farmer about to name her price – that is, if farmers are Afro-Caribbean, fierce and dripping in chunky gold jewellery, and with nails so big that if she picked her nose she'd give herself a brain haemorrhage.

'Wanna come to a casting on Monday?'

'Sorry?'

'I'm looking for Scousers.'

'Oh, are you a director?'

'Casting.'

'What's it for?'

'New advert. Can I take your number?'

So I found myself giving it to her while she punched it into her Palm Pilot.

'Who was that coloured lady you were talking to all night?' Moth asked on the night bus later.

'Her name was Laveenia and she's not coloured, she's black.'

Moth tutted. 'What's the difference?'

I couldn't be bothered to get into a semi-drunken discussion about the politics of racism – possibly because I didn't understand it – so I decided to show off instead.

'She's a casting director.'

Moth looked up. Until then she'd been slobbering a bit and leaning her head against the window.

'Really?'

There was a tangible hint of jealousy in her voice. As potential actors, casting directors were people to keep in with. They were part of the great food chain that got you work. I nodded.

'She wants me to go in for a casting on Monday.'

'You can't.'

'I know.'

'Rupert would go ape.'

'I know.'

And that was the truth. Students at L.A.D.S. were not allowed to go for professional auditions or take acting work while they were training. If you did you were kicked off the course. End of. Rupert felt we weren't ready. Rupert felt we could only be proper actors once we'd earned our stripes. And he was right, we weren't ready. We'd be lambs to the slaughter.

'What's it for?'

'An advert.'

'Oh,' and she rolled her eyes and looked back out of the window. Drama students didn't aspire to be in adverts, they aspired to play Shakespeare at the RSC, lead roles in Oscar-winning movies, kooky performance art pieces in out-of-the-way happening spaces.

'I thought it was for something good,' she added, then blew on the glass and wrote her initials in the mist with her fingers.

'She was really nice,' I said, which was true. 'She was a real laugh.'

'She was with that dreadful actress from *EastEnders*.'

'I don't really watch it.' I was more of an *Acacia Avenue* sort of girl.

'I hate soap actors. They just play themselves,' she continued. 'It's just like, the lowest form of acting.'

I was going to let it go, it was her birthday after all, but I couldn't help myself.

'What, just because she's working class and has a Cockney accent? And she plays someone with a Cockney accent? That makes her shit, does it?'

'I didn't say that.'

'So, what? You're posh. So if you play a posh character, that's not acting?'

'God you twist everything, Jodie.'

'Oh get over yourself, Moth.'

We completed the rest of the journey in silence. I thought she was pissed and pissed off with me, but when we got to our stop and she didn't follow me as I got up to get off, I realized she'd fallen asleep. I was half tempted to leave her there, but poked her in the arm with my bus pass and dragged her off with me.

That night I dreamed about Our Joey. I went for the audition for the advert and he was sat there behind the desk with Laveenia and they made me do one classical piece and one modern. I kept forgetting my lines and could hear Laveenia tapping her nails on her desktop, then there was a slurping sound. I turned to see that Greg had joined Our Joey and Laveenia behind the desk and was snogging the face off Our Joey. I woke in a cold sweat.

The next morning I had a big row with Moth, probably because we were both hungover and hanging onto the residual ill-feeling from our night-bus clash, but it centred mostly on me not being able to find my bus pass amongst all the rubbish she'd strewn around the flat. I must have dropped it on the short walk between the bus stop and home as I'd struggled to keep Moth upright, so I laid the blame solely at her door. She was completely non-plussed about my loss, and the mess in the flat, shrugging dismissively and going, 'It's just a bus pass.' I knew full well that if she so desired she could probably rent a Lear jet to fly into college every day, though when I pointed this out she harrumphed into her room and blared out Tracy Chapman till I thought my ears might bleed.

The music was so loud I only just managed to hear the phone ringing when Laveenia followed through (in a good way) to talk to me about Monday's casting. I had no intention of going really, but was too polite to tell her, and too fearful I'd blow my cover that I wasn't a proper actor and was still at drama school. But then, before she hung up, she said something that wetted my whistle.

'The money's not brilliant. It's a buyout. Two grand.'

Two grand! TWO GRAND.

I had no idea what a buyout was but . . . TWO GRAND?!

I was sick of having no money. It filled my every waking thought. Everything I looked at had an invisible price tag on it that only I could see. And even the smallest of tags were ones I couldn't afford. I'd learned all the tricks to make my money go as far as it could: dipping a stale loaf in a bowl of water and then heating it up in the oven to refresh it – or somebody else's oven to save on the lecky – walking as much as possible to save on bus and tube fares, I even pretended to be a Yugoslavian Princess in exile at the laundrette so the proprietress took pity me and let me use the dryers for free. Two grand was lottery-sized winnings. Two grand would see me comfortable for the rest of my student life. Two grand was . . .

But it was pointless even thinking about it. I'd never get the job. And even if I was offered it, I wouldn't be able to take it. I'd be chucked out of drama school. Rupert would never speak to me again. I'd be blacklisted in the business and never be a proper actress. I'd have wasted the last three years; thrown my whole life away.

No. No, I couldn't do it. But then again, it might be really good experience to go for a professional audition. I headed off to the newsagents with a heavy heart, carrying a passport photo of myself to get a replacement bus pass.

On the Monday morning I phoned in sick to college, even giving the performance of a lifetime to Moth to convince her I really did have food poisoning and couldn't go in.

On the Monday afternoon I was sitting in a damp room in Soho pretending to be able to smell a really nice barbecue in front of some advertising executives and a twinkly Laveenia.

On Tuesday morning Laveenia called me to say I'd got the job.

The Lord gives with one hand, and with the other he takes it away. There was just no way I could do it. I'd be kicked out of drama school.

Unless . . .

Unless no one at drama school ever found out.

FIFTEEN

Charlie Walsh was a cheeky chappy chef who had a string of subversive cookery programmes to his name with titles such as *Serving Up Charlie*, *Everyone Loves a Bit of Charlie* and *Charlie Delivered to Your Door*. A Liverpudlian by birth, he had worked in some of Europe's finer restaurants, and at the grand old age of twenty-six was now a full-time celebrity chef with a penchant for rapping while he cooked. He was mixed race, had a skinhead, a swallow tattooed on his neck and the piercing green eyes of someone on lithium. Most people I knew thought he was a knob, but I must admit that whenever I channel surfed late at night and ended up watching one of his shows because there was naff all else on, I usually finished the half-hour hungry and contemplating emulating one of his recipes, such as Funky Fish Pie or Rack 'Em Up Lamb. He made it look easy and, OK, I thought he was quite easy on the eye. In a borstal boy kind of way.

He had recently become the face of a well-known supermarket chain, the same supermarket chain I had stacked shelves for before moving to London to become all thespianic. In an attempt to make him more user-friendly for the home counties (and not just the late-night pub brigade who might get the cocaine references in his programme titles), he was shooting a string of adverts for the supermarket showing him at home with his family and friends, cooking for them, partying with them, having barbecues and the like. I had been offered the part of one of his nameless best friends, who was meant to hang out in his back garden and 'ooh' and 'aah' over his tasty burgers and salad dressings, thus making him look popular whilst lining the pockets of the supermarket. The fact that I could 'ooh' and 'aah' in an authentic Liverpool accent was the main reason I'd got the job.

I had originally said no, I couldn't possibly do it, and come clean to Laveenia, but when she'd explained that the adverts weren't going to be shown on the TV until mid-August – long after I had graduated from L.A.D.S. – I realized it, and the small matter of two grand, was too good an opportunity to miss.

Which is why I found myself in the back garden of a Surbiton semi on a Friday afternoon surrounded by cameras, cables, make-up artists and gazillions of blokes in windcheaters, commonly known as 'crew', waiting for the arrival of none other than Charlie Walsh. I had lied again to Moth and the school about another bout of food poisoning – prompting Moth to caution me about being careful what I put in my mouth – and then slipped away to Surbiton on a train from Waterloo.

A hassled looking woman with a side ponytail and culottes was clapping her hands like a sea lion, trying to get everyone's attention.

'OK, listen up, guys! Charlie's still travelling so we're going to shoot some cutaways. If I can have Jodie, Max and Loll by the barbecue please? I thank you!'

We shuffled over to the gas-fired barbie, where someone with red hair was concentrating hard on laying out some pre-barbecued food on the unlit grill, and we were ordered to generally tuck in and 'ooh' and 'aah' to our heart's content. There were cameras everywhere. The feel for the ad was going to be 'edgy', which I guessed meant there'd be lots of shots of us from different angles, having a great time and eating Charlie's fantastic grub. Ten minutes later someone called, 'Action!' and a hush descended as we tucked in. We were ordered not to actually say anything, just make appreciative noises, which we did, making eye contact with each other as if we were bosom pals. The grill was magically lit and the food didn't taste half bad, I had a chicken skewer and then grabbed something akin to a big fish finger. It was particularly nice, and as the voice called, 'And . . . cut!' I couldn't help myself. I said, 'God, them fish fingers are gorgeous.'

The other actors nodded and I heard someone murmuring, 'Did we get that? That was hilarious.'

And someone else saying, 'Yeah. Got that.'

'Excellent.'

I wasn't really sure what was hilarious about me liking fish fingers, but waited to be told what to do next. We spent the following two hours tucking into more and more food – so much so I was starting to feel a bit nauseous – before someone announced that Charlie had finally arrived.

He came into the garden in shades and a brightly coloured tracksuit top, and all I could think was that he was one surly bugger. He completely ignored me and the other people play-ing his friends, and got behind the various cameras to discuss shots, lighting and angles. When, eventually, he did some performing – he had to hand me a fish finger and say, 'There you go, babe,' – he continued to ignore me between takes and grin maniacally at me during them. Later on we had to dance to some music, like we were having the best time of our lives, with Charlie waving his barbecue tongs in the air like he just didn't care, while I shimmed near a rose bush. Except they didn't play any music for us to dance to, we did it to no sound at all, which was completely embarrassing and made us look like a gang of demented loons. As the sun faded we were told it was 'a wrap' and sent home. As he was leaving to get in his posh black car I said, 'Bye, Charlie. Nice working with you.' He looked at me, seemingly surprised that I'd spoken to him. He looked me up and down and, just as I thought he was going to say goodbye, said, 'Nice tits.' Then left.

I got the train to Waterloo, then a bus back to the Oval, which is when I started to feel a bit queasy. I got a weird tingling sensation in my legs and realized I was getting very clammy and my top was starting to stick to me. When I finally got off the bus I felt my stomach spasming and buckled over and threw my guts up in the gutter.

Those fish fingers might well have been gorgeous, but it seemed I had gone and got myself an unhealthy dose of food poisoning. Talk about karma. It was as if I'd brought it on myself by lying. Still, with two grand winging its way towards my bank account, I thought it was well worth it. As I walked up the Clapham Road towards the flat I swayed a bit. God I felt rough. I had to stop every now and again and clutch onto the railings as I felt the waves of nausea rise through me, but I reckoned I could make it back to the flat without chucking up again. Part of me was hoping no one would see me – just having vomited is not a good look. My fringe was plastered to my face, I was trembling and my breath smelled of regurgitated fish fingers – but the bigger part of me hoped someone from drama school would witness my hideosity so my food-poisoning claims could at least be verified. I toyed with taking a detour past L.A.D.S. and possibly shrieking loudly to get someone to look out of a window and gasp, 'Jeez, poor Jodie looks dreadful!' But the lure of my bed and the opportunity to wash my face and brush my teeth was too much.

As I neared our flat I plucked my keys from my bag and stopped to take a deep breath as I thought I was going to throw up again. It was then that I noticed someone sitting on the steps up to the main door of the house. Maybe it was one of the Polish tenants from the flat above me, having locked themselves out again. But they were dressed too well to be Bolek or Boleslaw (who Moth and I nicknamed Coleslaw – hilarious), in Adidas trainers, smart jeans, a Puffa jacket and a mop of blond curls. My stomach lurched. It was Greg.

As he stood up I felt my knees buckle, my head pound and a familiar spasm in my chest. I gripped the nearby railing and vomited so violently that bile bounced off the pavement and splattered up my legs.

'Jesus, Jodie, are you all right?'

I coughed and spat some bits out. Greg was stepping closer to me. This wasn't happening. I blinked quickly, hoping I was hallucinating, but no, he was still there, worst luck. I dry-retched again.

'Oh my God, I knew you hated me, but I didn't think you'd be sick at the sight of me,' he added. I shot him some daggers.

'I've got food poisoning, knobhead.'

'Oh,' he sounded almost disappointed. God, I wanted to get inside and clean myself up, but he was standing there, blocking my path to the door.

'How did you know where I live?'

This was the worse possible scenario imaginable. When I met my ex again I wanted to have arse-length sun-kissed Hollywood hair, an amazing complexion and Tom Cruise and our three triplets at my side. Oh, and an Academy Award poking out of my tote bag, which I'd won for a hard-hitting, gritty role playing a drug mule or a saviour of abused children. Not bedraggled and covered in sick.

'Your mum told me.'

I'd kill her. I would, I'd kill her. Not only had she given Our Joey my address at college to write to, she'd gone and told my cheating bastard of an ex-husband my personal address. She'd clearly set up a booth on Liverpool's main shopping street, handing out business cards with my personal details on, shouting, 'Roll up, roll up! Anyone who wants to know where our Jodie lives, come and get her details here! Preferably those of you who've done her head in or broken her heart. One day only. Roll up, roll up!' How *could* she?

'What do you want, Greg?'

It was so weird seeing him. Thus far every time I'd thought of him I'd seen him in the boiler room at his farm, eyes closed in pre-orgasmic ecstasy, Our Joey kneeling before him. And now here he was, in front of me, in human form. Larger than life. He hadn't changed a bit. He'd had at least two and a half years to change. Why hadn't he changed?

'I've missed you.'

'Yeah, well you should've thought about that before you started copping off with Our Joey.'

I tried to brush past him, but he stuck his arm out and grabbed mine.

'Please, Jodie. Can we talk?'

'About what? There's nothing to talk about. You're gay. End of.'

'I'm not!'

'My brother had sex with you. On more than one occasion.'

He blushed, realizing that Our Joey had obviously filled me in on everything.

'Doesn't sound particularly straight to me,' I added.

'OK, I fucked up. But don't we all fuck up at some point?'

'There's fucking up and there's fucking your wife's brother. Leave me alone, Greg.'

'I've thought about you non-stop since the day it happened.'

'Our wedding day,' I pointed out bitchily. I was on fire, literally, this food poisoning was really kicking in.

'Some days I've felt like me head was about to explode.'

'Oh spare me the poetics, Greg. I'm not gonna help your guilty conscience. You've got it for a reason.'

'I was confused. I'm not now.'

'What? You think I'd take you back?' I sounded hysterical now and he backed off.

'Course not. But, surely we can be . . . friends?'

Which is when I hit him with my handbag. It was a pretty pathetic hit – Joe Bugner wouldn't be quaking in his boots – so I hit him again with more venom.

'Friends? *Friends?!* Are you MAD?'

'What we had was good, Jodes.'

'Don't call me that! I'm nothing to you!' And I hit him with my bag again, which is when I heard a strangely familiar voice behind me.

'Everything all right, Jodie?'

I swung round. It was him. It was Stuart from a few doors up, looking concerned as I battered Greg with my tote bag. His chest was puffed out like he was itching for a fight. Oh my God, he was stepping in to defend my honour. And he'd called me 'Jodie'!

'Is this muppet giving you hassle?'

Essex, he was from Essex. I'd not been able to pinpoint it the day I'd stood on his doorstep, but now it was ringing out loud and clear. We'd done the Essex accent in dialect class.

'Who's this?' said Greg, frowning at Stuart.

'This', I said to Stuart, pointing at Greg, answering the question as if he'd asked it and not Greg, 'is my ex-husband.'

Stuart nodded. 'Ah, the one who was shagging your brother.'

'Exactly!'

Greg looked mortified. Clearly his misdemeanours were known far and wide in London town. Even random blokes on the street knew what he'd been up to. I couldn't help but give a valedictory smile.

'Is he giving you hassle?' Stuart asked, stepping closer to Greg, so that I was in the middle of them. Oh God, if I didn't feel so lousy this might almost be exciting.

'A bit,' I bleated.

'What's it to you?' asked Greg, perplexed.

Stuart smiled a rather nasty smile and folded his arms across his chest. 'She's my girlfriend.'

Greg looked shocked. I probably looked shocked, too. Even Stuart looked quite shocked that he'd said it. But his ploy worked; Greg immediately seemed to shrink before my eyes.

'So,' added Stuart for good measure, 'why don't you fuck off back to Fazakerley?'

Gosh, his knowledge of the Liverpool suburbs was good.

'I'm not from Fazakerley,' said Greg like a petulant child. 'I'm from Hunt's Cross.'

I lasered Greg with a steely look. A look that said, 'Well, you might have thought I'd've been sat in like an old maid pining for you, but no. Consider the evidence. I have been sowing my seed, throwing caution to the wind and my knickers to the floor.'

'I'm sorry,' said Greg. 'I just . . . came to apologize.'

'Well take your apologies, mate, and shove 'em where the sun don't shine,' Stuart replied. Gosh he was good at pretending, I had to give him that. Rupert would have been proud. I nodded in agreement as he added, rather melodramatically it had to be said, 'You're nothing to her.'

I shook my head in agreement. God this was the best outcome I could have hoped for when meeting Greg again, especially after the vomit-look start. This was excellent. Greg stuck his hands in his pockets and started shuffling down the street. He looked back sadly and added, 'See you, Jodie.'

'No you won't,' said Stuart. Greg narrowed his eyes at him, then kept on walking. Stuart looked at me, grimacing, as if he was checking he'd not overstepped the mark. I gave him the high-five equivalent of a grin, after which he relaxed.

'I'd better go into yours. Looks more real then.'

I nodded and stuck my key in the door. I don't know if Greg was looking back to see us retreating into my building, but if he had he'd have assumed we were living together, which was brilliant with me.

Once inside the hall I closed the front door behind me. Stuart smiled awkwardly. 'You all right? You look shocking,' he said.

I nodded. 'I'm fine.'

Then another wave of nausea hit me and I vomited all down the front of his shirt.

He took my bag for me, which looked so wrong but felt so right, and led me down the stairs to the front door of our flat, took my keys and let us in. Then he guided me to the bathroom, put the shower on and said he was going to make me some black tea. Before he left the room I said, 'When I'm better, can we go for a drink?'

He smirked – such a cheeky face – and said, 'Guess we'll have to, seeing as how I'm your boyfriend now.'

I smirked back.

It was only after he'd gone to the kitchen and I'd locked the door so I could shower in privacy that I realized I'd never even told him my name. And yet he'd called me Jodie. How had that happened?

SIXTEEN

'Mum? What on earth did you think you were doing giving Greg my address?'

There was silence on the other end of the phone.

'Mum?'

'Oh I'm sorry, Jodie. I didn't think it would do any harm.'

'D'you not think you should at least have warned me you'd given it to him?'

'I . . . just thought he'd send a letter or something.'

'He turned up on my doorstep. He came to London, Mum.'

'I know.'

'You know?'

'Yes he . . . he came round last night and told us.'

'He came to your house?'

'Bungalow.' She sounded accusatory, then added almost apologetically, like she knew she didn't have to say it but couldn't help herself, 'Dormer.'

'What?'

'Oh, Jodie, he's a broken man. He's never gotten over you. He didn't mean to hurt you.'

'Gotten? Did you just say gotten? Have you changed your name to Tammy Wynette?'

I heard her tut. The receiver shook in my hand. Had the

world suddenly gone mad? I spoke, incredulous, 'Why are you suddenly taking his side in all of this?'

'Jodie I'm not. It's just . . .'

'What?!'

'Well, I think he regrets it.'

'Er, rewind a second here, Mother. Why's he even going round to yours? How come you know so much about how he's feeling all of a sudden?'

'We did get close to him, Jodie, when he was marrying you. I tried to make an effort to get to know him and—'

'Yeah, well, you don't have to any more.'

'I know but . . . well, you're away in London and our Joey's there, too, and—'

'What? Our Joey's in London now?'

This was news to me. I felt weightless all of a sudden. Usually that would be a good thing as it would mean I'd lost so much weight I could float away, but this felt horrible.

'Yeah, he's working as a DJ. Didn't I say?'

'No.'

This was very bad news. So weightless, in fact, that I could float out of the front door and bump into my cheating, two-timing bastard of a brother at any time. No! I sat on the floor, hoping to root myself, weigh myself down.

'Well, anyway, the house feels so empty without you.'

'Bungalow. Dormer.' I was feeling mutinous.

'You never phone. You never write. You never seem that keen on coming back for a weekend or—'

'I'm skint, Mother. I'm a student. D'you know how much the coach costs?'

'We'd send you the money.'

'I'm too proud,' I lied.

'You're too lazy,' she countered. Cheeky mare!

'Oh what, so me and Our Joey have buggered off – quite apt for Our Joey – so you've moved my ex in to take our place?'

'You always were such a drama queen, Jodie,' she said, as if I'd never understand.

'You haven't answered the question!'

'Don't make a mountain out of a molehill, Jodie. I bumped into him in the Asda at Hunt's Cross a while back and we got chatting in the two-for-one section.'

I rolled my eyes, which clearly didn't translate over the phone. Oh the irony . . .

'And one thing led to another and he ended up coming back for his tea.'

Blimey, she'd be telling me they'd ended up in bed together next.

'We don't get many visitors now and he seemed so upset. And, well, I didn't think there was any harm in him just writing. I didn't think he'd go and see you.'

At least she was saying sorry. And it did sound like she was feeling guilty.

'I thought it might give you both some closure.'

'Closure? Bloody hell, Mum. From Tammy Wynette to Oprah Winfrey in one fell swoop.'

'Jodie.'

Now it was my turn to tut.

'Anyway, you might have told me you'd got a new fella. You never tell me anything any more.'

Oh God. Oh no. Greg had told them about Stuart.

'Well it's very early days,' I blustered.

'What's his name?'

'Stuart.'

'Is he from a good family?'

'Mother, what d'you think this is? *Pride and* fucking *Preju-*

dice?' Truth be told I had no idea what sort of family Stuart was from. He might have been raised by wolves for all I knew.

'I know you're upset, Jodie, but there's no need to swear.'

'I'm sorry. Greg shouldn't have told you that. Greg shouldn't have been here in the first place.'

'He hasn't got a Mum, Jodie.'

'I know. I went to the funeral. We all did.'

'I feel sorry for him.'

And how about feeling sorry for me? I wanted to say. But I knew it would sound petulant.

'Mum, I've . . . I've gotta go.'

I had to do no such thing, but I just didn't know what to say. The whole conversation was making me feel immeasurably sad.

'Jodie, I'll tell him. I'll tell him to stop coming round if that's what you want.'

Of course it's what I wanted, and her saying it actually made me a bit weepy, but agreeing with her might have made me sound unreasonably bitchy. Or would it? I really had no idea what was the right thing to do.

'Oh, Mum. You're a grown-up. You can see who you like.'

There was silence at the other end and I wondered whether she, too, was upset. I heard the scratch of a cigarette lighter and guessed she was.

'If I send you the money, will you come and see us soon?'

'Course, Mum. Course I will.'

'Oh good.'

'As long as my ex-husband's not gonna be popping in every five minutes for Rich Tea and sympathy.'

She chuckled.

'Er, Mother? I think the words you're looking for are, "Absolutely not, Jodie."'

'Absolutely not, Jodie. Oh you do make me laugh.'

'I have my uses.'

'What does Stuart do?'

'I'll tell you next time.' Because of course I had no idea.

'Oh, OK. Well, say hello to him from us. And don't slag us off.'

'As if. Bye, Mum.'

'See you, love.'

'Ta-ra.' And I hung up. I saw a shadow move on the wall and turned to look behind me. Moth was hovering with a packet of Scampi Fries, a startled look on her face.

'What?' I said, embarrassed.

'Jodie!'

'What?'

'Were you . . . married?'

Oh God.

'I'm psychic.' Stuart winked as we walked along the South Bank, eating some unpronounceable Vietnamese street food that we'd picked up from a bullet-shaped stainless-steel stall underneath one of the bridges. If I was to say he was wearing a navy duffel coat, I know it would sound like I was on a date with Paddington Bear, but I wasn't. He carried it off. In fact, it made him look cool. Especially as it was teamed with battered jeans and Nike trainers. His eyes were twinkling and his cheeks were pink. It was a crisp day for May, and I'd managed to stain the faux fur wrap I'd put on to block out the chill with something red that had popped out of my spring roll.

'Yeah, right!' I joked back.

So he went for the counter attack.

'All right then, I . . . I . . .'

'OK, this had better be good!' I teased.

'I . . . got some post delivered to you, wrongly, and I took it round, only you don't remember me doing it.'

He grimaced – could he get away with it? No. I rolled my eyes and asked him for the umpteenth time, 'How did you find out my name? Tell me!'

He looked out over the Thames, lifted his arm and dropped a noodle in his mouth, slurping it up like something out of *The Aristocats*. He didn't shut his mouth much as he proceeded to eat it, but I didn't care. It made more of a feature of his over-sized lips.

'I made it my business. And when I make something my business, I always get what I want.'

He looked at me and winked again, sending a jolt of promise through my body, then he threw his head back and emitted the dirtiest laugh I'd heard in a long time. I was desperate to know how he'd found out my name. You see, whereas I had been ambling along with the misapprehension that my newly dumped neighbour thought I was a 100 per cent certifiable loon, I now realized he must have been madly in love with me and done something terribly romantic like . . . hiring a private detective. Called Clint. I could just see the scene now:

It's late at Clint Machonohy's office. The ceiling fan's spinning but the room is muggy as Clint, a native New Yorker (in fact, he has 'Native New Yorker' playing on a scratchy turntable in the background), peers across his desk at Stuart Moses.

'So, this broad you need to find the name of. Whaddaya know about her?'

'Not much, apart from her address.'

Clint nods. That's a good start. Then Stuart adds, 'Oh. And the fact that she's a psycho killer, bunny boiler, kiddie fiddler.'

Clint nods, impressed. Women like that certainly don't come along every day . . .

'I'll find her, goddammit!' Clint bangs an angry fist on his desk, causing the ice in his bourbon to rattle. 'I'll find her if it freakin' kills me.'

Stuart nods, grateful tears in his eyes.

He must have done something like that to find out, mustn't he? But he was pulling something from his pocket.

'Truth be told, I found this.'

And he handed me my bus pass. The one I'd lost a few weeks ago. It was so lovely to be reunited with it I felt like kissing it. I didn't, that would have looked far too egotistical on a first date. Especially as I now realized that it wasn't a particularly good photo of me. In fact, as I imagined seeing it through Stuart's eyes, it was pretty hideous. The *Mona Lisa* may have bewitched many with her enigmatic smile, but I was going to win no suitors with my startled Goth look. I'd plumped for a – I felt – moody black and white passport-booth snap, which made my skin look albino white and my hair (criminally) dyed black. The smile was not so much enigmatic as, 'Shit, I think I've just sat on a pine cone!' What had I been thinking?

'Where did you find this?' I asked, conjuring an image of him breaking into my flat in the dead of night in a black balaclava with the bit between his teeth, desperate to find a keepsake to remind him of the woman who was clearly, and quite rightly, pervading his dreams. I imagined a mixture of the Milk Tray man and – less appealingly – the bloke with equally big lips in *Jagged Edge*.

'Found it in the gutter, down by the bus stop.'

Oh. Well that wiped out that fantasy, which was probably a good thing the more I thought of myself as Glenn Close in

Jagged Edge. In fact, she got drowned in the bath in the end. Or
was that *Fatal Attraction*?

'I meant to give it back to you the other day, but all that stuff
with your ex kinda . . . got in the way. Knew it was you soon
as I seen it.'

I pulled a face. 'Oh God. And here was me thinking I was
gorgeous.'

Again, the dirty laugh came, only this time he flung his free,
non-street-food-holding arm round my shoulder and guided
me down the esplanade.

'Oh shut it, Treacle. You'll do.'

Yikes. He called me Treacle. But with his big manly arm
around me he could have called me anything and I'd probably
have melted. Just as I was melting now. Funny how you can be
freezing and melting at the same time.

Food finished and wrappers sensibly disposed of in a metal
perforated bin, we walked almost as far as the Globe Theatre
and sat in a pub overlooking the Thames. The view was nice
but the design of the pub was a bit 1970s municipal car park,
and over a few drinks – vodka and sodas for me, pints of
Guinness for him – I realized that I fancied him. It was all a bit
embarrassing really, all I could think of was that I wanted to go
to bed with him. Hell, forget the bedroom, if he wanted to take
me over this pub table I'd have welcomed it. In fact, if he wasn't
careful I was going to shove our drinks floorwards, jump over
the table and pounce on him. It had been so long since I'd had
any sexual urges about anyone that the feeling was both alien
and all-encompassing, so I knew I had to get a handle on this
and distract. Distract! I couldn't exactly stick my fingers in my
ears and sing, 'La La La,' loudly and gaily, but I could blurt out
the first thing that came into my head, which I did: 'Let's play
twenty questions!'

He had been in the middle of explaining the off-side rule, so he looked a little perturbed. His smirk said, 'Women, huh?' Then his mouth said, 'Er, OK.'

So we played it. We each asked a question about the other and had to answer honestly. Several drinks were consumed during the playing of this game, as it was actually quite hard to come up with twenty original things we wanted to know. Repetition between players was allowed, but the offside was rule was not (whatever that was . . .).

I went first.

'What are you like in bed?'

I didn't really. Though it was the one I wanted to ask, natch.

'So. Karen. The writer of the card. Your ex. What was she like?'

'A bitch. My go.'

'No. I'm not happy with that answer. Say more.'

Cue roll of eyebrows.

'Er, I dunno. She was all right. She was a laugh. When she wanted to be. Moody, most of the time. She had big tits, blonde hair, most of it not hers.' He didn't look that impressed by the large breastage or extensions. Promising. He continued, 'She's a care assistant in a nursing home. Fuck knows how, all she cares about is herself. Enough?'

I nodded. He was right, she sounded a total bitch. 'Your go.'

'Did you always know your husband was gay?'

Er, OK. Good question.

'No. No I didn't. If I had've done I would never have married him. I'm not stupid and he hid it really well. He says he's not gay. I don't know if I believe him. It's the thing that's caused me the biggest, weirdest pain in my life and I just wanna draw a line in the sand and pretend it never happened. You're not gay are you?'

'Is that question two?'

'Yes. Was that yours?'

'Go on then. And no, course not.'

Relief.

Though he could've been lying.

Though that cheeky wink told me otherwise.

I continued, 'Question three. Who's Ricky?'

'Well.'

He was struggling for the words. This was good. Some fellas would just clam up and say they didn't want to talk about it. He was trying to be open. Promising.

'Look, I ain't supposed to tell you this, but . . . it's Ricky Martin. The singer? She's run off with him and they're living *la vida loca, por favor.*'

Oh my God. GOSSIP!

'You're joking!?'

'I am. He's some knob from her work. All Brylcreem and nerdy glasses. I can't stand him, never could, but apparently he's a better listener than me.'

He could see my embarrassment that for one silly second I'd been taken in, so he said, ever so fondly, 'You muppet.'

'Your question three. Come on.'

'Right. Right. OK, d'you still see your brother?'

I shook my head vehemently. And, God this was embarrassing, from nowhere I started to cry. I tried to stop myself but I couldn't. A wave of despair had hit me; a sudden, sharp, breathtaking sadness. I felt I was plummeting down a big hole at breakneck speed and it was futile to try and claw my way out. Stuart reached across and took my hand.

'Fuck, Jodie, I'm sorry.'

'God, this is so embarrassing.'

His look told me otherwise. Blimey he must have thought

I was a freak. Last time he saw me I threw up over him, now I was sobbing my heart out in a pub in broad daylight, though I have to say I was doing my utmost to cry as quietly as possible, and not *too* many people were looking over.

'Change the subject,' I gasped. So, bless him, he did.

'Question four. Are we gonna go back to my place or yours?'

My answer was a bit too quick for anybody's liking.

'Yours. Moth's not speaking to me coz I never told her about being married.'

He nodded, drained the dregs of his pint, then slapped his knees.

'Are we right?'

Were we ever! We continued to play twenty questions in the cab home and even on the pavement outside his house. We played it on the steps up to the front door. Inside the hallway. On the stairs up to his flat. And we carried on playing it as we undressed each other and tumbled onto his futon. OK, so the questions got a bit fewer and further between as we actually got down to the business of 'the sex' – that was question eighteen.

Me: What are we doing now?

Him: The sex.

And we rounded off with question twenty after we'd both, miraculously, climaxed.

'Stuart? Question twenty: How was it for you?'

'Fucking amazing.'

I grinned like the cat who'd got the cream and waited for his question twenty. And waited. Er, OK, maybe he was trying to make it a good one. Final one and all that. Or maybe he hadn't heard me. Maybe he needed a prompt.

'Well go on then. Your last question.'

Silence.

'Question twenty?'

It was then that I discovered Stuart Moses was a snorer.

That night I dreamed of Our Joey. He was doing something he'd often do at Christmas to make the family laugh. He used to play a Liza Minnelli track called 'Ring Them Bells' and mime to it, dancing round the through lounge. It was about a girl who went all round the world, only to fall in love with the boy next door.

I looked around the through lounge and saw Mum chuckling and smoking, loving the campery of it all. Blimey, even Dad was tapping his foot and clicking his fingers. I turned my head round a bit more and saw Stuart sitting there, shimmying in his seat. Panic rose in my chest. Was he shimmying because the Liza Minnelli lip-syncing appealed to his inner gay?

'Are you gay?' I gasped.

He shook his head. But I couldn't tell if he meant 'no I'm not' or 'not now, Jodie, I'm really enjoying your brother's song and dance routine. It's blowing my gay mind!'

I looked to Mum, desperation exploding in me like an al-Qaeda bomb.

'Mum!'

She tutted.

'No, Mum!'

'Jodie! Your brother's performing!'

'I know, but I need to know something.'

Mum turned and looked at me. 'It's true. Liberace was your father.'

In my dream, I already knew that, but it still made Dad look over and scowl.

'What did you say, Sandra?'

'Nothing, Alan!'

'Mum, no, it's not that.'

Mum rolled her eyes and swivelled her head in a very drag queen way – God, there was a running theme – then looked at me and issued a very impatient, 'WHAT?'

'Mother. I need to know. Is he gay?'

Another roll of the eyes and another swivel towards Our Joey.

'Take a frigging wild guess, love!'

I knew I was dreaming. Mum would never say frigging.

'No, not Our Joey, Stuart!'

Mum let out a coruscating laugh, so loud that Our Joey stopped lip-syncing to Judy Garland's daughter and stomped his foot petulantly.

'Er, I'm performing?'

'Sorry, love.'

That was Mum. Then she did a kind of 'as you were' movement with her wrist and Our Joey carried on. Mum looked at me as she lit up another cigarette.

'Jodie, relax. Not every fella you meet's a big bender. Look at Barry Manilow.'

I now realized Our Joey was no longer lip-syncing to Liza, but to the big-nosed vamper. This wasn't looking good. Especially as Stuart was now juggling suggestively with two nectarines and a banana in the direction of my boogieing brother. I jumped up and pushed Our Joey back against the fireplace.

'Jodie!' cried Mum.

'Aw, I was enjoying that,' echoed Dad.

I cast Stuart a steely glare and warned, 'Don't. Even. Think about it.'

The nectarines and banana vanished. Replaced by a mango,

which he raised to his mouth and started devouring. I relaxed. And as I did, I found that I was waking up.

As I discovered myself lying there, tangled up in his bed sheets and him, his muscly legs gripping mine like a vice, I realized, yes, it had all been a bad dream. I drifted off again, and when I woke in the half light of morning I could see Stuart scrambling about in his wardrobe for clean clothes, and a cup of hot, steaming tea sitting on the beside cabinet for my delectation. As my fuzziness cleared and I saw him pull on some fresh boxer shorts I saw again that his thighs were so chunky as to be almost cubist. Picasso would have been proud to have sketched them.

I did a little 'look at me, I've woken up' cough and he immediately looked over.

'I was trying to be quiet,' he whispered.

'It's OK. What time is it?'

'Six forty-five. I've got to get to work.' And he leaned over and pecked me like a woodpecker on the forehead. I'd puckered up for a long languorous tongue-fest, but I guessed he was in a hurry.

'I know,' I said. 'You have to leave at six fifty to get to Abbey Wood for eight ten, where you are plastering the walls of a semi-detached house.' Adding with a smirk, 'Question seventeen.'

He smiled and pointed to my tea. 'Milky. No sugar. Question twelve.'

I smiled back and lifted the cup to my lips. 'Thank God for question twelve.'

'Right, I'm offski. Just pull the door behind you on your way out, yeah?'

I nodded from the other side of the mug as he shot me a wink, then went.

SEVENTEEN

I should have known something was wrong when I walked the twenty yards from Stuart's flat to mine. It can only have taken thirty seconds maximum, but two schoolgirls who were walking past nudged each other, pointed at me, then burst out laughing. I immediately wondered what was wrong with me as they giggled their way past. Did I have bird crap in my hair? Had Stuart lampooned me with the biggest love bite you ever did see? Were my clothes not streetwise-funksy-spunksy enough for them? But then they both called back to me, in broad, mock Liverpool accents, sounding like a cross between a constipated Beatle and Sonia, 'God, them fish fingers are *gorgeous!*'

The words sounded familiar. I'd heard them before for sure. Where on earth had I heard that phrase?

And then I realized. My breathing went shallow and I felt a nausea, not unlike the one I'd felt the day I got food poisoning after filming the advert.

How did those girls know I'd said that? They must have seen the advert. But they were fifteen years old, sixteen tops. How would two schoolgirls have access to an advert that wasn't being shown on the telly for another three months? Were they part of a focus group, called in to road-test ads to see if they were attractive and accessible for the teenage market? Were they relatives of the director? His daughters? His teenage sex slaves?

As I climbed the steps to the front door, it opened. Moth was standing there, bewildered, remote control in hand. She looked at me like she didn't recognize me.

'Who are you?'

Oh God, and to top it all, now my flatmate was going mad.

'Moth, it's me; it's Jodie.' Then I laughed to make light of it. 'Big night on the sauce last night, was it?'

When at last she spoke, her voice was hollow. The sort of voice you'd hear in movies when the main character's been wrongly locked away in a state penitentiary for murdering her own triplets and she hasn't seen daylight, human kindness, or *Desperate Housewives* for years.

'I . . . don't know a thing about you any more.'

I tried to push past her into the hallway, but she raised an arm to the door frame, blocking my way.

'Er, Moth, I need to . . .'

'I don't want you living here any more.'

'WHAT?'

'First I discover you're married.'

'Divorced,' I countered.

'And now. Now! I discover you've been off filming adverts for the television, and not a word of it to me!'

There was absolutely no need for her to say 'now' twice, though she did sound genuinely hurt.

'Has it been on the telly?'

Moth nodded.

'Bollocks. It wasn't meant to be on till August. Laveenia swore! When was it on?'

'It was on last night in the ad break for *Acacia Avenue*, and it's been on about a million times this morning.'

'Oh FUCK! D'you think Rupert watches telly?'

Moth still wasn't letting me past. 'No, he's too Bohemian. But someone at college is bound to tell him.' The light in her eyes started dancing. She was enjoying this, as if she was considering marching in and telling Rupert herself.

'Anyway, can you let me in? I need to get changed before I go to college and get lined up in front of a lynch mob to have my showbiz brains blown out.'

But Moth wasn't budging. 'I meant what I said, Jodie. I want you out. I don't like liars.'

'Moth!'

'I really thought you were my friend.'

'I am! Jesus, Moth, you've proved your point. I'm sorry, OK? I can explain everything. Now can we just move on?'

Moth's eyes narrowed. 'I'll have your things sent on to your next quarters.' With that she slammed the door in my face and I heard it being bolted from the inside.

I lifted up the letter-box lid and called through, 'Quarters? Quarters? What *century* d'you live in?' Then I slammed the letter-box lid shut. It gave a satisfying clunk.

From inside I heard a muffled, 'Oh piss off, Peasant!' and the inner door slam.

Anger coursed through my veins like neat vodka. I felt murderous. I looked at the flat windows, wanting to smash them all and break in, grab my measly possessions, stage a dirty protest, set fire to the flea-ridden mosh pit and then leg it. Only I knew that something disastrous would occur if I attempted even a vandalism-lite version of that. I'd probably dissect a vein on the broken glass and have to be air-ambulanced to a special hospital on a special island that specialized in MONUMENTAL FUCK-UPS. Because that's what I felt like right now. Oh yes, an M.F.U. That was me.

Far beneath me a tube rumbled by, causing the steps I was standing on to vibrate softly. In a way it felt like I was standing over an earthquake. The very earth itself was going to crack open. Lightning jags would split Clapham Road in two. Buses would fall in. I'd be crushed by an uprooted traffic light. Vultures would swoop and peck at me like relentless overeaters at a finger buffet.

In many ways that was preferable to what I knew the day had in store for me.

I trudged disconsolately down the street and headed off to college, even though it was far too early. How I wished I'd stayed longer at Stu's and used his shower. I had yesterday's clothes on, yesterday's knickers, yesterday's make-up. I was dressed for a date, not a morning pretending to be a tree in a movement class. Not only would I look like an M.F.U., I'd also scream S.W.N.W.H. (Slag Who Never Went Home.) I had no books, no ballet blacks, no money for lunch, nothing. Literally just the clothes I stood up in, including the patent red leather high heels I'd purloined from a charity shop which, as the assistant had said at the time, leant me an air of Hollywood glamour. When I caught sight of myself in a shop window, I looked more like Courtney Love after a weekend of dirty living than Courteney Cox after a weekend in a spa. The faux-fur wrap that, when I'd bought it, I was convinced made me look like Joan Crawford in her Coca-Cola boardroom days, actually made me look like a mentally deranged bag lady.

I comforted myself. Maybe no one had seen it. Maybe no one else apart from Moth was watching television this morning. Or last night. Maybe they'd all nipped out to see something fantastic at the theatre. Maybe Rupert's house was ransacked and burglars took not only his umpteen bunny rabbits, but also the telly in his lounge. Oh, and the portable in the kitchen. Oh, and the huge one in his bedroom, which Mum had described as obscene in a disapproving way that suggested she assumed that anyone who had a TV in their bedroom used it as some sort of sexual aid (I knew not how!). Maybe there had been a power cut in his street and he'd been forced to read up on some classics, have friends round or trim his armpit hair. Then I reasoned that even if he *had* been watching the box, there's no *way* he'd be watching *Acacia Avenue*. Intellectuals and free-thinkers like him weren't glued to soap operas. The more I thought of it, the more I realized I was probably worrying over nothing. People liked me in my year, no one was going to grass me up. Everyone knew I struggled for money; they weren't going to be hacked off that I'd earned myself a couple of thousand pounds by eating a few fish fingers. And if I told them I'd got food poisoning during filming, they might even pity me. As long as Rupert didn't tune into ITV, everything would be OK and no one would know, nothing would be said. My place at L.A.D.S. was safe.

'Jodie!' I heard someone screech behind me. I turned to see Amanda bounding along the street, looking like she was about to go and spend the day on a yacht: white culottes, stripy blue top, naval blazer, espadrilles and shades perched in her hair like an Alice band. I stopped myself from saying, 'Oi, Oi, me hearties!' as she got nearer, but as I went to greet her she butted in.

'You never told me you knew Charlie Walsh, you dark horse!' And she linked arms with me as if we were best mates and walked along at my side. That was weird. Amanda has rarely touched me before. She was the sort that, if she did, she'd be reaching for some Wet Wipes afterwards.

'What's he like? Is he gorgeous? I have to say I *love* his shows. God I can't believe one of my best friends has actually worked with, shot an ad with, hung out with, my, like, number one total crush?'

'Right.'

She'd seen the ad. Amanda, who claimed to only watch 'really serious drama on Channel 4 about twice a year? Stuff about wars? And mother on daughter child abuse?' had clearly been watching *Acacia Avenue* the night before. I couldn't imagine her having time to watch breakfast telly in the mornings. She'd once confessed that it took her two hours to do her hair, never mind her make-up, in a rare moment of intimacy down the pub one night when she'd cried on my shoulder, fearing she had OCD about her appearance.

'Do you . . . still see him?'

'No, I just met him that day.'

'Oh, right. I thought you must have known him from Liverpool.'

'No, I just had to pretend to be his mate. It's called acting.'

She looked surprised. Big time. 'What? All the people in that advert, they're not his real friends?'

I shook my head.

'They're actors?'

I nodded my head.

'Shit. I just assumed it was, like . . . a documentary-style advert. It's really misleading.'

'It's just really good acting, Amanda, that's what it is.'

'I just assumed you were buddies and you hung out and a camera crew popped in one day and shot you having a party and stuff?'

'Well, that's what they want the audience to believe.'

'Was he nice?' she asked, like she wasn't sure she was interested now her bubble had been burst.

I sighed. 'Well, he said I had nice tits.'

'Wow! He likes them small then.' She sounded frustrated that hers might be too big for him. Clearly her self-obsession was so all-encompassing that she hadn't stopped for a second to think how her words might impact on me. To be honest, I was so used to her inadvertent put-downs they no longer upset me. She continued, 'God, I can't believe that. I laid in bed last night thinking about it and thinking, well, about this exciting life you must lead. Hanging out with Charlie Walsh and partying in his back garden. I was a bit jealous actually. You're such a closed book, Jodie. No one knows anything about you. Ask you something personal and you just kind of . . . clam up. I wondered last night whether it was because you were hiding this secret celebrity lifestyle. Isn't that silly?'

'Very.'

'Oh shit!' She stopped dead in her tracks.

'What?'

'Rupert will go ballistic.'

'I'm rather hoping he won't have seen it.'

'Oh, he will.'

'Maybe his telly exploded.'

'No, he will have.'

'But it was on during *Acacia Avenue*.'

'He adores *Acacia Avenue*. Never misses an episode.'

This was as surprising as learning that Margaret Thatcher secretly took in homeless people off the streets and fed and watered them for the night because she had one hell of a social conscience.

'Really?'

'Yes.' She started walking again, brisker now. I tried to keep up with her as our arms were still linked. I felt like a slow fat kid teamed up with a fast sprinter in a three-legged race, so dazed was I by what I was hearing. 'He says there's a really good actress in it. He used to go out with her when they trained together with Stanislavksi. Or it might have been Alan Ayckbourn. Yvonne something.'

I gulped. 'Carsgrove?'

Amanda shrugged. 'Possibly. Is she any good?'

I nodded. 'She plays Nona Newman.'

Amanda could see the look of blind panic on my face.

'But you never know. He might have been out last night.'

Rupert hadn't been out the night before. He had seen the advert. And his distaste for my betrayal shone out like a light-house, illuminating the rehearsal room as I walked in. He didn't say anything, so I just sat in a circle with the rest of the class, ignoring the odd cod Scouse whisper about the qualities of fish fingers, and waited for the lesson to start. I'd found a pen and pad in my locker and managed to have a wash in the girls' toilets, so I looked semi-decent, even if I was dressed like I was about to hit the casinos. As a hooker. Rupert looked at the floor and waited for us to settle down. We did. Still staring at the parquet, he said, 'Miss McGee. Stand up.'

All eyes were on me as I rose.

Rupert broke into a smile. 'Firstly, what have you come as today?'

'A street walker,' I said a bit quickly. 'It's a project I'm doing about how different costumes elicit different reactions from the general public.'

I saw Moth roll her eyes.

'And how have they responded to this one?'

'They've found me quite slutty on the whole,' I lied, glad to be communicating in a positive way with He Who Must Be Obeyed.

'Aha. And secondly, congratulations! You got your first job!'

He started clapping his hands. He beckoned the rest of the group to join in and soon I had my first standing ovation. I blushed and smiled; this wasn't the reception I'd been expecting and, I have to say, it felt really pleasant. I could have done without Moth scowling and giving a slow hand clap, the only one in the group to remain seated. Rupert flapped his hands, indicating that the group should sit, and they did so like obedient dogs at Crufts.

'Jodie, I am very happy for you. Very happy that you have entered the big bad world of television and secured your first professional job. It is commendable and shows great industry.'

Well, this was a surprisingly nice turn up for the books.

'Thanks. Thank you,' I blustered in a 'gee shucks it was nothing' kind of way.

'And with it you have shown you no longer need us.'

Gulp. What? Oh dear.

'That your time at L.A.D.S. is done. You clearly have what it takes to be a professional actress, so why on earth would you need to be trained? You, after all, have been in an advert for a top supermarket chain. You see, I was under the misapprehension that you weren't quite ready yet. Clearly, I was wrong.'

'No, I still need training, Rupert,' I gasped, unable to hide the panic in my voice. If he booted me out, where would I go? I couldn't go back to Liverpool a failure. I couldn't go back to Liverpool full stop. I'd never know who I was going to bump into round my mum's kitchen table. Probably my ex-husband seeking a mother replacement who could understand his fluctuating sexuality.

Rupert raised a hand to silence me. I wasn't aware I was still talking.

'Do you know why I didn't think you were quite ready?'

'Coz the course doesn't finish for another few months.'

'No. Because you never really shared with us your pain.'

'Right.'

'Which I think is a shame. We only ever truly progress as actors once we have stripped ourselves bare, revisited past traumas, explored them, understood our emotional reactions to them. This, I don't think you have done.'

I shot a cursory look around the group. Everyone, bar Moth, was looking uncomfortable. There was a lot of shifting in seats, staring at the floor and watch-checking. Moth, meanwhile, sat with her arms crossed and head to one side, nodding.

'When your drama teacher contacted me she told me you had been depressed. Laid low. She told me the reason for this. Yet you never shared it with the group.'

'I was upset.'

'The group you have been part of for three years. I feel you have held back. Yes, you can act. Yes, you can make people laugh. Yes, you can make people cry. You are good. Very good. But you could be brilliant.'

I really didn't know what to say to that.

'But you never will be. Because you've never owned your pain. Would you like to tell the group what the cause of your pain was?'

My mouth was dry. I could feel my cheeks burning. I looked around the group and saw it: pity. I cleared my throat to speak, but the words literally ran dry. How could I say it? It sounded so stupid. Rupert had built it up so much that anything I said would sound like an anticlimax now. Everyone would be expecting me to say that I'd been involved in a massive paedophile ring or had been raised by wolves.

'Jodie?'

'Well, it was nothing really.'

I felt so stupid. Why had I hidden it from everyone all these years? Everyone carried some pain around with them, no matter what shape it took. It still left an ache in the heart, no matter what had caused it. Why did I think I was different from anyone else? What made me so special, so superior? Everyone else had loved unburdening themselves to the group each week during our course. Why had I held back and felt I didn't need to? It was time to bite the bullet and show everyone else I didn't think I was superior, possibly just more scared of being ridiculed than most.

'I got married. Only the day I did, I discovered my husband was having an affair.'

People were nodding sympathetically. Some looked disappointed. Not very salacious.

'With my brother.'

A few eyes widened at that.

'I think about it every day.'

Rupert nodded sagely, a parent whose child has finally owned up to stealing from the cookie jar and is apologizing for it. Maybe I was in for a reprieve.

'Finally,' he said. 'Now, you know the drill. You have broken the terms of your contract. Please collect your stuff from your locker and vacate the premises. You are no longer a student at L.A.D.S.'

'But . . .'

'I wish you all the best in the future, both personally and professionally. I am sure you will do some wonderful work on this journey you have already embarked on.'

'I'm really sorry, Rupert.'

'As I am, too. I liked you, Jodie. I gave you a chance. And you betrayed my trust.'

I wasn't going to win. I was in the same room where, a few years earlier, I had stood, overdressed, as my mum came in to berate Rupert for keeping me so late when we had a train to catch. Then I had been hopeful about my glittering career in showbiz. Now I had blown it.

'I'm so sorry.'

'Yes, you said.'

I couldn't look at the group. It was too embarrassing. I headed for the door. As I did I heard Rupert brightening and clapping his hands to energize everyone.

'Right! Come on! Let's do some great work.'

At the door I hesitated. Possibly because this was so scary. I was stepping into a whole new world. The last time I had done this was when I'd stepped out of Sandalan to head to the wedding. Then I was full of excitement, the air heavy with promise. This time there was no positivity, only the knowledge that I had messed up. Big time. Now I had no flat, no college course, no future basically.

M.F.U.

I stood on the street outside L.A.D.S. weighing up my options. I had very few. I walked slowly up and down, unsure where I should go. I checked in my purse. I had the grand total of three pounds and eighty-two pence. That wouldn't get me to Liverpool, so I had to rule that out. It might get me a Big Mac happy meal, so I wouldn't go hungry and have to sell a kidney just yet, but it wouldn't see me through the day. Now, I was by no means a spiritual person. I didn't sit cross-legged on a floor each morning chanting for world peace and a house in the Cotswolds. Nor did I genuflect at the drop of a hat or mistake shooting stars for UFOs. In fact, I'd never even seen a shooting star and doubted their existence, never mind God's. But in that moment, I'm not afraid to admit it, I said a little prayer. I looked to the skies and said, 'Dear God. Please help me see what I am meant to do right now. I have no bloody idea. Sorry for swearing. Is bloody still seen as swearing these days? Well, anyways, you were around yonks ago so it probably is – sorry about that. I just need some guidance. A sign. Your loving daughter, Jodie.'

That made me feel a bit icky.

'OK, so I'm not really your loving daughter coz I hardly ever believe in you. But any guidance gratefully received. Thanks. And I mean that. Amen. Over and out.'

Just as I finished saying my prayer, a sky-blue Volkswagen Beetle slowed down and pulled up. The passenger window slipped down and I stepped forward. Who was in the car? Surely this was a sign from God! Blimey, he did exist. Inside the car, in the driver's seat, sat a balding man in his fifties with – bizarrely – dandruff on the collar of his jacket.

'Yes?' I bleated, eager for words of wisdom. This would be . . . the sign!

He looked at me, squinting through varifocals. Gosh the Lord's messengers were a funny-looking lot.

He opened his mouth and I waited.

He said, 'How much, love?'

'Sorry?'

'How much?'

I screwed my eyes up. Then realization hit me like a slap round the chops.

'Sorry, do you think I'm a prostitute?'

He nodded.

'Well, I'm not.'

'Oh. Sorry.'

'It's OK.' I smiled, backing away.

As he pulled off I heard him call, 'It's just you really look like one!'

I pulled my faux-fur coat around me and tottered off up the street. Surely God was going to send me a sign? And then I saw one. Straight ahead of me. Almost glowing in the sunlight.

A phone box.

It reminded me of something.

I dug in my pocket and pulled out a scrap of paper, ripped from the back page of a Thompson's Local Directory. It had a number scrawled on it. I went into the box, ignoring the faint whiff of urine, took a fifty pence piece from my purse and put it in the slot. I dialled the number, heard it ring, then . . .

'Hello?'

'Stuart, it's Jodie.'

'All right darlin'. How's it going, babe? I was just thinking about you.'

He sounded genuinely thrilled to hear from me. Not, as I had feared, pissed off that I'd rung him on his mobile while he was at work.

'Er, not well.'

'Hang on, I'll just get down me ladder.'

I heard the clanking of Puma on metal.

'What's up?'

'Oh it's just . . . I'm sorry to phone you on the mobile, but you said to call you any time and I just didn't know what to do.'

'Why? What's happened?'

'Well, I've been kicked off my course and, well, Moth's kicked me out of the flat.'

'Fuckin 'ell. With friends like her, who needs enemas?'

'I just don't know what to do.'

'Right,' he sounded decisive. It thrilled me. 'What you do is this. You go round my gaff and you ring flat three and ask Jennifer for the key. She's in the flat below me and she keeps a spare. I'll call her now and tell her you're on your way. Then you let yourself in to my place. You chill out there till I get back tonight and we'll have a talk and sort it all out. All right, Treacle?'

'Yes. Thank you.'

God I felt relieved.

'Now I've got to get back to work, but listen, Jodie, yeah? It's all gonna be OK.'

'OK.'

Was it? Was it really? There was something about his confidence that made me think he could be right.

'Have a nice bath. Watch some telly. Use my phone, do whatever. I'll be back about six and I'll bring a takeaway. D'you like Chinese?'

'Yes.'

'Cushty. And remember.'

'What?' I felt helpless and fragile in the glow of his no-nonsense go-getting dynamism.

'If this is sink or swim, I'm blowing up your armbands.'

I smiled.

'Easy,' he said, and hung up.

I hung up.

Easy.

EIGHTEEN

86C Clapham Road
London SW9
15 January 2010

Dear Joey,

God, you don't know how weird this feels after all these years!

And now I've started writing, I'm not sure what to say. So I'll start with the boring option and say how are you? Well, I hope.

I have been wanting to write for ages now, but I've been putting it off and putting it off. And then last week I broke my leg! So I'm laid up in bed with nothing to do but think and reflect and watch daytime telly, so there's no avoiding it. I'm confronting my fears, feeling the pain, or whatever it is they say. Here goes!

(Sorry. I seem to be using exclamation marks a lot. Will try not to! Sorry. I mean, will try not to.)

As you can see I'm still living in London. After I got kicked out of drama school (did Mum tell you? I was mortified when she phoned up the boss of the school and called him a 'silly Yorkshire pudding'), I got a little bit lucky coz I was in a run of adverts with Charlie Twatface, the chef off the telly. You probably already know this, but what you won't know is, I still have people screaming shite about fish fingers in my face whenever I leave the house. Imagine. Your sister. Famous. And for being in a fucking fish finger advert. Whatever happened to art, darling?!

(Sorry. Exclamations *again*. Grrrr!)

The other thing that happened when I left drama school was that I moved in with my new fella, Stu. And I've been with him ever since. He's gorgeous, Joey. I was going to say you'd fancy him, but I don't want to tempt fate! (Only messing.)

No, Stu's straight. I made him sign an affidavit when we got together saying that if I ever caught him indulging in anything from heavy petting to full-on dirties with a male member of a) my family or b) the species, I had every entitlement to chop his bollocks off and use them as earrings. So far, so good. (Touch wood – oh, that's Formica, hang on . . . Wood touched.)

OK, so I'm being slightly flippant, but I just wanted to show you I've moved on and hold less of a grudge now than I did five years ago. Call it the healing power of love. Or call it finally going out with someone who actually knows who they are and what they want. If only I'd found that in the first place!

I was completely gutted when I found you doing what you were doing, and I'd be lying if I said it didn't still hurt, but I appreciate your writing to me (ages ago, I know) and I understand that we were all that bit younger, and of course I also understand the beguiling, magical powers of Greg Valentine. Even if I do think he's a complete twat now. (Do you know Mum has him over for dinner? Feels sorry for him she says. *Bitch!*) And I suppose me having the current boyf puts everything in perspective a bit, if that makes sense.

Not sure what Mum's told you about Stu. I can never work out whether she likes him. She laughs at his jokes, but he's so blokey he like . . . fills the room when he's there, and I think she likes that and feels threatened by it all at the same time. Like, if he was to breathe out too quickly, all her knick-knacks would vanish in the slipstream. She sometimes looks at him like she's not sure whether to slap him or snog him. And I feel a bit the same. (Ha ha, don't tell him I said that if you ever meet him. Ah, I hope you do.)

What's your fella like? God, I feel so bad, I can't remember his name. I remember you saying he was dead nice, though, and I hope you're still together and all's going well. (I could ring Mum and ask, but I'd rather she didn't know I was writing to you – she'll only get excited and I'd rather play this by ear for now, just between you and me. Does that make sense? Hope so – God, the subterfuge I had to go through to get your current address! I had to get Hayls and Debs involved. Hilarious.)

Anyway, listen, I'm rambling now, so I'm gonna sign off and say ta-ra for now. I don't half miss you, Joey, and it'd be dead nice to see you soon.

Loads of love,

Jodie AKA Fish Finger Woman (easy on the breadcrumbs!)

P.S. You may be wondering how I broke my leg. Let me just say, I was dressed as a mermaid promoting frozen crab sticks in a shopping centre in Bethnal Green when I slipped my flippers on some spilt olive oil. Arse over tit. Thwack. Ouch.

P.P.S. Nightcap?

P.P.P.S. Daytime telly is shite. Just gonna lie here now and wait for Stu to get back from work and ask him to fly to the postbox. Laters!

Wow! Two years I'd been with Stuart now. How had that happened? It seemed to have whizzed by in the blink of an eye. Two years was twenty-four months. Twenty-four months was one hundred and four weeks. A hundred and four weeks was seven hundred and thirty days, which was a shitload of hours if you could be bothered to work it out. We'd rarely had so much as a night apart, and all in his tiny flat on the Clapham Road, which had gradually morphed into our tiny flat, my few possessions crammed up against his. The slim IKEA wardrobe, perfect for a single man, was now obese with a mixture of Fred Perry shirts and glittery disco tops. The sad shelf in the bathroom packed with so many Calvin Klein for Men products and girly Clarins tubes it reminded me of one of those boats you saw on the news, packed with people escaping a war-torn country. Our tastes were intermingled on the walls, Blues Brothers posters rubbing up against Audrey Hepburn looking elegant with a cigarette holder (and not a little disapproving of her wallmates).

The road outside remained the same, but Moth had long gone. I'd seen her moving her stuff out one day and she'd deigned to give me a teary hug as I ran out to say goodbye, her tweedy parents looking on disapprovingly as they'd parked their four by four on a red route. She'd wished me luck with my adverts, then hopped in the back of the car and disappeared without so much as a backwards glance. I knew from the college website that there were regular reunions of everyone in my year, but for some reason I was never invited. I knew full well the reason. I was persona non grata because I'd been kicked off the course with a month or so to go. It felt so unfair. I'd done the majority of the work. OK, so I'd fucked up and broken the rules, but I hadn't exactly broken the law or anything. I hadn't broken any hearts either, I'd been that wrapped up in my steely determination to succeed. Or in my steely determination not to disclose the dreadful secret of my doomed marriage. In the clearer light of hindsight I saw that Rupert had had a point. Not regarding booting me off the course, but in terms of my reluctance to open up. I'd been so scared of appearing a fool. I'd had too much experience of that particular sensation to want to go there again. Some days I wished I had. Some days I wished I'd blurted it all out in one of our group bonding exercises. Other days I was glad I hadn't. Other days I understood why I'd chosen that path. But the pitying looks the rest of the class had given me that last day could make my cheeks redden, even now. I'd become a self-fulfilling prophecy. One of my biggest fears at drama school was that everyone would find me out for who I really was: a fraud. Someone who didn't deserve to be there. A supermarket shelf-stacker who'd been a minor success in a theatre club equivalent of a school play, but little more. Certainly not sophisticated or articulate or worldly wise in the ways of the theatre world. Certainly not someone who deserved a place amongst them. I had been so determined to fit in, to excel, but I hadn't. I'd hidden my bad times, my messy times, my emotional bad hair days, and they'd found me out. I just thought they'd find me out for not being a very good actress, not for attempting to cover up my pain.

On other days, though, I didn't give a damn. I'd film another advert with the cheeky chappy chef, two grand would drop into my bank account and I'd think, Screw the lot of them. Who needs to treat drama school as some sort of unqualified psychotherapy course when there was money to be made?

But the two grands wouldn't last very long – not with London prices – and as I got overdrawn again, and relied on Stuart to bail me out and pay for . . . well, everything really, then the worries about my behaviour would resurface.

Stuart was unsentimental about the whole thing.

'Listen, Princess,' he'd say. 'How many ads have you done since leaving college?'

'Ten.'

'Ten, babe. At two grand a pop. You've earned more in your first two years of acting than most of those muppets'll earn in a lifetime. And you earned it *acting*. Not temping, or being a traffic warden, or robbing a bank, or on your back with your legs splayed, but doing what you love doing. What you were trained to do.'

That always perked me up. Though I could have done without the prostitute analogy, truth be told.

I kept an eye out for what my fellow ex-students were up to. Amanda appeared to be doing, bizarrely, quite a bit of musical theatre. I'd seen her name – in tiny writing – on a board out-side a theatre on Shaftesbury Avenue in a new musical based on the back catalogue of some obscure Britpop band. It ran for all of four weeks, but by the time I bit the bullet and decided to go and see it, and maybe pop backstage afterwards to congratulate her, I found the show had been pulled and a stand-up comedian was playing there instead. I saw Moth in a *Crimewatch* reconstruction about a somewhat overweight estate agent who'd been brutally maimed. I sent a card to her parents' address telling her how good she'd been, but never heard back. Oliver had set up his own website to promote himself, which I sometimes looked at, but it mainly consisted of moody black and white snaps of himself, and his 'latest news' section boasted little more than a play called *Foosteps on my Heart* at a pub theatre in Highbury ('pics to follow!' – they never did). Everyone else seemed to have disappeared into oblivion.

Two years of being with Stuart meant we were well and truly

past the lovey-dovey stage. Or, as I called it, the 'cute sandwich' stage. Let me explain:

The Cute Sandwich Stage (definition):

A phrase I invented to describe the opening months of a relationship, where you think everything your partner does is undeniably gorgeous, adorable and cute. For instance, on our first trip to Liverpool for Stuart to meet Mum and Dad, we bought a load of sandwiches from W.H. Smith at Euston Station. When Stuart nipped to the loo on the train I gazed lovingly at the empty sandwich wrappers that littered our table. I sighed warmly at his discarded, half-eaten tuna and sweetcorn on brown and thought, Ah. That's his sandwich. It's so . . . cute. Coz it's his – Aw – and caressed it lovingly.

Yes, I caressed a sandwich.

Because that sandwich told a story. OK, so it wasn't the greatest story ever told, as it was a story about him popping to the loo while I gazed at our snacks, but it spoke of us working as a team; it spoke of mystery. And even if that story was about us doing something mundane, it was still unbearably romantic, because everything about him then was cute, as everything about him was still new.

N.B. Now if I saw a half-eaten sandwich of his I'd be more likely to roll my eyes and moan about starving black babies in Africa before eating it myself. Which is exactly what I did on this particular morning as I lazily tidied up the flat.

My broken leg had healed, and the promotions company who'd employed me were elated that I didn't want to sue them for exposing me to dangerous puddles of olive oil.

I plumped the cushions on the couch. Our special couch. *The* couch. It had been the one concession to this now being a love palace for two rather than a bachelor pad for one. It soon became obvious after I moved in that the couch was the centre of our universe. Nothing could beat snuggling up together after a long day, drinking wine and watching crap TV. Stuart's original two-seater had been more practical than comfy and it had always been a tight squeeze for both of us. Our legs dangled off the side and once we'd found a position we were comfortable with we'd have to stick with it for the duration of the evening. One Saturday we went to Tottenham Court Road and spotted a huge big, lumpy, bumpy three-seater in Designer's Guild fabric – turquoise and bright yellow check – which was reduced in the sale. Once we'd established it would fit into the flat through the various doorways from the street we stuck it on the joint – get us – credit card. It was huge. It looked more like a double bed than a sofa and, of course, it dwarfed the tiny living room. But we didn't care. It was *our* couch. Now we could spend all the time in the world on it each evening, and daytimes at the weekend, and not only could we both fit on it side by side, there was plenty of spare room to fit plates of Hobnobs and other TV-centred snacks on it, too.

As I straightened out the turquoise and yellow beauty that was the centre of our universe, I found some stray biscuit crumbs mushed between the cushions. Oh, this wouldn't do. I would have to get the handheld Dustbuster and get to work.

You see, Stuart isn't like many other men. Stuart has a thing for cleanliness and hygiene. He doesn't mind mess, as long as it's clean mess, and he likes the cleaning done a certain way. I know this makes him sound a bit prissy and house-proud, but it's not a girly, camp, gay thing, he's more OCD about it than that, which I put down to his childhood. Stuart had spent a few years of his childhood in a local authority children's home, which had been run like a boot camp. I always assumed children's homes were like the ones I'd seen on the telly in dramas aimed at children, where everyone has a bit of a laugh, midnight feasts and treats their care workers like avuncular uncles or best mates. Not Stuart's. His care worker ran the joint like an army barracks, forever doing spot checks and making the kids stand by their precision-made beds, practically saluting him as he ran a finger along the bedstead, checking for dust and measuring the angles of their eiderdowns with a protractor. The picture he painted of the place was one of isolation and loneliness. The few friendships he made never lasted long as new-found pals were often plucked to go and live with foster parents at the drop of a hat, so Stuart became wary of making friends.

The reasons for him ending up in the care of the local authority were as Dickensian as they were complex. The shorthand version was that his mother walked out on his dad when Stuart was a toddler, then his dad hit the bottle, so Stuart went to live with an aunt who heard voices in her head. One day he walked in and found that she'd hung herself, possibly because the voices were telling to, so in the absence of a grown-up who could get their shit together enough to look after Stuart it was decided he'd be better off in a home. He didn't open up much about this period of his life, understandably, but the memory was ever present, especially if I, or anyone in our company, told a funny story about growing up, or their family. Stuart's inability to match like for like floated in the air like a Zeppelin, blocking out the light and thinning the atmosphere.

When Stuart first told me about this I was going through the 'cute sandwich' stage, so I was more than a little moved. It made me like him even more, as every time I looked at him I didn't see the macho man with the cropped hair in his plastering gear, I saw a lost little boy in a duffle coat and mismatching wellies with a label round his neck saying, 'Please help'; the last evacuee that no one wanted to take in (sometimes I pictured him with a gas mask and ration book for good measure). But on days like today, when I approached each room with Stuart's 'top down' approach to cleaning – you start dusting at the highest level, say, a picture rail, and work your way down, then hoover etc. – I resented his upbringing and the way it manifested itself in his current behaviour. Don't get me wrong, he didn't march home from work and make me stand by my bed as he peered suspiciously at the skirting boards, but it was very clear that if the flat was anything other than spotless, he found it very hard to settle. Sometimes, if I'd neglected a stray corner of a room, he had been known to get the Dyson out and go over it again. He wasn't always like this, some days he could be really relaxed and up for a laugh and not even notice the state the flat was in, but if he was feeling stressed, or things weren't going well at work, he'd retreat to the comfort of attempting to control his environment. I spent a lot of time second guessing which mood he'd be in, so always erred on the side of caution and cleaned the place anyway. It wasn't a sexist thing – if he'd been home more than me he'd willingly have tackled the dust on the ceiling fan himself – it was just the way he was. It had been conditioned into his DNA.

The nights I liked best where when it didn't seem to matter. He'd return, plastered in, well, plaster, drop his overalls on the bedroom floor, stick his jogging bottoms and a fresh T-shirt on and flop onto the sofa. I would then dive bomb on top of him, he'd zap the telly on and we'd cuddle up with a bottle of Pinot Grigio to watch the soaps, and then possibly a documentary on a cable channel about a fat person with a sibling or two growing inside them.

But on the nights when it did matter, he'd tidy his overalls away and spend ten minutes in the shower. He'd then sit rather formally on the couch, like he was waiting for a job interview, and I'd see his eyes flitting round the room, anxiously looking for mucky spots or neglected cobwebs. Eventually his anxiety would shift onto me, as if by osmosis, and I'd join him in the eternal search for dirt.

His hygiene obsession extended to the bedroom and 'physical intimacy'. It was one thing cuddling on the couch after a long day and me inhaling his none-too-unpleasant man-musk, but we never went to bed without showering first, no matter how late it was. We might have been drinking till 5a.m., but if sex was on the cards, he'd say something like, 'Bedtime, babes. I'm just gonna jump in the shower. Or d'you wanna go first?'

I didn't mind at all – it felt like old-fashioned courtesy and it touched me. A bit like he'd then touch me as soon as the lights were out and the duvet was over us. But if one of us wasn't in the mood, the shower would be our way of communicating this.

'Actually, I'll just get into bed. I'm knackered . . .' and so on.

I sat on the couch and rested the Dustbuster in my lap. We'd not had bedtime showers for over two weeks now, even though my leg was better. Oh God, had it happened? Had the sexual magic gone out of our relationship? Surely this was normal after two years of living together. But then I remembered the last time we'd showered and then started fumbling about in bed. And for the first time in all the months (and years, and days) I'd known him, he'd not got an erection.

I hate the word erection. It sounds so . . . industrial. And it's not exactly a word you'd use every day.

'Oh, you have an erection. How nice.' Or, 'Get me with my massive erection. Sort it out, babes.'

When he'd not managed to get one, he didn't exactly say, 'Sorry I haven't got an erection, Jodie, this is mortifying.' Instead, we both ignored it for a while and just carried on kissing.

After a while I could tell he was tiring and he just said, 'Sorry, babes. Not really in the mood. Sorry, love.'

To which I'd said, 'Don't be daft, we'll just cuddle. I love cuddling you.'

And he'd said, 'Yeah, me too.'

And we'd spooned till we'd fallen asleep.

Since then, though, spooning was all we'd done.

Now, in the clear light of day, and with two weeks having elapsed and the shower only being used each morning, I came to a pretty decisive conclusion: Stuart had gone off having sex with me. And, worst of all, I knew why. It was a fear I'd been fighting for a while now, but I had to face facts.

Stuart was having an affair.

I'd never voiced this suspicion before. Any time an insecurity had pinged its way into my head, I'd pinged it right back out again with a mighty thwack! But the pings and thwacks had worn me down and now I knew. I just *knew*. Before, the ping and thwack had been because I'd surmised, It's just you. You think everyone's having an affair because of what Our Joey and Greg did. You mustn't tar everyone with the same brush. Some men are nice. Stuart's nice. OK, so he is a bit weird with his cleaning thing, but at least he loves you.

He did love me. He'd told me after we'd been together about five months. We'd gone to Brighton for the weekend to celebrate the slightly ridiculous anniversary, and on a moonlit stroll along the pebbly beach we'd giggled at some skinny-dippers, then he'd wrapped his arms around me and told me.

OK, so I told him first and he said, 'Me an' all.' But he was a *bloke*. Blokes never make the first move, I thought. And at least he'd said it and not backed off roaring, 'Whoa, whoa, whoa, mad crazy lady alert!' before running into the sea and drowning himself.

To make sure he'd meant it and hadn't just been high on wine, an Italian meal and the sight of naked swimmers, I'd double-checked the next morning as we lay in the discomfort of a B & B bed together.

'Last night you said you loved me,' I said lightly, with a chuckle in my voice. My subtext was, God I bet you're mortified. How pissed were *you*?

But he just shrugged, like it was nothing, as if he said it all the time, and went, 'So? It's the truth.'

But now, sitting here on our couch, that felt like a very long time ago. I closed my eyes, wanting to block the whole thing out. But closing my eyes helped not one jot. With eyes shut I only had my imagination and my memories, lurid in the brightness of their detail.

The phone started to ring. I opened my eyes and looked at it, convinced it was Stuart. He'd read my mind and was ringing to tell me it wasn't true. I wholly believed this as I got up and walked towards it. I waivered. What if he was ringing to tell me the opposite? Sod it. I'd been here before. I could handle anything. I picked it up.

'Hello?'

There was a familiar but strange female voice on the other end.

'Jodie?'

'Yes?'

'It's me. Amanda.'

Amanda? How did she . . .

'How d'you fancy doing a little play with me?'

What?!

NINETEEN

'Jodie, you're going mad. I am *not* having an affair,' Stuart whispered urgently.

'Whatever, Stu,' I whispered back, not so urgently.

'I am *not* your prick of an ex-husband.' He was getting louder.

'Well something's going on and you're not telling me.' So was I.

'Don't be ridiculous. You are, you're being ridiculous.' Back to the whispering.

'So what's with the no sex thing?' Me too.

'I've told you. I'm just not feeling very sexual at the moment.'

'Bollocks, that's the sort of thing women say. Blokes don't say it. Blokes have one-track minds, and if it's there on a plate they jump on it.'

'Oh shut up, Jodie, you don't half talk shit sometimes.'

'Ah, so *that*'s why you're having an affair. Because I talk shit? Well now we're getting to the bottom of it.'

'Jodie, do you really think this is the sort of discussion we should be having in a lift full of strangers?'

I looked around the tiny lift. Four pairs of eyes darted away rapidly, not wanting to be seen to be eavesdropping.

'You're drunk.'

I gasped. 'It's my opening night! I can be drunk if I want to!'

When we arrived at our floor I stomped out and tried to lose him, attempting to make as grand an entrance as possible at our first night party.

It was the opening night of my new play, *Things My Mother Told Me*, in which I was playing Claudie, a wise-cracking broad from the Bronx, while Amanda was playing her virginal sister Cissie. I got all the best lines, but Amanda got to have special needs: something that, she claimed, would get her noticed. Cissie's back story was that she'd been raped by her uncle on a fishing trip in Utah, and had retreated into a childlike world where she felt no one or nothing could hurt her. Claudie, meanwhile, spent her life drinking whiskey and going to all-night parties, sleeping with men in cornfields and coming home with a bra full of corn on the cob. Truth be told, much as I had a laugh playing Claudie, I hated the play. It was very long at three hours ten minutes (including an interval), but the upside was I was only in three scenes which, fortunately, if the opening night audience was anything to go by, I stole.

Amanda was onstage the whole time, crying for a lot of it, and she relished each second of her – as she see saw it – tour de force performance. She actually asked me in the interval, 'D'you think any of the critics'll say, "She puts the tour de force into performance"?' I looked at her blankly, so she tried to explain. 'Tour de performance?'

I'd shaken my head and she'd looked hurt. 'But only coz it sounds a bit shit,' I'd reassured her. She'd looked appeased.

The play was being performed in a tiny pub theatre in Camden. It had been funded by Amanda, cast by Amanda and the director was Amanda's current boyfriend, Joshua Hammerstein, who I guessed might have been Jewish. Amanda had designed the set, the costumes and the poster, so tonight was Amanda's night, and she wasn't going to let us forget it. Following drinks in the pub after the show Amanda, in an attempt to bring a bit of glamour to the proceedings, had organized for us to have drinks in the fifth floor bar at Harvey Nichols.

I saw her by the bar, throwing her head back and laughing in a manner that told me whoever she was talking to was someone important. A casting director, or an agent, or a producer. I wasn't interested. All I wanted was a drink. I wanted to obliterate my row with Stuart in the lift and I didn't care what I had as long as it hit the spot.

A tiny Asian waiter was passing with a tray of champagne flutes, all tantalizingly full, so I swiped one from him with a wink that said, 'Don't mind me, dear, I was in the show,' and took a big swig. Mmm, the bubbles tickled the back of my throat. God it was gorgeous. Good stuff, too. But when I looked back, the diminutive tray carrier was looking alarmed.

'Sorry, Madame, that's for table fourteen.' And he indicated a table of very pissed-off-looking women in business suits in the corner.

'Sorry?' I gasped. What did he mean? This was the after-show party, wasn't it?

'Oh, Jodie, you absolute CARD!' bellowed Amanda from the bar. 'It's not free drinks, darling. Come on, I'll get you one if you're brassic. Where's that hunk of a spunk boyfriend of yours?'

Oh bollocks. I looked around and realized that, despite the place being nose to nipple full, hardly any of these people had been in the pub beforehand.

'Oh. Sorry.' I smiled at the waiter and put the half drunk glass back on his tray.

'Sorry, Madame, erm . . .'

'Get your own fucking drink!' shouted one of the women in business suits. I turned to her.

'Sorry,' Stuart intervened, putting his hand in the small of my back and grinning pathetically at the women on table fourteen. 'I'll pay for that, don't you worry.' And his macho-man cheeky-chappy grin won them over. 'I'll take this and get you ladies another one. Sorry about that.'

Stuart handed my guilty glass back to me, then dragged me to the bar.

'You wanna slow down, Jodie,' he whispered in my ear. 'You're making a show of yourself.'

'Don't say Liverpool things in a cockney accent, it's really unbecoming.'

'And don't channel your mother, it's not a good look,' he spat as he tried to get the barmaid's attention. I pulled a face at him as he turned his back on me and saw Amanda leaning over.

'That's what we all need, darling. A knight in shining armour.' She rubbed Stuart's back lasciviously, adding, 'Darling, there's someone you simply *have* to meet.'

She pushed Stuart out of the way so she could drag me to meet her barside pal. I recognized her immediately. There are only so many fierce black women who could wear a morello cherry poncho with leggings and lipstick to match, and get away with it.

'Laveenia!' I gasped.

'Jodie, Jodie, Jodie!' she said, shaking her be-bangled wrists at me, then dragging me in for a momma-bear hug.

'You played a blinder there tonight, kid.'

It was nice, resting my head in her bosoms. She felt maternal. And possibly because of that, my barriers went down. I relaxed. And as I did, I burst out crying.

'Bottom line is, mate,' said Laveenia, twirling her cigarette between her fingers like a mini baton. 'If he's dicking you around, you need evidence. No point shouting the odds unless you've got cold hard proof.'

We'd come outside for a ciggie and were standing on the pavement, beside a window display showing a pyramid made out of gold lamé hotpants with a burning torch of artificial flames at the top. Quite what this represented, I had no idea, but that may have been because I was drunk. I must have been if I was smoking.

'How do I do that?' I asked lamely.

'Behave yourself, keep your composure and watch the fucker like a hawk.'

I nodded. Laveenia had a way about her that made me conform. She could have told me to stick my hand in the artificial flame on top of the pyramid and I would have smashed through the glass and done so.

'Follow him. Read his texts. Hack into his emails. Be suspicious when he works late, goes for boys' weekends, or has a few too many trips to the gym. Blokes are shit at covering their tracks. Us girls are way better. Believe me, I know.'

She flicked her ciggie onto the concrete and ground it with her morello cherry moon boot, which, amazingly, didn't catch fire. I realized that part of me had a bit of a crush on the fabulous Laveenia.

'Now. We'd better get back in. And when we do? Smile. Apologize. You were drunk. You're sorry. First-night nerves. And then he'll think he's got a reprieve. And then?'

I nodded eagerly, wanting to learn from the oracle.

'Wait.'

In the express lift up to the fifth floor she added, cursorily, 'I'm working on *Acacia Avenue* now, you know.'

'Really?' I had no idea. Wow!

She nodded nonchalantly.

'We should get you in for a meeting.'

I must have looked shocked – in a bad way – because she frowned.

'It'll pay better than the shite you're in at the minute, kid.'

'No. No. No, it's just . . . I've always wanted to be in *Acacia Avenue*. I had an audition when I was younger to play Paige the paper girl. Only I blew it.'

Laveenia was smiling now.

'I've only ever had three ambitions in my life: to be in *Acacia Avenue*, to win an Oscar and to get married.'

As we arrived at the fifth floor and the doors whooshed open, she winked. 'Well, I'd put number three on hold.'

I pushed my way through the throng and found Stuart looking bored with a couple of people I didn't recognize. He caught my eye across the room and I stopped and shrugged and mouthed, 'Sorry.' He nodded, then jolted his head to tell me to come over. I did. And as I stood next to him he enveloped me with his right arm and kissed the top of my head tenderly.

'I ain't husband number one. All right?'

I nodded. All right. I looked up at him and pretended a smile.

All I had to do now, apparently, was wait.

I didn't have to wait long. The week after, Stuart announced that he was going to be late home from work that night because he was going to someone from work's birthday drinks. As the job they were doing at the moment was in Hendon – miles away – he didn't see the point in me joining them when I suggested it, so I just shut up and nodded compliantly. When I asked which pub they were going to, trying to look blasé as I flicked through *Bella*, he shrugged and said he had no idea, pecked me on the head and left. As soon as he'd gone I paced the flat angrily. Laveenia had said this would happen. Why? Why did this always happen to me? Was I too much of a doormat? Was it because I dutifully cleaned the flat to his exacting standards instead of flinging down my feather duster and screaming, 'It's only a bit of bloody DUST, Stuart!'? Was it because I was too, I don't know, nice?

'You're not that nice,' countered Mum on the phone a few days later. I'd phoned for my weekly catch-up and had done exactly what I'd promised myself I wouldn't do as I'd picked up the receiver – I'd told her what I was worried about.

'I'm quite nice.'

'OK, so maybe I'm choosing my words wrong.'

Oh, the insight.

'You're not a pushover. Look, for what it's worth I don't think he is having an affair.'

'And how would you know? You've only met him three times.'

'I think you could be going out with Mother Teresa right now and you'd think she was playing away.'

'If I was going out with Mother Teresa that would make me a lesbian. A lesbian who was into dead, old Asian nuns. And I'm so not.'

I heard her sigh.

'I just think your experiences with Greg will have made you extra . . .' she searched for the word.

'Paranoid?'

'Suspicious sounds nicer. OK, so have it your way. He's having an affair. Leave him.'

'What? No.'

'Why not?'

'Coz I love him. And I don't know for sure.'

'Why d'you love him if this is what you think of him?'

'Coz he's been good to me. He looked after me when I was down on my luck. We have a laugh together. I . . . I fancy him.'

'So who's he having an affair with?'

'This new girl from his work. Mandy.'

'What's she like?'

'I don't know. I've never met her.'

'Is she single?'

'No, she's got a girlfriend.'

'She's a lesbian?'

'It's a cover story.'

'He's having an affair with a pretend lesbian?'

'Yes.' I was sounding rather timid now.

I had done what Laveenia suggested and checked the text messages on his phone one night when he was in the shower. He had several from someone called Mandy. Mandy, I knew from what he'd told me, was a new painter and decorator who did the odd bit of work with his company. He claimed she had a shaved head and had a tattoo saying Julie on her left forearm. And yet the texts read:

STUART: Oi oi sexy wot time u in?
MANDY: Running late. M25 nightmare.
STUART: L8rs.

Then on another day:

STUART: Marry me?
MANDY: Grow a vag.

And another day:

STUART: Back killing. Need one of your messages.
MANDY: It's massage, you thick git.

STUART: Bloody predictive texting.
MANDY: I know. Fack off you old cult.

'I have it on very good authority, Mother, that he not only receives massages from her, but has also proposed to her.'

'And who told you this?'

'Someone who knows them.'

'So, he's proposed to a pseudo lesbian from work who looks like a bloke?'

'I imagine the bloke thing is also a cover. She probably has long brown hair and legs from heaven.'

'Mark my words, Jodie. You meet this Mandy? She'll have legs from Devon.'

'I don't know what Devonshire legs look like.'

'It's all in your head, Jodie.'

I sighed. 'Can we talk about something else?'

'Well, you brought it up.'

Like a fur ball, I wanted to say, but didn't, as I wasn't sure if cats bringing up fur balls was a good or bad thing. Whether it was something they enjoyed or not. And whether the fur ball itself was yucky. Though I kind of reckoned it was.

'How's the play going?'

'Yeah, all right.'

'We're really looking forward to seeing it.'

'Don't lie.'

'No, I am. I'm gonna bring some knitting.'

'Why?'

'Well, you said it went on for hours.'

'You can't knit through it, Mother.'

'Why not?'

'It's not becoming.'

'Oh. But I like to keep busy.'

'You can't knit in a play, Mum. It's not like watching telly.'

'You said the theatre was so small it was just like watching telly.'

'I know but . . . Just don't bring your knitting.'

'And when the play finishes, what then?'

'Nothing. I've got an audition for *Acacia Avenue*, but I doubt I'll get it.'

'*ACACIA AVENUE*?!' she practically screamed. I had to hold the receiver away from my ear.

'Don't get excited, Mother, I'm not going to get it.'

Truth be told I'd not given it much thought. I'd had more urgent things to attend to, like pacing the flat all day wondering what Stuart was getting up to with Lesbo Mandy, before heading off to a pub in Camden to pretend to be a New York slapper.

'What's the part?' Mum said, trying to conceal her delight as I heard the scratch of her cigarette lighter. She was clearly settling down for all the soap-based goss.

'Well, this is the thing. It's for the part of a nun.'

'Oh.' And there it was, the deflation of disappointment. Like a burst balloon. I thought I could hear her stubbing out her ciggie sadly, though I might have been wrong. But she and I both knew that if I was going to be good at something, if I was going to be convincing, it certainly wasn't going to be pretending to be a sweet and saccharine nun. Julie Andrews I was not.

'When's the audition?'

'Next Friday.'

'Oh. Well, good luck. Will you have to come to Liverpool?'

'No, they're doing it in London. They're putting me on tape and then sending it to the producers.'

'What you gonna wear?'

'I dunno.' What's more, I didn't care.

'Well, I suggest you go in something quite nunsy.'

'And what does "nunsy" mean exactly?'

'Well, you know. High collar.'

'Wimple?'

'Maybe a beret.'

'Nuns don't wear berets.'

'No, but a lot of Christians do. I've seen them, Jodie.'

'Where?'

'Going to church! I've seen at least two people in berets going to St Hilda's in the past month. I pass by it when I'm going for my *News of the World*.'

'OK, I'll wear a beret,' I lied. I just wanted to get her off the phone now.

'But nothing stripy. Otherwise you'll look like something out of *'Allo 'Allo*.'

'Yes, Mother. I'll avoid a string of onions as well. And not turn up on a bike.'

'Maybe have a bible poking out of your tote bag. Hmm?'

'Mother. Enough of the Americanisms. People over here don't have tote bags, we have massive handbags or holdalls.'

God I was being unnecessarily argumentative. I'd had a tote bag for years. And loved it.

'If I'm honest, Jodie, I don't even know what a tote bag is. I just saw it in a magazine article and liked the sound of it.'

I sighed impatiently. There was silence for a bit.

'Jodie?'

'What?'

'We're really looking forward to your last night. Will there be a party afterwards?'

'Probably.'

'And, Jodie?'

'What?'

'I really don't think he's having an affair.'

Bless her. She was trying to be nice. I just wasn't in the mood to hear it.

The coming weekend promised to be a big one. Not only was it the end of my play, but Stuart was going away for a boys' weekend to Brighton. Which meant only one thing: he and Mandy were shunting off down there to spend all day Saturday and Sunday massaging each other in some vile B & B.

Brighton, for God's sake! The place where Stuart first told me he loved me! Did he have no shame? It showed he had no imagination. He'd had lovely romantic times with me there, and now he was going to have lovely romantic times with *her* there, too. It was clearly where he went to fall in love.

And of course he'd organized it for a weekend when he knew I'd be busy. Well, busy till the Saturday night anyway. No doubt he assumed I'd have a hangover on the Sunday after my closing night party, but I had other plans. Because Sunday . . . well, I was going to get on a train to that there Brighton and catch them at it.

On the Saturday morning he packed a little overnight bag and gave me the biggest hug as he set off to Victoria for the train. I hated every second of that hug; the way he clung to me spoke of a very guilty conscience. I pulled away after a while, smiled – God, this was some of the best acting of my life – and said, 'Now you have a brilliant time with the lads. Misbehave. Have a wild time and remember . . .'

'What's that?'

'I love you.'

He nodded and almost welled up before hurrying out. Seconds later there was a bang on the door. I rushed to open it. Stuart was stood there looking anxious.

'Babes?'

'Mm?'

'You gonna be in Sunday night?'

I nodded.

'Only . . . I wanna have a chat with you.'

'What about?'

'Look it's nothing but . . . make sure you're in. We can have a nice dinner and . . . talk.'

I gulped and nodded. He pecked me on the forehead then ran down the stairs.

A chat. Sunday night. After his sordid little weekend away. One thing was clear. He was going to dump me. *He* was going to dump *me*. No. No I had to get to Brighton as soon as I could on Sunday, catch him at it and dump *him*.

I didn't sleep much that night. I'd chosen not to drink at the closing night party as I'd wanted to be alert and unemotionally unhungover on the Sunday morning. But as I'd stuck to Diet Cokes all night I then couldn't sleep. I wished I had a car so I could jump in it right then and drive the hour or so to Brighton and punch the pair of them in the face. Lesbian my arse! They were at it now, I just knew it, and I couldn't bear it. The last night of the show had whirled by in a breeze of disconnection, as if I wasn't in the play at all, but hovering in the wings, watching someone else act. Someone who wasn't very good or funny, come to think of it. As we'd headed to our dressing room after the final bow, Amanda had commented, 'You really found the sadness in the character tonight, Jodie. It was almost moving.'

I'd nodded. Whatever.

'Did you hear that clicking noise all through the second half?'

I'd nodded again.

'It was my mum,' I explained, 'knitting.'

Amanda looked suitably horrified.

I was so distant at the drinks do afterwards in the pub that I couldn't even be bothered to chastize my mum when she pulled out the jumper she'd finished off during the play. My face must have belied my disinterest because she whispered, 'I know you told me not to, love, but it was boring as hell.'

Mum and Dad had booked themselves into a B & B in Victoria as they'd got the coach down. Dad seemed disappointed when I told them I couldn't meet for breakfast the next day, but Mum smoothed things over. I think she could tell where my mind was.

The problem with not being able to sleep that night was that, despite my best intentions, the next day I had zero energy. I lay in our tiny bath for about an hour, letting the water grow cold around me, and by the time I stepped out to dry myself I looked like a huge wrinkly scrotum. I then spent another hour putting my make-up on and choosing an outfit. I wanted to look my best when I delivered my shot across the bows. I wanted him to be gutted and her to be jealous. I caked my poor face in half a ton of slap, backcombed my hair so it was bigger than a volcanic ash cloud, spritzed myself in Vivienne Westwood perfume, pulled on some skinny jeans, a glittery gold vest top and battered brown suede jacket, quietened down my cleavage with a clunky gold necklace, then headed for the door.

It was a lovely day and the world, his wife and their pretend lesbian mistresses seemed to have got on the train from Victoria to Brighton. I took out the pages of the *Acacia Avenue* script that Laveenia had sent for my audition and studied them.

INT. CHAPEL – DAY
SISTER AGNES SITS WITH JOAN, WHO IS CRYING.
SISTER A: Joan. I have to warn you. I'm not a priest.

JOAN: I know that. I know that, Sister.

SISTER A: But anything you tell me is, of course, in the strictest of confidences.

JOAN: Thank you. Thank you, Sister Agnes.

SISTER A: You might look at me and see just a woman in a wimple, but before I took my holy vows, you and I were not too dissimilar. I, too, knew the love of a bad man, the comfort of the whiskey bottle. I, too, knew loneliness and despair.

JOAN LOOKS SURPRISED.

SISTER A: What I'm trying to say is. I'm . . . not easily shocked, Joan.

JOAN NODS. AND WORKS UP THE COURAGE TO TELL HER THIS AWFUL, AWFUL THING.

JOAN: I did it.

SISTER A: Did what, Joan?

JOAN: I'm a bad person. Gary . . . Gary . . .

SISTER AGATHA LOOKS SHOCKED.

SISTER A: What are you trying to say, Joan?

JOAN: He didn't die of cancer. He asked to die. And one cold and lonely November night, just after the Neighbourhood Watch buffet and mingle that no one attended because they were trapped in the kerfuffle of the supermarket fire—

SISTER A: Fire? It was an inferno. The memories of that horrendous night will stay with me for the rest of my life.

JOAN: He begged me to finish him off. I took his pillow and I smothered him with it. I . . . I killed Gary.

AS JOAN BREAKS DOWN, WE STAY ON SISTER AGATHA, A KALEIDOSCOPE OF EMOTIONS CARTWHEELING ACROSS HER FACE.

CUT TO: END OF EPISODE 7564

Bloody hell it was shit.

I turned the pages over and, taking a biro from my bag, started to write a list. The list of what I would do with the rest of my life.

What I am going to do with the rest of my life:
1 Dump Stuart.
2 Punch Mandy.
3 Tell Mandy she looks like a lesbian even if she doesn't.
4 Punch Stuart twice – that's the feminist thing to do.
5 Track Our Joey down and punch him for never replying to my grovelling (I now realize far too grovelling) letter.
6 Move out of Stuart's flat.
7 Sleep rough or use last of savings on cheap B & B till decide what to do.
8 Audition for *Acacia Avenue* and try not to burst out laughing when reading the scene.
9 Not get the part.
10 Starve to death on the streets of London.
11
   Go back to Liverpool and move back in with Mum and Dad.
12 Eat.
13 Put on weight.
14 Become size of house.
15 Not care because I am a fabulous, strong, independent woman whose life will no longer be ruled by a man.
16 Never have another relationship with a man as long as I live.
17 This doesn't make me a lesbian.
18 Unless I meet a *really* hot woman (i.e., Cameron Diaz) who tries it on with me and think, What the heck.

19 Why did I write 'what the heck'?
20 Give up acting and find a real job.
21 Go back to the supermarket, I guess.
22 Move out of Mum and Dad's and into a spinster flat in a spinster part of Liverpool.
23 Kill myself.
24 But change my mind at the last minute because even being a spinster is better than being shat on by yet another bloke.
25 Learning to love yourself is the greatest love of all.
26 I hope to God that's not a song about self-love/flicking.

I knew which hotel to go to, as I had made the booking for Stuart. I had checked the route from the station and decided to walk, as it was such a lovely day. The salty sea air would invigorate me, I decided, as I plugged in my iPod and took courage from the thumping bass of Destiny's Child's 'Survivor'. I found myself doing what I often do when listening to music and started walking in time to the beat, but as it was quite slow I snapped the iPod off and quickened my pace. Why had he let me book it? The silly boy had obviously been calling my bluff.

The Palladino, which had described itself as a B & B with rock 'n' roll aspirations, was located in one of the cute little side streets of white stucco Regency houses that run up the hill from the seafront. I was there within fifteen minutes. I looked up at the building, which was trying its hardest to look like faded glamour with its cracked plaster work and leopard-skin drapes, walked up the steps and into the narrow hallway. In the absence of a reception I wandered into the first room I found, a bar. All the tables were empty, but there was a Gothy looking girl behind the bar painting her nails black.

'Yo,' she said, and blew on her nails as she waggled her hand in the air.

'Hi, is there a reception?' I ventured, all smiles.

'Like, this is the bar and the reception, but we're fully booked. Shit.'

She looked really disappointed that she couldn't offer me a room, so I quickly made her feel better about herself. I was good like that.

'Actually I'm here to surprise one of the guests? Stuart Moses? He's in the Blues Brothers room.'

When I'd booked it I'd felt it was apt.

'I'm his sister,' I added quickly, in case she realized I was in fact his lover come to catch him at it with his pretend lesbian lover. She looked even more disappointed.

'Shit, he's gone out. Shit.'

'Oh.' I tried my hardest to hide my disappointment.

'For, like, brunch.'

'Right. With his girlfriend?' I asked, just to make sure she got the message. I *was his sister*! I even started modulating my accent to vague Essex in an attempt to sound similar.

The receptionist/barmaid/gothic monstrosity shook her head.

'No, he's on his own.'

'Oh.'

'Shit.'

Odd. Very odd. Ah, now I got it. He'd gone to meet her for brunch. Maybe she was staying somewhere else. Some pretend lesbiany hotel.

'You don't know where he's gone, do you? Only I've come all the way from London.'

'Shit! That really sucks.'

I nodded. It did indeed suck. A bit like Lesbo Features would be sucking him post eggs benedict, no doubt. I saw that Gothy Golightly was smiling.

'I do know where he's gone, though, coz I made the booking

for him.'

'Oh brilliant.'

'I shouldn't really tell you coz it's, like, health and safety and stuff . . .'

'Client confidentiality?' I corrected her.

'But he's gone to Mollie Maguire's. It's really cool.'

Brilliant.

'Molly Maguire's?'

She nodded. 'On Church Street.'

Brillianter.

'Was the booking for one or . . .?'

She shook her head. 'Two. Definitely two. I guess he was meeting someone.'

I nodded. Bingo!

'Unless he was really hungry.'

'Can you tell me how I get to Church Street?'

She nodded. 'God this is so exciting. I love surprising people. Oh he's going to be over the moon.'

I nodded. 'I can't wait to see the look on his little face,' I beamed.

She took a Post-it note and drew me a pretty crap map.

Seven minutes later I was standing outside Molly Maguire's. It was a rather jolly, rough-and-ready bistro with a black canvas awning covering a few tables outside. I pretended to read the menu, which was framed outside the front door, before peering inside at the busy, bustling eaterie. The waiters and waitresses were wearing long, almost floor-length black aprons. The customers on the whole tended to be twenty- and thirty-somethings eating fry-ups and reading the Sunday papers.

And then a waiter moved off from a table and I saw him. He was sat right at the back, his hand stretched out across the table. He was talking to someone. Not animatedly, quite calmly.

What was he doing with his hand?

My heart was thumping in my chest. This was it. This was the moment of truth. My moment. Come on, Jodie! You can *do* this!

I joojed my hair up, smoothed down my top, rearranged my necklace, then headed inside. The air was rich with jovial conversations and I walked slowly through the restaurant as T'Pau's 'China In Your Hand' was playing. I didn't take my eyes off Stuart, but he didn't see me. The nearer I got, the more of his arm I could see. Then I saw that his hand was in someone else's. And as I arrived at the table I finally caught my first glimpse of her.

I got a shock. She was old. She wasn't decrepit, far from it. She was rather beautiful in a downmarket Catherine Deneuve kind of way, and she wasn't dressed too dissimilarly to me. She was looking at Stuart intently, hands clasped. I was behind him now, staring at her, amazed. She had to be fifty. She might have had work done on her eyes, but her neck was a giveaway. Suddenly she looked at me and I glared back.

'Can I help you? she asked. She was quite posh. This couldn't be Mandy, surely. This woman didn't look like a painter and decorator who texted things like 'grow a vag'. This had to be someone else.

Stuart looked round and saw me, and his eyes widened in shock.

'Do you love him?' I asked, looking back to her.

'Jodie!' There was no hiding the anger in Stuart's voice.

'Yes,' the woman said.

She was sitting on a bench that ran along the side of the wall, so I nestled in next to her, resting my bag in my lap. She reluctantly budged up to accommodate me. I clocked her handbag on the floor. Expensive.

'And do you love her?' I asked Stuart.

'This is not what you think,' he said, then looked at Granny Features. 'This is Jodie.'

The woman looked at me and smiled. I frowned back.

'Are you Mandy?'

Stuart looked confused. So did she. She shook her head.

'I'm Jan,' she said.

I looked back at Stuart.

'I didn't know you were into arl biddies.'

Stuart rolled his eyes.

'Jan's not my bit on the side, Jodie.'

Yeah, right!

'She's . . .' He struggled to find the words.

'An old slag?' I ventured, then looked at Jan, whose lip was curling in what I took to be fury. Ha! Good!

'Tell her,' said Jan, sounding pissed off. I felt like slapping her.

Stuart swallowed, took a sip of his orange juice, then said, 'She's my mum.'

I gulped.

TWENTY

I had screwed up. Much as I'd like to be able to say this was the first time I'd ever screwed up, that would, of course, be complete nonsense. I'd screwed up many times. My life appeared to be one long series of self-inflicted catastrophes. I may as well have walked round with a big sign around my neck saying, 'AVOID. I SCREW UP. I SCREW MYSELF UP AND I'LL PROBABLY SCREW YOU UP, TOO. BUT I WON'T SCREW YOUR SHELVES UP BECAUSE I AM CRAP AT DIY.' And yet again, post screw-up – a phase I was used to being in, though it brought me little comfort – I felt stupid. I must have been completely stupid if I felt stupid so often.

Many of the details of what had happened I could cope with. I could get my head round the fact that Stuart had gone behind my back and made contact with his mum. I wasn't particularly happy about it, but I got it. I could see that when his mum had got in touch, via letter, he'd been so startled and confused that he'd kept it secret, unsure how it would pan out. I felt he might have handled it better if he'd been honest and shared his anxieties – and this pretty major life event, let's be honest – with me, but I understood why he'd kept it quiet. I understood when he said that he'd never been so afraid in his life, afraid she was going to be a nightmare and that it would be as messy as the circumstances when she'd left him as a toddler. I understood when he explained that he had clammed up and had no idea why he'd chosen to hide it, apart from that he was afraid of the outcome. I could deal with all that. I could also deal with the relief that he wasn't in fact having an affair. This was good news.

I sat in the reception of Crystal TV's London offices, dressed in a dowdy cardy and lopsided beret, contemplating all of this. I contemplated the fact, too, that Stuart hadn't really spoken to me since the previous weekend in Brighton. He'd arrived back at the flat about four hours after me. I was sat waiting on the sofa, ready to talk and apologize, but he just ignored me and stomped round the flat doing mundane things like putting dirty clothes in the washing machine and returning his toiletry bag to the cupboard under the bathroom sink. But the seething silence that accompanied his actions made them full of foreboding. How long could he keep on ignoring me? Eventually I got up and went to find him in the bedroom, where he was, for reasons best known to himself, remaking the bed.

'Stu, I'm sorry,' I said, almost inaudibly. But he ignored me and carried on flattening sheets with the palms of his hands, plumping up scatter cushions. There was something oddly anachronistic about it. The huffy male in a foul mood doing something so stereotypically feminine as making a bed.

'Stu,' I repeated, but he wouldn't even acknowledge my presence. He picked up a silky throw from the floor and launched it into the air so it fell on the bed like a landing parachute. It fell diagonally and as I bent to straighten the corner nearest me, he . . . Well, it all happened so fast. But at the same time it felt like slow motion. I saw him lunging towards me. I stepped back. But not soon enough. He pushed me away from the bed so that I stumbled backwards and fell ungracefully to the floor.

I landed on a hummock of shoes. He jolted back, landing on the bed, stared at me and hissed. Yes hissed.

'I can make my own fucking bed.'

'Wanker,' I heard myself saying. Which was neither big, nor clever, nor even witty. He stared at me for what felt like ages, then he stood up and looked down at me. I actually thought he was going to kick me. He didn't.

'Why am I even bothering?' he asked. 'I don't want to be anywhere near you.'

And with that he walked out of the room.

I sat on the shoes for a bit longer, then hoiked myself up and slipped onto a corner of the bed – much more comfy on the arse cheeks. I stared at the mess of shoes, processing what had just happened. He had never raised a hand to me before. OK, so he still hadn't. He'd lunged at me and shoved me, jabbing me in the arm to be precise. But it was so out of character. No matter how much I might have deserved it – well, not it exactly, but deserved some comeback for my blatant display of mistrust – I was pretty sure I hadn't deserved that. And now I didn't want to leave the room. I was scared of what he might do next. Rather than irritate him further, or throw more fuel on the fire, I decided to stay put. But before I had time to deliberate about when I might venture into another room – I'd have to go to the loo at some point, unless I found a novel use for my faux Mulberry handbag – a piece of paper came floating through the open door. I flinched, unsure what it was at first. Then I saw it was, in fact, a paper plane. Why had he thrown a paper plane into the room? It landed in the corner. I got up and bent to pick it up, then returned to the safety of the bed and unfolded the plane. In the centre of the creased paper Stuart had written, 'That was out of order. Sorry, bit mad.'

Feeling it was now safe to leave the room I got up and

headed into the kitchen, where I dropped the former plane into the bin. I put my coat on, headed out and walked. I walked for hours with no sense of direction or purpose, just the need to avoid. Once I returned home I saw that he'd camped out on our sofa, leaving me to sleep alone in our three-quarter-size bed. Even though it was tiny, it felt cavernous. The empty side of the mattress was stained with longing and regret. He'd marked the sofa out as his territory and, OK, so 'not speaking' was a bit of an exaggeration, we spoke, it was just that the pinched, cursory sentences we uttered to one another were served with a side order of bitterness and a huge sprinkling of resentment. Getting the cold shoulder made me retreat into myself, question myself, punish myself – nothing new there then. On the upside, though, on that week in particular I had just the distraction I needed to take my mind off it all. That week I had an audition to prepare for.

I decided that although I was never going to get the part of Nun Features on *Acacia Avenue*, I may as well approach my audition professionally, just as we'd been taught at drama school. So I set about writing a character study of her, trying to work out who she was, where she came from, what made her tick, that kind of thing. I bought a new Hello Kitty jotter from Paperchase and wrote on the front of it in big glittery pen, 'SISTER AGATHA CHARACTER STUDY'. Here's what I wrote inside:

SISTER AGATHA
What I know about her from the miserly, tiny bit of script I've seen:
- She's a nun.
- She has people confessing murders to her.
- She knows someone called Joan.

- Before taking her vows she knew the love of a bad man and the comfort of the whiskey bottle.
- She knew isolation and despair.
- She has lived through the horror of a supermarket fire.

My thoughts on Sister Agatha:
- Probably Irish. All nuns on telly are?
- Not too interested in clothes or make-up.
- Before becoming a nun she was going out with an Irish farmer who was also her half cousin, and because of in-breeding was also her half brother. On discovering this she took to the bottle, took an overdose of pills and had to have her stomach pumped. When she came round the hospital chaplain was so nice she decided to become a nun and never looked back.

God she sounded dull. It was all so dark. There was no *way* I was going to get this part. At college I'd been praised for my comic timing and scene-stealing abilities. I was never going to be able to do that with the constraints of a wimple and a life full of pain, so I decided to make her a little bit more interesting. I crossed out all of the above and wrote a new back story for her. One I could have some fun with. One that might make me, Jodie McGee, stick out from all the other actresses going for the part.

Page 2:
- She is from Liverpool and has a strong Liverpudlian accent. (No one will make her a Scouser, so I'll stick out. Brilliant.)
- She *does* have an interest in clothes, and will always try and glam her habit up with some clever accessorizing. When she was young she dreamt of being a fashion designer, even going so far as to design her own wedding dress (sounds familiar!).

- All of her friends were very surprised when she decided to become a nun.
- She likes a laugh.
- She's a compulsive liar. She'll make up stories to show people she empathizes with them.
- She became a nun in the way Whoopi Goldberg did in *Sister Act*, coz she was on the run from someone or something. Not the mafia, but maybe she had some dodgy dealings with Liverpool's underworld, lived with a gangster, saw him kill someone and ran away to find Catholicism to avoid being fingered by the fuzz, and coz she felt guilty about it.
- She is a laugh. She'd be great fun in the pub. But she can't drink too much or she gets maudlin and runs the risk of blurting out her guilty secret (gangster murder, blood on her Capri pants etc.).
- She started the supermarket fire?
- Note to self: Remember what Rupert said when I played the secretary in that Pinter thing. 'You are blessed with the arched lip of a true comedienne.' ARCH THE LIP. NO ONE ELSE WILL DO THAT.

I had grown to really like Sister Agatha now. So much so I was desperate to get the part, if only to stop someone else getting it and playing it the boring way, where she was just another humdrum nun. A nundrum. In fact, I wrote on Page 3, 'Use phrase "nundrum" in audition. Shows you've thought about it. Shows you care etc.'

I was hungry for it. Thirsty for it. Gagging for it.

'Jodie McGee?' the receptionist called out. I stood up and adjusted my puffball skirt (I wanted to show she was quirky). 'If you'd take the lift to the eighteenth floor.'

I nodded, looked back at the other three actresses waiting to go in after me and headed for the lift. Their berets weren't as nice as mine, and they were all sporting pleated skirts. The *idiots*. I got in the lift and hastily applied some lip gloss.

The audition lasted about twenty minutes and just involved me, Laveenia and a director called Tubby, who nodded and smiled his way through my character analysis, and then grinned all through the reading of the scene I did with Laveenia playing Joan. The meeting was recorded and sent to the producers and powers that be at 'the network', and they said I should hear something in two weeks.

Two weeks later I had to go up to Liverpool with two other actresses and screen test for the part on a Saturday morning. I had to be in Liverpool by lunchtime, so I'd booked myself onto a nine thirty train from Euston, which meant setting the alarm for seven thirty to give myself time to shower and grab some breakfast before heading out. My plan was to do my make-up on the train, but clothes were less important (the beret, for instance) today, as I would be put in costume on arrival in order to do the screen test.

But, horror of horrors, I slept fitfully the night before, as Sister Agatha's dialogue from a new scene they'd sent me was spinning round in my head. When I woke, feeling rather refreshed, it has to be said, for someone who'd not got off till about 3a.m., I looked at my curtains and mused to myself, 'Gosh, the light outside seems very . . . light . . . for what must be before seven thirty of the a.m. variety.'

It had to be before seven thirty because my alarm hadn't yet gone off.

But when I turned to the alarm clock, I saw that Mickey Mouse's hands were entangled in an awkward position. A position that was just plain wrong. I grabbed the clock and thrust it in front of my eyes, checking I wasn't going blind or mad or both.

SHIT! IT WAS FIVE TO FRIGGING NINE!

'Stuart, you big KNOB!' I yelled as I tumbled out of bed and started scrabbling around my room. 'It's five to nine. Have you been messing with my alarm?!'

I heard a mild groaning from the living room as I stumbled into the bathroom, whipped the shower on and jumped in. It was cold. It woke me up. It would be hot soon. This was a nightmare. What would I do? Stuart came in, naked, and bashed down his morning glory to pee in the loo. He groaned again. This time it had an upward inflection, which meant, 'What are you on about, Jodie?' (I was fluent in Boyfriendspeak.)

'I'm going to miss my train.'

Groan. This one meant, 'Shit.'

'I can't believe my alarm didn't go off.'

Groan. This meant, 'Really?'

'Stu, what am I going to do?!'

He flushed the toilet and turned towards me. I averted my eyes from his rapidly decreasing penis and watched him yawn and scratch his left armpit with his right hand. Then he seemed to snap awake.

'Get a later train? I thought you were getting an early train anyway.'

'No, I was cutting it fine coz the nine thirty was cheaper than the one before. Oh God, this is a *catastrophe*.'

He burped.

'Find out the time of the next train, I'm going to dry my hair!'

I jumped out of the shower, threw a towel around myself and ran through to the bedroom again. Head down. Dryer on. Five minutes later my hair had taken on some sort of semblance of shape and I wrestled into some jeans, a Nicole Farhi sweater and some patent court shoes. I was just fixing a faux pearl Topshop necklace round my neck when I realized Stuart was still on the phone.

'For God's sake, Stu! How long does it take to ask about bloody train times?!'

I threw my script into my bag, chucked in a Tampax, *just in case*, and legged it into the lounge. He was just hanging up. He looked excited.

'I want you to say,' then he put on an American accent, 'how do you pull that shit out of the bag?'

'What time is it? The next train!'

Infuriatingly he said, 'How do you pull that shit out of the bag?'

I shook my head. There was no time for this.

'I'm going.'

But he blocked the doorway with a swift pincer movement.

'Babe,' he said, 'we're flying.'

'Stu, I need to go. I don't need an appraisal of the mood you're in. You're actually scaring me, let me out!'

'No, you're getting the plane. Flight leaves from City Airport at eleven. Gotta check in by half ten.'

'I can't afford to bloody fly!'

If only. It would be the answer to all my problems.

'No, but I can. And I'm coming with you. To hold your hand. This is a big day for you and the bottom line is, what you can't afford, Jodie, is to miss the audition.'

He held my hand in the cab – yes cab – to the airport after telling the driver to put his foot down. Bit of a wasted sentence in Central London, but we were both now caught up in the drama of it all. He talked to me all the way. During the past two weeks there'd been a defrosting between us, as if one of us had taken a hairdryer to the freezer of our relationship and switched it on. He'd mostly perked up once I was recalled for the part of Sister Agatha. He wasn't the world's biggest fan of *Acacia Avenue*, but I'd hear him bragging about me to his mates on the phone, or his mum when she called. (She had a habit of calling most evenings at six on the dot. I'd say, 'Guilty conscience calling!' And fortunately he'd take it the right way.) He even sat down each night and read the lines with me so I knew them. Sister Agatha, if you like, had brought us back together.

'I'm sorry I never told you about my mum, Jode,' he was saying, 'but when something big happens I just retreat into myself and bottle it up. I'm a knob.'

I would have argued, but he was hardly drawing breath.

'I needed time to think, to work it all out, and I shouldn't have been such a knob about you coming to Brighton. Least I know you care. It's just in my head. I get scared that any woman I'm with's gonna leave me, like she did. But she's back, and it's made me think, Maybe they don't all go away after all.'

But she did go away, I wanted to say, she went away for twenty-five years, but I didn't want to spoil the moment – he was holding my hand now – so I kept it buttoned and he carried on. All the way to the airport. All the way through check in. He'd said he'd hold my hand till we got there and, bar me slipping off to use the lav on the plane, he did.

Turned out he'd checked his bank account the night before and found that his mum had paid a thousand pounds into it. He'd phoned her and she'd explained it was in lieu of all the birthdays and Christmases she'd missed over the years. I wanted to say she was manipulating him, trying to win him over, buy his affections, but as it was paying for the cost of our flights, I didn't dare.

We made it to the TV studios with plenty of time to spare. A really sweet actress showed us round the set. Her name was Trudy and, as we didn't recognize her, she explained that her character had only just started, so she'd shot about three weeks of scenes, but hadn't appeared on our screens yet. She seemed to flirt a bit with Stuart, but as he held my hand through most of the tour, I didn't mind a bit.

We saw everything. The avenue itself (it was tiny) with the mocked-up houses and the Sleepy Trout on the corner. We saw the Chinese takeaway, the outside of the factory and the florist's. Trudy showed us round a bit of the studios, too, so we saw the insides of all the houses on the avenue, laid out with walls missing and lights everywhere (all the sets looked dirty. They were tiny, too). I didn't really care if I got the job now, just seeing all this was a treat in itself. But the more we looked and nosed, the more I got butterflies in my stomach and the more I wanted this to be the place I came to work every day. Something about it felt right. It felt familiar. It felt like home.

A runner came and found us while we were pretending to serve each other pints in the Sleepy Trout. They were ready for me to go into costume. I turned to Stuart, who winked, then hugged me. And as he did, he whispered in my ear, 'You're amazing. Go knock 'em dead.'

Forty-five minutes later I walked onto the set of the Our Lady of Great Sorrow, dressed in my wimple, habit and wrapover blouse – my suggestion – where I greeted the director and the actress doing the screen test with me, who was none other than Yvonne Carsgrove/Nona Newman – that *had* to be a sign! I felt at home again. I felt a million dollars. Stu had poofed some air beneath my wings and I knew I was going to fly. I just knew I was going to be Sister Agatha.

*

Two days later.

'Mum?'

'Hiya, love. Any news?'

'I didn't get it. I'm not going to be Sister Agatha.'

'Oh, Jodie, I'm devastated for you.'

I could hear her calling, a hand over the receiver, 'Alan? She didn't get it!' And then my dad saying something like, 'Told you!' but I couldn't be sure.

'Your father's very upset, as you can imagine.'

'Yeah, they've offered it to another actress. I mean, she's really good, I've seen her in a few things. She's called Colette Court.'

'Oh. Sounds like a block of flats.'

'I know. Looks like one as well.'

Mum laughed at that.

'Oh Jodie, never mind. Your time will come. And maybe next time you'll be up for something you can do really well. You know, something a bit more slutty, tart with a heart.'

'Thanks.' Though it was fringed with sarcasm.

'Is Stuart looking after you?'

'Yeah, he's gone for a takeaway. He's really angry about it. Said he wanted to ring up Crystal TV and lodge a formal complaint.'

'Would that help?'

'No.'

'Coz your dad's good at complaining. He's just got a twenty-five-pound gift voucher from Marks & Spencer for writing a letter about their toilet paper.'

'Right. Anyway, I . . . better get off, Mum.'

'Oh OK, love. And it was lovely to see you when you came up for your screen test.'

She loved saying that. I knew it made her feel like her daughter was Joan Crawford or something.

'You and Stu seemed to be getting on so much better.'

'Yeah, we are. I think I can hear him coming up the stairs. I'd best be off.'

'OK, Jodie. Love you, kid.'

'You too, Mum.'

'You'da been a crap nun anyway. Ta-ra!'

'Ta-ra.'

Two days later.

'Mum?'

'Hiya, love. Twice in one week, I am lucky.'

'You'll never guess what?'

'You're pregnant!'

'No!'

Pregnant? Where did that come from?

'I'm going to play Sister Agatha!'

Silence at the other end of the line. Ten seconds later I heard a cigarette being lit.

'That actress who they offered it to? She's only gone and got a part in *EastEnders*.'

'The one with a name like a block of flats?'

'Colette Court, yes. Mother, I'm going to be on *Acacia Avenue*! I start filming next week.'

Silence again. And then a crash – it sounded like something heavy falling on the nest of tables in the hall – followed by silence again.

I was pretty sure my mum had fainted. I turned to Stu, who was stood before me with a bottle of champagne and two flutes (the glasses not the musical instruments) and said, 'She's over the moon.'

He winked and I heard the line go dead.

TWENTY-ONE

The third time I met Yvonne Carsgrove she screamed at me, 'KNOCK FIRST, YOU STUPID BITCH!'

Whoops.

I'd accidently walked into her dressing room, mistaking it for mine. As I beat the hastiest of retreats, I bleated a staccato apology and closed the door firmly, wondering how on earth I could have made this mistake. It said in quite definite letters on her door 'MISS Y. CARSGROVE'. I was hurrying down the corridor, slightly panicky after being yelled at, trying to locate my own dressing room, when I heard a door open behind me and footsteps, followed by her dulcet tones – if dulcet meant furious and hissing venom à la pantomime villain.

'Do you know how difficult it is to learn one's lines when one has random runners barging into one's own personal private space willy nilly, hmm?'

I turned, panic rising in my chest. I could feel my cheeks burning. Her face was contorted with disgust. It was a shock. She was always so lovely onscreen as Nona, everybody's friend. It was as if Goldilocks had announced she'd had a foursome with the three bears.

'I'm . . . not actually a runner.'

'Oh are you not, *actually*? And do you think I *actually* care? Because *actually*, dearie, I do not.'

'Sorry, Nona. YVONNE! It won't happen—'

'MISS CARSGROVE TO YOU!' she countered. She was almost bent double in seething anger now.

'Miss Carsgrove, sorry.'

'Name?'

'Sorry?'

'You do have one, I presume?'

'Jodie.'

'Well, Jodie. Whatever you do – and from your behaviour I'm guessing you're on work experience from the special school – whatever it is, if this happens again I will make it my personal mission to see that you are fired. *Comprendez*?'

'I'm actually in the show.'

'Well extras aren't allowed on this corridor.'

'No, I'm an actress. A proper one. I play Sister Agatha. We met at my screen test.'

She flinched and pulled herself back up to her full height, examining my face with a stealthy look of concentration. Then she broke into a smile, chuckled, flung her arms out and walked towards me before engulfing me in a lung-flattening hug. From wicked queen to Snow White in the blink of an eye.

'Oh, Jodie. Lovely, lovely Jodie. I recognized you the minute I laid eyes on you. And yet you still fell for my cheeky little prank.' She was rubbing my back so vehemently now it felt like she was searching for my bra strap. 'One thing you'll get to know about me is . . . I'm a *huge* practical joker. Fancy a snort?'

'Sorry?'

'I always have a little snort in my dressing room with new cast members.' She'd linked arms with me and was guiding me back to the dressing room she had, just a minute earlier, kicked me out of.

Oh God. What was a snort? Was she offering me cocaine? At eight thirty in the morning? How was I going to get out of this one without incurring her wrath all over again? 'It's a little *Acacia Avenue* tradition, darling. Like wanting to hurl the producer under the wheels of an oncoming truck.'

She let go of my arm so that we could both fit through the door, single filee-stylee.

'Who is the producer at the moment, my lovely?'

'Eva.'

'Oh yes. Ghastly piece.'

'I quite like her.'

'No, dear. Never trust a woman with more facial hair than Jesus.'

She pointed to a lumpy chaise longue, which appeared to be her sign language for 'please take a seat'. I practically threw myself at it.

'So, is it your first day?' she enquired, full of faux bonhomie, whilst grabbing two Disneyland Paris mugs from a shelf with one hand and procuring a whiskey bottle from her dressing table drawer with the other. Boy could she multitask!

'Yes.' I nodded.

So a snort was a quick drink. Bullseye! I quickly scoured the room for somewhere to chuck the alcohol while she wasn't looking. There was nowhere, unless you counted the burgundy crocodile skin cowboy boots in the corner, which I didn't. She'd no doubt be kicking a runner in them later.

'And tell me . . .'

I looked back at her.

'Are you feeling paranoid yet?'

'Paranoid?' I asked, becoming immediately paranoid. 'Why would I be—'

'Oh, it's the culture of a soap, darling. It's just the way it goes. The way the cookie crumbles. You could cut the feeling of paranoia in this place *en ce moment* with a rather blunt cake slice, because we're filming that ghastly fire. Everyone thinks they're for the chop. Trust no one. Particularly those bitches in make-up; they're all on a retainer with the *News of the Screws*. The walls have ears and the ceilings have eyes. And the toilets in the green room are bugged.'

Somehow she had managed to unscrew the top of the whiskey bottle and upend two large glugsworths into the mugs. She handed me one.

'Up your bum and no babies.'

'Cheers.' We clinked glasses. 'Thanks.'

I took a hard, quick glug and felt the familiar burning at the back of my throat. Well, familiar for half eight in the evening, not half eight in the morning.

'Even when you've been on the show as long as I have, and darling when I joined even Croesus had a paper round' – Who was Croesus? I didn't remember a character with that name on the show – 'I still spend every waking hour in this building thinking, They hate me, they're going to fire me.'

'They wouldn't fire you, Yvonne, you're Nona Newman. You *are Acacia Avenue*.'

She chuckled ironically. 'Christ, what an epitaph. I can see the headstone now. Here lies Yvonne Carsgrove. She *was Acacia Avenue*.' And she knocked back her whiskey.

'Actually,' I said, 'I feel fine. I feel really good.' Which was the truth. Maybe it was the warmth of the whiskey.

'It'll come to you,' she added, leaning forward in her seat like she was an American high-school coach and I was her soccer team.

'It starts innocuously enough. You're thrilled to get the job, why shouldn't you be? You've not worked for months, and even then it was a cough and a spit. You up sticks. You move to Liverpool. You have an income for the first time in your life. You're in *Acacia Avenue*, for God's sake, life is sweet. And then a few months down the line you think, Hmm, I don't really do much in the show. I'm a glorified extra. But you overcompensate for your dissatisfaction by eating a lot. You can afford to eat now. You probably do your food shop at Marks & Spencer. If you can find one anywhere near this godforsaken *hole*. And then they use you. As part of a story. It's not much, but it gets you on the cover of a handful of magazines. You go on *Brunch With Bronwen*. Graham Norton knows everything about you. Paul O'Grady declares you're one of his favourite characters. People start clocking you on the treadmill at the gym you've joined to lose all the weight you've gained since being on the show. But that's OK. You like it when the Lycra-clad lotharios double take you. You like it when people strain to see if you have a credit card made of solid gold in M&S. And then . . . well then, some younger, prettier, blonder upstart with tits like Zeppelins rocks up and steals your limelight. Your part gets small again. You're not in the show for weeks. People clam up when you walk in the green room. You request to see the boss. You ask her, 'Does everyone hate me? Do you hate me? Am I on my way out?' She tries to make you feel better, but it's lip service. The whole time she's speaking to you she's looking at floor plans for the newly redesigned Sleepy Trout. You hit the bottle. You sleep with a groupie and catch an STI. Your boyfriend leaves you and sells his story to the papers about how you once went to Lanzarote where he tied a dressing gown cord round your wrists, and suddenly everyone calls you the Queen of S&M. You go to a Travelodge just off the M62 and drown yourself in a bath of pills of liquor.'

I actually felt a bit sick listening to Yvonne bulldozer on in such a depressing way. I made a mental note: never *ever* allow Stuart to tie me up with a dressing gown cord. Or anything else come to think of it.

'You know my best advice to you now, Jodie?'

'Be professional and remember it's just a job?' I asked hopefully.

'No, my dear. Stand up, walk down the corridor and out of those gates. And never, ever, act again.'

I gulped.

Possibly because Yvonne Carsgrove had been part of the furniture at Crystal TV for so long, a lot of what she predicted came true. Well, I never actually slept with groupie or caught a disease, and I didn't need to join a gym as I didn't put on that much weight, but I didn't see the point of moving back to Liverpool for what was, to all intents and purposes, a part-time job. I was lucky if I was in the show once a week. And when I did go in I usually just said stuff like, 'Yes, Father. Right away, Father,' or Father? We're low on Communion wine and I've just come on my blob.' (I made one of those up. Can you tell which one?)

For the first few months of the job I acted pretty much as a one-line sidekick to the resident priest, Father Parr, played by Greek hunk Aristotle Turisas, otherwise known as Ari Turisas. Or, as I nicknamed, him Hally Tosis. Because although he had chiselled cheekbones and abs you could bounce a fifty pence off, his breath was 100 per cent creosote. When I eventually made it onto the screen and some reviews came out, I was praised for holding myself in his company as if I really, really 'wanted to' (screw him, I guessed they meant), but held back because of my allegiance to the Lord. Actually, I was just flinching from his smelly breath. At first I tried to subtly offer him peppermints and chewing gum before we shot our scenes, but he always batted them away claiming he 'didn't do sugar' and 'only ate protein'. The make-up artists empathized with me as they spent hours with him up close and personal in make-up each morning, so they had a word with the sweet guy who dressed the sets of Our Lady of Great Sorrow, and soon there were plug-in air fresheners galore on set, as well as a bowl of pot pourri on the vestry table. What made his odours worse was that the windows of the vestry set were stained glass and the directors liked to spill loads of light through them, so they could get arty shots of us with multi-coloured faces. All the lights caused heat and the heat caused even more of Ari's aromas to evaporate in my direction.

Mum wasn't keen on Ari either. She said he had shifty eyes and a sticky-out bum. And in my mum's book, having a sticky-out bum meant one thing: you were a show-off. Whenever she saw him she'd tilt her head to get a look, as if to check whether it was still sticking out or not. She'd then wrinkle her nose, which I would impersonate for Dad at home, only for him to roll his eyes and say, 'She's checking him out. Always been an arse girl has our Sandra.'

Mum had taken to being an SSM – Soap Star's Mother – like a duck to water. Even the simplest of tasks were jazzed up for her now, just by having a daughter in the soap. Here, for instance, is a typical conversation she would have at the checkout at the local supermarket:

'Do you . . . watch TV?'

'I do.'

'Right. Right. Do you . . . watch any soaps?'

'Oh God yeah, love me soaps, me.'

'Right. So. Which is your favourite? *EastEnders*?'

'Oh God no!'

Because it pretty much went without saying that most Liverpudlians' favourite television drama was its own homegrown soap.

'I really like that *Acacia Avenue*.'

'Do you?'

'Yeah.'

'Really?'

'Yeah.'

'You know, it's funny you should mention that, coz my daughter's actually in it.'

'What? She's in *Acacia Avenue*?'

'Yeah.'

'She's actually in it?'

'She is, she's an actress.'

'Oh my God, your daughter is actually an actress who's actually in *Acacia Avenue*?'

'Guilty as charged!' Mum would chuckle. She used that sentence a lot these days and it got on my tits.

'So who does she play? Does she play Finchley? I love Finchley. Well, I love her hair.'

'No, she's not Finchley. And that's actually a wig.'

'Go'way! So who's your daughter?'

'My daughter plays Sister Agatha.'

'Who?'

'The nun.'

'I've never seen no nun.'

'Well, no, she's not been in it yet. Although the proper technical television term is, she's not been onscreen yet.'

'So she's not in it?'

'Not onscreen yet, no. But she's got quite a few eps in the can. Eps is another technical television term. It means episodes. And in the can means—'

Unfortunately, Mum didn't know what it meant, so it was just as well she was interrupted.

'So you've come in here, showing off about something that hasn't happened yet?'

'I'm not actually showing off. You were the one banging on about *Acacia Avenue*, love.'

'Wait till you see my daughter's wedding dress.'

'Sorry?'

'It's gonna be gorgeous.'

'Oh, right . . .'

'The only thing is, me daughter's not actually been born yet. But, you know, may as well brag about it now, know what I mean? Nothing better to do.'

'I'm going to report you. Where's the manager? The customer's always right, you know.'

'Well, this customer's getting right on my tits, love.'

Mum's excitement at being an SSM didn't stop there. As I was in the show so infrequently, I remained living in London with Stuart and just kipped at Sandalan on the nights when I needed to be on set in Liverpool. And although it was only a short bus ride from the bungalow to the studios, Mum claimed my new-found celebrity status – for new-found please read non-existent, I'd still not been on the box, so I was hardly being mobbed in the Netto – ruled me out of using public transport ever again. Just as I was about to say, Fine. I'll walk in, the exercise'll do me good, she said, 'I've got the perfect solution. I'm just going to Maureen's.'

And off she went. On foot. But returned thirty minutes later in Maureen's lime green Fiat Uno. After wrenching some furry dice from the rear-view mirror, she hopped out and did a 'da-dah!' to me from the path as I watched from the living room window. Then she came in, jangling some car keys in her hand.

I said 'What's going on?'

'I've borrowed Maureen's car.'

'What for?'

'To take you into work.'

'I'm not in till tomorrow.'

'I know.'

'Does Maureen not need it before then?'

'Well, she said she had to go and visit her mother up the hospital. But as I said, Jodes, the buses these days are really quite reliable.'

'Are you sure she didn't mind?'

'Course. Like I said to her, "Jodie can't actually get the bus at the moment, Maureen, so just thank your lucky stars you still can."'

'Right, only I'm not sure that's very—'

'"And besides," I said to her, I said, "Think of all the money you're gonna save on parking up the hospital." She goes, "We've got a special pass coz Mam's dying." I said, "Maureen, it's the principal of the thing. Why should you be taxed for losing your loved one? Make a stand. Take the bus." She completely agreed by the time I left. Even nipped to the Esso and filled the car up for me. Well, as I said to her, "I'd hate to put the wrong stuff in. Petrol, diesel, unleaded, you know?" She's a good friend.'

She's a mug, I thought.

Needless to say, after that it's doubtful that Maureen saw much of her car when I was in town. And now Mum could throw herself into a role she relished: SSD (Soap Star's Driver). She always wore her Sunday best to drive me and littered the back seat with duvets, pillows, cushions and throws. It might have been a Fiat Uno, but journeying to the studio was like being lifted in a Bedouin tent.

The journey from Sandalan to Crystal TV took approximately twelve minutes. We always drove in silence so that, as Mum put it, I had the perfect ambience for last-minute line learning.

Mum soon knew all the security staff at the studios better than I did, and as we glided under the lifted barrier she would shout out things like, 'Morning Villandro! How's your Giuseppe's gout, my love?' Or, 'Morning, Woody! Any news on your Muriel's smear yet?' Or 'Morning, Arthur! What's the latest on your Toni's gender reassignment, my darling?'

Basically, whenever Mum came in to pick me up, she made sure she got there early so she could go round gabbing to all the various members of staff, pumping them for gossip. She already knew some of them as they lived locally, but all of them seemed dusted with the fairy glitter of showbiz to her.

If I thought she was excited now, when I hadn't even appeared onscreen, I had a gut feeling that once my face was in millions of living rooms five nights a week, she'd be bloody unbearable.

TWENTY-TWO

I didn't even get a chance to say hello this time when I picked up the phone.

'Jodie?'

'Oh hiya, Mum.'

'Love, I've checked your schedule and you're not at work next Monday.'

'No, I know. I'm not in at all next week.'

'But, of course, it's your big night.'

How could I forget? The following Monday was the night the nation first got see my be-wimpled ugly mug on their screens as Sister Agatha.

I was kind of excited. My first episode boasted three scenes. The first saw me answering the phone and giving Father Parr a telling off. It went like this:

SISTER AGATHA: Hello, Our Lady of Great Sorrow, how can
   I help you? Well, no, you won't recognize my voice. I'm the
   new nun, come to help Father Parr in this inner city parish.
   Of course, I'll just get him for you.
SHE PUTS THE PHONE DOWN.
SISTER AGATHA: Father Parr?
FATHER PARR ENTERS, DRIPPING WET, FRESH FROM

319

THE SHOWER. HE IS NAKED BUT FOR A TOWEL
AND A SMOULDERING GLINT IN HIS EYE. SISTER
AGATHA BLUSHES.

FATHER PARR: Please, Call me Gino.

SISTER AGATHA: I'll call you no such thing, Father, and
please, never let me see you without your dog collar again.

SHE WALKS OFF IN A HOLY HUFF. FATHER PARR PICKS
UP THE PHONE.

FATHER PARR: Father Parr speaking? (ALARMED) What
was that? The supermarket's burning down? Of course.
I'll come straight away. (PUTS PHONE DOWN. CALLS)
Sister Agatha!

My first appearance coincided with quite a big episode in
Acacia Avenue's history as it was also the night of – da-dah! –
the big supermarket fire.

Acacia Avenue's resident supermarket was called Salisbury's.
During the past year it had had a revamp, becoming quite a big
employer in the fictional north west borough of Liverchester,
where the show was set. Quite a few of the main characters
had taken jobs there. Even Nona Newman worked there in
the evenings, stacking shelves to get some extra money to help
put 'their Jeannette' through beauty school. This Monday an
unexploded Second World War bomb would be discovered
under the five items or less till during some minor building
work, and then explode before the manager had the chance
to clear the store. Nearly every major character on the show
would be trapped in the rubble of the towering inferno of the
supermarket. The emergency services would arrive en masse.
Father Parr and his new sidekick Sister Agatha would leg it
round there, administering the Last Rites. But who would die
in the huge disaster?

No one.

Well, no one that important.

The 'Supermarket on Fire' episodes would be spread over a whole week. And no one was going to die.

Rumour had it that several highly paid members of the cast were in the firing line to be written out during the blast, therefore saving the TV company money on their wages. But according to the same rumour mill this had been scotched when the first of said highly paid stars had caught the producer sitting on the face of a new young hunk brought in to pretty up the bar staff at the Sleepy Trout.

Anyway. Back to Mum.

'I would hereby like to invite you, and Stuart, of course—'

'Hereby?'

'Don't interrupt – to Sandalan for a bit of a do to watch your first episode.'

Oh God. I'd planned on getting pissed with Stuart and watching from behind the sofa shouting, 'Do I look fat? The camera puts six pounds on you!' etc. But now I could just see the hell my mother had in store for me. Me, Stuart, Mum and Dad, all sat round in party hats drinking warm fizzy wine and having to listen to Mum passing comment on every actor in the show, which was her current obsession. ('Oh she's got a lovely car, her, Alan. Drives herself in. Volkswagen Beetle with a single red rose in a vase on the dashboard.')

'I'm not sure Stu can get the time off work to come all the way to Liverpool.'

'Well then, just bring yourself. Oh go on, Jodie. I've told everyone you're coming.'

'Everyone?'

'Well, I've invited a few people.'

'How many?' I was sounding alarmed.

'Just a couple of neighbours. And Maureen. Well, she has been very kind in lending us the Uno. I think she'll be disappointed if you're not there.'

Blackmail, that's what this was. There was no way I was going to go. I decided to say yes right now, then phone in sick on the day and claim I was unable to get out of bed with a lurgy. My plan was genius. It was foolproof. And I wouldn't be letting too many people down if she'd only asked a few neighbours and Maureen round.

I told Stuart of my genius plan when he got in from work that night, but as I lifted the Marks & Spencer moussaka from the oven (Oh God, Yvonne Carsgrove was so *right*) I heard a bit of huffing and puffing coming from Stuart's direction.

'We have to go, Princess,' he said.

I couldn't believe it. I looked at him as I threw the moussaka onto the work surface. Damn! I should have worn oven mitts.

'Your mum's been really generous, putting you up. Most actors'd have to pay for a hotel or rent a room, but she hasn't charged you a dime.'

I ran my fingers under the tap, turning the cold water on first.

'And she's been driving you in every day.'

'Once a week. If that. And only coz she wants to. She's obsessed.'

'It's the least we can do.'

'We? You'd take two days off work – one to get up there and one to get back – for me?'

He winked. 'You're not the only one who can pull a sickie.'

Every subsequent mouthful of moussaka made me want to choke. I looked at Stuart's face as we ate – well, as he ate greedily and I pushed some overcooked aubergine round my plate and doodled patterns in the residual grease stains with my fork – and tried to work him out. His winks these days had less of the cheeky chappy about them; they were more mournful, plaintive, like I was looking anew at that lost little boy in the children's home instead of the big butch plasterer I'd fallen in love with.

He'd become very pro-Mum lately. My mum, not his. It was as if the reconnection he'd made with Jan had made him more aware of what he'd missed out on over the years and therefore more approving of everything my parents had done for me. All the stuff I'd taken for granted, the things most families did – meals on the table, clothes on our back, an ability to laugh at your camp brother's high kicks – he now saw as the stuff of Arthurian legend. Award-winning, medal-deserving acts of bravery, courage and endeavour that went far beyond the norm. Sandra and Alan had stopped being Mr and Mrs Average in his eyes and were complete and utter heroes. An act as simple as coming back from the shops with carrier bags of frozen vegetables had been elevated to the drama and majesty of, say, those fellas running along the beach in *Chariots of Fire*.

He'd stopped wanting to talk about his mum. When they'd first met he'd been full of it, bubbling over with tales of her racy life in Paris as the muse to an artist called Geko. How she'd snorted drugs off the belly of a well-known Spanish television presenter. How she'd worked voluntarily for a few years on a Greek island rescuing Labradors or something.

'She's . . . she's . . .' he'd say.

And I'd say, 'A compulsive liar?'

And he'd look at me with such hurt that I'd backtrack.

'I'm messing. It's just she's had such a colourful life, Stu. I'm jealous.'

And he'd nod, encouraged again. Encouraged to think that

it was fine that she'd bummed around Europe most of her life being glamorous and selfish, instead of sitting at home cooking egg and chips and telling him she loved him.

Recently, though, he'd started saying that she 'did his head in'. He'd return from their meetings and not want to talk about her. It would appear that the honeymoon was over. When I'd ask how it had gone he'd just shrug and ask about the show. My part in *Acacia Avenue* had become a comforting distraction from having to talk about any mixed emotions he might be feeling about the reappearance of the woman who'd given him life.

He didn't want to talk about much any more. Time was he'd come in from work and be full of funny stories, off-colour jokes, the usual stuff people bring back from a day spent with other human beings. But these days he'd just come home, flop on the couch and want to watch *Acacia Avenue,* asking me what I knew about all the different people in it. The show was the balm that soothed away anything bad in the world. However I felt about the job – some days I was daunted by it, other days exhilarated – it certainly felt like a bit of a gift as it allowed Stuart and I a common interest.

In my darker moments I thought back to a recent storyline on the show where a man had tracked down his long-lost daughter, not told her who he was, then started an un-surprisingly ill-fated affair with her. Apparently a lot of previously faithful viewers had switched off their TV sets in their droves because of it, which was why Eva decided she wanted the supermarket to burn down. She wanted 'Fire Night' and 'Fire Week' to make *Acacia Avenue* must-see TV. One of the people who defended the incest storyline almost as loudly as Eva was Mum. She'd even written a letter to the *Radio Times* about it. And it was published.

Dear *Radio Times*,

In response to your article in the last issue 'Jumping the Shark', I would point you in the direction of the findings of lots of scientific research by psychologists and psychiatrists that shows that genetic sexual attraction is a part of everyday life and often happens when siblings or parents and children who have been adopted meet for the first time. If you Google it, you'll find it. End of.

Also, about your claim that Trudy-Jo Patterson's performance as the 'abused daughter' has more wood on it than your average bonfire, I disagree. I find her a wonderful actress who portrays the confusion of post-adolescent trauma with a truthfulness rarely found in other so-called 'soaps'. She is also a very proficient driver who drives herself to and from the studios each day in a convertible Mondeo, and always stops at the security gates to sign autographs for her legion of fans. (I do not know this because I work on the show as a driver or in any other role, but because I live not far from the studios.)

In future, check your facts.

Yours sincerely,

Maureen O'Flaherty (Mrs)

Liverpool.

She had appropriated Maureen's name as a disguise in case the letter came back to bite me on the bum in the future. She had ripped it from the magazine and posted it to me. Each time I looked at it a fist clasped my heart. Could Stuart be doing the same with Jan? It didn't bear thinking about; it was too horrible a thing to consider. But was Mum trying to tell me something? No. She was just showing off that she'd been published, even if it was under a nom de plume. I banished all thoughts of Jan-on-Stu hot love action from my head.

The weekend before my first episode was transmitted Stu said he wanted to have a big romantic soppy weekend having fun in London. He was clingier than usual. We walked round Islington Green, pootling in bookshops, sipping cappuccinos on pavement cafés, mostly holding hands, sometimes stopping to kiss in the street like lovesick teenagers who'd got off with each other at the school disco the night before. We went to the pictures on Tottenham Court Road and saw a very girly rom-com, something he usually detested but this weekend seemed to be right up his *strasse*. We went on the London Eye, giggled at silver painted people in Covent Garden pretending to be statues and had a moonlit picnic on Hampstead Heath. For two days solid my life was a love montage, like the one in the film we'd just seen. And when we curled up in bed together on the Sunday night he said, 'I just wanted to feel like you were mine this weekend. Coz from tomorrow you'll belong to everyone out there.' And he pointed towards the window.

It felt weird. I wanted to belong to him. Not in a downtrodden, under-the-thumb, I-am-not-worthy kind of way, but in a way where I wanted him to be more important than a faceless public who only knew me as 'that nun off the telly'. I'd been recognized many times over the last couple of years as 'that girl off the ads', but it rarely created a problem. It was usually just people staring on the bus or in the shops, wondering if they knew me, and trying to work out where from. Was all that about to change? I'd always kidded myself that it was quite lucky that onscreen I'd be a dowdy piece in a wimple, so it was unlikely I'd be recognized much. But I'd have been lying if I'd said that a part of me wasn't a little bit excited by the prospect of imminent fame.

And I'd also be lying if I'd not considered that somewhere in London a certain gay DJ might be watching the telly and kicking himself that he'd really messed things up with his now superstar sister. Was it bad to think like that? Was it punitive and immature? I didn't care. Our Joey had caused me so much conflict and heartache over the years. Maybe this was payback time.

Sometimes, your parents lie. The party was one of those times. What my mother had told me about the party:

1 It was going to be tiny. Just a few neighbours and Maureen. I'd imagined some nibbles on the coffee table, revolving on the electronic lazy Susan that Our Joey had got them for Christmas. Hopefully they'd switch it off during the programme as it made a loud whirring noise. Every time I looked at it I wanted to stab it through the heart. Even though inanimate objects don't have hearts.

2 Well, that's about it really. But tiny was the operative word.

What the party was really like:

1 It was huge. Alarm bells started to ring when we arrived at three o'clock on the Monday afternoon to find a marquee in the garden.

2 I say marquee, it was really a gazebo that could fit about twenty people under it, but it was still massive and dwarfed the garden.

3 Mum's opening gambit as we arrived was, 'Oh there's been a slight change of plan. It's a fancy dress party now. You have to come as an *Acacia Avenue* character.' On seeing our looks of dread she calmly reassured us that they'd reserved a fireman's outfit for Stu from a nearby fancy dress shop ('Coz it's the "Big Fire" episode!') and as I went to protest

she produced my actual Sister Agatha habit from the hall cupboard. ('I had a word with Costume, Jode.')

4 The bungalow was a hive of activity as we arrived, so we got pinned to the wall as jobsworth caterers whizzed up and down the hall and in and out of various doors, preparing the spread. I also saw one caterer pinning a sign to the door to the through lounge that said, 'This evening's party was catered by LESLEY SPREADS OF HUNT'S CROSS'.

5 Some electricians turned up and erected a huge plasma screen telly in the gazebo with loud speakers on either side. At this point I started to feel sick and had my first drink.

6 When Ming from the press office arrived with her assistant I felt even more sick. It turned out Mum had suggested she invite a few local journalists along, and a couple of national ones, too, to run a 'local girl makes good' story. This was completely mortifying. The only centimetre of silver lining on a very dark cloud was that although all the local papers had jumped at the chance to attend the party, none of the national papers had.

7 When I told Mum I didn't want to dress up as Sister Agatha she looked like she was going to hit me. Stuart intervened and said I 'owed it to her'. We then had a massive row, which ended with me locking myself in the bathroom and refusing to come out.

8 I stayed in there for eighteen minutes before being forced to evacuate for Lesley of Lesley Spreads, who put a note under the door which read, 'Please come out. I have bladder issues. I can't say this out loud, though, as it might be bad for business. Thank you, Lesley (Lesley Spreads).' I wasn't sure if Mum had put her up to it.

9 Mum's second cousin Cath announced very loudly in the kitchen, whilst dressed in an A-line skirt, platforms and a

bobbed wig (Nona Newman in the Seventies, apparently), that if I put my habit on she'd 'donate fifty pounds to brain-damaged kids'. A round of applause went up from the caterers and I duly ventured into my old bedroom to get changed.

10 By six o'clock Sandalan was rammed. Anyone who was anybody on Flaxton Road was there. Teachers from my primary school. A guy with special needs who'd once flashed at me in the swing park. A dinner lady from the comp who proudly told anyone who'd listen that 'Jodie always loved her custard'. She even told me. Then she added, 'She's like a daughter to me. Is she here yet?' I told her I was Jodie. That shut her up.

11 Hayls and Debs came. Debs was dressed in a big furry costume as she'd come as the avenue's resident poodle, Cheeky. Though on closer inspection, many people commented that she was actually dressed as a rabbit. Hayls had come as herself in a protest 'against the lack of visibility of disabled characters and actors'. She had a placard resting behind her in the through lounge which read, 'IF A CRIPPLE'S YOUR TIPPLE AVOID "AA"' When Stuart, in an uncharacteristic display of political correctness, suggested the wording was slightly offensive, she snapped at him, 'I can say it coz I am one,' then got up to dance to 'Sisters Are Doing It For Themselves'.

12 Mum had got 'someone from down the road' to make a mix tape of nun-themed songs. From what I could make out this involved listening to 'Sisters Are Doing It For Themselves', a disco version of the 'Singing Nun' and 'I Will Follow Him' from *Sister Act* again and again and again. I challenged Mum that she had invented this person from down the road and that the tape had in fact been sent to

her by Our Joey, but she poo-pooed this idea, claiming I was in the doghouse with Our Joey because he'd written to me apologizing for his behaviour re Greg and that I'd never written back. When I said I'd written back she accused me of lying. I then accused Our Joey of being the liar (even though he wasn't there) because I *had* written back and he was pretending I hadn't so that he could continue our feud, something that probably suited him because he was no doubt jealous of my new-found fame. Dad then pointed out that Our Joey was enjoying a certain level of fame as a DJ in London called Mr Milk, to which I retorted that just because you played a few nights in a gay club in Charing Cross, it didn't make you Tony De Vit.

13 Mum and Dad had no idea who Tony De Vit was. Neither did the woman from *Merseymouth* (the free local newspaper) who carried out our interview in the gazebo. It took the best part of forty minutes because she painstakingly wrote down everything I said in a notebook. 'Do you not know shorthand?' I enquired. She shook her head and said, 'I know a bit of sign language.' From what I could see of her writing, she didn't know how to spell either. I said, 'You've spelt wimple wrong. There's no "U".' She said, 'My editor spellchecks everything, she's really good.'

14 Stuart spent a lot of the early part of the evening chatting in the garden with Dad's fellow postmen from work and Maureen's husband Tony. They were all dressed as firemen. A tipsy Debs kept shimmying up to them and asking if she could slide down their collective poles.

15 Maureen got very drunk on the free champagne (supplied by Bargain Booze on the parade, who had sponsored the evening). She then started to row with Mum about the car. It transpired that not only was she fed up with her

borrowing it all the time to ferry me to work while her mum lay dying in the Royal, but she'd also heard that Mum was toying with getting the windows blacked out. The row that ensued in the kitchen consisted mostly of Mum's fears that 'after tonight life will never be the same again' and I 'might get a stalker who chooses to try and storm the car at traffic lights'. Maureen countered that it was her car and she could no longer use it. Mum accused her of 'showing off in front of the journalists'. Maureen said, 'She's only from the frigging *Merseymouth*!' picked up a quiche and threw it at Mum, then stormed out. Mum then spent the next ten minutes trying to get runny egg off her wimple (she had come as Sister Agatha, too).

16 Fortunately the only local journalist who had turned up was that dopey one from the *Merseymouth*, a publication most people used to line their cat litter trays or wedge under wonky coffee-table legs.

17 Half an hour before the show started, Stu complained that the plasticky material his fireman's outfit was made from was bringing him out in a rash, so he went and got changed into his normal clothes. Cue cries of Dad shouting, 'Play nice, Stu lad! Play nice!' Stu ignored him. It might be worth pointing out at this point that Dad was dressed in thigh-high leather boots, a PVC miniskirt, a leopard-skin boob tube and frizzy red wig as he'd come as fierce queen of the one-liner, barmaid Sorrel Slatterthwaite.

18 At twenty-five past seven Mum banged a gong, which silenced no one, and announced, 'Ladies and Gentlemen, please make your way to the marquee for the *Acacia Avenue* debut of my wonderful daughter Jodie.' As we headed towards the back door Mum poked me in the ribs. 'D'you want to make a speech?' 'No,' I said, 'I want to make

331

a sharp exit.' As he walked into the garden, Dad said the grass was playing havoc with his heels.

19 I couldn't actually describe what watching the episode was like. It was all too mortifying for words. I started panicking when Ming from the press office said to me, 'Have you seen a preview tape of tonight's ep?' I shook my head and asked, 'Why?' She blushed and twitched. 'Nothing. Nothing.'

20 And what an apt word 'nothing' was.

Taken from the *Merseymouth,* 16 April 2010.

A BAD HABIT . . . FOR ACTING!
By our entertainments reporter Penny Haynes.

The great and the good of Hunt's Cross were out in force last night to celebrate the success of resident Josie McFee, 38, of Flaxton Road, who has just bagged herself the part of Sister Agnes in the controversial soap opera *Acacia Avenue.* Josie watched her first appearance on the show in a specially erected marquee in the back garden of the council house she shares with Mum Sandra, cross-dressing Dad Alan and brother Joseph. 'Joseph really wanted to be here,' said the proud mother, 'but his DJing commitments in London prevented him attending. He and Josie are so close. They have an almost telepathic relationship, like black identical twins.'

Acacia Avenue recently hit the headlines when it depicted the incestuous relationship of Derek DeVere and his long-lost daughter Finchley, but its reputation certainly didn't put off Josie, who has already found fame in a string of TV roles, including playing top TV chef (and fellow Liverpudlian) Charlie Walsh's love interest in those zany commercials. 'Being in *Acacia Avenue* was always my dream,' says Josie, who trained for six years at the Myrtle Mendelson School of Drama and

Disco in Allerton. Other famous alumni of Mendelson's include Sacha Walker, who last week was seen being decapitated in some heart-wrenching scenes in *Casualty*.

'I've always wanted to play a nun,' said Josie. 'I saw *The Sound of Music* eighteen times, plus I feel I have a personal relationship with Jesus. He's kind of one of my best friends. So this really is my dream come true. When I first walked onto that famous crazy paving and saw all those familiar icons I was really nervous, but I hope I've done OK. Touch wood.'

Josie, who turned up at the party dressed as a nun, has been dating her boyfriend Stuart, another actor, for two weeks. 'I think he's the one,' she gushed. 'We've already talked about marriage.'

Last night's episode of *Acacia Avenue* – one of the most talked about in months – depicted the horrific fire at Salisbury's, which left several characters' lives hanging in the balance. What was it like to shoot those scenes?

'Tough. Emotionally and physically,' said Josie, 'I did a lot of crying – on screen and off! It was almost like I'd been in a major national disaster myself. Scary.'

But although the party went with a swing (thanks to Bargain Booze of Allerton Road and Lesley's Spreads of Hunt's Cross), attendees were left disappointed when they only managed to catch a glimpse of the back of Josie's head during the actual show.

'Stuff like this happens all the time,' explained Ming Marshall-Nkoko, a spokesperson from Crystal TV who was there to support Josie on her big night. 'Scenes get cut all the time. And not because of wobbly sets! On a big night like "Fire Night" you need to show the audience the drama, the characters they love. Josie wasn't cut from the episode because she was rubbish. I'm sure we'll be seeing lots more of her in the future.'

'Acting's like a drug for me,' explained Josie, 'and every day I need another fix. Crystal TV is my crack den. And I just can't wait to get back there for more.'

The article was accompanied by a dreadful photo of Mum doing a thumbs up to the camera. Underneath it said, 'Excited Josie – Back in the habit.'

Mum wrote a letter, which appeared in the next edition of Merseymouth.

Dear *Merseymouth*,

I have to take issue with your article in yesterday's paper by so-called entertainments reporter, Penny Haynes, about our local superstar Jodie McGee.

Ms Haynes made several 'inaccuracies' in her so-called piece of investigative journalism that I feel I have to correct, for fear that the readership of Liverpool may otherwise be 'misled'. Firstly, Jodie's name is Jodie McGee and not Josie McFee. Also, the picture you printed of her was actually of her mother Sandra. I understand why you made this 'mistake', however, as Sandra is a very youthful mum and people have always said they could pass for sisters. It is also worth pointing out that she has never had surgery and is a lovely woman who a lot of people say reminds them of our latterday Queen of Hearts, Princess Diana of Wales (before she died).

Also, Sandra's husband Alan is not a cross-dresser. The party was a 'fancy dress party' and people had to come dressed as their favourite character from the show – a wonderful 'theme', I'm sure you'll agree – and Alan came as Sorrel the tarty barmaid. Claiming he is a cross-dresser is libellous. He is an upstanding pillar of our local community and a very popular postman (three hundred pounds in 'Christmas tips' can't be wrong).

Sandra and Alan do *not*, I repeat *not*, live in a 'council house'. It is an ex-council house, and actually, when you think about it or care to drive past it you will find it is in fact a very attractive dormer bungalow with a beautiful Spanish villa-style theme to the outside that is very evocative (of Spain). It is the only residence on Flaxton Road to have a wagon wheel attached to its edifice and many people have commented on how unique that is. Only the other week a complete stranger knocked on Sandra's door and told her quite blatantly, 'I think your house is the nicest in the whole street.' But Sandra is modest and has never told a soul about this incident. She is not a bragger.

When Sandra said her children were like black identical twins, this makes her sound 'racist'. She is not. She has many black friends at her workplace and enjoys much banter with them, none of it of an off-colour nature. She actually said, 'like those black twins off that TV play in the Eighties.' I forget the name of it now, but it was really good and the actresses in it were really good (whatever happened to them? Maybe you could do a piece on it. *But get their names right!*). I know she said this because I was standing nearby at the time. I really want to clear this up as I would hate to think that her black friends would phone and ask her what she meant, and point out that she is racist. She is one of the least racist people I have ever met. Phone calls of this nature would really upset her and I would urge anyone who may have made one of these calls (not that I know they have, but just say they had for instance) to apologize to her at work next time they see her. She really does have a heart of gold. (Her favourite light entertainment personality for many a year was Rustie Lee and her favourite pop song is 'Ebony and Ivory' by Paul McCartney and Stevie

Wonder, who is not only black but blind as well. That's just what she's like.)

You claim Jodie has only ever studied drama at that place on Allerton Road. This is a *lie*. She went to one of the 'top London drama schools', where she shone playing lots of 'upper crust' parts such as Lady Bracknell and 'the like'.

Her partner Stuart is not an actor. He has a very high-powered job in London and, although he is dishy enough to be a Hollywood action hero in the style of 'Jean-Claude Van Damme', he's never been in front of a camera in his life.

Finally, Jodie never said those things about her workplace being like a crack den. What she actually said was 'acting is like a drug to me'. I find your comments 'obnoxious' and, actually when you think about it, offensive to Scousers. We are not all crackheads, we are nice, sensible people with good jobs and dormer bungalows with through lounges and serving hatches we pass Sunday roasts through, *not* heroin, smack or any of those other stereotypically Liverpudlian things. I have a feeling Ms Haynes had a Manchester accent and would actually question why she is 'employed' by *Merseymouth* in the first place.

The people of Liverpool will not stand for this. It was a lovely party, beautifully organized by Sandra McGee, who is one of the nicest people I have ever met.

Yours sincerely,
Maureen O'Flaherty (Mrs)

That afternoon a note was pushed through the door at Sandalan. It read:

Sandra,

Stop writing shite and pretending to be me, it is a cause of deep embarrassment. Also, Mum has taken a turn for the

worse so I will do as you suggested at your party and shove
my Fiat Uno up my arse.

Maureen.

PS Tony's offer of a job for Stuart still stands. Jodie's the
innocent in all this.

'A job?' I gasped as we all bent round the letter to read it.
Mum immediately tore it into tiny pieces and hurried to the
bin in the kitchen to dispose of it. I looked at Stu.

'I'll tell you later,' he said.

'What a *bitch*!' Mum called from the kitchen.

'Tell me now.'

'After all I've done for *her*!' Mum continued. Dad hurried to
her side.

'Don't let her get to you, love.'

'I think we should move to Liverpool,' said Stuart.

Whoops. Rug-pulled-from-under-feet time.

'Y'what?'

'How would she like it', said Mum, hysterical now, 'if I stuck
a note to her Tony through their door telling him what she got
up to with Ged from the Elephant after she won on the bingo
that night?'

Stuart shrugged. 'We'll talk about it on the train.'

'No, we'll talk about it now.'

'He only did it coz he was after her money. She only won a
hundred and eighty quid.'

'Look at us, Jode.'

'What about us?'

'I'm gonna phone him,' Mum was saying.

'No you're not,' Dad was saying.

'It's at times like this I wish I could text,' Mum said before
lighting a cigarette and going into the garden. Dad followed her.

'We live in that tiny flat,' Stuart was saying, sounding all needy. 'Up here we could buy somewhere, get a mortgage. The cost of property's much cheaper here than in London.'

'But your job's in London.'

'And yours is here.'

'I'm hardly ever in the show.' Now I was sounding needy.

'But that's gonna change.'

'How do you know?'

'Minge said. Last night.'

'It's Ming. You know it's Ming. But what about your lovely flat in London?'

'Our lovely flat,' he corrected.

Actually, if he'd corrected me properly he'd've just said, 'Jodie it's tiny.'

'We can rent it out, charge a bit more than the mortgage and we'll have a bit more money to spend each month,' he added.

Well, that made sense.

'But who would we rent it to?'

'Mandy from work said she'd be interested.'

'Mandy the lesbian?'

He rolled his eyes and nodded, and I felt a bit daft for calling her that, so I made out I was joking.

'Lesbians . . . are allowed to live indoors?'

He chuckled. Then looked all serious.

'And if you must know . . .' his voice trailed off and he shoved his hands in his pocket. A sign of defeat. But where was the battle? 'It's Jan.'

Ah, there was the battle.

'Your mum? What about her?'

Turned out his mum had started turning up at whichever house he was working at towards the end of each working day and hassling him to go for a drink or dinner. He'd not told her where he was working – he was often in a different house each week – but she'd taken to ringing up the office and saying she was his mum and needed to get a message to him. It was starting to piss his bosses off, not to mention him. It was as if she was stalking him. He showed me his phone. He'd had thirty missed calls from her in the past twenty-four hours. He wanted to escape her.

'God, she sounds like a nightmare,' I said, deflated rather than defeated.

'She is.'

'You should call the police,' I said. A genius idea.

'She's my mum. I can hardly say to the rozzers. "My mum keeps ringing me. Keeps coming to see me. They'd go, "So what?"'

He looked so beautiful, stood there in our hall. And he'd been so lovely to me this past weekend. These past few months, really. Part of me pitied Jan. Of course she wanted to see him, he was her beautiful son. The other part of me wanted to scratch her eyes out, messing with his head like this. How dare she!

'She's on some sort of medication,' he ventured.

'And I'm guessing it's not for hay fever.'

He shook his head sadly.

I thought about it. He had a point. Up here we'd be able to buy somewhere eventually – if my number of episodes went up, and if Tony was offering him a job.

'I can understand you not wanting to be here coz of Greg,' he said. And that sealed it.

'My past's not gonna rule my life, Stuart.'

'I just don't know what to do for the best.'

He sounded so helpless. I stepped closer and hugged him. He took his hands from his pockets and put them on my bum.

'Best get to London and get packing then, kid,' I whispered. I felt him chuckle.

'I love you, babe,' he said, which was nice, because usually it was me who said it first.

I came back with his usual reply, 'Affirmative from me, too, Captain.'

TWENTY-THREE

The first few months back in Liverpool, Stuart and I moved into my old bedroom at Sandalan and kept our stuff in storage in Our Joey's old room. Mum said there was no likelihood of him paying a flying visit at the moment because he was working through the summer in some clubs in Ibiza. I warned her he'd probably be off his face on pills and injecting vodka into his eyeballs, she said I had a very narrow-minded view of DJs. No, I countered, just a very narrow view of my brother. Stuart started working for Maureen's husband Tony's building firm and I started to get more episodes of *Acacia Avenue* as my character eventually stopped being just an adjunct of Father Parr and started talking to other people outside of the church. Gradually I was needed at the studios three days a week, then four, and before I knew it it felt like I was there full time. Without access to Maureen's car I took a taxi to the studios at a cost of five pounds eighty each way, much to Mum's chagrin. She scoured the pages of the used-car section of the *Merseymouth*, desperate to be my driver again, but as I'd found out from Dad that she'd been bunking off work to drive me in I put my foot down and told her I insisted on getting a taxi in. She'd had a disciplinary hearing about it apparently and – if Maureen's Tony was to believed – she'd actually said to her manager at the hearing, 'Don't you realize who my daughter *is*?' The *shame*.

One day I got a text from Mandy in the flat in London:

Jodie. I have found a necklace of yours behind the bed. Shall I post it up or will you collect it next time your down?

I texted back,

The correct spelling is "you're".

No, that was too bitchy.

Jodie: Thanks, Mandy. Will pick up next time I'm down.
Mandy: Cheers Jode. Loving your work.

Contrary to popular belief an actress in her first few years on a soap does not earn gazillions for her efforts. I got about £400 for each episode I was in, and although the show was on five times a week, I wasn't in each episode, so earned roughly the equivalent of an office manager in a medium-sized company. Of course, office managers didn't have cameramen camping on their doorstep each morning, and neither did they run the risk of headlines in the papers such as, OFFICE MANAGER RUBY WAS CRAP IN BED, sold by former lovers, so a lot of the other actors felt we should be paid more because of this inconvenience. I appreciated that it came with the territory, and it was up to me not to roll out of nightclubs hammered at 4a.m. with my bits hanging out. Damage limitation was pretty much a ball in my court. Living rent-free meant me and Stu became cash rich, especially with the few extra quid coming in from Mandy's rent on the London flat, so we were able to save up our pennies. So much so that very soon we had enough for a deposit on a small flat. We eventually moved into a new-build block overlooking the River Mersey on the outskirts of the city centre. It had pale wooden floors, bare white walls and – on one side at least – floor-to-ceiling glass windows that gave us a stunning view of the river but, on the downside, made you feel you were living in a greenhouse. The building had silver-doored lifts; thick, biscuit-coloured carpet in the communal areas and you used a key fob to let yourself in through the main door to the lobby. In said lobby was a full-time security guard, pretentiously known as our concierge. Usually it was a foghorn-voiced Nigerian woman called Godfavour, who said things like, 'Oh look. It is you. That lady from the television.' Or, 'I watch you on the programme. You are not really a nun, correct?' Or, 'You have walked in the dog dirt. You need to wipe your shoe or you get it all over the biscuit-coloured carpet.' (This is how I knew it was biscuit coloured. Otherwise I would have said it was beige.)

I was advised by many to take on an agent, but as earning money was new to me and agents took at least 10 per cent of your earnings – sometimes 20 per cent – I didn't really see the point. It's not like I was looking for other work.

Life was sweet for a while. I felt more at home and less of a fish out of water here than I did in London. It was great hanging out with Hayls and Debs again and being able to put my hand in my pocket to repay the kindness they'd shown to me during my povo student years. I had a night out with them every Friday, a night out with Stu every Saturday and a roast round at Sandalan every Sunday. Weekday nights I sat in and learned my lines for the next day while Stu prepared ready meals and opened the odd bottle of wine.

I was starting to get semi-famous as well. I was lucky that

I could leave the house without getting recognized by every single passer-by. That wimple was blooming handy to hide behind on screen, so as of yet no one knew what my hair looked like, or what shape I was in normal clothes as opposed to a grey A-line skirt and matching wrapover cardi (costume had liked my suggestion that Agatha was quite funky). I only ever got recognized by the people waiting at the gates as I arrived in the morning or left in the evening. I always made a point of telling the cab driver to stop while I wound down my window to sign autographs and pose for leaning-out-of-the-car-window photographs for the fans. I sometimes looked through the sea of faces to see if I could spot the fat specky guy who'd hung around the gates that day when I'd gone with Mum and Our Joey all those years earlier, but I never saw him. Maybe he'd died. Or worse, started watching *Coronation Street*.

There would be more people at the gates if it was a sunny day or a school holiday. There would certainly be less, or none, it if was raining. Sometimes there would be paparazzi there, too, but they were never interested in me, which suited me fine. It didn't, however, seem to suit my new best friend on the show, Trudy. Much as I loved Trudy – she was funny, hilariously indiscreet and could be very thoughtful – she was someone who measured her own self-worth by how many column inches she took up in the tabloids or celeb magazines. Most of us turned up to work in clothes that would make the average plasterer look skanky (And I should have known, I had a joint mortgage with one), because let's face it, once you were in work you were hurried through to your dressing room and then spent the rest of the day in your costume. But Trudy usually turned up as if she was heading to the beach at Magaluf and was determined to get the sun on as many naughty bits as possible. One look was guaranteed to grab headlines: cut-off T-shirt with 'SLUT' written on it in pretend lipstick, tiny denim hotpants and saggy knitted Uggs. Her hair was up in a scrunchie and her lips were painted bright white. *And* she always made her taxi driver drop her on the street outside the entrance, so she had to walk through the autograph hunters and paps before hitting the security barrier. She would perform this little self-created catwalk strut with her mobile clamped to her ear, signing their books like she was swatting away flies, refusing to take her sunglasses off and scowling at the paps as if she was channelling Victoria Beckham on the toilet.

One of the things I was less enamoured by was the nickname she gave to the autograph hunters at the gate. She called them the door knobs. I was fascinated by her attitude to them, she barely disguised her contempt for them, unlike the rest of the cast who would practically rub themselves off over them whenever they passed by. Yet the ruder she was, the more they seemed to like her. Possibly because the men wanted to shag her and the women wanted to be her. Disdain, it seemed, was a sure-fire way to be popular.

She had a weekly column in the glossy magazine *Hiya!*, in which she wrote short paragraphs about which pop groups she liked, or what shoes she thought were cool. I first saw evidence of her propensity to be two-faced when she wrote stuff like, 'Quick shout out to all the guys at the gate at Crystal. Sorry if I sometimes don't say hi, but I'm like MAD busy right now. Kisses!'

When I jokily challenged her about it she giggled, peered over her shades and said, 'You really think I actually write my column, hun? I can just about write my own name.' I asked her if she was dyslexic. She didn't answer, but sat there chewing her bottom lip. The next week her column informed her admiring readers that it was 'a little known fact that I actually suffer from dyslexia, and my heart goes out to anyone reading this who does, too. Take your time, read from left to right, you'll get there in the end. Kisses!'

I frequently got recognized on my girly nights out with Debs and Hayls, but that was only because they enjoyed showing off about who I was in the hope that it'd get us free drinks. Hayls had even started keeping a small pile of my publicity shots in the tote – yes tote – bag hanging off the back of her wheelchair – yes, wheelchair; she now claimed to have ME. Debs was prone, after too many WKDs, to aggressively accost passing fellas and say, 'Oi, do you know who this is?' pointing to me with the severity of Orla Guerin indicating a war-torn hot spot. Cue blank looks from the innocent bystander. 'It's Sister Agatha from *Acacia Avenue*, you *knob!*' Cue polite nodding from said bystander, or a completely blank stare before she'd add, 'She's really thirsty and so are we.' She'd then fold her arms and wait for them to offer to buy us a drink. Bizarrely, it often worked, if only so the poor guy could find an excuse to get away from us, in the same way that people give money to *Big Issue* vendors as a means of escaping them. When they'd return with the round of alcopops, Hayls would produce a postcard-sized picture of me from her bag, together with a marker pen, and get me to sign it for them. A similar ruse was played with doormen to get us into clubs for free, and security guards to get us into VIP areas.

Unsurprisingly, Mum got in on the name-dropping act, too, even if dropping my name at the moment felt more like dropping a clanger to me. I would often hear her trying to book a table at the local Harvester.

'You're fully booked? Oh I see. It's just I'm bringing Jodie McGee from *Acacia Avenue*. She was really looking forward to it.' Pause. Pause. 'Oh right. Well that's wonderful then. And maybe you could throw in the desserts for free. She'd be more than happy to pose for pictures with you and the staff. You could frame it and stick it behind the bar.'

But then something exciting happened. Sister Agatha got a big story. Well, she was on the peripheries of one. As predicted in my original audition script, she became the confidante of assisted-suicide pillow suffocater Joan Jones and suddenly, not only was I in the series every day saying stuff about holy water and itchy wimples, I had big dramatic scenes that were pages long. I knew it was make or break. If I messed up these scenes it was a given that my time on the show would be limited, so I threw myself into them with gusto.

Someone from the Crystal office arranged for me to go to a convent to interview a few nuns. OK, so none of them had ever been put in the position of being in on a big murder secret, but just seeing how they lived, and what Sister Agatha had left to be part of the outside world, was really helpful for me to consolidate where she'd come from. The office also arranged for me and the actress playing Joan to visit a man in Burnley who'd actually smothered his wife with a pillow when she'd had enough of her MS.

Trudy was appalled: 'He killed her coz she'd had enough of Marks & Spencer? But their prawn cocktails are amazing.'

When I explained what MS actually stood for she chewed her bottom lip. I knew what was coming. The next edition of *Hiya!* included the following: 'If anyone reading this has MS, I just want to say my heart goes out to you. It must be a nightmare. I once deaded my arm in a playfight at school and it really freaked me out. Kisses!'

The man in Burnley was so sweet and gentle as he sat drinking PG Tips from the bone china tea service he'd got out because he obviously saw this as a special occasion. Hearing his story was heartbreaking. And having met the nuns, too, it made me understand even more why Sister Agatha would want to protect Joan. As the story unfurled, Joan was sent to court for the murder of her husband and Sister Agatha was then arrested because she knew about the killing but didn't report it to the police. Because it was a big story for the show, the press office started lining up interviews for me. I was excited. Surely they'd all be highbrow affairs to do with assisted suicides and life in the convent?

No.

In one Sunday supplement I had to talk lovingly about the contents of my fridge. In another I did a makeover as a 'naughty nun' in rubber mini-habit and leather wimple etc. And in an even more embarrassing interview called 'They make me sticky, Nicky' I had to talk to a 'journalist' called Nicky from some tits and ass magazine about who I fancied on TV. The only bit of highbrow coverage I was offered was Relative Values in *The Sunday Times*. The press office had heard that my brother was an up-and-coming DJ and wanted us both to talk about our alleged close friendship, as once heralded in the *Merseymouth*. I told them he was like Banksy and never agreed to be interviewed or photographed. That intrigued them, making them push for it even more. At this point I told them he didn't exist and that my mum had made him up for publicity purposes. There was no *way* I wanted anything about Our Joey in the papers. Scratch the surface and no doubt soon I would become tabloid fodder, with lurid tales of how my first marriage had ended like a soap-opera storyline. It didn't bear thinking about. If I'd been embarrassed about letting my fellow students at L.A.D.S. in on my turmoil, I'd have been suicidal at the whole world knowing.

I'd not thought about Greg for ages. Well, I had, but I'd not spoken about him. He'd long since stopped coming to see Mum for his tea. And now, rather than hating him when I thought about him, I just worried, hopefully unnecessarily, that he might go to the press and sell his story. I couldn't talk to Stuart about it – it didn't feel right discussing my ex with him even now – but I did talk to the girls one night, sat outside the Blue Lagoon at a pavement table. It felt almost continental, if you didn't look across the road and see the chippy and a hardware store.

'There's no way he'd go to the press, Jode,' said Hayls after taking a hit off her inhaler. She'd recently been diagnosed with asthma. She then lit up a cigarette and took a long drag of that. 'It would only make him look bad. He's saying he's not gay now. He's got a girlfriend by all accounts. He's not gonna wanna mess that up by going to the papers and talking of his gay shame.'

Debs said nothing, she just stared into her cocktail empathetically.

'Not that being gay is something to be ashamed of,' added Hayls. 'I've met a lot of lovely lesbians at my disability book group.'

Debs looked up from her drink. 'Do you have to read the books in Braille?'

'I'm deaf, Debs, not blind.'

'Yet,' she said, then returned to staring at her drink.

'Are you all right, Debs?' I asked. She seemed in a funny old mood.

Debs nodded, took a sip of her drink, then said she had to go to the loo. After she'd gone I looked at Hayls, who was now also deep in thought.

'What's got into her?' I asked.

Hayls shrugged. 'I'm just trying to think. It's not like she's part of an oppressed group or nothing.'

'Well, she's a woman,' I countered, half-joking.

Hayls nodded. 'I was thinking smaller than that.'

And then she snapped the brakes off her wheelchair and shunted herself a bit closer to me.

'I know she's met some fella online and she's been . . . getting her end away with him. Don't tell her I told you!'

'What's the big secret?'

'Well, you know. It's just for sex. It's one of those weird websites.'

'Weird in what way?'

'Well, you just meet for sex, nothing more. He's called Mickey, and apparently he's gorgeous.'

This was news to me. I thought we told each other everything.

'Sorry, babe. She swore me to secrecy. I think she's a little bit mortified.'

'Why doesn't she want me to know? I'm not judgemental, am I?'

'She only told me when she was pissed up at the Legion the other night. And Jodie, you're a big star now. She wants you to think she's great.'

'I'd think she was great even if she was Rose West. She's my mate.'

'Fame doesn't change the person; it changes those around them,' Hayls said philosophically, which made me feel a bit sad.

'I hope you still feel you can tell me stuff,' I offered up hopefully. Hayls nodded.

'Course.'

'So why d'you think she's on a downer?'

Hayls shrugged. 'Maybe she's fallen for this guy, only he just wants to keep it as fuck buddies. I dunno.' Then, with a sense of urgency, she added, 'She's coming back.'

Hayls wheeled herself a few centimetres back. Debs seemed

a bit more smiley now and sat down and took a big slurp of her drink.

'So,' she said, looking at me, 'how's it going with your one?'

My one. How was it going with Stuart? As if she'd summoned him up I heard my phone beep and saw I'd got a text from him:

Where r u?

I ignored it and sighed. 'I dunno. He seems a bit fed up really.'

'Fed up? Why, babe?' Debs maintained her interest as she withdrew a ciggie from Hayls' packet and lit up.

'I don't think he's too happy with the move.'

'From your ma's to the flat?'

'No, you dozy melt!' tutted Hayls. 'From London to here.'

'Oh.'

'Hang on, I'd better text him back.'

So I quickly texted,

At Blue Lagoon XXX

I told them how I'd been feeling lately. Everything was going all right for me. I was back in Liverpool, saw my family and friends regularly and was really enjoying work. Life was good. But the more content I got, the more it seemed to highlight the fact that Stu's life wasn't great.

'In what way is it not good? He's going out with a soap star,' said Debs. 'He's got a gorgeous flat, too – it's not just yours.'

'I'm not a soap star,' I argued. 'I'm an actress.'

Debs pulled a face. Yeah, right!

'Anyway men aren't arsed about things like that. Flats and stuff. My Lotan could live in a wheelie-adapted shoebox and still be like a pig in shit,' countered Hayls, before looking at me. 'Is it the stuff with his mum?'

I shrugged my shoulders and took a sip of my dirty Martini. His plan to extricate himself from Jan had worked. They'd not spoken in months.

'Maybe he just misses London,' I suggested, but they both pulled faces like I'd suggested the impossible.

'Is he going to the party with you tomorrow?' asked Debs.

I was off to a big party the next day in London, which was being thrown by the controller of the channel. It was being held in a hotel on Park Lane and it was all anyone on the show had been talking about for weeks. I'd bought a silver lamé halter-neck catsuit for the occasion.

I shook my head, 'No, it's just the talent.'

'The talent?' asked Debs.

Hayls tutted. 'The stars, knob.'

'Oh right,' said Debs, taking it in.

'No partners,' I explained.

'God, I'd love to go to a party like that,' said Debs dreamily.

'I bet the wheelchair access is shocking, mind,' said Hayls sadly.

'Is Stu bothered?' asked Debs.

'I don't think so. I don't know what he thinks any more. He's more monosyllabic than a Moomin.'

Debs looked confused. Hayls tittered. 'Do you know what monosyllabic means, Debs?'

'Course I do. And there was that girl in our class who was a Moomin. Michelle Thingy.'

'She was a Mormon,' said Hayls and looked at me, shaking her head despairingly.

They wanted to know if I'd asked Stuart what was wrong, and when I told them I had and he'd just shrugged and said,

'Nothing, I'm fine,' or similar, they decided I was inventing it all because I had a guilt complex about making him move from the south east to the north west. That didn't fit, though, as he'd kind of made me move. I mean, he'd not put a gun to my head or anything, though I had, of course, taken very little winning over.

Debs leaned forward in her chair and fingered her drink suggestively with a straw. It immediately made me feel uncomfortable.

'Jodie?'

'Aha?'

'Can I ask you a . . . dead personal question?'

'Aha?'

'Do yous two still do it?'

I felt Hayls' eyes on me, too, gagging to know the answer. I could feel I was blushing, though it probably didn't show as it was dark and we were sitting outside, basking in the reflected glow of the neon Blue Lagoon sign flashing behind us.

What I really wanted to say was, 'Er, hang on a minute. You're shagging some random bloke off the internet and can't be arsed to tell me, yet I'm supposed to share with you the innermost secrets of mine and Stu's bedroom habits?' But instead I found myself nodding, then shrugging, then leaning on the table, then resting my chin in my criss-crossed hands, then sighing, before admitting, 'I mean, it's not like it was. It's not that regular.'

'How regular?' Debs leaned in further.

I blustered, 'I dunno. Once a week? Sometimes more if we've got nothing on at the weekends.'

Hayls emitted a dirty laugh.

'I mean in our diaries!' Then I emitted a dirty laugh.

'What about you?' Debs asked Hayls. Hayls smiled like a cat that got more than its fair share of cream.

'I didn't really understand what love-making was till I met a paraplegic.'

The look on Debs' face was priceless. She quickly turned to me and gabbled, 'Do you think people go off sex the longer they're with their partners?'

'No,' Hayls butted in. 'Take me and my Lotan. Only last night we experimented with—'

'I WAS ASKING JODIE!' Debs practically shouted.

Hayls looked stunned. People were looking over from the other tables.

'Erm,' I said quickly, aware that Debs was keen to avoid hearing about Hayls and Lotan's adventurous sex life. 'I wouldn't say you go off it. It's just that things change, I suppose.'

'In what way?'

Fortunately I was spared having to answer as we heard a woman on the next table saying, 'Oh my God look, Raj. It's her. Sister Thingy off *Acacia Avenue*.'

Instinctively I turned and smiled. Two spotty teenagers were staring at me. They immediately looked away. I looked back to the girls, before hearing a male voice say, 'Bollocks! Sister Agatha's a moose. She's fit.'

'That's a back-handed compliment if ever I heard one,' I said, trying to make Debs and Hayls laugh. But they didn't. They were looking behind me and Debs was rolling her eyes. I looked back, seeking the object of their disapproval.

Stuart.

He was shuffling along the pavement, kicking chip wrappers out of the way, hands in his pockets, nodding a greeting.

'All right, ladies?' He said, then pulled a plastic chair over to our table and plonked himself down on it. 'Who's gonna buy me a bevy?' He said this in a mock Scouse accent.

Hayls rolled her eyes. 'You're the one with the soapstar girl-friend.'

'She's not a soapstar, she's an actress.' He slurred. OK, so he'd had one over the eight. Maybe he'd fall asleep soon and we'd sidetrack the trouble I could sense was brewing just because he still had his hands in his pockets.

'You've got him well-trained,' said Hayls, and any fool could tell she was joking.

'Piss off you pretend mong,' Stuart said, again in a false Liverpool accent.

OK, so he was the fool who couldn't tell she was joking. I decided to intervene to save us all the hassle.

'Shall we go home, Stu?'

'No, Jodie. You're on a night out with us. If he can't bear his little lady having some fun that's his lookout.' Hayls was sounding arsey.

'Jodie can do what she likes,' Stuart said, reverting to his own voice.

'Where've you been?' I asked. He didn't usually get this drunk.

'Out with the boys. Pub crawl down Picton Road.'

'Maybe I should get him home,' I said to the girls. They said nothing, though their silence spoke volumes. Stu stood up, the plastic chair ricocheting back behind him so it knocked into Raj and his girlfriend.

'So it's a fucking criminal offence to come and meet your bird on a Saturday night? Sorry. I had no idea that was the law in Liverpool.'

'Don't be daft, Stu, it's just you're a bit . . .' I searched for the word.

'Cuntified,' said Hayls.

355

I just knew it was going to kick off when salvation arrived in the form of a passing black cab. I waved at it, doing a very Hollywood movie screech of 'TAXI?!' Miraculously it pulled over.

'I'm gonna go,' I said, fishing a twenty-pound note out of my purse. 'Get yourselves some bevies with that.' And I shoved the money in Hayls' direction. Hers and Debs' eyes lit up so much they were shining more light on the table than the neon sign. I could see they weren't going to argue with that.

'Lovely seeing you, girls. Sorry about this.'

We issued a few 'Ta-ra, babes' and hugs and kisses, then I grabbed a swaying Stuart and bundled him into the cab.

'Is he gonna be all right, Queen?' the cab driver grimaced, a ciggie hanging out of the corner of his mouth. But before I could apologize and answer he looked a bit startled and said, 'Oh, it's you. Get in.'

So in I got. Fame didn't just open any old doors, it opened taxi doors as well.

Throughout the journey home Stuart mumbled on about how much he hated 'this fucking city' and how all my friends were 'knobs'. Pissed, he had been picking up on the speech rhythms of his drinking buddies, and unfortunately, mixed with his cockney it made him sound like he was from Birmingham. I just sat in silence, ignoring him. When we finally got back to the greenhouse, Godfavour was just putting the phone down at reception.

'Stone my crows,' she said, alarmed. 'Mr Moses looks a bit worse for wear.'

'He's on medication,' I said. God knows why I said it, it was none of her business if he was drunk or not, but my instinct was clearly to protect. As I linked arms with him down the corridor I heard Godfavour calling after me, 'I was not on the phone to my mother in Nigeria when you came in. That would be unprofessional in the extreme.'

But as we got into the lift I'm sure I heard her tapping out a very long number on the reception phone and then saying, 'It is me. They have gone.'

Once back in the flat, Stuart opened the bottle of vodka we kept in the fridge. I went to bed and he stayed in the living room. A few moments later I heard some American rock blasting out from the stereo. I put the pillow over my head and tried to block out the noise, and the events of the evening, and get some much-needed beauty sleep. Big day tomorrow, maybe I'd dream of my silver catsuit.

TWENTY-FOUR

I was woken by the sound of my mobile phone beeping. I looked at the digital clock on the bedside cabinet: 1:05a.m. Who on God's earth was texting at this time in the morning? Assuming it was Hayls, possibly having a go for being under his nibs's thumb, I grabbed my phone from the floor where I'd left it. But when I looked at the screen I saw the text was from Mum. She had recently been 'learning to text' (her words). Panic rose in my chest and I put the bedside light on and sat bolt upright. Parents texting in the early hours could only signal bad news. Had Dad had a heart attack? Had they been broken into? Had she got early onset dementia and was texting to say she'd just Hoovered the lawn? I jabbed the phone, opening the text.

Dear Jodie are you awake, Mum. Lol xx

Obviously no one had informed her that 'LOL' didn't stand for lots of love. I texted back,

What's wrong?

The landline rang. The landline was in the living room. I looked around and saw Stu, fully clothed, lying next to me on top of the duvet. I got up and hurried through to the lounge.

'Hello?'

'Jodie, love, you all right?'

She sounded all bright and breezy.

'What is it, Mum?'

'Oh, just ringing to see how you are, you know.'

'No, I don't know. Mum it's one o'clock in the morning. Is Dad all right?'

'Oh he's OK, you know.'

'So why the text?'

'Well, we went to a lovely barn dance tonight.'

I sat on the sofa. The leather deflating under me sounded like a soft fart.

'OK?'

'Over in Cheshire with Val and Vernon.'

I'd never had the pleasure of meeting Val and Vernon. They were a couple from Halewood that they'd met on holiday recently. She had poker-straight hair (I swear, that was all Mum ever said about her) and he was very big in stretch covers.

'Well, anyway, we were driving back – Vernon doesn't drink coz of his bypass – and we went past Greg's place. The farm, you know?'

Of course I knew.

'Aha?'

OK, so she'd piqued my interest now.

'When who do we see getting out of a taxi but your friend and mine . . . Debbie.'

'Debs?'

I might have been groggy when she first phoned, but in the space of a millisecond I was wide awake.

'That's right. So I told Vernon to slow down, he's got a delightful Daewoo . . .'

I got the impression that Val and Vernon were posher than Mum and Dad as Mum's voice went a bit affected when she spoke about them.

'And your Greg came out of the farmhouse and they went inside together.'

My heart was pounding in my chest. Well, it would have been odd for it to have been pounding in my handbag. Though maybe it was, actually, as the whole flat seemed to be vibrating in time to it.

'Like Val said – oh she is funny, Val, you'd love her.'

'What? What did Val say?'

Why was it so important to me what frigging Val said?

'She said, "That could only be a booty call." Do you know what a booty call is, Jodie?'

I nodded, and then realized she couldn't see me.

'Yes, Mother.'

'I just thought you'd like to know. Sorry if I woke you.'

'No, it's OK.'

'I mean, it might not have been a booty call.'

'No, I suppose not.'

Yeah right, what was she doing? Going round to milk his cows?

'Anyway, I'd best get to bed. Vernon's taking us to the Peaks tomorrow. I've bought a kagool especially and your father's got binoculars.'

'OK, Mum.'

'And they are both big fans of the show.'

I nodded, said goodnight and hung up. I looked around the room. Stuart had left a half-pint glass of vodka on the coffee table. I grabbed it, took a sip and sat there, stewing. It all made sense now. Debs had been seeing a guy for sex and had asked Hayls not to tell me. This is because that guy was Greg. Was it any of my business? We'd not been married for years, there was no love lost between us and he was nothing to me now. So why was anger coursing through my veins? No wonder she didn't want me to know. No wonder she'd not told Hayls his real name, inventing the nom de shag Mickey. Mickey! What sort of a name was that?

Actually there was nothing wrong with the name Mickey, I reminded myself. But how dare she? How dare she be all sweetness and light and accept drinks off me when she was bonking my bloody ex?!

I stood and paced the room, taking greedier and greedier glugs of the vodka. I looked out at the black Mersey, the lights from the prom shimmering on its restless slurping waves. No wonder it was restless tonight. Maybe it had just found out its ex was sleeping with its best friend, too! I walked angrily to the kitchen and grabbed the vodka bottle. The top was off, so I upended it into the glass and knocked it back. Then I grabbed my phone.

Hayls. Hayls would know what to do. I texted her:

Are you awake?

I waited. And waited. No response. I texted again:

Hayls?

Nothing. I waited another fifteen minutes. Staring at the clock on the wall. Staring at the Mersey. Staring at the sad, sad stars in the sky. Of course they were sad. Life was a fucking bitch! I grabbed my phone and texted Debs,

I'm so glad you're shagging my ex-husband.

I waited. Nothing. So I sent another:

You dirty bitch.

I waited. Nothing. In frustration I threw the phone across the room. It hit the skirting board in the corner and ping-ponged back into the middle of the room. When I heard it vibrate, I ran to it, knelt on the floor and looked at the screen.

Text from Debs.

I opened it.

I asked Hayls not to tell you. It's casual. I hope she told you that, too. Nothing to be jealous of. Speak tomorrow.

The phone shook in my hand. So Hayls knew. She had told Hayls? No wonder Hayls had said he'd got a new girlfriend.

Another text came through from Debs.

Some of us are not as lucky as you, Jodie, btw. And I am very lonely. Night night xxx

I threw the phone across the room again.

The party the next day was going to be horrendous, I just knew it. I'm sure that if I'd been in a better frame of mind and had had my requisite eight hours sleep I'd be like a kid on Christmas Eve. But I hadn't. I'd stayed up pacing my flat, drinking enough vodka to flood a medium-sized island, and I'd woken up groggy, arsey and feeling like death. I'd had a bit of a barney with Stu, as he'd woken feeling even worse than me and assumed my bad mood was to do with his drinking and general rudeness to my (then) friends. I didn't want to tell him the real reason why I was furious. It wasn't really his issue, and who wants to know that their girlfriend is upset by something to do with her ex? It didn't seem fair on Stu. Telling him how angry I was would have shown him I still cared about Greg, which I didn't. Or I thought I didn't. So why was I seething?

As I travelled on the train down to London I decided I was seething because not only had Debs kept something from me, but Hayls had, too. I realized that the whole thing was bringing back uncomfortable emotions and feelings from when I'd found Greg with Our Joey that fateful day. I was seething because it was a recurring theme. Maybe in a few years' time I'd find out that Mum and Dad had moved Greg in and were living in a Sandalan-style ménage à trois. It all felt so gritty, so dirty, and as well as leaving me with a blood-boiling anger, it made me feel more than a little sad. OK, so I hadn't exactly been close to the girls while I was at drama school, but since my return to the Pool of Life we'd slipped back into that cosy familiarity that best friends never lose. Or maybe they did. Maybe now I'd lost it. And that's what left me feeling flat. As with the wedding debacle, when I'd realized I was losing Greg and Our Joey from my life, I thought that Hayls and Debs might have to be consigned to history, too. Or was I over-reacting? Was it that important? Would we be able to get over it? Could we in fact weather the storm and come out the other side?

As the train careered through countryside I didn't recognize I was struck by the navy blue and white sticker on the window that said 'FIRST CLASS'. I couldn't help but smile to myself. I felt like a first class fool for feeling the way I did.

Look at me, I thought, Jodie McGee. The girl who was thrown out of drama school for breaking the rules. The girl who used to stack shelves in a supermarket for a living. Sat here in a first class carriage, heading to a glitzy showbiz party in London, all expenses paid, where there would be be loads of famous people, free champagne and hair extensions, boob jobs, party dresses and heels. This was the sort of journey most girls dreamed of making. So why couldn't I enjoy it? Why couldn't I feel buoyant with excitement, rather than anchored with pain? Because with me, it was a physical pain. Heartache wasn't just something conjured up by Patsy Cline's songwriters, they must have got it from somewhere, from their own shitty lives maybe, because it was real, and I hated feeling like this. Just because I had a job that lots of people would covet, and the alleged accompanying fabulous lifestyle, didn't mean the crap stuff went away. I still had shit to deal with. For God's sake, I seemed to be a magnet for it. I believe Dolly Parton once said that if you wanted the rainbow, you had to put up with the rain. That I could deal with, that made sense. I just wish God, or whoever was up there pulling the strings of my puppet-show life, could send me an umbrella when the raindrops started to fall.

My phone was telling me I had three voicemails. (Well, it wasn't telling me using words as such, but there was a written message on my screen). I dialled and listened to the first one.

'Jodie, it's me.'

Hayls.

'Before you start getting your knickers in a twist about me knowing, think it through. Debs has put me in a shocking position. I wish to God she'd never told me she was seeing him. I didn't tell you coz I didn't want to upset you. Anyway, it's up to her to tell you, not me. I don't see why I should have to do her dirty work. I'm sorry I lied in the pub about, well . . . making that internet stuff up. I'm a knob, what can I say? But listen, Jodes, it's not going anywhere. He's only in it for the sex, and he's told her that, but she's practically picking out rings at Boodle and Dunthorpe. So I didn't see the point in upsetting you. And I knew it would. D'you know what I mean?'

Yes, Hayls. I do know what you mean.

'Oh God, I can't believe this has happened. How did you find out? I'm mortified. Ring me. I'm going out of me mind here, I'm dead panicky for you. I can't settle. I've just got to look at a piece of toast and I feel like spewing. Anyway, I'll speak to you later, yeah? Love you.'

There was another message, thirty seconds later. Hayls again. This time with music blaring in the background.

'I can't believe this has gone to answerphone. That's really unprofessional of you. LOTAN, TURN THAT FUCKING SHITE DOWN. Sorry.'

The music went quieter.

'Can I order two large pepperoni pizzas with extra chilli on one and extra cheese on the other. Two lots of dough balls and two death by chocolates. We're at three Stuart Road. Thanks'.

Then another message. Hayls again.

'Jodie, ignore that. That was for Domino's Pizza. Lotan's forcing me to eat. Love you!'

Just then Trudy returned from the buffet car clutching cans of ready-mixed gin and tonic, a plastic beaker of ice and another lemon. She handed me a can. I cracked it open and slurped. I didn't even bother with a beaker.

'Good work, babes.' She nodded, impressed. 'Everything OK?'

I smiled. 'Never better, babes.'

'Oh good.'

No point telling someone with a weekly magazine column about my private life, eh? Although a few hours later I couldn't help but blurt out something I'd rather not have told her.

When we got to Euston there were no taxis. Irritated beyond belief – we had more bags than a convention of Anne Widdecombe lookalikes – we started walking towards the hotel, where not only were we staying the night, but the party was taking place, too. Walking down the Euston Road, dragging wheeled suitcases behind us, frocks and catsuits slung over our arms in plastic wrappers, all Trudy did was moan about her heels hurting.

'For God's sake, babes, we can't turn up at the hotel on foot. The paps'll be there already and they'll have a field day.'

'You turn up for the studios on foot. Well, you make the taxi drop you off outside and you walk through.'

'I know, but this is a proper posh party, babes. We're so not gonna look like VIPs.'

I didn't really care, as long as the walk wasn't too long. But having lived in London I knew it was more than a stone's throw from Euston to Park Lane.

'We could get the bus?'

Trudy laughed, thinking I was joking. So I laughed back, pretending I had been.

We weren't sure if we were going in the right direction for the hotel, but we marched on regardless, past constipated lines of traffic waiting for lights to change and start moving again, hoping to see a taxi sooner rather than later. Suddenly Trudy stopped and shouted, 'THESE FUCKING HEELS!'

I looked down and she'd got one of her pin-thin stilettoes caught between two paving stones.

'Come here,' I said and dived down to wrestle it free.

As I did I heard her go, 'Oh my God, Tony De Vit!'

'What? Where?'

I stood up and looked at the stationary traffic, wondering if Mr De Vit was at the wheel of a Merc or something, but then I saw that Trudy was looking at a billboard pasted with a patchwork of club posters.

'Tony De Vit's playing tonight. D'you know who Tony De Vit is, babes?'

'Course,' I tutted. What did she think I was? Untrendy? Cheek! I looked at the poster she was considering. In big letters at the top, done in the style of neon lights, was the name Tony De Vit. But underneath was another name that drew me like a spider to a web.

'You heard of him?' I said, pointing at the name below as I felt excitement and panic compete like a rhythm section in my ribcage.

'Mr Milk? Course, babes. He's well fit.'

'He's not fit.'

'He is fit.'

'He's gay.'

'So? You can still be gay and fit. All my gay mates are well fit. And his music's brilliant.'

'You heard him play?'

'Once or twice.'

'Did you meet him?'

She shook her head, then kept on walking. She didn't even say thank you for freeing her foot. I grabbed my case and followed her, unable to believe I'd seen my brother's DJ name on a poster in central London, announcing that he was playing with an A-lister DJ at a club that night. I felt a stupid amount of pride, which was now blotting out the panic I felt at seeing his name. That *was* his name, wasn't it? I was sure that was his name. I'm sure that's what he'd told me in his letter. Or maybe Mum had told me, or Dad.

'D'you know anyone who knows him?' I asked, calling after Trudy who'd now built up some speed. God she could work a heel.

'Babe, if you wanna get VIP'd into a club just speak to the press office,' she called dismissively.

'I don't.'

'Aw, d'you wanna meet him, babe? Where are the fucking TAXIS?'

'I don't need to meet him. I've met him.'

'Have you, babe? Oh this is taking the PISS.'

'He's my brother.'

She stopped and looked at me like I was mad. And in a way I was. Why had I blurted that out? To her of all people?

'Don't you dare put it in your column,' I warned aggressively.

'Take a chill pill, babes, that column's about promoting my brand.'

Of course. Phew.

We eventually found a taxi. As we drove to the hotel I lied through my back teeth that me and Our Joey were close, but that we kept our siblinghood quiet as we didn't want to cash in on each other's success. Trudy was in turns fascinated, amazed, then bored. It was, of course, because I was talking about me and not her and her so-called brand. When we eventually arrived at the hotel she opened her purse and said, 'Oh, babes, I've only got cards. Can you get this? It's such a kerfuffle.' Then practically leapfrogged over my case and out of the cab. I paid, got a receipt and toyed with asking the driver to take me back to Euston so I could return to Liverpool. Anywhere. I just knew this party was going to be dire.

By the time I decided to leave my palatial room, complete with its own Jacuzzi, having drunk most of the complimentary bottle of champagne provided by the hotel for 'Miss McGee with our warmest wishes' and head to the party downstairs, I realized I was pissed as a newt. This wasn't good. My producer would be there, the controller of the channel, everyone paying my wages basically, and if I couldn't stand upright, well, what would they think of me? I checked my watch. It was just after six. OK, one more for the road and then I'd be ready to go down to the ballroom. But pouring another glass of bubbly I tripped over a Persian rug in my silver wedges and fell over, bottle in hand. Standing up I caught sight of myself in one of the many full-length mirrors in the room (which was about four times the size of my flat) and saw that I'd spilt the champagne. Over my crotch. Even in my tipsy state I realized that venturing down in the lift to an area where there might be photographers looking like I'd wet myself was not a good idea. I tried drying myself with the hairdryer in my dressing room (yes, there was a special room that you could get changed in) but the silver lamé started to singe a bit, so I decided to sit open-legged on the couch and turn the air con up full pelt. There was a little bit of champagne left so, to save further spillages, I drank it straight from the bottle. It was then that Stu rang.

'Why didn't you tell me?'

'Tell you what?'

'About Debs and Greg.'

'It's not important.'

Silence.

'How do you know anyway?'

'It's Sunday, Jodie. I had to go to your mum's for a roast.'

Oh yes, I'd forgotten that.

'She couldn't believe you'd not said anything.'

'Is it important?'

'Are you pissed?'

'No.'

'Well, it is kind of important. You find out your best mate's done the dirty on you with your ex-husband, and—'

'You hate my friends,' I interrupted.

'I don't.'

'You did last night.'

'They just get on my tits a bit.'

'Yeah, well you're not the only one.'

'Jodie, you're slurring your words. Have you been to the party?'

'Just about to go.'

'Jeez.'

'What?'

'Don't you think you should try and sober up first?'

'I am not pissed.'

I heard him sigh.

'Just don't go showing yourself up.'

'I'm fine, Stuart.'

I looked down. Crotchwise I was looking quite dry now. Excellent.

'You sound like you're in a wind tunnel. Where are you?'

'Oh, I just turned the air con up a bit. It was a bit . . . warm.'

'Well, drink water.'

I hated it when he told me what to do. Nine times out of ten it made me desperate to do the exact opposite.

'You didn't stop when I told you last night.'

'I ain't a face, darlin'.'

A face. So that's what I was reduced to was it? Just a bloody face?

'D'you want pictures in the paper of you falling out of a club at three in morning looking like you've pissed yourself?'

I sharply closed my legs. How did he know? *How*?

'Say something nice to me,' I said in a really irritating little-girl-lost voice. I'd meant to sound vulnerable, but I just sounded a bit mad.

There was silence on the end of the phone. Then he said, 'I just worry about you sometimes.'

Aw. That was quite sweet. Very sweet, in fact. If a bit paternal, so therefore a bit pervy as he was my boyfriend. He continued,

'It's just. The show. That world. It's full of wankers. I don't want you turning into one, too.'

'I won't.'

'Promise?'

'Promise. Stu?'

'What?'

'Do you still love me?'

Silence again. Oh God, why had I asked him? I was only being vain, wanting to hear him say it. And now he was going to say no. Oh *God*.

'Do you really have to ask that?'

Now he sounded pissed off. Oh bollocks. Maybe I was pissed.

'I moved cities coz of you. I've got a whole new life coz of you.'

'You're not happy, though.'

Oh God, I'd said it. This was pathetic. I was miles away from home and dragging up white elephants like nobody's business.

'Jodie, as long as I've got you I'm fine.'

I smiled and checked my crotch again. Bone dry.

'Thanks, Stu. What you gonna do tonight?'

'Drink with the lads.'

'Get completely wrecked.'

'I intend to. Behave yourself with all them good-looking men.'

I laughed. 'I wish. I'll bell you later, yeah?'

'Yeah, babe.'

'Love you.'

'Affirmative from me, too, Captain.'

When I put the phone down, a text came through.

Mandy: Jodie. Stu says your in London. Wanna come get necklace? Or I could bring to you.

I punched, irritated, on the keys.

Jodie: It's "you're" and no am bit pissed. Next time. XXX XXXX

A few seconds later I got another one.

Mandy: Rude. Lol.

The ballroom of the hotel was rammed. I didn't recognize anyone there as there were so many finance people attending from the channel. I floated around on a cloud of contentment, looking for someone from the show. For the first time that day I felt like I didn't have a care in the world. OK, so it was probably the high you get from the bubbles in the champagne, but I now saw my future with crystal clarity. How apt. Here I was representing Crystal TV at a big posh party and . . . oh the irony made me giggle. Was it irony or was it something else? Was it coincidence? I decided to ask someone, so I poked a nearby middle-aged man in the arm and asked him. I talked at length, explaining my predicament, and he nodded patiently and agreed that irony was probably apt enough, before adding that he was very high up 'upstairs' and we should 'do breakfast'. He gave me a business card and I tucked it into my clutchbag (silver, to match the catsuit). Then I walked on with a spring in my step. So what if I never saw Hayls or Debs again? I'd survived without them before, I'd survive without them again. Who needed that pair of two-faced bitches when I had my lovely Stu to look after me? I felt a hot wave of love wash over me as I realized how much I loved all my co-stars on the show. If only I could find them. I walked around some more.

The room seemed to be mostly full of fat middle-aged men. I thought there were meant to be bloody celebrities here? Oh well. I mustn't be a snob, I should talk to the people behind the scenes, without whom I wouldn't be in work. I caught sight of a buffet along one side of the room, so I went and grabbed a plate and tucked in. Prawns, filo parcels of who knows what, cucumber sandwiches, I had the lot. And very nice they were, too. I chatted to several guys there, who told me they were in IT, or finance, or . . . well, words I didn't understand really. They hung on every word I said and laughed more than was completely necessary. My champagne glass was rarely empty either, as they kept rushing to get me topped up by passing waiters. I'd told myself in the lift coming down that I wasn't going to drink, but it was a bit nerve-racking otherwise, chatting with these powerful men who were in charge of my career, and it would have been rude to say no to such powerful people. I got lots of business cards and handed my mobile number out willy nilly. When the music started up in the ballroom I even did some impromptu booty bouncing with some of them. They were old but they definitely went for it. Who said people in telly were dull? I was a bumpin' and a grindin' with one old codger called Roger (oh the poetry!) when he grabbed hold of my arse and rammed himself into me so hard I could feel his doodah through the shiny cotton of his suit trousers. I jumped back, a bit surprised, and he looked bewildered.

'Oh I see,' he said. 'I've got to pay. Well, I've got a room up-stairs. Why don't we go and . . . make ourselves comfortable.'

'I've got a room upstairs, I don't. . .' I was slightly bewildered. Was he offering me a pay rise in exchange for sexual favours? This party was bizarre!

'I'm not paying for that!' he said quickly.

'I know, the company is,' I was confused.

'My company? Really?'

I nodded.

'Glasto Smith Watson is paying for a room for you?'

'No. Crystal TV.'

'I beg your pardon? You're a TV? A . . .' He gasped. 'A trans-sexual?'

He was looking horrified, and a penny was beginning to drop for me.

'You're not from Crystal TV? You don't work for the channel?' I asked.

'Channel?' he said, shaking his head. He didn't get it, and I was starting to realize why.

'TV Channel.'

He was looking completely perplexed. Yes, well, he looked the way I felt. I shot a quick look around the room.

'Have you still got your penis? If you have, it's kind of a deal breaker.' He was sounding tetchy now, and changing the subject.

I looked back. I still didn't see a soul I knew. 'Is this not the TV party? The controller's party?'

He looked horrified.

'This most certainly is not a party for submissive transsexuals. This is the annual dinner and dance for the National Union of Account Managers for Glasto Smith Watson. The medical company?'

I nodded. And gulped.

'Tell me, is there more than one ballroom in this hotel?'

He rolled his eyes, then nodded.

'Thanks for the dance,' I said, then walked out as fast as my legs would carry me.

I'd been mistaken for a prostitute before, but never a pre- or post-operative transsexual one. I ended up running into the lobby, where I accosted what looked like a bellboy.

'Is there another ballroom?' I gasped. He nodded and

pointed to a door opposite. Eva was stood outside it, shouting into her mobile phone.

'IF YOU DON'T GO TO SLEEP, ALICIA, I WILL GET NANNY JANET TO PUT A SCARY FILM ON, THEN YOU KNOW WHAT WILL HAPPEN!'

'Hi, Eva!' I said brightly as I bounded into the proper party.

What a silly bitch. Me, not her.

I'd just finished my first drink in the Crystal TV party and had a nice chat with the controller of the channel, who thought it was completely hilarious that I'd been mistaken for a tranny in the party over the way.

'You're one of our brightest stars, Jodie. And in that catsuit it is more than clear that you are all woman.' Then he threw back his head and laughed.

Oh God. Did I have camel toe? I did a quick check. No. Well, not from this angle anyway.

'I think I might get another drink,' I ventured.

'You can probably get one in the bar, we're finishing off in here now.'

'Oh.'

Oh indeed. I'd come all the way to London for a party and only made fifteen minutes of it. As I looked around I saw lots of my fellow cast members slowly making their way to the door. What a waste of time. I said my farewells to the controller and thanked him for a fabulous party. 'What you saw of it!' He grinned.

I left the ballroom and traipsed into the lobby. My feet were feeling heavy now and the floor seemed to have got slippier – maybe they'd polished the carpets in the last fifteen minutes? I was having a recuperative sit-down on a ruby-coloured circular velvet banquette when I saw a familiar face approaching. Ari

Turisas, my partner in crime at Our Lady's. He came and plonked himself next to me.

'Looking good, Jodie.'

'Ta.'

Oh please don't tell me he was going to perve over me as well.

'I feel a bit pissed.' That was him, not me.

'Me, too.' That was me, of course.

'What did you think of the video montage?'

'Video montage?'

'They showed a video montage at the party.'

'Of what?'

'Highlights of the next few months. You were in loads of the clips. People were pissing themselves.'

Oh. That sounded a bit rude.

'In a good way,' he added quickly.

Oh. That sounded lovely. Oh God I really was pissed. I was forgetting to speak.

'You in tomorrow?'

I shook my head.

'You coming to the bar?'

Part of me wanted to. I'd come all this way and then spent the majority of the evening at a party for middle-aged men who managed medical reps. But I knew by now that I was more than a little tipsy and Stu had told me not to show myself up. I owed it to him to go back to my room and sleep, but the pull of the bar was strong. Ari stood up.

'I'm going.'

I stood up.

'D'you know what, Ari?'

Just then I heard a blast of raucous laughter from the bar. Ari and I both looked at the door. It was rammed. That nailed it.

'I'm knackered. I'm gonna get to my bed.'

'I miss you,' he said. I looked at him. He was pulling a funny face. Sticking out his bottom lip like a petulant child. 'I remember when you did all your scenes with me. Now you're off being brilliant with other people.'

I laughed – bless him – and pulled him in for a hug. 'Well, you know, wherever she strays, Sister Aggie'll only ever have eyes for one man and that's you.'

He squeezed me, planted a kiss on my lips and grinned naughtily.

'I feel old.' He was sticking his bottom lip out again. He must have been pissed. His breath smelt fine.

'You're only as young as the woman you feel, love.'

He nodded.

'So get in that bar and start touching up the teenagers.'

He rubbed his hands together lasciviously.

'Let me at 'em!' he chuckled, then turned and headed to the open door. I headed for the lift before calling back.

'See you in church!'

It took me half an hour to find my room – I kept getting out of the lift at the wrong floor. I peeled off my catsuit, texted Stu that I loved him, then went out like a light.

The headline in the paper the next day read, SINNERS. It showed two pictures of me and Ari in the hotel lobby. One of us hugging, then one of us kissing. The story took up less space than the photos. How we'd misbehaved behind our partners' backs at the party last night. Spent the night together. How a 'source' at the hotel had seen us going to Ari's room together. All complete and utter bollocks, of course, but it didn't stop me feeling ill. I spent the train journey back to Liverpool texting and phoning Stu. But either his phone was off or he was ignoring me. I'd had Ari on the phone panicking (he had slept with someone last night and assumed the spy at the hotel had got their wires crossed. His wife was going mental and he feared he'd never see his kids again). I'd had Mum on the phone, disgusted, then angry when I told her the truth. I'd had the press office promising me they were going to sue (fortunately Ming from the office had been at the do and seen Ari getting off with one of the make-up girls). I'd even had Eva on the blower saying, 'Welcome to Soapland, Jodie. And here's where you start paying. In column inches.' If I hadn't felt so rotten I might have laughed, but I couldn't.

When I got out of the taxi at our flats there were three photographers waiting. As they clicked away I hurried to swipe the entrance fob reader and one of them shouted, 'Time to face the music, sweetheart.'

I told him to piss off. Godfavour was on reception.

'Is Stu in, d'you know, Godfavour?'

She just nodded. It wasn't like her to give me the silent treatment. I hurried to the lift.

I put my key in the door, let myself in, dragged the case inside and parked it in the hall. Then I shut the door and called out, 'Stuart?'

No reply. I could smell stale cigarette smoke. This didn't bode well. He rarely smoked unless very drunk.

I looked in the bedroom. Empty. The bathroom was empty, too. I anxiously entered the living room.

The paper was on the coffee table, alongside an overflowing ashtray and a couple of discarded lager cans. Stuart was sat on the floor, his back leaning against the window, his feet bare, he held an empty glass in his hand. Beside him was an empty bottle of vodka. He looked for all the world like a hunger striker or careworn hostage.

'Stuart, you have to believe me. Nothing happened.'

He didn't look at me.

'Stuart, please.'

He had been crying and his eyes were red. Judging by the state of him he'd not been to bed. I went through to the kitchen and put the kettle on.

'Coffee?' I called out.

Which was when he jumped into action. He stood and started pacing the room, shouting louder than I'd ever heard him shout before. Louder than I thought was humanly possible. The pain in his voice was primal, he was gabbling his words so quickly that it was difficult to keep up with them. It started with a criticism of my suggestion that coffee might be the answer to our problems, which mutated into a critique of everything bad I'd ever done to him. Then it morphed into how he'd given up his life for me 'only to be treated like a cunt'. He was in my face now, cornering me in the kitchen.

I finally snapped. 'You didn't give it up for me, you were running away from your mum!'

Which is when he did it. And it wasn't in slow motion this time. As soon as the words were out of my mouth he swung his arm round and punched me in the face. Hard. He was pissed, so the swing and the punch sent him off balance and he slipped and banged into the kitchen units. I fell backwards and hit my back on something hard, but seeing a route out as he steadied himself, I pushed past him and legged it to the bathroom. I slammed the door and locked it, then snapped the toilet seat down and sat. I could taste something metallic in my mouth. I didn't dare look in the mirror. I touched my lips. Shit they was sore. When I took my hand away my fingers were red. I looked at the floor of the bathroom. My route to the toilet was marked by little red circles of blood. I wanted to cry. I wanted to scream. I wanted to go back to the kitchen and batter him.

But I was scared. Out in the living room I heard a smash, like he'd thrown something at the wall or the window, possibly his glass. I heard stuff being moved, kicked, then glass smashing again. I buried my head in my hands, wanting to block out the noise, but I couldn't. And every time I touched my face it stung, and something felt wrong, like my chin wasn't there. I could hear him mumbling and shouting in the other room as he went about his rampage, then he hammered on the door.

'I'll kill him!' he yelled. 'I'll kill the fucking dago bastard!'

I got up to push myself against the door, hoping he wouldn't be able to break it down. I was crying now. I closed my eyes. I reckoned if I couldn't see it, it wasn't happening. I pushed and pushed against the door with all my weight. And waited. Waited for it to stop. Please God, let it stop.

PART THREE

TWENTY-FIVE

Two Years Later

From *Hiya!* magazine, 23 March 2012:

With typical understatement Jodie McGee lets us into her executive apartment in Liverpool's fashionable dockside area and sighs. 'Please excuse the mess. I keep meaning to get a cleaner, but then I promise I'll do it myself. Oh well. Champagne?' It's this mix of down-to-earth modesty and out-and-out glamour that not only makes her a joy to meet, but explains why the nation has taken her to their hearts. Although it feels like she's been around for ever, Jodie only burst onto our screens two years ago as feisty, no-nonsense Sister Agatha in the ratings-busting soap *Acacia Avenue*. Against all the odds, Jodie has made the wise-cracking nun one of the best-loved characters on British television. As we settle down in her plush dwelling – spotless, in fact, cleaner or not – overlooking the sumptuous River Mersey, we can't help but note how happy and contented Jodie looks with her long-term partner Stuart Moses. Stuart has joined us on a rare day off from his job with a building company, and let's just say he cuts quite a dash as he drifts bare-foot – and sometime bare-chested – around the apartment.

Hiya!: Jodie. We're here in the beautiful home that you share with long-term partner Stuart, and it's clear the two of you are madly in love. What's the secret to everlasting happiness?

JM: Two and a half litres of water a day, not taking *The X Factor* seriously and 300 pairs of shoes, of course! (At this point she throws back her head and guffaws as Stuart pats her appreciatively on the knee.) But seriously, it's about finding your soulmate. The one. Call it what you like, but I guess I'm just really lucky. I'm going out with my best friend. Isn't that right, Stupot?

SM: Affirmative to that, Captain!

Hiya!: We can see you both share a zany sense of humour. Is that important, do you think?

JM: Who was it said, 'If you don't laugh you'll cry'? I think that's so true.

SM: Except for the times when you're not laughing or crying, I guess.

(And again the pair of them laugh their adorable heads off. They are so cute together, aw!)

JM: Yes. Though can I point out to the readers that I don't spend too much time crying in real life. I do enough of that at work!

SM: Tell me about it.

JM: I just did!

(And again, that infectious laughter.)

Hiya!: Yes, if we could talk about Sister Agatha for a bit. She does do her fair share of crying, doesn't she?

JM: I've been really lucky to get some great stories this year. Big, meaty, dramatic stuff requiring the whole gamut of emotions. I love the way *Acacia Avenue* treads such a joyous line between tragedy and comedy. In a split second you can be bawling your eyes out, then wetting yourself with laughter.

SM: Why d'you think we had to get a leather sofa?

(Hilarity ensues in the McGee/Moses household.)

Hiya!: What first drew you to the role?

JM: Look. I've got to be honest. I didn't get too much work when I left drama school, so I'd've played the invisible man on *Acacia Avenue* if they'd paid me. But getting the part was such a surprise, a joy. I never in a million years expected to get it, because Sister Agatha and I are so dissimilar.

SM: She's not actually a nun.

(They clutch each other's hands and have a no-holds-barred laughathon.)

JM: I thought I'd be more suited to tarty, brassy parts, so it's lovely doing the kind of job that stretches me as a performer.

Hiya!: Did you think your recent storyline with Father Parr was far-fetched?

JM: Not really. Look, it's a soap. I think a lot of the time the writers see some chemistry on screen and think, What if?

Hiya!: There were several complaints to Ofcom. How did that make you feel?

JM: Look, priests and nuns fall in love every day of the week, it's just that nobody talks about it. I thought it was a privilege to be able to present the Roman Catholic church in a non-stuffy way. They get such bad press sometimes, what with paedophilia and the like, I thought it was interesting to show a different side to them.

Hiya!: How did you feel seeing Jodie kissing another man, Stuart? Was that hard?

(Stuart shifts a bit in his seat before placing his hand on Jodie's knee again.)

SM: At the end of the day, Jodie's an actress. Of course I don't particularly enjoy seeing her doing a tongue sandwich with another man, but if I can't cope with it, then I chose the wrong girlfriend.

JM: And the love-making scenes were very tastefully shot. Considering there was S&M involved.

Hiya!: Yes. Very risqué for a pre-watershed audience.

JM: What amazed me was the number of people who stopped me in the street and said, 'I too love to be chained to the hostess trolley of a Friday night while my husband tickles me with a feather duster.' It was a real eye-opener.

(Jodie and Stuart look at each other and nod. Their chemistry is almost telepathic.)

Hiya!: Can we talk about the abortion?

JM: Of course. Talk about what you like, I'm an open book.

Hiya!: Do you think it was a step too far?

JM: At the end of the day I'm not just playing a nun, I'm playing a woman. And I strongly believe that abortion is a women's issue and it's a woman's right to choose.

Hiya!: But a nun would be dead against abortion, wouldn't she?

JM: Which is why she tried to kill herself. I think it was all very sensitively handled.

Hiya!: They were quite shocking scenes.

JM: Thank you. I did a few takes where I tried to find some comedy in it, but in the end me and our wonderful director Kunz said, 'You know what? This is going to be so much better if we play it for real.'

Hiya!: While we're talking about the show, we hear that a serial killer is going to be stalking the avenue sometime soon. Can you give us any inside info on that?

JM: I could, but then I'd have to kill you! Seriously, I know very little about it. I hear it's a bit of a way off yet, and as actors we only really learn what's going on when we get our scripts. But believe me, I'm nervous! Everybody's nervous! Who knows what the future holds? But I can tell it's going to be another exciting chapter in the life of *Acacia Avenue*.

Hiya!: Now, moving on to more personal matters. Sister Agatha
  doesn't have much luck with men.

JM: She doesn't have much luck full stop. Did you see what
  those horrible yobs did to the church last week? I'm still in
  shock!

Hiya!: Oh yes, they set fire to it.

JM: I couldn't watch. It made me so sad. That church feels like
  it's actually mine!

Hiya!: Getting back to you, Jodie, for one minute. You certainly
  have more luck with men. You and Stuart are so blissfully
  happy . . .

JM: We are.

Hiya!: He's adorable. How did you guys meet?

I couldn't read any more. I folded up the magazine and
stuffed it in my bag as my cab pulled up outside the greenhouse. Godfavour was reading *Hiya!* on reception, her head
bowed, her tortoise-head tongue peeking out in a study of
concentration. She didn't even look up, though as I reached the
lifts I heard her call, 'It's a good job they did not come when
you were having one of your ding-dongs.'

I went to press the button to my floor, but had second
thoughts. I marched back to reception, letting the doors shut
behind me.

'Er, excuse me, Godfavour, but you're paid to stop intruders
coming in, not voice opinions on the state of my love life, OK?'
I knew it was harsh, but she'd pissed me off. She didn't look the
slightest bit bothered.

'You also have a cleaner. Your cleaner is called Sandra.
Sandra I like,' she commented, looking confused more than
anything. I half expected her to bang her fists on the counter
and cry, 'None of it makes any sense!'

'Godfavour. Sandra's my mum and . . . the press, they twist things.'

She nodded. I turned on my Uggs and left.

As I slipped the key in the door of the flat I called out to Stu to be on the safe side, but I knew he wouldn't be there.

The living room and kitchen were just as we'd left them that morning, breakfast dishes piled in the sink, a bit of water run on them to stop the Weetabix from moulding to the plate like cement, an open magazine on the couch, DVDs scattered on the floor by the telly. I checked the big brass nautical clock on the wall. Half past six. Stu was out tonight, going on a pub crawl with some blokes from work. Even if he came home at eleven that gave me four and a half hours of peace. Four and a half hours to catch up on my emails. Or four and a half hours to be naughty. I chucked my breeze block of scripts on the break-fast bar – learning lines was for wimps – and sprinted into the bedroom.

I threw myself onto the bed, powered up my iPad and watched the screen flicker to life. I ignored my email and went straight to my Facebook page. I chewed my lip and felt my heart beating faster. Would I have a message from him? I looked at the top of the screen and caught my breath: I had *three* messages. I opened my inbox. Message number one was something dreary about keeping Bangladesh afloat. The second was from a girl asking if I was the Jodie she went to school with. I felt like replying, 'Yes I am, but I couldn't stand you at school, so I don't see why, fifteen years later, I'm gonna suddenly think the sun shines out of your arse,' but instead I deleted it. And message number three was from him. I felt my breath become shallow as I read it. What *was* happening to me, for God's sake?

From: Matthew Martin Maxwell (France)
To: Jodie McFee (Liverpool)
Subject: LAST NIGHT. WOW!
Hey Baby Girl,
    The weather's scorching here today. Just been lazy and sat
in the sun. Jealous? Keep thinking about last night. Hope you're
not embarrassed. I'm not. It was intense, it was fun and it felt
good. I swear I've never done that before. But I hope we can do
it again. No one else need ever know, so who are we hurting?
I might go to the pictures later. There's an arthouse cinema in
Juan Les Pins which shows everything with English subtitles.
Hope you've had a good day. Sending good vibes.
    Matthew x

I blushed at the memory of what we'd got up to last night.
Stu had gone to bed early and I'd cracked open a bottle of red
and chatted online to Matthew. He'd cracked open a bottle of
red, too, and one thing had led to another until I'd sampled my
first taste of cyber sex. He'd said what he'd like to do to me, I'd
said what I'd like to do to him, and suddenly I was in a fantasy
land, sharing my innermost sexual thoughts with a guy I'd not
even met! God, I was mortified. I clicked reply.

From: Jodie McFee (Liverpool)
To: Matthew Martin Maxwell (France)
Subject: SAYONARA CYBER LOVER
Me? Embarrassed? No way. I do that sort of thing all the time.

I was about to add 'only joking!' when I heard a key in the
door. I panicked and clicked send instead, and the message
vanished from the screen.
    'Jodes?!' I heard Stu calling from the hallway. I shoved the
iPad under a pillow and jumped up to put the telly on.

'In the bedroom, babe!'

Shit! Now Matthew was going to think I was a cyber slut. 'I do that sort of thing all the time'?! I was shaking when Stu walked in with a pizza in a box. God I hated these close shaves. I was convinced I must have gone the colour of ketchup and look like a walking advert for high blood pressure. *Get high blood pressure and you can look like THIS!*

'What's that?' I said, pointing to the pizza box, my voice three octaves higher than usual. It was a stupid question, it looked like a pizza and smelled like a pizza so the options were limited. He didn't seem to notice, though, and grinned mischievously.

'Sloppy Giuseppe, extra cheese.'

'Lovely. I thought you were out tonight, drinkswise?'

Had I really just said drinkswise? Was that normal? Jeez, Louise. How much more blatant could I be?!

'We're not meeting till eight,' he said, disappearing off to the kitchen.

'Eight. Great.'

I was a poet and I didn't know it.

I'd joined Facebook a few months earlier. Everyone in the green room had been talking about it for ages, bandying about phrases like 'writing on walls', 'poking' and 'tagging' with the conspiratorial excitement of members of a religious cult. Trudy showed me how to use the website, although she herself paid someone to manage her page and write (and presumably spell correctly) her updates. She seemed to use it primarily to look at photographs of her exes or people she hated from school, and spent most of her time slagging off their taste in soft furnishings as displayed in photo albums called things like 'Randoms!'. I sat home one night and explored the site with her, telling her to enter the names of Debs and Hayls, and within seconds I was reading all the banal things they'd been up to. I even told her to look up Greg, claiming he was an old mate. At the push of a button I saw crystal-clear images of him at various parties and clubs. It totally appealed to the nosey side of my nature, and once she'd gone, I set up my own page. I wanted to be incognito on the site. I wanted to snoop rather than be snooped on, so I gave myself a false name – Jodie McFee – uploaded a photo of me from a few years back, which made me look carefree and reckless, and so the snooping began. I added a few friends from the show – some of them also used noms de plume – and before I knew it I was being inundated with friend requests as people on their friends lists realized who I really was. I ignored most of them, but soon couldn't wait to get home of a night to delve into other people's lives. Or other people's lives as they wanted to present themselves on the internet. I could start clicking through pictures of strangers' holidays and, before I knew it, hours had slipped by and I'd not even noticed. Hayls and Debs seemed to be compulsive posters, bantering with each other on their walls, posting photos of themselves doing everything from cleaning the bathroom to visiting Magaluf. And because they had no privacy settings, any fool – and in particular, this fool – could follow their every move without them knowing.

The other good thing about the whole set-up was that Stuart was a Luddite as far as technology was concerned. He had no interest in social networking and its relative merits, so Facebook became something that was mine alone, my hobby, my waste of time, and he had nothing to do with it. No idea who I was looking at, who I might be chatting to, or what I was saying about myself on there. It was my private world.

He therefore had no idea that I was spying on the lifestyles of the non rich and famous who had once been a part of my life but who I'd long since consigned to the status of 'used-to-be friends'.

Most of the friend requests I got on a daily basis were from fans saying, 'Are you really Jodie McGee? What's with the false name? I think you rock as Sister Agatha.' Or words to that effect. I was occasionally approached by people I actually knew – some I accepted, some I didn't – but I never accepted people I hadn't met.

After using the site for a month I had uploaded half a dozen photographs (all incredibly flattering – you'd have thought I was Gwyneth Paltrow on some of them. If you squinted or were pissed) and wrote generic updates that gave nothing away about my work. I called the studios 'the office', so it was usually 'another long day in the office' etc. Honestly, I bored even myself with my uncatchy one-liners.

Then one night I found a message in my inbox from someone I didn't know called Matthew Martin Maxwell. It said, 'Hey. You don't know me and I don't know you. But can I just say you look pretty damn hot in that photo with the snake.'

I had recently been to a fancy dress party as Britney Spears in the 'Slave 4 U' video. I didn't look half bad in the picture; I didn't look half bad in any of the pictures. In fact, all the pictures in the entire world in which I felt I didn't look half bad were on Facebook, which explained why there were only six. In this particular shot, in an attempt to look like Ms Spears, I was wearing a curly peroxide-blonde wig, bra, miniskirt, shiny body glitter and an inflatable snake.

I was about to delete the message – I didn't know him and he didn't know me, as he'd pointed out – when suddenly it struck me that this was the first Facebook message I'd received from a complete stranger. I clicked on his name in the message and a second later I was on his page. Why didn't he know who I was?

Was he taking the piss? Did he not have a television? I wasn't being big-headed – well, maybe just a little bit – but most people recognized me now, I'd been on that many magazine covers. At the top of his page I saw that his location was France. Ah, that explained it. He really was an *Acacia Avenue* ignoramus. And, judging by his profile pic, an undeniably cute one. I clicked on the picture and the page changed so that I was confronted by twenty different pictures, all of him looking undeniably cute. The first thing that struck me was that on every picture he was laughing. I found myself smiling in response. The chiselled jaw, with varying amounts of stubble, dimpled chin, shiny Malteser eyes and floppy Merchant Ivory locks were always punctuated by a flash of pearly whites as he guffawed and grinned – without so much as a hint of gurning – at whoever was taking the pictures. The other thing that struck me was that he was an outdoorsy type. He was dressed in a variety of wetsuits and sports gear, sometimes holding a surfboard, often on a beach, sometimes topless (I lingered on those shots possibly a bit too long). He wasn't so much sunkissed as sunsnogged. He was fit, active and probably ate his five a day. In summary, he was the complete opposite of me. I replied to his message with a brief, 'Not so bad yourself in some of those pics, Mr Speedo.'

The next day he requested to be my friend. For the subsequent fortnight we had messaged each other sporadically with the odd sarcastic, 'Have you got that wetsuit in nipple pink?' (I said that, natch.) Or, 'Worried about your snake. Is it still alive?' (Him to me. For now.) His messages always made me smile but, truth be told, I didn't give him too much thought. Until one night he popped up in the chat section of the site and we got . . . well, chatting. He'd write a sentence in the little chat box and I'd write one back – instant communication. It was like being on the phone, only you had to write everything down.

It was silly banter at first, but through it I discovered that he was a Yorkshireman by birth, but was now living the life of Riley in the South of France, working in a beach club by day as a waiter and partying by night. When he asked what I did for a living, I told him I had a very boring job in an office. I enjoyed the pretence. I had been playing Sister Agatha for two years now, and it was an adventure, an escape, to play Jodie McFee, administrative assistant at Crystal Plastics. I just hoped he never asked me anything about plastics. I basically had the same personality, though I started writing the rather irritating LOL to show I was joking sometimes – it's hard to be ironic on the internet – and soon we'd built up a cosy intimacy. All through the written word.

I was upfront about being in a relationship. That didn't faze him. But as our chats got longer and our messages more detailed I found myself, even in the guise of Ms McFee, becoming more and more honest. If I read our messages back I realized that for some inexplicable reason, Matthew was the only person in the world I was being completely honest with. The anonymous contact and lines in a chat box sometimes felt like I was talking to myself, his responses like voices in my head. At times he felt like a counsellor, someone I was able to open up to without fear of being judged. And if he was going to judge me, simple. I'd just stop talking to him and delete him as a friend. And because of my honesty I soon started to find this contact incredibly important. It was like a drug. I began craving it, but at the same time tried to exert some form of control over it. I wouldn't chat with him at work, despite being able to get Facebook on my phone, but I would find myself becoming increasingly excited about finishing for the day, getting home and getting on the iPad. Rationally I knew it was ridiculous. Matthew didn't know who I really was – Jodie McGee, television actress – but somehow it felt like he knew the real me – Jodie McGee, mess.

The one thing I didn't tell him was that Stuart had hit me. I described our relationship as fiery. Volatile. In my eyes this gave an impression of Burton/Taylor passion, or Italian-style shouting and gesticulating; the fights would be fun, and the making up afterwards even more so. But then neither of us was Italian, even if we were fond of takeaway pizza.

I would be lying if I said I lived in a constant state of fear and anxiety about Stuart battering me. I didn't. But I would be more of a liar if I said that everything between us was hunky-dory. Following the 'kitchen incident' I'd had a fat lip for a week. I'd had to phone in sick to work and claimed to have a virus. Fortunately they believed me and didn't ask to see a doctor's note. And in that week, Stuart was the most delightful he'd ever been. After the shock of the punch I had lain in bed, or on the sofa, distracting myself with daytime telly while he waited on me hand and foot, tears never far from his eyes, remorse writ large on his face. If he apologized once, he apologized a million times, and I had to say part of me enjoyed not only this, but the knowledge that I could pretty much do or say anything and he would agree and jump to it. I could do no wrong. During that period I thought maybe he was the guy for me, a good choice for a life partner. I began making excuses for him. He had been drunk. He had been jealous. He'd not been thinking straight. He had asked me not to get drunk and I had, and because I was drunk I'd put myself in a vulnerable position while there were cameras around. In the clear light of sobriety he believed I wasn't having an affair with Ari. He told me he'd never doubt me again, he'd always check the facts with me first instead of jumping to insane conclusions. And of course I believed him. I wanted to believe him. I had to believe him. Because I didn't want our time together to have been wasted. I knew he cared for me. He'd taken me in when I had nothing. He'd uprooted himself to a city he wasn't particularly fond of. He'd made so many sacrifices for me, what had I done for him? We entered a golden age in our relationship. I even thought that maybe the punch had been a good thing. Not pleasant to go through, but at least it had made us both stop and think. It was a low point we could move on from; neither of us wanted to sink to that level again. And he'd not hit me since. See? Life wasn't always like it was on the TV or in films, where if the guy hits you he's always going to do it again. Human beings do have the ability to change, and Stu had.

But I would also be lying if I didn't admit that after he hit me, a little bit of my love for him died. A troubled childhood was no excuse in my book, that fear that I would leave him, just as his mother had, wasn't a reason to lash out. I veered between loving him and feeling indifferent about him.

The thing I disliked most was how I'd gradually become a trouble avoider. I stopped going to showbiz parties, not wanting to have my behaviour misconstrued or misrepresented by a tabloid. I didn't talk too much about guys at work, in case Stuart thought I had a crush on any of them. I didn't stay out longer than necessary whenever I left the flat in order to avoid any 'Where have you been?' discussions. I was very careful about what I said in interviews in case it upset him. I turned down most public appearances I was offered through work, and there were a lot: would I go on *Saturday Kitchen*? Would I open a new pound shop? Would I do a PA at a nightclub? I no longer spoke to Hayls or Debs. I had been toying with forgiving them and making contact again, but Stuart insisted that would make me a loser and that they didn't deserve my friendship and generosity – they were users.

The other bit of trouble to avoid was Stu when he was drunk. I now knew the triggers for his angry behaviour. Although he hadn't hit me again, he still got arsey after a big night out and my reaction to his beefed-up belligerence was to take myself to bed and ignore him. If I stayed up and disagreed with something he said, a row would ensue. This happened less if he'd eaten before drinking, so tonight at least I could feel reasonably relaxed as he had brought a pizza home to gorge on before heading out to sink an ocean of booze.

'I've had untold texts about that interview,' Stu said through a mouthful of Sloppy Giuseppe. 'Got the piss taken big style at work.'

'I bet you did,' I said, though I could see just how excited he was by his brief taste of fame. 'Best wear a balaclava when you go out. Don't want people recognizing you now you're a huge star.'

He chuckled and wiped some stray tomato sauce from his chin.

'Fuck that, babes. I'm gonna wear the exact same outfit I had on in the pictures. Take the magazine with me, leave it open on a few tables.' Then he added dramatically, 'Don't you know who I am?'

We both chuckled, but I wasn't thinking about his night out. I was thinking, If only you knew. If only you knew I spent my evenings chatting to some random bloke online. If only you knew that we had cyber sex last night.

Some people might say that a man who hits a woman is weak. Some might say it gives him power. Although the dust had settled on that hateful incident many moons ago, I found myself relishing the power that having a secret from him gave me. And he was never going to find out.

Once he'd disappeared for the evening I returned to my iPad

and checked who was available online to chat to. Result. He was there. I knew he would be. I clicked on his name and a little white box appeared in the bottom right-hand corner of my screen. I took a deep breath, wriggled my fingers like an athlete preparing for some exercise and wrote, 'Matthew? Are you there?

Seconds later I got a reply: 'Hello gorgeous. How's you?'

TWENTY-SIX

Mandy: Jodie. It is nearly three years that I have had your
    necklace now.
Jodie: Sorry, Mand. Can you post it to me?
Mandy: No. Pop round next time your down and you can sign
    some AA stuff I've got for my mum. Deal? (You owe me.)
Jodie: Cool. Not sure when down next but defo will. XXX

I pressed send and heard the landline ring. I snatched it up.

'Hiya, Jodie love!'

'Hiya, Mum!'

Golly our voices were perky today. But then she lowered
hers dramatically and purred, 'How's it all going then?' with
her best Denise Robertson faux concern that, had it come from
anyone else's lips, would have elicited a sharp 'Mind your own
bloody business.' But this was my mum, so I replied, 'Yeah, not
bad thanks.'

'Oh good. Good.' (Though she elongated the second good so
it sounded more like Goooooooooood.) I heard the scratch of
her ciggie lighter and realized we were in for a marathon gab.
'Only me and your dad were wondering, you know.'

'No, I'm fine, yeah.'

Kirsty MacColl was on the stereo, singing a song about

waving or drowning. The irony was not lost on me as I zapped her off with the remote.

'Oh that's great. No that is, that's really great.'

She was slowing her words down with an insincerity that made me think she wasn't really concentrating on what she was saying, but carefully planning where to go next.

'Only me and your dad were just. I dunno. A little concerned, that's all.'

'Why?'

'Oh, no reason.'

I let the words hang in the air for a second or two, like the halos of smoke that were no doubt hanging above her head.

'But there must be some reason. You don't go all concerned for no apparent reason.'

'Well, it's a parent's job to worry, you know.' And she added one of those patronizing chuckles that people with kids do when they really want to say, You know nothing. You are childless. I am omniscient. Screw you (type of thing). And which also often infer, when it's your mother who's saying it, One day you will thank me for providing you with a bedroom with a single bed and Spice Girl posters and umpteen school uniforms that made you look like a Weeble. One day you will know the pain of childbirth. It's like shitting a basketball. It was one of my least favourite laughs.

'I just worry, you know?' she continued.

'Yes, I do know. When I said I was moving next door to the Mersey, you told me you wanted me to buy a boat, in case it flooded.'

'I didn't say a boat, Jodie.'

'You did.'

'I said a dinghy, there's a difference.'

'A dinghy *is* a boat.'

'Boat suggests something like the *Marie Celeste*. I was thinking more along the lines of something plastic you could keep in your bottom drawer.'

'What, like a vibrator?'

'Jodie, don't be coarse.'

'Sorry. Well anyway, I'm on the sixth floor of a block of flats. If the river does burst its banks I think I'll be all right.'

'Unless there's a tsunami.'

'Of course. Why didn't I think of that? Forgive me. Unless there's a tsunami.'

'There's no need to be sarcastic.'

'I know. Liverpool is famed for two things: The Beatles and plentiful tsunamis.'

'You might think what happened in Japan was funny, Jodie, but—'

'I don't!'

'Your father showed me a clip on YouTube last night. A whole street disappearing. Flats collapsing. And on my life, Jodie, it was seven eleven all over again.'

'Nine eleven.'

'What's seven eleven?'

'It used to be my local shop in London.'

'Where the guy short-changed me on that Vienetta?'

'Yes, Mother. It ranks alongside the Great Train Robbery as one of the most heinous crimes of the century. Myra Hindley's got nothing on Furqhan from the Seven Eleven.'

She seemed to process this for a second, then continued, 'You're in a funny mood tonight, Jodie.' It sounded like a leading statement. She was no longer a daytime telly agony aunt, but a full-blown psychotherapist with a practice in West Hampstead. Certificates on her wall, cat hair on her couch.

'Mother. Why are you so worried?'

'Well, the last the few times we've seen you . . .' and her voice trailed off.

'What?'

'Well. You've just seemed a bit distant, that's all.'

'Distant?'

'It means far away.'

'Oh right, I thought it meant something else.'

'Well, you've seemed a bit quiet, withdrawn. Like you were treading on eggshells with your Stuart. I could be wrong.'

'You are wrong, actually. Everything's fine.'

'And then, of course, you've cancelled the last few Sundays. Coming here for your dinner. You used to do that all the time at one point, and now . . .'

Her voice trailed off again sadly.

'We've just been busy. We like to . . . mix things up a little anyway.'

Truth be told, things had been a bit tense between me and Stuart recently. And they tended to get worse when people wanted to talk about my job. Stuart got completely overlooked. In the early days of my time on the show he'd not minded, in fact he'd enjoyed basking in the reflected glory of my new-found fame and was happy to take a back seat, it was like my 'success' was a sunlamp and he was happy to stick on some protective goggles, lie back and soak up the rays. But lately he seemed to find it a drag. And as Mum was still as obsessed with *Acacia Avenue* as ever, even going to Sandalan had become something of an obstacle course. *OK, great, we got through taking our coats off without Mum rhapsodizing about my latest storyline. Result! Oh, hang on . . . Bollocks! She mentioned my latest* TV Times *cover while putting the kettle on . . . etc.* When caught in those situations these days I grew more and more uneasy, always trying to involve Stuart in the conversation I was having, but increasingly people seemed to want a slice of me and nothing of him. I was the rocky road pie to his marzipan square. It was part of the reason I'd suggested he do the *Hiya!* magazine interview with me. So he felt a part of it all. I was amazed when he'd jumped at the chance.

Mum was going on . . .

'Of course, I'm not expecting you round here every Sunday for a roast but, well . . . We get so lonely, Jodie.'

I sat down and actually heard violins start to play. That's when I realized I'd sat on the remote control and the radio had come on playing some old Electric Light Orchestra song. I quickly switched it off.

'Well, I'm sure we'll be round soon.'

'When?!' She nearly bit my ear off.

'I dunno.'

'Shall we talk dates?'

'I'm nowhere near the calendar.'

'Only, what I was thinking was, Val and Vernon would love to meet you, so I thought I'd do a little dinner party. Kill two birds with the one stone.'

'Right.'

'I mean, nothing fancy. It'll be nothing compared to the level you're used to these days, but . . . well, you know. Never forget your roots an' all that.'

'That sounds great,' I murmured, with all the enthusiasm of a death-row prisoner who'd just been told what sort of perm they'd be getting before heading for the electric chair.

'Oh good. Well, text a few dates over to me and we'll take it from there. And, you know, it'll all be very casual.'

*

Mum was wearing a long dress when she answered the front door.

'Jodie! Stuart! Entray!' she bellowed in a very posh accent that made her sound almost as ridiculous as she looked. She saw my bewildered glance at her red floral-print maxi dress, which I now realized was actually a very flared strapless jumpsuit. The sort of thing J-Lo wore to go to Kwik Save.

'You look nice, Sandra,' Stuart said as he handed her a bottle of white in a Tesco's bag.

'Thanks, Stuart. Alan says I look like Liza Tarbuck.'

'I didn't say Liza Tarbuck, I said fucking Jimmy Tarbuck.' That was Dad coming out of the bedroom.

Mum spun round – on what I now saw were cork platforms, her dangly silver hooped earrings whiplashing her cheeks in the process – and hissed, 'No swearing in front of our guests!'

Dad rolled his eyes and carried on into the through lounge.

'I don't mind a bit of swearing, San,' insisted Stuart.

Mum cast him a contemptuous look, then boomed, 'Val and Vernon are already here. Shall we follow through?'

She flung an arm out towards the open door and marched into the living room. She had to really lift her feet up in the jumpsuit to stop herself tripping over her flares. It made her look like she was doing some kind of army-based keep-fit routine. We did indeed follow through.

'This is Val!' Mum was pointing to a woman on the settee sporting a similar flared jumpsuit to Mum's, except hers was orange. They must have got a job lot on one of their many days out together. Val had a coquettish look on her face, a bit like Cilla Black used to have before she sprung a surprise on someone. It was an unsettling mixture of excitement and confidence that something fantastic was about to happen. She jumped to her feet, flung her arms wide, like that big statue of Jesus in Brazil (but with a maxi-dress-that-was-really-slacks on), and went, 'Jo-DEEEE! Come and give Vally a hug!'

Great. That's just what I needed. Physical contact with someone who spoke in the third person. She enveloped me in bingo wings and nylon, and I was overcome with a heady aroma of Elnett and Anais Anais as she scratched my back enthusiastically with what felt like Swiss Army Knife nails. She rested her head on my shoulder and whispered, 'Mummy's told me so much about you. And now I'm beginning to see. Everything really is true. You're a poppet.'

What was I, six?

She then pushed me away, but clung onto me, looking me up and down like a new rug she was considering buying, shook her head – with no moveage of hair – and repeated, 'An absolute poppet. Isn't she a poppet, Vern?'

I contorted my head round to see her husband, Vernon, stood by the serving hatch, jingling some change in his pocket with one hand and holding a pint of frothy lager in the other. The most striking thing about him was that he had bright orange hair, worn in a style similar to Chucky from the horror films. He broke into a smile when I looked round and raised his glass towards me.

'I bet you drink champagne, don't you, Jodie? Hmm? Nice cold, ice cold champagne, my lovely? Hmm?'

'Erm.'

'You telly box stars are all the same, I'll bet. Now!'

And she left me standing in the middle of the room as she turned her back on me, bent over and went rummaging in a handbag the size of a small elephant.

'And this is Stuart,' Dad added from the kitchen, coming

through with two glasses of something fizzy for me and Stu. Stuart wasn't a big fan of champagne, so it was obvious they were doing this for show, to impress Val and Vernon. The whole evening was clearly turning out to be a mission to impress.

'Hi, Stu my lovely!' Val called, still rummaging, arse in the air. I could make out some serious VPL. The lines appeared to be a mile apart. I looked away. Mum appeared from the kitchen with a plate of tiny white plasticky blobs.

'I did quail's eggs with celery salt. Hope that's acceptable.'

'Vern can't eat celery, San. Not since the bypass. Has an unfortunate effect on his rectum, doesn't it, Vern?'

'Well, it's only celery salt.' Mum was sounding wounded.

'On your own head be it, San. Well, your own toilet, actually.'

And with that she sprang up. I could see she had a paperback in her hand and was jabbing it towards me. It was one of several books that had been published recently, allegedly detailing the back stories of various *Acacia Avenue* characters. This one was the one about Sister Agatha, *They Know Not What They Do*, and displayed a watercolour painting of my ugly mug on the cover, staring pensively into the middle distance. It was a look that either said, I'm just concentrating on Jesus, or, Can't for the life of me remember if I left the iron on.

'Now,' she said, 'would you mind signing this for my lovely neighbour Pauline? She's gone blind with her sugars and I just know you'll make her day.'

'Sign it big, Jodie. If she's blind,' Mum urged.

'I could puncture it in Braille if anyone's got a pin?' I suggested.

'Have you got a pin, Vern?' Val worried.

'That . . . was a joke,' I explained.

'Just as well, coz she can't read Braille,' Vern said, and I couldn't tell if he was being serious or joking.

'Dyslexic,' Val mouthed, like it was a curse.

'Stuart's a plasterer, aren't you, Stu?' Dad was trying to bring Stuart out of his shell.

'That's right.' And out of his shell he popped.

'Always good to have a skill.' There was something of the bossy primary school teacher about Val, as she practically took my eye out passing me a permanent marker to sign the book with. 'Vern's rag-rolled the whole of my downstairs.'

'Too much information,' Stuart murmured under his breath, and I took this as a good sign that he was in a positive mood, content to be my 'plus one' in what was turning out to be a very intimate personal appearance. I giggled nervously and Dad chuckled into a serviette.

Val was going, 'What? What was that?'

Mum offered her a quail's egg – hopefully to distract her or shut her up – but Val shooed her away with the shake of a heavily braceleted wrist.

'Saving myself for my starter, San.'

'I'm not doing a starter,' Mum gasped, with all the panic of a murderer who'd just had their alibi quashed.

'Oh, well pass 'em here, kid.' And with that she grabbed a handful, like she was nobbling some M&M's, and bobbed them into her mouth in one go. Eating didn't stop her speaking.

'Be good to lose a bit of weight anyway, eh Vern?'

'We could always stop for fish and chips on the way home!' He pulled an 'Aren't I hilarious?' face and Val guffawed.

'Oh wait till you hear about this dinner party we went to last night, San. Oh you'll howl.'

'Shall we sit down, Stu?' I ventured. He nodded and we set up camp on the settee as Val sashayed up and down the through lounge, calling through to Mum, who was having a nervous breakdown in the kitchen and alternately turning her head to look at us.

'We went to Ruby and Naveen's house. Lovely semi round the back of the Polish drive-through? Jaroslaw and his boys bring the Daewoo up lovely. Anyway, Ruby's always trying to show off with her alleged culinary skills. Well, you'll never guess what she served us for the main course. What was it called again, Vern? Karen Carpenter sang a song about it.'

'Solitaire?' he joked, doing his funny gurn again. Stu and I laughed politely.

'Jambalaya?' offered Dad nervously, then shot a look towards the serving hatch.

'Jambalaya! That's it. Oh it was hideous, wasn't it, Vern? I had to tip some in my clutch while she wasn't looking. It was like chicken and mussels and yellow rice. Yellow rice, San! Oh I could've vomited, couldn't I, Vern? We had to stop at the Chinky on the way home and get a portion of chips.'

'That's racist,' said Stu quietly, with the air of a man seriously losing the will to live. I knew how he felt.

'No, it's a really lovely Chinky,' argued Val. 'I've written them letters in the past. They've got one of them pinned up on the corkboard.' Then she looked at me. 'Jambalaya, Jodie. What on earth was she thinking?'

I gave an 'I don't know' look.

'Jamba-friggin-laya, Jodie,' said Vern in a 'Would you believe it?' way.

'Anyway,' Val said, brightening as she turned towards the serving hatch, 'what you cooking, San?'

We heard a plate smash in the kitchen.

Mum's Jambalaya was much nicer than Ruby's, according to Val and Vernon, though Mum went frostily quiet as we pushed the mulchy ricey mess around our plates and gurgled appreciative hums. Of course her silence went unnoticed by Val, who hadn't shut up since we arrived, and she continued her breathless monologue once we sat down. Mostly she wanted to know *all* about *Acacia Avenue*, so she fired off a list of questions to me, which she invariably answered for herself before I'd managed to get my words out. Mostly it went like this:

Q: The one thing I've always wanted to know, Jodie, is how you learn all those goddam lines? What am I like, Vern? I shout at the screen! 'How do they do it? How do they learn all those goddam lines?!' It drives Vern mad.

A: Well, I suppose what I'd do if I was learning lines would be, I'd get a bottle of plonk out and just read and read and read and read. And hopefully it would sink in, d'you know what I'm saying, Jodie?

Q: What's Nona Newman really like?

A: I bet she's lovely. I saw a gorgeous *This is Your Life* about her and she came across lovely, didn't she, Vern? When her husband sang 'The Rose' to her, I was in bits. All that success, that gorgeous house on the Wirral, and she still had to have a mastectomy. I take my hat off to her, I really do.

Q: Oh I hear there's a serial killer going to be let loose on the avenue. What's the goss?

A: Well I suppose you can't tell me, coz you'd have to kill me and all that. But I'd really like to know, wouldn't I, Vern? You see I'm quite clever. And what I try and do is, I try and predict the outcome of each storyline. Don't I, Vern? It drives him up the wall, Jodie, it really does. I think, but obviously I'm not a hundred per cent sure on this, but I think it's going to be that street sweeper, don't I, Vern? Coz he's got a sly look in his eyes and, well, we all saw what he did with that Lambrini at the factory Christmas party. Oh, I thought that was evil.

Q: How many wimples does Sister Agatha actually have?

A: Coz I say to Vern, don't I, Vern? I say, I bet she's got—

At this point Mum practically spat across the table, 'Val, if you want to ask so many questions, maybe you should try and let Jodie answer them.'

Val didn't appear to blink for the longest time.

'You're hogging the airways again, Val,' grimaced Vernon. But instead of appearing upset, Val flickered back into life and chuckled, finding herself a complete hoot.

'Oh, what am I like? I'm always doing that, Jodie. Aren't I, Vern? I'm always hogging the airwaves. Drives him demented, doesn't it, Vern?'

'I know the feeling.' Mum sounded bitter and a hush descended on the table.

At this point I didn't know where to put myself. Stu was looking as tormented as a BNP member forced to attend a rehearsal of the London Gospel Choir. He was holding his head at a funny angle, as if he'd cricked his neck, as though if he averted his gaze from the table and stared at the china praying hands ornament that my mum loved so much and thought looked 'distinguished' on her nest of tables, then he wasn't really here and this wasn't really happening. Mum looked as if she was going to burst out crying; Dad and Vernon were chomping away as though nothing had happened – typical men – while Val kept nudging her Jambalaya round her plate as if Mum had served up dead baby's entrails. Mum cleared her throat and looked at me, trying to smile, and said, 'Any news on the Soap Awards, love?'

Oh God. Did she have to keep this thread of conversation going? Couldn't we talk about something else? I looked at Stu, half expecting him to have a gun pointing at his head and a

sign round his neck reading, 'Don't think I won't do it, bitch.'
He was still intrigued by the praying hands.

I shrugged and replied, 'Well, I know I'm on the long list.'

'What's a long list?' asked Val.

And so I explained the ins and outs of the selection process
for the awards. Although I was awkward, tentative at first, I soon
got on a roll, seasoning my explanation with provocative bits of
gossip about the other cast members, which, of course, Val and
Mum lapped up. By the time I'd finished my impromptu stand-
up routine, I noticed that Stuart's plate was tellingly clean, like
he'd lifted it up and licked it repeatedly. I hurried to finish mine
off as I noticed I was lagging behind even Val. As I hoovered
the last of my yellow rice down I prayed that someone would
ask Stu something. Anything – 'What was it you do again, Stu?'
'How's life in plastering, Stu?' 'Should I fake my orgasms, Stu?'
– But they didn't. And as I heard Val asking me, 'What did
it actually feel like when you got the part of Sister Agatha?' I
decided now would be a brilliant time to go to the bathroom.

'I'm so sorry Val, but I need to visit the little girls' room.'

'See, Vern? Even celebrities need to poop!'

I quickly looked at Vern and gushed, 'I'm only going for a
wee!' quickly.

'I'm mad like that, Jodie!' Val was saying as I stood up from
the table and gave Mum a thumbs up about the empty plate,
'I say to Vern while we're watching telly. "You might think
Hyacinth Bucket's got it all, Vern, but even she poops like the
rest of us."'

'Well that's true, Val,' Mum chipped in, 'coz I've actually
been in the loos at the green room at the studios.'

'I imagine a lot of them are hooked on laxatives, am I right,
San?'

I pecked Stu's head and ruffled his hair as I passed. He

flinched, alarmed at my sudden advance and probably sensing I was doing it for effect, as if to say, I'm not the only person here who works. Stu's here and he does, too. But it made no difference to Mum, who continued to describe, in minute detail, exactly what her olfactory senses recalled from her brief visits to the ladies' loos at work. Amazing what could pass as acceptable dinner party chat when laced with the spectacle of celebrity.

I didn't actually need to go to the toilet. I was going in the hope of instigating a conversation change, so I touched up my make-up and sat on the side of the bath, looking around, bored. The bathroom wall opposite the bath was festooned with framed family photos from across the years. Me and Our Joey in an awkward school photo, Dad and Mum on their wedding day, that kind of thing. But on the right-hand side a new picture had been put up, taken from a magazine. It took me a few seconds to decipher who it was. It was Our Joey. It was a gorgeous black and white photo, taken by some really cool photographer, and Joey looked amazing. The image was startling. Black background. Our Joey lit from below in a faded denim jacket, which was half falling off his toned, naked flesh. Taut neck, square chin, his lips pouting in ecstasy, his eyes shut, like he was reaching orgasm. In his hand he was holding a bottle of milk. The lid was off and what looked like a cloud of talcum powder was exploding all around his head, so it looked like he was being showered in either milk or cocaine. The caption alongside the image read, 'MR MILK. The white stuff's good for you.' I looked closer, my pupils practically touching the frame, and saw that it was in fact a page from *Wallpaper* magazine. I felt at once insanely jealous – that magazine was so cool, much cooler than any publication I'd ever been in – and insanely proud. That was my little brother! No wonder Trudy had said he was hot. He looked incredible. He looked like a big, butch, grown-up bloke. A proper full-on bloke!

My brother, who used to traipse round the back garden with a sleeping bag round his shoulders pretending to be Miss World now looked like a bruiser. He had bloody pecs, for God's sake! And he was obviously doing so well in his job that he was becoming famous.

The other feeling I had was one of sadness. There we were in those childhood snaps, looking like two peas in a pod, the best of mates, and we were, we had been. But now our lives had taken us in different directions and we had absolutely zero contact. Our Joey would have been able to make me laugh tonight. He'd have found Val camp, entertaining, delightful. He'd have made it all bearable. There he was, off being successful in his chosen field, and here I was, doing well and feeling miserable. And part of that misery, if that wasn't too dramatic a word, was because I no longer had him in my life. And that was his choice. And I didn't know why. I'd written to him when I'd broken my leg, but never heard back. The truth was probably that I just didn't register any more. He'd managed so long without me, what need did he have of me now? And if he worked in nightclubs and was doing so well, he was probably never at home to see *Acacia Avenue*. He probably hated the soaps these days. He probably only read trendy magazines like *Wallpaper*, so what would he care about my career, my life? Fair play to him. He'd apologized for his bad behaviour, waited two years for a reply from me, received it and no doubt decided to move on.

I suddenly had a memory of Our Joey. Dancing round the through lounge in one of Mum's skirts. He must only have been about eight. I remember watching from the kitchen, transfixed. I wanted to laugh, to call out that he was a knobhead, but I couldn't. I admired him too much. I admired the way he could dance, not caring who saw or what people thought. I wanted to walk back into the through lounge and find it empty, table folded away, and Sister Sledge on the CD as Our Joey, eyes shut, lost himself in 'We Are Family'.

There was an urgent knock at the door. I hurriedly flushed the toilet and approached the door. I wanted it to be him. I wanted him to be stood there, tears in his eyes, all big and butch like in his photo, but with a sleeping bag round his shoulders, saying, 'I fucked up, Jodie.'

And for me to say, 'I fucked up, too, Joey.'

I turned the handle nervously. Stuart was stood there with a face like thunder.

'I'm going home.'

'What?'

'It's doing my head in. I've told them I don't feel well, been off-colour for a few days.'

'I'll come with you,' I said as panic rose inside me like mercury in a thermometer.

'No, stay. You're in your element.'

'No, I'm not.'

'You love it.'

'I hate it.' The look he gave me told me he didn't believe me. He was heading for the front door. I ran into the through lounge and grabbed my bag.

'I'd . . . better go with Stu,' I said breathlessly as I grabbed my bag.

'But I've defrosted an Arctic Roll,' said Mum, stung.

'I know, but if he's not feeling well.'

'Let her go, love,' Dad said awkwardly.

Val was looking at me despondently. I kissed, hugged, air-kissed again and ran to the front door, which Stu had left open. I saw him dawdling at the end of the street, head down, hands in pockets, and in that moment I knew the night was not going to end well.

'Stuart!' I called out as I cantered down the path. 'Wait for me!'

He didn't look back. I ran to catch up with him and tried to link arms, but he shrugged me off.

'Stu, what is it?' I bleated, despite knowing exactly what the problem was. He didn't reply. 'This isn't working, is it?' I ventured, hoping to elicit a response.

It worked. Without looking at me he said, 'So what do we do? Split up?'

'No, we work it through. Unless you want me to go.'

'You make me feel like a nobody,' he said sadly. Not that you could really say those words and sound thrilled.

'I don't. That's not fair.'

'Is that right?'

'It's knobs like Val that make you feel like that, not me.'

The streets were so quiet. The only sound was my heels on the paving stones. Stu made no sound in his trainers.

'You love it,' he repeated, this time disparagingly.

'Oh shut up. Will you listen to yourself? You didn't mind gegging in and getting a slice of the action when we did that interview for *Hiya!* magazine. You loved me being famous then.'

'Yeah, well I was a knob. And now I hate it. OK?'

'Then I'll go,' I offered. I wasn't sure why, I wasn't sure where, but it had to be better than coping with Stu's attitude to my work.

'You can't. We've got a joint mortgage. We're trapped.'

'Oh piss off, Stu, that's fucking ridiculous.'

'Oh, is it?'

Anger swelled in me.

'Yeah, you're being a fucking knob now. So I'm on the telly, so people wanna talk about it, deal with it.'

He looked at me, anger burning in his eyes.

'You don't mind the benefits it brings you. Posh flat, money to burn. Maybe I should just go on the dole and we'll see how much ale you can sink then.'

It was provocative. It was meant to be provocative. But what I was trying to provoke was an apology. An admission that he was in the wrong. Reassurance that things weren't good and we could sort this out.

What I actually provoked was a smack in the face.

TWENTY-SEVEN

From: Jodie McFee (Liverpool)
To: Matthew Martin Maxwell (France)
Subject: HELP!

Matthew if you there will you go into chat and talk to me? Please? I in a bit of a mess and need someone to talk to. I am in work and I'm a bit pissed. That's bad, right? And when I say pissed I mean tipsy rather than American pissed which means pissed off. I'm not completely pissed but I can tell I've had a drink. You'll probably think I'm a driunken lush and never want to speak me again but at least I'm being honest. Thing is I something really bad last night. I was a bit tipsy (running theme) and I fell over on my way home from my Mum's and now I a big black eye. It's really obvious. Now I know usually having a black eye would be no big deal when you work in plastics company as administrative assistant stroke secretary but today is a special day when they are filming us and we have to go in front of the cameras and talk about our jobs for a website or something so there was no getting out of coming in and now I have I wish I hadn't. I only had a drink this morning coz my eye was hurting so much and I thought numb the pain, plus I was a bit shaken up by it all and thought it might steady my nerve. Me and Stu aren't getting on at the moment (but he didn't push me over

or punch me I genuinely fell. Bit worried folks here will think
he did) so I can't talk to him. He just seems pissed off all the
time, like he's jealous of my success. (I am a really successful
administrative assistant, in the Plastics world I have a really
good reputation) Anyway I have come into work, think I said that,
and this woman in the office Yvonne (sometimes I call her Nona
in old messages), saw my eye when I went into her office by
mistake and she's told Eva (the boss) and Eva is coming to my
office to see me in a bit and all is too hideous for words. I want
to run away but I've got nowhere to run to. If I don't hear back
from you I'll understand. I'm a nightmare. My life is chaos. I'm
burdening you with all this shit and all you've ever done is be
nice to me and are not a bastard and have the nicest smile (and
the dirtiest way with words when you want to, but it's not about
that) but if you've got a moment it'd be good to hear from you.
Jodiexxx

    PS. I am a bad person.

Who was it that said a woman is like a tea bag? You don't know
how strong she is till she's put in hot water. I didn't feel strong
as I turned from my iPad and looked at my reflection in the
dressing-room mirror. The only thing I was strong about was
lying. I was the tea bag that came out scorched and insisted,
'I fell into the hot water. I was a bit worse for wear and just
slipped in, then couldn't get out.' People fell over all the time
and had injuries to show for it. This was fine, it was going to be
fine. If only this black coffee would sober me up. I was shaking,
I now realized. Was that the shock of seeing myself? No. I'd
done bugger all except check my reflection every few minutes
since it happened. Each urgent glance found me hoping against
hope that the purple swelling around my left eye would have
miraculously gone down, but each time the colour darkened

and the puffiness increased. And with every passing moment I could feel my eye closing. I struggled to keep it open, feeling it weeping slightly, but it was hard to dab it with a tissue as every time I tried it felt like I was taking a hot needle to it.

It was all my fault. I hadn't made Stuart punch me; this was divine retribution for sure. The universe knew I had been misbehaving online with a man in the South of France and had accorded the correct punishment. I'd been waiting for the longest time for my misdemeanours to come back and slap me round the face, and now they had. Literally. Stuart was just a conduit, the universe's messenger. God that sounded dark and apocalyptic. I knew on one level that he'd just done it because he was a wife-battering prick, but my guilty conscience had gone into overdrive.

Maybe the coffee was making me shake. Maybe if I put some vodka in it that might stop me shaking? But as I took the smallish bottle from my bag – Hmm, it was almost empty, had it leaked? No, the bag was dry – there was a knock at the door and Eva barged in. I hurriedly tried to return the bottle to the bag, but in my haste dropped it on the floor. OK, so that didn't look good. Plus it was spinning round like I was playing some sort of daring party game. I looked up. Someone was with Eva. No doubt Ming, ready to tell me how we could play this with the press. God, we didn't have to tell the press, did we? But as my seeing eye focused, I saw that Eva's henchwoman wasn't Ming. It was Mum.

'What are you doing here?' I asked as she sat silently on the settee while Eva shut the door. Eva then joined Mum on the couch, the whole thing done so elegantly I realized they must have choreographed their approach before arriving. They looked like Cagney and Lacey sat there staring at me, waiting for me to break down and confess to my crime. Eva even had a beaker of takeaway coffee, just like Lacey would have done. Or was it Cagney? I bet Mum wished she had a coffee, too, just so she could look the part. One of them would start talking about their husband Harvey soon, pronouncing it Hoivee, because they came from Noo Yoik.

'Jodie, did Stuart do this to you?' asked Mum.

God she was loving this. She was loving the excuse to be back in the studios, at the centre of the action. I bet she'd phoned Val on the way in and squealed with excitement, 'I'm going in!' I said nothing. But when she spoke again, I could hear her voice breaking and I realized I was wrong.

'Jodie, please. Don't cover up for him.'

I had to make her feel better. I had to continue the lie.

'Mum. I was pissed. I fell over.'

I knew this was serious when she didn't tell me off for swearing. Eva looked at my Mum, who shrugged. I came up with a genius idea and blurted it out before thinking it through.

'Maybe I've got a drink problem. Did you ever think of that?'

And as if to illustrate my point, I bent, picked up the vodka bottle from the floor and waggled it before me like Charlie Walsh used to do with one of his trademark chilli-infused olive oils.

'Well, you're obviously drunk now,' Eva concurred, clearly thinking I was under the impression that the bottle was a maraca and I was part of a salsa band.

'I'm not actually,' I said and threw the bottle in the bin. Except I misjudged and it hit Eva on the shins. 'Whoops. Sorry, Eva.'

Eva rolled her eyes. Oh God, was she going to fire me? Had she brought Mum in because she wanted me to clear my dressing room and needed Mum to help?

'At least I came in,' I went on. 'Last time I just bunked off and made out I was . . .' My voice trailed off as I realized I was incriminating myself.

Mum paled and gulped, 'This has happened before?'

'The last time I fell over,' I explained.

'Fall over a lot, do you?' asked Eva, not losing eye contact.

'I . . . guess I'm kinda clumsy.'

Eva shook her head. Mum sighed.

'Jodie,' Eva said, losing patience. 'Whatever has or hasn't happened, you are in no fit state to film. No matter how brilliant our make-up artists are, there's no way they can cover up that monstrosity.'

I flinched, feeling slightly offended. It might have been a black eye, but she was still criticizing my looks.

'Never mind what scenes you are meant to be shooting today.'

Oh yes. We were slap bang in the middle of a domestic violence storyline. Sister Agatha was meant to find a bloodied and bruised Finchley in the vestry and tell her, 'They always do it again. No matter how many lies they peddle. Oh they're full of apologies, sweetness and light, butter wouldn't melt. Pay no heed. Get out, Finchley. Get out.'

Guess that wouldn't look too brilliant if the soothsayer looked worse than the beneficiary of her wisdom. I nodded my head. Alanis Morissette would've had something to say about that particular irony.

'OK, well here's my solution,' she continued. 'I am not a detective, I haven't got time, frankly, to find out whether you're telling me the truth or not. And as such, I have to take what you say at face value, even if I do think it's a crock of shit.'

I shifted uncomfortably in my seat. And there was me thinking I was such a good liar.

421

'Actually, it's funny you should say that, coz I was thinking you looked a bit like Lagney and Casey.'

Oh God. Did I really just say that? Shut up, Jodie! Eva ignored it and carried on. Maybe I hadn't actually said it. Maybe I'd just said it in my head.

'You've told me you fell over when drunk. You have presented yourself to film in no fit physical state. You are also intoxicated on the premises. I will therefore give you a written warning that this cannot continue. I am going to insist you have two weeks off to get yourself together. But in two weeks' time you present yourself here, ready to film, no injuries and no alcohol in your system. Whatever you need to do in the next two weeks to make sure that happens, you do it.'

Wow! Two weeks off? But . . .

'But I'm involved in a major storyline.'

'You were. We'll give all your lines to Ari. No one is indispensable on this show, Jodie. Just remember that. This is incredibly inconvenient for everyone. Schedules will have to be reworked, scripts rewritten, the lot. Maybe you'll consider that before you next decide to have a drink and fall over.'

I nodded contritely.

'I've arranged for a car to take you home. It's waiting just outside the green room. Your mum will go with you.'

I nodded. Oh God.

'Thanks, Eva.'

I stood up. Mum rushed to my side to take my arm, but I shrugged her off.

'I'm not an invalid.'

Eva stood and straightened her pencil skirt.

'I'd put some sunglasses on if I were you. The other actors will be told you've had a fall and are recuperating. If you choose to disagree with this it'll be you that looks like a liar, not me.'

'No, Eva. Thank you, Eva.'

'Yes, thank you, Eva,' Mum echoed.

Eva opened the door and hurried out. I looked at Mum.

'Where d'you want to go?'

But before I could answer, someone else was coming into the room. I turned and saw Yvonne. Mum practically fell into a curtsy.

'Miss Carsgrove!'

'Could I have a quick word with Jodie? Alone?'

She could've asked to crap in Mum's handbag and she'd have agreed.

'Of course. I'll step outside.'

Yvonne nodded. No pleasantries here. I got the feeling she, too, was about to give me a stern ticking off. She sank onto my settee, her housecoat billowing around her. When she looked at me, it was as if she was staring straight into my soul.

Although we rode home in silence, Yvonne's words rang like tinnitus in my ears. I'd thought she was going to be horrible. I'd thought she was going to go all prima donna-ish and accuse me of being unprofessional. But instead she'd said, 'I, too, was in a relationship like yours. I thought he loved me and that his volatility meant great passion. And when he hit me I thought I'd let him down, because surely he was my protector? He wasn't. He was my tormentor. And the only person I let down was myself, for not getting out of there sooner. Run for the hills if you have to. But whatever you do, don't go back.'

And then something else popped into my head and kept spinning around like a psychotic glitter ball. Something Yvonne had said to me on my first day at the studios: 'One day I'll tell you all about me and Rupert Dale.'

Had she? Had she just told me? Was Rupert the man who'd beaten her? Mild-mannered, if slightly arrogant Rupert? Was he the man she'd had to get away from? Oh God, this was too much for my little brain to handle. And surely I needed to concentrate my energies on my own situation and what I needed to do now. I closed my eyes, trying to block out the confusion, but even that made my eye shoot with pain. I felt something touch my arm and I flinched, but turning to look it was, of course, only Mum.

'We're here, Jodie. There's no press or nothing.'

I looked out of the window. This wasn't my street. This was her street. She'd brought me to Sandalan. I turned back, confused.

'Thought you'd want to come here,' she said gently. Oh please would she stop being so nice? I shook my head. 'Why would you want to go back there?'

'It's where I live.'

'Well . . . we could go back. You could pack a few things, then we could come back here, if you like.'

Meaning it's what she would have liked.

'No,' I said, trying to muster a strength I couldn't feel. 'I need to work out what to do next.'

She turned away now, looking out of the window, sighed, then looked back at our confused driver. She apologized and told him my address. As we drove along I spoke softly and calmly, 'Can Dad get someone over to change the locks?'

'He wants to murder Stu.'

'Can he?'

'Of course.'

'Thanks.'

We continued to drive. I saw all the familiar sights of Liverpool passing me by as if in slow motion. As I caught my first glint of the Mersey, I added, 'Can he do it this morning? Stu'll be back later.'

'Of course.'

As we drove alongside the river and round the side of my apartment block, for the first time I thought how lovely it would be to jump in the river and swim in it. To just float to the bottom and live with the plankton and the bullrushes, or whatever you found on riverbeds. Feet wedged in the sand. A sunken relic that no one cared about and who didn't have to make any decisions, good or bad. Who breathed in water and blew out bubbles and just had fish for company.

From: Matthew Martin Maxwell (France)
To: Jodie McFee (Liverpool)
Subject: Black Eyed Pea!
Hey Pea!

How's it going? Are you still sat inside all day licking your wounds? Or would you like me to come over and lick them for you? Actually, that sounds a bit gross. The image of you licking your wounds conjures up you laid there on your day bed (you have a day bed in my imagination. Deal with it!) in a towelling robe, with an impossibly long lizard-like tongue, lapping at your bruised eye. Poor poppet. It both tickles me and makes me feel a bit blurgh. Not that you make me feel blurgh. It's just the image.

Moving swiftly on.

You know when you asked me what I thought of Stu? Well, I don't really know what to say. It's almost like you want me to say I hate his guts! But I don't think I do. I know you guys are going through a hard time at the moment, but I don't really see what he's done that's all that wrong. Unless he's fallen out of love with you. And as you're so lovable, I'd say that was completely wrong. So yeah, I hate his fucking GUTS! But listen, he can't be all that bad. You're a bright girl. You chose him. He chose you. Hang on, just munching on some sour grapes here as it was yet another case of wrong place, wrong time. #storyofmylife!

It's probably good that you've chosen to take two weeks off work. It would drive me nuts working in a big office like that (no offence) and if, like you say, your life's feeling a bit out of control just now, it's probably a really good idea to chill and sort out all the shit that goes on in our heads from time to time. Sure you'll feel better by the end of it. Sometimes just knocking the booze on the head for a bit sorts out most of our problems.

Anyway, chooks. I've got to head to the beach now. Gonna be around later, see how you're fixed. And I hope you're fixed soon.

One day at a time . . .

Take care, Miss Pea

M xx

From: Josie McFee (Liverpool)
To: Matthew Martin Maxwell (France)
Subject: Black Eyed Pea!

I am alternating between bags of ice and raw steak as a fetching eye mask. OK, and sometimes frozen burgers. Three days on and the swelling and purplosity is subsiding. Thank GOD. Don't think I'll be winning any beauty pageants soon, though with the amount of meat about my person I could give Lady Gaga a run for her money. Might even start calling you Alejandro (Alejandro) (the repeat is important).

Mum's brilliant. She's round here again, cleaning, ironing, rambling on about the neighbours (hers and mine) or what Val and Vernon have said etc., etc.

Stu hasn't come back. He might be off with some fancy piece. I feel a huge sense of relief. Gonna have a snooze now and listen to that video you posted on my wall. I love the Lightning Seeds.

Love you, Jodie xxx

I was such a liar. I didn't love him, I didn't know him. How could you love someone you didn't know? Plus, I had seen Stu. He'd been back every day. I knew full well where he was. But the lies I told online were fine. They were a fantasy, just like my online relationship with Matthew. It didn't mean anything because it wasn't real. What was real was the pain in my heart and the pain in my cheek and eye. Well, if that was real life, no wonder I wanted to retreat into this golden land of the inter-net. It was my pill. Matthew only ever said lovely things to me. It was as if I plugged myself into him for short bursts at a time and came out feeling cleansed. Maybe he was dialysis in human-ish form.

But then, in the middle of the night, I might wake with a fright as I heard a noise outside, convinced it was Stu breaking in, and I'd realize that it wasn't Jodie McGee who was healed by Matthew, but Jodie McFee, office administrator. And she was just a persona I'd magicked up. I'd not been 100 per cent honest, he'd only heard a fictionalized version of what had happened to me. But the balm he poured on, with his constant messages and the rapidity with which he replied, soothed and relaxed me. Madness, I knew it was madness, but it was my secret. It was special to me, mine and mine alone. And for someone who felt pretty much like public property most of the time, it was a fresh and exhilarating feeling.

Stuart had been very sackcloth and ashes since the punch. I'd somehow managed to scramble to my feet afterwards and run. I'd lost a shoe as I bolted but didn't stop to pick it up. I'd got a cab home and put the chain on the door so he couldn't get in. I'd heard him rattling the front door about half an hour later, but after five minutes the rattling stopped and I assumed he'd gone away. I'd not slept, I'd sat up drinking. I'd played a mix tape that Our Joey had made me years ago, which I'd found in his room at Sandalan while we'd been staying there, and I'd put it on at full blast and danced round the living room. It contained a lot of Ace of Base. All that she wanted was another baby, apparently, and as I sang and danced along it was like the night hadn't happened. But then, before I knew it, it was morning and time to go to work. When I stumbled into the communal hallway I half expected Stu to be sleeping on our doormat, but instead, where I thought he might be, I saw the shoe I'd lost the night before. He must have left it there. I didn't touch it.

Dad had called a locksmith out who changed the locks, so that when Stu returned from work that night – after sending me millions of apologetic texts and numerous answerphone messages, all of which I'd deleted – he couldn't get in. He'd cooed several more apologies through the letterbox, then asked for some clothes as he was going to sleep on a mate's couch. I threw some out of the window for him.

Every day since then a bouquet of flowers had arrived for me, each with increasingly contrite messages on the cards. The flat was beginning to look like a chamber of rest. I was pretty damn sure it was going to be his funeral and not mine.

He texted every day, phoned both my mobile and the landline, to the point where I unplugged the phone and didn't bother charging my mobile – cue frantic visit from Mum who'd convinced herself I'd thrown myself, like Stu's clothes, headlong out of the window.

I hoped by pushing him away and cutting him out of my life I'd be able to surf along on a wave called denial, but of course the shooting pains to my eye and cheek were a constant reminder that this *had* happened and there was no escaping it. If we wore other people's love on our faces in smiles, we wore their hatred in bruises. Or I did. Many couples existed in seething bitterness without resorting to physical violence, why did ours have to be so complicated? There was love, there was camaraderie, but there were also huge pockets of indifference and anxiety, and I spent so much time walking gingerly on egg-shells I was surprised my lower limbs weren't deformed, like some travelling circus freak: Roll up! Roll up! See the battered lady! See her negotiate a thousand eggshells and get a punch for her labours!

But was there hatred? Did I hate him? I thought about this almost constantly. I hated what he'd done. I hated the physical evidence he'd left on me of his own frustrations about life, but hatred seemed too strong a word. I was disappointed in him, I was frustrated by him, I was furious with him, but if there was hatred there then it was a low-level crackle of interference, interrupting the radio show of our relationship. But what did I do with the radio now? Switch it off? Silence it once and for all? Or re-tune it and let the show play out more clearly, and hope against hope that there'd never be interference again?

As the purple bruising faded, so the scales fell from my eyes. If it wasn't already clear to Mum and Dad that I'd not really been tipsy and fallen over, then it was confirmed when Stu appeared on their doorstep one night and broke down and apologized. They visited me the next day to tell me, and I knew I couldn't lie to them any more. If there'd been no surge of hate before, then there was now as they sat in the apartment politely drinking tea and talking in hushed, mournful tones. I hated Stu for what he was putting them through. The pain and confusion etched on their faces. The quietly bubbling anger in Dad, the plaintive ache of Mum. What had they done to deserve this? How dare he? How *dare* he?

Dad was all for me reporting it to the police, but I was adamant I wouldn't. My biggest fear was that it would end up in the papers. I didn't mind, on one level, them knowing the mistakes I made, but I didn't want it to be fodder for the hungry mouths of the gutter press. Dad was all for getting some fellas from their estate to 'sort Stu out'. I told him I could fight my own battles. Dad's eyes flitted to mine; he didn't look entirely convinced.

All the time they were there I was looking past them to the breakfast bar in the kitchen, where my iPad was. It was as if it was pulsating with a neon glow, off and on, off and on, drawing me to it. I couldn't wait to get rid of them so I could rush to it and see if *he* had sent a message. Completely irrationally my excitement was like bicarb burning in the pit of my stomach. I knew I was becoming restless, fidgeting in my seat. No doubt Mum and Dad interpreted it as an unease with the conversation, and maybe on one level it was, but really I was feeling like a heroin addict. And there was my next fix, all ready to smoke/inject on the breakfast bar, calling me to it.

'Jodie. What are you going to do?' Mum asked.

I sighed, and for once in my life I was completely honest.

'I don't know.'

They nodded. They could easily have said, Don't take the bastard back. But they didn't have to, because the words floated from their brains and hung above their heads, like in some scary cartoon, curling round like cigarette smoke. I breathed out deeply, hoping to blow them away.

Trudy was less subtle.

'Babes, you've gotta kick him to the kerb. This is totally a well dodge situation and stuff.'

Trudy came round on the seventh day of my incarceration. I heard a ring at the doorbell and, convinced it was Stuart again, approached the front door with some trepidation. But when I looked through the tiny spyhole I saw Trudy's face distorted in the glass and reluctantly let her in. I'd not had a drink since the day I'd been to the studio, but she arrived bearing a large vodka bottle and two more of diet tonic water. I got some ice from the freezer and a dried-up lemon from my veg rack, and before you could say 'second glass' I was opening my heart up to her. My black eye had all but gone by now and she looked shocked when I explained what had happened. By glass number three I'd even told her about Matthew.

I knew that in the morning I'd regret telling her. I could just see the article in *Hiya!* now . . .

You know I never shy away from being too deep in my column, so . . . a big shout out to all you ladies (and guys, too, coz let's face it, it happens to some poor dudes as well) suffering from domestic violence right now! It's a real toughie, and it never goes away. Talk about taboo and stuff! Foundation and blusher might be able to help those bruises, but what about the mental scars? Anyway, I hope you all find the strength to get through it. If Finchley can, you can. Kisses!

She wanted to know what Matthew was like. And now that she was asking, I had no idea how to answer. This is all I knew about him:

1 He lived in the South of France but was originally from Yorkshire.
2 He was three years older than me.
3 He worked in a bar type place on a beach.
4 He wore his hair in a floppy centre parting.
5 He had a sister.
6 He had a nice smile.
7 He was very good at cyber sex (I didn't tell her this bit)
8 He was really nice.

And I was ashamed to admit that's all I knew. But Trudy didn't seem fazed.

'I fell in love with a guy on a bus once. I only saw him twice. We never spoke, but it was a deep, emotional love.'

'I'm not in love with Matthew,' I protested, thrown somewhat by her bizarre declaration.

'But you could be.'

'But he's in the South of France.'

'So go and see him.'

'I can't.'

'Why not, babes?'

'Coz . . .'

'You've got another week off. Have a little holiday. Go and say hi. He might be a plonker. He might be really nice. But at least that way, you won't always wonder what might have been.'

No. No! I couldn't just up sticks and fly to France.

'Babes, if anyone needs a holiday it's you. And let's face it, we can't walk down a street in this country without someone trying to take a picture. At least in France you won't get no hassle, babes.'

I couldn't.

'What else you gonna do? Slob round here all week? Go to France. I would. Top up your tan. Well,' she corrected herself, 'get a tan. Drink wine, surprise him. What have you got to lose?'

My dignity? A sense of pride?

Yet how much dignity and pride did I have now, hiding away in my Mersey-view ivory tower?

No I couldn't. I really couldn't.

Could I?

TWENTY-EIGHT

SPLAT!

There was one.

SMACK!

And another one. I turned to my companion, alarmed. She circled her glass in her hand and explained, 'You know, dear, if the archetypal sound of England is leather on willow on the village green, then the Provençal equivalent is people slapping their flesh to kill the mosquitos.'

I loved the way she spoke. Part olden-days BBC travel presenter, part aristocratic lush.

'Now if you'll excuse me, Miss McGee, I need to visit the little girls' room.'

She got up and waddled away. She was old school. I liked that. I addressed her as Mrs Bathing and she called me Miss McGee. Although it sounded formal, it actually felt rewardingly intimate. I cooed a warm sigh of contentment, had a dainty sip from my glass of rosé and took in the view from the terrace of my villa.

My villa. Get me.

Well, of course, it wasn't *my* villa. I was only renting a room in it, B & B stylee for a few days from Mrs Bathing. But sat here, alone, as the light faded over the bay beneath me, I could pretend it was my house, my lavish steeply sloping garden, and those sprinklers that had just come on to water the tropical plants? Why, I'd planned that meticulously with my gardener, Patrique, of course! I didn't even know if Patrique was a real French name, my French having been taught to me at school by Mrs Byrne in her strong Liverpool accent. But in my head, Patrique was my rock. Sometimes, when I bossed him about in the garden or the house – he was an odd job man, too, it was quite some building – I would shorten his name, playfully, to Rique. But he always, *always* called me Madame Shhodee. Anything more familiar and he knew he'd be for the high jump. I took another baby sip of rosé. I'd never really liked it before, but here, in the baking dusk, palm trees poker straight above me like imperious cranes on the skyline, the oily blue sea darkening beneath me, I don't know, it just felt . . . right. The South of France was clearly bringing out the poet in me, I realized with a wry smile.

For the first time in ages I felt completely relaxed. Maybe it was the wine. Maybe it was the heat. Maybe it was the fact that as soon as I'd stepped off the plane, not a soul had recognized me, pointed at me, sniggered at me, or squawked, 'Oi, love, where's your wimple?!' at me. Being abroad agreed with me. Feeling the warm breeze from the Mediterranean, as opposed to the chill wind from the Mersey, agreed with me. Doing nothing and just *being* agreed with me. And Mrs Bathing's fantastical villa agreed with me so much we were in danger of becoming co-dependent.

Thanks heavens for the internet. I knew nothing about the South of France before coming here except, well, it was in the South of France. But remembering that Matthew had mentioned he lived in a place called Mandelieu-La Napoule, I looked it up on Google Maps and saw that it wasn't that far from

Nice Airport, which was nice. I then looked up 'luxurious B & B's Mandelieu-La Napoule', and before you could say, '*Bonjour, je m'appelle Jodie,*' in a thick Scouse accent (thank you, Mrs Byrne) I had tickets booked and accommodation sorted. Stu and I had saved a lump sum for a rainy day in a high-interest account, and that rainy day had just come. With a valedictory tap of my fingernails I texted Stuart and announced,

Spending all our money on a nice holiday. ON MY OWN.

I got one back almost immediately: 'Hope you have a nice time and find some peace.'

Oh Jeez. He'd turned into some tree-hugging earth mother all of a sudden? I couldn't help myself, I texted back,

Very peaceful thanks. Now you're not around.

The only fly in the ointment was that I messaged Matthew on Facebook to tell him I was coming. And then didn't hear back. Oh well, it all added to the anticipation of the journey. It would be just my luck that he'd have gone off on holiday while I was heading over, but he'd not told me if that was the case. He was probably just working and missed my message. He'd probably read it while I was airborne. I was sure I'd get to France, turn on my iPad and see that he'd replied, overexcited by our impending meeting. And if I didn't hear from him, well, nothing ventured, nothing . . . No, I would hear from him. He'd never let me down so far. He wasn't going to let me down now, right?

Wrong. After half an hour in a cab from Nice to Mandelieu along a motorway called the A8, and stopping at something called a *péage* for the driver to pay for the joy of using the motorway, we arrived in Mandelieu. Wide avenues alongside the yacht-dotted port led to narrow cobbled streets of olde worlde shops and terraced cottages, then we climbed a hill to streets that put me in mind of Beverly Hills. Soon the driver was pulling up outside the most gorgeous white villa that looked equally LA, except for the very French blue shutters on the windows. The owner of the villa, a pleasantly posh English lady with a beetroot nose, black and white scraggly hair scraped back in an Alice band and mismatching flip flops, showed me to my room. I gave it a cursory glance, 'Yes, Mrs Bathing, it's gorgeous. What's your Wi-Fi password?'

I fired up my iPad.

Opened the app.

Entered Matthew's name in my Friend search.

And came up with the error message: 'Did you mean Matthew Martins?'

No! I meant bloody Matthew Martin Maxwell. I retyped the words, assuming I'd spelt something wrong in my over-enthusiastic haste. I was here. He'd be over the moon!

But the same error message came up.

I tried again. And again. And again. Then, with a sinking feeling, I realized that Matthew had deleted his profile. He wasn't on Facebook any more. In fact, Matthew Martin Maxwell had ceased to exist.

I deflated onto the bed, closed my eyes and tried my hardest not to scream. But I must have made some kind of noise because Mrs Bathing came sliding into my room – note to self, that must be one hell of a highly polished parquet if even flip flops could slide – gasping, 'Are you OK, sweetness?'

I sat up, straightened my dress and nodded with an embarrassed, 'Yeah I just . . . stubbed my toe.'

'I know what you need.'

I looked at her. What?

'A glass of rosé. Why don't you unpack and I'll see you by the pool in fifteen?' She winked, clicked her teeth, then slid away again in those flip flops.

I looked at my computer, hoiked it back onto my lap and entered those three words one final time.

Nothing.

Merde! MERDE!

I sighed and looked round the room. It was beautiful, there were no two ways about it, with its parquet flooring, iron framed bed, lacey white linen, white timber walls, model ships painted white and displayed in cabinets on top of the wardrobe and above the door. There was even a painting on the wall that looked like an original David Hockney. But right now, like many beautiful things, it just felt . . . pointless.

What was I even doing here? I'd come halfway across the world. Well, Europe. To find a bloke I'd chatted to for a few months on the internet. Someone who'd chucked me a few platitudes when I was feeling down and confused. And now he'd done a bloody runner as soon as I'd threatened to come and visit. Why? Why?

I knew why.

Because he wasn't daft. He had a brain in his head. He saw me for the chaotic, crazy, mixed-up, lying fool that I was, probably. Oh God. Why did I always do it? Why did I always make a complete and utter mess of my life? I had done it again. My recurring theme. Oh, Jodie, you complete and utter *tit!*

I stood up and moved to the open window, where a hot draught hit me as I looked out. The sun was high in the sky and I pulled my sunglasses down off the top of my head, covered my eyes and admired the view. And what a view! The velvet green garden, the pool at the bottom. I could see Mrs Bathing fussing about at the far end of the pool in her billowing kaftan, arranging a table under a canvas awning. Looking further afield I could see the sea, twinkling like it was full of diamonds. Ironic, I'd just got over my black eye and here I was having to wear sunglasses again. I took a deep breath, considering the view and what I'd been through, and came to a positive conclusion. I was here. I was on holiday. I needed a rest and, Matthew or no Matthew, I was going to enjoy myself.

Je vais m'enjoyer, I told myself. And I actually found myself smiling. Instead of the usual mortification of, Oh, Jodie, you stupid cow! I actually found it funny that I'd been so ridiculous. My only bit of stupidity had been witnessed by one person – if I didn't count Trudy. God I wished I'd not told her – and as it appeared that he was no longer in my life, even if he had just been a picture on my computer screen and some, admittedly charming, words, then I had no one to feel embarrassed in front of.

Come on, Jodie. You're here. In a beautiful part of the world. You've been miserable for ages. Time to lighten up and have some R & R.

Oh. And . . . possibly do some Jessica Fletcher-style detective work to track down the elusive surfer dude while I'm at it.

I'd find Matthew. Somehow I would. But not so I could pounce on him or proclaim undying love, but to apologize and show him I wasn't a nutter. And to thank him for being so kind. But mostly to say sorry for being a psycho bitch from hell.

I headed down to the garden with some suncream and a smile to meet my rosé companion. We sat and chatted into the late afternoon before she excused himself to make a trip to the supermarket. I moved from the pool area up to the terrace and watched the sun set. I felt no sadness as the fierce orange circle dropped into the sea like an egg yolk. Tomorrow was going to be the start of my adventure. And as the evening got darker, bright sparks exploded in the sky. It must have been a firework display down the hill in either Mandelieu or Cannes (Mrs Bathing had pointed out the geography of the view). It was odd, seeing it happen so far below, but I allowed myself the pretence that they had been laid on to welcome me to the area.

I heard some doors shutting in the house and footsteps behind me. Then Mrs Bathing gently touched my shoulder.

'Miss McGee? Shall I crack open another bottle?'

'I think it would be rude not to, Mrs Bathing.'

The next day, after a terrace breakfast of pain au chocolat and fresh fruit salad washed down with a fierce black coffee, I took a cab to nearby Cannes and started the seafront promenade back to Mandelieu. Having spoken to Mrs Bathing about 'an old friend I wanted to look up, but all I knew was his name and the fact that he worked in a nearby beach club', Mrs Bathing had informed me that there were practically millions of them between Cannes and here. I'd foolishly worn some impractical cork platforms for my journey, which started to rub after the third beach club, all of which seemed to consist of bars or restaurants with their own private sections of beach.

I ventured into a couple of them and practised the sentences Mrs Bathing had written down for me on a scrap of paper. At first she'd advised me to say, '*Je cherche un homme,*' but then realized it made me sound like I was after a shag, or 'connubials' as she delicately put it, so we altered it to the more difficult to say, '*Je cherche mon ami qui travaille par ici.*' Then I'd show them a picture of Matthew that I'd printed off on Mrs Bathing's computer.

How, you might wonder, did I manage to have pictures of Matthew when he'd deactivated his Facebook account? Well, little stalkery me had, many moons ago, created a folder on my iPad called MMM, standing for Matthew Martin Maxwell, and into it I'd saved all the photos from Matthew's page, so that I could moon over them in the awful event that my internet went down. Although I had felt like a total stalker at the time, I was really glad I'd done it now, and gave myself a congratulatory pat on the back.

However, no matter how many photos of the floppy-haired one I showed to the bar managers . . .

'*Il est Anglais et il s'appelle Matthew Maxwell?*'

. . . all I got was the shaking of French heads, the shrugging of shoulders and the offer of a sunlounger.

'*Non merci, au revoir!*'

As I trudged along the waterfront I noted that nearly every guy I saw appeared to be wearing Vilebrequin shorts, and all the older women, glamorous as they were, had skin the colour and texture of their bulging leather handbags. Between the beach clubs of chic restaurants and glorified pizza parlours I took in a heady haze of Franglais menus and fashion victims, oligarchs on yachts and Eurotrash on the sands. The tables of the clubs were adorned with the heads of sunflowers, and skinny, facelifted Madames flicked cigarettes into yellow and blue (the colours of Provence) covered ashtrays. Teenagers whizzed past on motorbikes without helmets, creating the rarest and most welcome of breezes.

After the twelfth club I decided to call it a day, pay my silly amount of Euros and rest up in a club at the far end of Cannes. I'd done Cannes today, Mandelieu could wait till tomorrow. After a light lunch of lobster salad and a glass of rosé, I settled down on a lounger, shielded from the two o'clock sun by my clay-coloured parasol, untied my platforms and prepared for a snooze. Before I shut my eyes I vaguely noticed a stout woman on the next lounger who was rubbing lotion into her tree-trunk thighs whilst concurrently munching on a croissant and reading a paperback. I didn't give her much thought, except to comment to myself that her skin was the colour of the average British sideboard.

A few minutes later I appeared to be awake again. The stout lady turned towards me and smiled, pastry wedged between her teeth. I smiled back pleasantly but uncomfortably and emitted a girly, '*Bonjour!*'

When she replied, she had a Geordie accent.

'You don't recognize me, do you pet?'

I shook my head. Who was she?

'First up, I've got to apologize.'

'Apologize? What for?'

She swung her legs round so she could sit facing me. Her swimming costume was tight around the crotch and my eyes were drawn to the hairs from her growler, which were poking out of either side of the paisley patterned costume.

'For shutting down me account, like. I'm sorry Jodie, like.'

I had no idea what she was going on about, so I tried to change the subject.

'Have you ever thought about having your growler waxed? I'm sorry, but I can't help noticing you've got a bit of a pedestal mat down there.'

'I like it au naturel,' she insisted. 'I'm a feminist.'

I nodded and tried to turn away to read my book. I had a book all of a sudden.

'I'm also a twenty-stone lesbian,' she continued.

I had no idea what to say to that, so I answered politely, 'Really? You don't look a stone over seventeen.'

'Thanks, pet. I knew you were a good 'un. How's life at the plastics company?'

I looked back, putting my book down. How did she know about that? Gosh this woman was confusing.

'Plastics company? I'm Jodie McGee. I'm an actress. I play Sister Agnetha in *Acacia Avenue*.'

For some strange reason it made complete sense that my character had morphed into one of the singers from Abba. The woman looked hurt.

'But you said your name was Jodie McFee. And that you was an administrative assistant.'

'Only to Matthew,' I confided.

'But don't you see, Jodes? I *am* Matthew.'

Gulp.

'I'm sorry, pet. I used the name and the photos as a pretence. I knew you wouldn't look twice at us if I put me normal pictures up, like, so I borrowed some off our Declan.'

Gulp.

'That's why I shut me profile down when I knew you was coming over, like. Didn't want to have to tell you the truth.'

Gulp.

'Anyways. Now you do. So, would you like to go for a drink with us tonight? I won't try to grab your snatch or nothing.'

Gulp.

'Well, not unless you want us too, like.'

'I don't!' I called quickly, a few people on the adjoining loungers looked round to see if I was OK.

'Well, what about I put some tanning lotion on your pearly white skin, like. I hear the tops of your thighs can be quite sensitive, pet.'

'I'm terribly sorry,' I seemed to be channelling Joyce Grenfell. 'I'm not actually a lesbian.'

'Sure about that?' a man's voice said behind me. I turned to tell him to shut up. Why were there so many English people here? I saw Stuart behind me in Vilebrequins and a frown. 'Are you sure you're not a total, full-on lez?'

'Stuart!' I gasped. 'What are you doing in Cannes stroke Mandelieu?'

'I mean. Maybe that's why you left me?'

'I left you because you hit me, you stupid twat.'

'And maybe I hit you because you're a lesbian.'

'How many times? I am NOT A LESBIAN.'

Now the whole beach was looking over.

'But you've been chatting to one on Facebook behind my back.'

'Oi! The name's Gwen!' the woman beside me reprimanded.

'I thought she was a bloke!'

'Look at the pictures, Jodie.'

He produced the originals of all the pictures of 'Matthew' from the website. He laid them out on my chest. Looking again, I could see why Matthew had floppy hair. It was actually an asymmetric bob, because Matthew was, in fact – how had I not spotted it before? – a *lady*!

I wanted the sand to open up and swallow me whole, but just then Ace of Base came on the tannoy from the Beach Club DJ, playing 'All That She Wants'. I turned to look at the DJ's booth and saw Our Joey standing behind the decks. He was sun-kissed, but twelve years old. He waved over and started gyrating in time to the music. One by one everyone on the beach sprang up from their loungers and started to dance along with him. It was all too much. I'd come on holiday to get away from all this. Gwen was dancing with Stuart, fondling his arse quite obscenely. I thought she was a lezzer! I clambered up from my lounger, intent on heading to the DJ's booth to have a word with Our Joey, but the tide had come in without me looking, and my feet sank into the gooey sand beneath me.

I tried to move my feet but couldn't. How come everyone else was dancing in the incoming water and I couldn't budge? I was trapped, frozen in the heat. I bent and gripped onto the sun-lounger, trying to squelch my feet up, but the lounger started floating away. I would be trapped here for ever, like an Antony Gormley statue on Cannes beach. The sad bitch who came to France and made a holy show of herself.

I woke with a start.

'Gwen' was picking her nose, distracted by her paperback. Europop was coming from the tannoy. Stuart was nowhere to be seen.

I asked a waiter for a bottle of water.

The second full day I wore more sensible shoes, flip flops actually, and worked my way through the beach clubs of Mandelieu. Once again I drew a blank. I rested up on a lounger for the afternoon, listening to my iPod and flicking through some *Paris Match* magazines that Mrs Bathing had lent me. I nodded off again, but only dreamed about swimming in the sea. No mad encounters with monstrous boyfriends, bogus internet trolls or twelve-year-old gay brothers. Just me, paddling through what looked like a mirror.

I decided to be healthy and walk back to the villa rather than take a cab, and soon discovered the hill was steeper than it appeared. I passed a huge development of apartments that looked like a berthed ocean liner, very much the *trompe l'oeil*, and headed through the cobbled streets of what must have been the old town. I stopped to take a swig from the bottle of water I'd bought from the club to replenish me on the walk home when I heard music coming from a bar down a side street to my left. It was music I recognized. Why was it so familiar? I took a nosey down the side street and soon identified it as a song that had been in the charts ages ago, that really annoying *Bob the Builder* song. What a bizarre thing to hear in the South of France, where even the blokes on bikes carrying onions wear head-to-toe Nicole Farhi. And then I saw a wooden sign hanging above a pub. Nell Gwyn's. Traditional Olde English Pub. It had a painting on it of a titian toothless hag holding two oranges where her boobs should have been and a wobbly Big Ben behind her looking like the Leaning Tower of Pisa. Oh well, in for a penny, in for a Euro.

A girl whose name badge told me she was called Sandrine served me a warm pint of bitter and, on realizing I was English, added, 'Cor blimey, strike a light,' in her thick French accent, never once cracking a smile.

I looked around the place, taking in the spit and sawdust floor, which was making my flip-flopped feet itch, the various framed photos of English 'celebrities' on the oak-panelled walls: Su Pollard, Desmond Tutu – yes, Desmond Tutu – and Anita Dobson looking like someone was pinching her. Maybe it was Brian May (unseen).

Half a pint in and I was feeling chatty, so I asked Sandrine in my pidgin French if there were any English people working there. It went something like this – remember, I was going off piste as Mrs Bathing hadn't written this one down – '*Excusez moi, monsieur*' – she didn't look too pleased about that – '*Les Anglais de pub. Behind le bar. Excusez moi ici? Por favor?*'

She narrowed her eyes at me in a way that made me think she might be in the Mafia and I had just crossed some hideous line and told her that her mother was a cock-sucking whore in Antibes, but then the eyebrows bounced back and she called to an open door behind her, 'Matthieu!' Then continued to ignore me.

Matthieu? Matthieu? But . . . wasn't that French for . . . Matthew? My breath became shallow and my heartbeat raced.

Was my Matthew going to appear, *Stars in their Eyes*-like, from behind a curtain with his floppy hair and neon smile?

I looked again at the picture of Anita Dobson, trying to distract myself. Where had they got it from? No wonder Dirty Den dumped her.

'Yes, can I help?' a chirpy Australian voice chirruped at me cheekily. I turned to see where the voice was coming from and was met by a spindly guy in bifocals and a Union Jack waistcoat who had far too many teeth for the one face.

'Matthieu?' I asked, heart sinking.

He nodded. 'Well, Matt. But that stupid bitch can't pronounce it.'

I regained my composure, pulled out my photos of Matthew and, after a brief explanation of my quest, he sifted through them thoughtfully. I garrulously rabbited on about how he was a friend from school and how we'd lost touch, and how I knew he was working in a bar somewhere in the area but had so far drawn a blank. He looked through the photos again, then opened his mouth as if to say something. Then he sighed and handed them back to me with a chirpy, 'No, mate. Never seen him before in my life.'

Oh. I put the pictures back in my bag and drained my pint.

'Can I ask you something?' he asked. I nodded. 'Are you that bird off the telly?'

I nodded and grinned a 'guilty as charged' smile.

'I thought so. What are you in again? Oh, it's on the tip of me tongue, mate.'

'*Acacia Avenue*,' I said.

'Acacia What?'

'*Acacia Avenue*. The soap.'

'Oh yeah. We have it on Sky here sometimes. Coz it's an English pub and that. And you're in it?'

'I am.'

'Oh right. Fair play to you, mate. Personally I can't stand the fucker.'

'Right.' I gathered myself together to leave.

'Yeah. On account of the fact I think it's total shit.'

As I was heading to the door I heard him call after me, 'Have a good day, strike a light, yeah?'

I'm not embarrassed to say, I gave him the finger.

Mrs Bathing thought the sun shone out of my proverbials. Her phrase, not mine. And I thought they shone out of hers, too, pretty much. She'd told me I could treat her plentiful wine supply as my own, so I cracked open a bottle of rosé when I got back to the villa and went to sip some by the pool. I didn't understand how she'd made her money – something to do with investment banking: a subject likely to cause my eyelids to close over any day of the week – but she must have been loaded to afford a palace like this. I mean, it was posher than the posh bits of London, and properties there were eye-wateringly expensive. She had to be a millionaire, had to be! I'd told her I was an actress off the telly, but she said the last thing she'd seen was *Bouquet of Barbed Wire*, whatever that was. We had a camp old giggle together most evenings, and I think she was touched that I chose to sit in with her rather than venturing into the town to hit the bars. She always cooked a lovely meal each night and made enough for the two of us. I promised her I'd bung her a load of cash at the end of my stay for her generosity, but she'd poo-poo the idea with a flick of her wrist.

I gazed into the shimmering pool. Oh well, I'd tried my best. And now that it was pretty obvious I wasn't going to find Matthew, and that he was probably some bored housewife getting her kicks on the internet, it was time to get over it and enjoy my holiday. The one thing I had to be grateful to 'him' for was that he'd brought me to this beautiful part of the world. I would never have come otherwise. So it was now time to luxuriate, stop worrying and get on with relaxing. Having some me time. Taking a swim in Lake Jodie.

I had bigger fish to fry than Matthew Martin Maxwell. I had some decisions to make about my battering boyfriend back home. But as I started to feel all warm and fuzzy from the lunchtime wine, the warm bitter and now the rosé, I decided that worrying about real life could wait till tomorrow. Tomorrow I would decide what – to quote the Spice Girls – I really, really wanted. Today I would remain serene, fabulous and calm. Chilled. If you can be chilled and baking at the same time.

'Miss McGee?'

I turned. Mrs Bathing was standing up on the terrace at the French windows that led into the hallway. Her face was red from too much sun or too much wine, it was hard to tell which.

'Yes, Mrs Bathing?' I replied, faux haughtily. She liked it when I put on a posh voice. She grinned back at me, a little out of breath as she lit a cigarette in a holder. She took a deep, satisfying drag, then blew out the most enormous smoke ring.

'I think I've found your man!'

TWENTY-NINE

'My friend Petronella in the greengrocer's tells me that the people up the hill in the pink house – ghastly thing – have an English cleaner. And they're pretty sure her surname is Maxwell and she lives in Mandelieu with her brother. They don't know the brother's name and they've never seen him – she's pretty much a recluse who just nips out to do her cleaning jobs – but it stands to reason he's English, too, and that his surname might be Maxwell.'

Hmm. Was that a lead?

'So, Miss McGee. What do you think to that?'

'I think, Mrs Bathing, it might be worth pursuing. Bathing? We're back on the case!'

She grinned like a little girl who'd done well in a spelling test.

'Excellent!' she said, unscrewing the top off yet another bottle of rosé. 'Tomorrow we should head on up there and see if we can find her. Then you can introduce yourself and be reunited with your chum in a matter of hours, I'm sure.'

Chum? Oh gosh, yes, I'd told her Matthew was an old pal.

'Or do you know the sister? You must do! He must have mentioned her? Or are you pals, too? Though you didn't mention her. D'you know her name?'

I felt my cheeks burn, hot with shame. I hoped she might

just think it was the reflection of the citronella candle flickering away on the table. I waited for her to top my glass up, took a bulimic slug, then it all came pouring out of me like I was her very own overactive water feature. I told her everything about me. Everything good. Well, I couldn't really think of much that was good about me apart from the fact that my ugly mug was on TV five times a week – big deal, it didn't make me a nice person, it just made me a lucky bitch. And everything bad. That took a while longer. I told her about Stuart and my drinking at work, about Greg, Our Joey, everything. I even showed her some pictures I'd taken of my black eye on my phone. She said nothing, just nodded, shook her head and topped up our wines whenever we hit a tight spot. And, of course, I told her about Matthew Martin Maxwell, and how I didn't really know him. And yet I'd come to another country to seek him out. I'm not sure how long I spoke for, but I noticed she smoked two cigarettes during my urgent monologue, and she wasn't the sort to chain smoke, so it must have been ages. When I realized there was nothing more to say, and nothing to gain from randomly repeating the whole thing, I shut up and waited for Mrs Bathing to pass judgement. She sat and stared at the black sea, before lighting up cigarette number three and saying, ever so softly, 'My poor, poor angel. What you've been through is ghastly. Ghastly. But,' and here she took a drag on the fag before continuing with, 'I'm worried.'

'That he'll be a weirdo? A freak? A gorilla in Y-fronts?'

She shook her head.

'Or that he *is* the sister? The thought had crossed my mind.'

It had, fleetingly. I'd pushed it to the back of my mind as soon as it had entered, but jeez, Louise, what if his sister was . . . Gwen?!

'I don't wish to offend you, Miss McGee, but you appear to

be one of those women who defines themselves completely by the men in their lives. And it surprises me. And frustrates me in equal measure.'

Oh. Oh right.

'The old can't tell the young how to live their lives, but I often wish they could. I was just the same, till my divorce. That was in 1972. Since then I have lived my life for me, nobody else. And can I tell you something?'

I nodded.

'It's fan bloody tastic.'

She went on to describe a song from the seventies about a woman roaring. How anyone with fallopian tubes could become strong, basically, and on her own terms.

God, I felt embarrassed. Not only had I owned up to being a complete loon, but in so doing I had levelled a criticism that was so pertinent it was making my pulse race at about thirty times its normal speed. I wasn't just a fuck-up, I was an uber fuck-up. I was an anti-feminist fuck-up.

'I might go to bed,' I said, wanting to hide from her all-seeing eye.

'Or we could talk about something else?' she suggested, pity in her voice. I shook my head.

'I'm a fuck-up, Mrs Bathing,' I said clinically.

'Yes, dear. But even fuck-ups can roar.'

I said goodnight as I stood, then I leaned over to hug her. We'd thus far not had physical contact, but so many lines had been crossed tonight, who cared? She certainly didn't. She didn't flinch or push me away, instead she wrapped her skinny arms around me and held me. Long enough to show she cared, but not too long as to cause embarrassment. There was tenderness in that hug. And fragility, too. She felt so emaciated under her clouds of kaftan, she felt like a little old lady. Which I guessed she was. And yet, she was far stronger than me. She had the life she wanted, she enjoyed it, and it was all on her terms. No man in the picture. No rules to follow, only those that she set herself. OK, so she must have had the money to fund her self-appointed lifestyle, but I kind of got the impression that even if she lived in a studio flat on a council estate, living on benefits, the steely determination would still be there, she would still have lived by her own rules.

I lay on top of the bedcovers with the fan whirring away at me. Sleep came slower than Christmas that night as I pondered over what Mrs B had said. Since my teenage years I had lurched from one relationship to a relationship with drama school, and then jumped on the first guy who showed an interest in me. Now that had soured, I'd jumped on a cyber relationship as if that was the answer to all my problems. And clearly it wasn't. That had been inappropriate, I saw that, but had my decision to be with Stu been inappropriate, too? Could I only define myself in terms of the men in my life? Mrs B thought so. And I must have, too, or else why did her words hit home so much? I didn't feel the anger of injustice, just the shame of being caught out. Why did I depend on others to make me happy? Why couldn't I make me happy?

I suddenly remembered that months earlier I'd taken part in a photoshoot on *Acacia Avenue* for Feminism Awareness Week, or something. Three women from the cast – including Trudy in hotpants, four-foot heels and no sense of irony – smiled into a camera wearing T-shirts emblazoned with the logo, 'THIS IS WHAT A FEMINIST LOOKS LIKE'. The pictures had appeared online and in various trashy magazines under headlines as corny as GIRL POWER! and ACACIA SISTERS ARE DOING IT FOR THEMSELVES. (Cue Trudy commenting, 'It sounds like we're pleasuring ourselves, babes' – again, no sense of irony.) Could I really claim to be a feminist if I defined myself solely through men? No. But the magazines didn't care, it was all about getting a picture of three 'pretty girls' pouting with lips that spelt juxtaposition. I'd not given it much thought at the time – we were always being asked to pose for various causes wearing T-shirts with 'STAMP OUT HOMOPHOBIA' or 'BREAST CANCER – GET IT CHECKED!' etc. – and this was just another in a long line. But the memory of this particular photoshoot, and the resultant snaps, made me feel like a hypocrite. Maybe to the casual onlooker I was a feminist. I had a good job, people respected me and considered I had at least a modicum of talent. I was, as they say, going places. Only I knew the truth, and so did Mrs B now.

I wanted to be the woman Mrs B hoped I could be. Fabulous, fantastic and self-sufficient. After all, it's not like I'd had very good taste in men to begin with. So why did I think they were so marvellous? One turned out gay, the other turned out violent, the latest vanished in a puff of smoke as soon as I showed an interest in meeting him. Nice. Of course I was bloody ready. Apart from anything, it appeared I had no choice but to be ready.

I decided to write a list, to try and crystallize in my mind what I wanted from life now that I was at a crossroads. I got my pen and Hello Kitty jotter from my suitcase and returned to the bed, scribbling away: 'What I Want by Jodie McGee'.

That took me ages to write because I did big swirly writing for my name like this:

By Jodie McGee

I sighed, unable to think of anything, so added, 'Aged 28 and a third'.

And then the sad thing was, the really sad thing was . . . I couldn't think of anything to write. How bloody tragic was that? I didn't know what I wanted from life. Had I been that wrapped up in pleasing Stu, and working, and trying to keep my head above water that I no longer knew what I wanted from life?

But then, had I ever known? Memories flooded back of Mum sitting me down before I married Greg, trying to pin me down about what I wanted from life. My mantra in those days had been, 'I just wanna marry Greg.' How awful that sounded now. How tragic. Like I didn't have a brain in my head. God, this was even worse than I'd thought. I had to write something. Anything. So I just wrote the first things that came into my head.

1 To be happy.
2 To sort it out with Stu. One way or another.
3 To keep my job.
4 To carry on being happy.
5 To work out what I actually want from life.
6 To sort it out with Our Joey.

I paused. I couldn't believe I'd actually written that.

7 To find Matthew and apologize for being a nightmare. Not to start seeing him, just to explain where I am at and why I was such a tit. Do I owe him that? Or is it just me wanting to feel less embarrassed? Who cares? But it would be nice just to be able to put a card through his door. Maybe give one to his sister to give to him. Yes. That's what I would do. Save us all the embarrassment then.
8 To learn to roar.

I put my pen down and felt myself melt into the pillows, as if relaxation was engulfing me. I had a plan of action for the remainder of my vacation, and I had a plan of action for the rest of my life, because as I saw it, if I kept my nose clean at work then I'd keep my job. If I kept my job then I would be happy. I would speak to Stuart on my return and either dump him (good option) or get back with him (non-roar option). But if I'd sorted it and it was my choice, I would be happy. I would then write to Our Joey for one last time or, even better, go and see him DJing in a club in London, or wherever, surprise him and hold out the hand of friendship and see if he shook it or slapped it away (in a camp manner, perhaps).

And before that, first thing tomorrow, I would write a nice card to Matthew and get it to this cleaner bird up the road. And if she wasn't his sister, sod it. At least I'd have tried, and at least I'd have got my feelings off my chest. Maybe that would help me find some – God I hated the word – closure.

Over breakfast the next morning I informed Mrs B of my plan. She was so rapt by it she flicked her ash in the pain au chocolat basket by mistake. She went digging in the dresser in her living room and produced a box full of greetings cards in French and English, for all occasions. She was a veritable Paperchase in flip flops. I might have expected any other seventy-something ex-pat to have a selection of chintzy cards showing flowers in vases or pussycats licking brandy glasses, but not Mrs B, she had up-to-the-minute ones with comedy captions on the front, the sort I might have picked myself. I loved her even more for them. I chose one with a Sixties photo on the front of a telephonist at a switchboard looking up at a guy who was hovering over her desk. He had a speech bubble coming out of his mouth that said, 'Have you tried switching it on and off?' And she was replying, 'Have you tried shoving it up your arse?' We both agreed it was cheeky, decadent and tied in with the theme of our computer-based relationship. I asked her how much it cost as I went in my purse for some change, but she just said she would 'stick it on the bill' – my bill was going to be extortionate at this rate, I'd taken so much from her! I took it onto the terrace and wrote inside:

Dear Matthew,
    I'm sorry if I scared you off by saying I was coming over. It was foolish and inappropriate and I am sorry. I enjoyed our chats. You were there for me when I needed it and I'll never forget your kindness for that. But I also appreciate that you don't want to take this any further. And now I've had time to think, neither do I. But here's to a brief, lovely, cyber friendship, and I wish you all the best for now and for the future.
    Your mad friend,
    Jodie xx

I stuck the card in the envelope, licked the flap and wrote his name on the front. Now all I had to do was find this pink house and find this sister.

'One person's pink is another person's lilac,' I pointed out to Mrs B as we sat on a bench opposite the entrance to the 'pink' house. Mrs B had come to keep me company, and brought a bottle of rosé and two glasses. The bench, she told me, was what approximated a bus stop round here. The house we were staring at, by anyone's standards, was not only lilac but also not a house but a mansion. Poking up behind a tall wooden fence I could see lilac turrets, solar-panelled higgledy-piggledy roofs, circular stained-glass windows, plus the usual – for round here anyway – palm trees.

'I don't decide what colour people's houses are, Miss McGee. Someone else called it the pink house, I just followed suit. Hard to tell behind these bloody things.' And she tapped her humongous sunglasses.

'Sheep,' I said cheekily.

She raised an eyebrow. I saw it move behind the grey Perspex. 'Not like you to follow the herd. I thought you'd prefer to buck the trend.'

She shrugged and lit another cigarette, her fourth since we'd arrived. I topped myself up with some water from a bottle I'd brought. It was too hot, even in the shade, for me to be drinking just yet. I also wanted to be sober when I approached 'the sister'.

'Baaah!' she suddenly bleated, sheeplike, and we both giggled.

I sighed, bored. 'Why can't I just go up and ring the bell? Ask to see the maid?'

'I've told you. It's like Fort Knox over there. And they never answer to strangers. They have a security camera on the gate.'

'They'd recognize you.'

'And ignore me. We had a falling out when I accused them of mistreating their cat. Poor thing looked like he'd been in Belsen. I don't see it any more.'

'That's terrible.'

She gave a par-for-the-course sigh. It was a noise she often made, as if the rest of the world never quite met with her exacting standards.

'Mrs B?'

'Miss McGee?'

'Can I ask you a personal question?'

'I'd rather that than an impersonal one.'

'What's your first name?'

'Lar.'

'Sorry?'

'Lar.'

My eyes nearly popped out on stalks. 'That's a Liverpool word. It's like a term of endearment, short for lad. So if your friend's called Michael, you might call him Mickey Lar. I've never heard the name Lar before.'

'It's English.'

'Is it?'

She nodded.

'How d'you spell it?'

She rolled her eyes like I was the ultimate nincompoop and said, 'L.E.A.H. Lar.'

Which gives you an idea just how posh she was. I didn't have time to tell her how it should really be pronounced, because suddenly there was movement over the road. The slatted wooden gate of the lilac/pink house slowly slid to one side with an electronic purr – not opening at an angle as I'd expected it to – and a slim woman in her mid-twenties came out wearing a pale pastel green uniform, a bit like a nurse's. She had her hair scraped back into a medium-sized chestnut ponytail and she stopped to take a thirsty swig from a bottle of water before starting to walk down the hill. Mrs B and I jumped up.

'Miss Maxwell?!' Mrs B called, nudging me.

The woman looked round, trying to place where the voice had come from. It didn't take her long as we were running across the street, waving and saying, 'Hi. Hi.'

'Do I know you?' She had a Yorkshire accent. This was perfect. I remembered Matthew saying he originally came from Keighley.

'I'm Lar Bathing from down the road, I know your employers. This is my friend, Jodie McGee.'

'Hiya!' I gasped.

She was looking startled and a bit scared.

'I'm sorry. This is going to sound mad,' I was a bit out of breath after the mini dash, 'but have you got a brother called Matthew?'

Again, she looked startled and shook her head.

'Matthew Martin Maxwell? Floppy brown hair? Very sporty? Nice smile?'

She shook her head, swallowed and uttered an apologetic, 'I'm sorry. I don't know who you're talking about.'

'He's an old friend, and—'

'I'm sorry. I have to get on.'

And with that she carried on down the hill, drinking her water as she went. I looked at Mrs B, who whistled between her teeth.

'Well, Miss McGee. I'd say that was that. We'd better put that card in the bin and consider it closure.'

I turned away from her and watched Miss Maxwell marching down the hill. Something didn't add up about her delivery. It had been all wrong. If that had been a take, the director would have asked to do it again.

'What? What are you thinking, dear?'

'Mrs B. I work on a soap. I know bad acting when I see it.'

'What d'you mean, lovely?' She placed a hand on my shoulder.

'That was bad acting.'

'You think she's lying?'

I nodded.

'Well then, let's get in the car and follow her!'

And she ran off down the hill towards her villa.

Minutes later we were in her car, zooming down the hill like something out of *The Streets of San Francisco*. My mum had recently got the whole series on DVD from eBay because she had a bit of a thing for Michael Douglas. Every time I'd been round to Sandalan – apart from the fateful dinner party – I'd see Michael Douglas, looking about twelve, bouncing down the various steep hills of San Fran in one of those really long American cars that I imagined only existed in TV programmes.

Well, that's what it felt like now. It had to be said, Mrs B's car wasn't the best vehicle for being incognito. For a start it was a vintage navy blue Bentley from the Sixties, so everyone you passed stopped and stared, and secondly, it was a convertible, and we'd not had time, in our haste, to put the roof up.

'There she is!' screamed Mrs B as we caught sight of the green uniform at the bottom of the hill. By now Miss Maxwell was trudging quite slowly, so we had no choice but to drive past her. About twenty yards ahead Mrs B swerved over, hit the kerb, uttered an expletive and killed the ignition. Oh, this was her idea of parking. She then started the ignition again, remembering something, and hit a button on the dashboard. Very slowly – like, *really* slowly – the roof rose up from the boot and arced its way across the car, like the hood of an old Victorian pram being gently closed by a nanny. Only slower. By the time Miss Maxwell walked past us, we were still exposed to the elements. She looked at us warily and we both smiled warmly. Then she passed. About five minutes later the roof had locked into place and we were kind of hidden from view, though it was a bit late now.

'Sorry about that, dear.'

'It's OK.'

'I had the roof modernized last year. It's still bally slow.'

I realized I was shaking. Because I was wondering, like in my dream, whether the online Matthew might be some weird woman pretending to be a man. And maybe I'd just met her/him. Had I actually just met Matthew?

As Mrs B put the car into gear and drove, equally slowly, into central Mandelieu, a thought suddenly hit me.

'Are you safe to drive this thing?' I was remembering the rosé she'd been drinking at the bus stop.

'Never,' came the reply.

Every time she turned a corner I shrieked, thinking she was driving on the wrong side of the road because she was pissed – although Mrs B was never so vulgar as to use that word; she preferred 'past the post' – before remembering we were in France and it was, to be a little French for *un moment*, de rigueur. If not, le law. God my French was getting good. I felt I was almost fluent.

'What are we doing?' I asked.

'Just driving around in the vain hope of . . .' and then she suddenly squealed. 'Thar she be!' and pointed ahead.

Miss Maxwell was coming out of a greengrocer's with a carrier bag crammed with, no doubt, veg. She was checking something on her phone as she walked along a street to our left, then she looked up suddenly and started to run.

'Has she seen us?' I gasped, even though I knew it wasn't possible. We were too far away and stuck at a red light.

'No, I think she's running for that bus.' Mrs B pointed again and I looked. The lights changed and we saw Miss Maxwell hop on. 'Bingo.'

We followed the bus for about ten minutes, driving at a sluggish pace that annoyed other drivers, who beeped their horns and did road-rage gesticulations, making us giggle. It was impossible to drive any faster without overtaking the bus. Every time it stopped, Mrs B stalled the car and gasped, 'Has she got off?' With me straining to see round the side to the pavement. Eventually, the Maxwell girl got off. Mrs B then pulled over and we sat and watched. Again, she was stood on the pavement, fiddling with her phone. We were on the outskirts of Mandelieu; there were a few dull shops on either side, then a tree-lined avenue swept up the hill to our left. This is the road that Maxwell Features took when eventually she put her phone away.

'Of course,' I said, 'she could just be going to her next job.'

'With a bag full of shopping? I don't think so.'

I nodded. Miss Marple had a point. A minute or so later, Mrs B put the car in gear and swerved across the road and into the avenue. She drove at a snail's pace, the green uniform a hazy shadow in the distance. And then we saw her turn into a property on the right. Mrs B put her foot down and sped up to it, parking outside. Again she hit the kerb.

I looked at her and grimaced. What now? Mrs B grimaced back. Then her face fell.

'Rats!'

'What?'

'I left my bloody rosé at the bus stop.' She shook her head, incredulous at her mistake.

'What do I do now?' I ventured.

'That, Miss McGee, is up to you, but I'll wait here. You could always just post it in their box. She has got a brother. Petronella said. So . . .'

I looked up at the house. It was more modest than the houses in Mrs B's neighbourhood. It wasn't exactly a council block, but the fence was in need of repair and the shutters had seen better days. It looked like a bungalow. Taking a deep breath, I opened the car door and clambered out.

'Wish me luck!' I said, looking back into the car. Mrs B nodded and I shut the door as quietly as possibly.

From inside the house I could hear raised voices, muffled through the walls. I edged closer to the fence and peered through a hole in it. On the other side I could see a lush green lawn sweeping down the hill we'd just driven up, and to my left, the house. It wasn't a bungalow, I now saw, though it was quite squat, like it had been squashed. I could feel my heart pounding in my chest as the voices seemed to be getting nearer. I saw some open French windows leading onto a patio, not too dissimilar to Mrs B's. And then the shouting stopped.

And then.

And then.

And then Matthew came out onto the patio.

I knew it was him immediately. I just knew it. I'd recognize those eyes anywhere.

But the second I saw him I realized. I realized why he had had to shut down his account. I realized that he had been living in a fantasy world just as much as me.

THIRTY

My heart was in my mouth as I hurried to his gate and opened it quietly. I took a deep breath and stepped onto his drive. Clutching my card I made my way quickly round the side to the terrace, where he was sitting, staring at the view. I froze. He'd not heard me.

'Matthew?'

He looked round. Our eyes met. I gave an embarrassed smile and he just froze, as if he was seeing a ghost. I heard footsteps and then his sister came out on the terrace.

'Oi, what d'you think you're playing at?' She was heading towards me, furious. 'Get off my land, you're trespassing!'

I dodged her and headed towards Matthew, holding out the card.

'I just wanted to give this to—'

'He doesn't wanna see you!'

'I'm sorry,' I whispered as I held the card out to him. But he didn't raise his hand to take it.

The sister intervened, snatching the card from me and placing it in his lap.

'He can't move his arms. He can move his fingers, but he can't move his arms.'

'I'm sorry.'

Matthew was still frozen.

'Right, you've given him your card, now get lost. And make sure you shut the gate on your way out.'

I couldn't take my eyes off him.

'I had no idea,' I said.

'You had no idea coz he never told you. Go on, out.' I really did feel like slapping the sister. I looked at her. I'd met bullies like her before.

'I'll go when Matthew tells me to go, not before.'

Her eyes narrowed and her top lip curled unflatteringly. She snapped a look at Matthew and pulled a face, as if to say, 'Well?' Matthew sighed.

'Rosie, if you could get Jodie a drink.'

Her eyes widened in horror. 'You wanna give your mate a drink? You get her one. Let's see how far you get!'

And with that she spun round and stomped back into the house.

'My sister's . . . quite hot-headed,' he said, though the explanation was unnecessary. I sat myself down on a garden chair a few feet away from him and smiled.

'It's OK. I'm not thirsty.'

He nodded. He caught me looking him up and down and I was instantly mortified.

'How . . .? How did it happen?' I asked, my voice dry.

'Snowboarding,' he said sadly.

'When?'

'Eight months ago now. I used to count it in days. Then weeks. Now months.'

He'd put on weight since the photographs I'd seen online. That must have been through lack of exercise, sitting in his wheelchair all day. But his face was still as kindly as ever, even if the delightful smile was now locked away in those photos.

'I'm sorry if I freaked you out,' I said.

'I'm sorry if I'm freaking you out,' he echoed.

I shook my head. 'No it's . . . lovely to meet you.'

'Likewise.'

And then he did it. He gave me that amazing smile. He might have been a paraplegic, but his teeth were stunning.

'I'm sorry, Jodie. I'm sorry I . . . never told you the truth.'

'Snap,' I admitted.

'I know you're an actress.'

Oh God.

'I didn't when we first got chatting, but I was channel-hopping about a month ago and suddenly I saw your face on the screen.'

'You should've said.'

'I liked it. It felt like a good fit. You were pretending and so was I.'

'You weren't pretending, Matthew.'

'Well, I was pretending I was how I used to be. And I'm not. I hate my life. I hate depending on Rosie to . . . do the sort of stuff a sister shouldn't have to do, but . . . well. When I was chatting to you, my life felt normal again. That's what I liked. And I liked the symmetry of us both pretending.'

Symmetry. He used words like symmetry in everyday conversation. He was fabulous.

'But then you said you were coming over and I panicked.'

I nodded.

'The fantasy had to stop.'

I nodded. 'Or you could've just told me the truth.'

'Too scared.'

I nodded. 'I know that feeling.'

'I enjoyed our chats, though. And the other stuff, too.'

I blushed. He was referring to the cyber sex, I just knew he was.

All She Wants

'But even that . . . that was just a fantasy of a memory and . . . God, I wish I could shrug.'

He smiled. I smiled.

'How's Stuart?'

'I don't know.'

'Did he hit you?'

I nodded. He looked pained, looked at his lap, shook his head.

'But I know this much,' I said, 'he'll never hit me again.'

'How long you here for?'

'Couple more days.'

He nodded and looked out at the view.

'Sea's amazing, isn't it?' I said, looking out, too.

'I had the option of moving home after the accident, but I like the heat, though it doesn't like me. And I hate the idea of going back to England a failure. Here, I can just hide away.'

I gulped. I actually thought I was going to cry. Jesus, this was ridiculous.

'The fantasy me wanted to run away with you. Protect you from that bastard.'

I looked at him. He was an unlikely knight in shining armour, but it was lovely to hear all the same.

'And the real you?'

'The real me isn't ready. I'm a moody, selfish, arrogant twat, Jodie. And I've still not made peace with what's happened. I'm not ready for anyone else in my life. You know?'

I nodded. I did know.

'Well, when you read the card, you'll see I feel the same really.'

He smiled sadly.

'Bad timing?' he offered and I nodded.

'Bad timing.'

A thought suddenly hit me.

'You know . . . you know when you were typing to me? You weren't dictating it all to Rosie, were you?'

He laughed. 'No! Don't worry, you've not had a cyber three-some with a brother and sister.'

Thank God for *that*.

'I have me own computer. I can move the fingers in me hands, but mostly I use this stick thing on me head.'

And relax.

'I give good head,' he continued.

I could have sat there and chatted all day. He was as charming and delightful as his internet chat had been.

'Sorry if this trip's been a waste of time.'

'No. No it hasn't. I've become really good friends with the woman I'm renting a room from. She's mad as a box of frogs and I love her to bits.'

'Well that's good.'

'And the area's lovely. I'd definitely come again. Also, it's nice not to be recognized everywhere I go.'

He nodded. 'Well, in the plastics world you're a force to be reckoned with.'

I nodded. Jeez, we were like a pair of nodding dogs, 'Best administrative assistant slash secretary around, mate.'

Mate. He liked that. It was northern and pally. Laddy. And diffused any fears about potential sexual tension.

'I've . . . I've got a doctor's appointment in a bit. Takes me a while to get into the taxi, so . . .'

I stood up.

'It was nice meeting you. Come back online some time. We can still be mates, can't we?'

'Maybe.'

I walked towards him. Underneath his wheelchair I could see a white sort of fleece, like the kind you put in dogs' beds. For some reason it broke my heart. I leaned over and pecked him on the forehead, then stood back. He didn't look very impressed.

'That was a bit patronizing. You should always kiss a cripple on the lips. It's the law.'

'Shit. Sorry.'

I squatted down and moved my face to his. His lips were soft. Wet. It would have been so easy to turn it into a snog, but both of us knew that wasn't on the cards. It didn't stop us lingering a bit longer than we should have, though. I pulled back and stood.

'Bye, Matthew.'

'Jodie?'

'Mm?'

'You're a good woman. You're wicked. Don't settle for second best.'

I nodded, trying not to cry. Why did he have to be so *nice*? Then I turned and walked back down the terrace. Before I slipped round the side of the house, I turned to smile at him again. He was already smiling back at me.

'If I could wave I would!' he called, chuckling.

'Don't worry, I can wave for two,' I replied, and raised both my hands and waved.

'Bragger.'

'See you.'

'See you, Jodie.'

I walked round the house to the gate. To the car. Got in. Mrs B was strumming her fingers on the dashboard.

'Well? Closure?'

'Oh yes. Closure.'

'Come on. There's a bottle of rosé at a bus stop with our names on it.'

She turned the key in the ignition and pulled off. We made

the journey in silence. I was overcome by waves of sadness as I imagined everything Matthew had been through these past eight months. But I knew Mrs B wouldn't be full of questions. By the time we started chugging up her street I started to feel happy. I couldn't help but smile. I'd achieved one of the things on my list from last night. I had apologized to Matthew and realized I wasn't the only person who acted impulsively and lived in a fantasy land occasionally. Maybe I was on my journey to contentment. A one-way ticket to Roar.

But then, as we neared the villa, I saw a bloke standing outside the gate with a pull-along suitcase. My pull-along suitcase.

There, in a straw pork-pie hat, Adidas tracksuit top and baseball shorts, was Stuart.

Oh God.

'I've given up the booze,' he said.

'I haven't,' I said, 'though I'm hoping I'll have drunk so much rosé by the time I leave here that my system won't be able to take any more alcohol.'

'I've started an anger management course.'

'Three gold stars.'

'And counselling.'

'Don't. You'll be dragging me on *Jeremy Kyle* next.'

'I'm sorry.'

'So am I,' I said. 'Anyway. How did you know I was here? I haven't told a soul.'

'You paid a deposit on the credit card. I saw it online. Tracked you down that way. This is a big romantic gesture.'

'Thank you. It makes it all the more special, you pointing it out to me.'

'Sorry.'

We were sitting on sunloungers by the pool. I'd made him

put sunblock on his nose because it had a tendency to burn in the sun. He looked slightly comical. I could hear Mrs B clattering away in the house. She never usually made any noise, so I guessed it was for my benefit, reminding me that there was someone around in case Stu decided to whack me one. I expected to feel scared when I first saw him again but actually, seeing him there outside the house I'd just felt annoyance. Annoyance that he'd interrupted my nice holiday. Annoyance had led to acceptance, and now I just felt pity. It was a bit like looking at a version of myself at various points in my life, someone who had majorly screwed up, but it made me realize that at least when I'd screwed up I'd not hurt anyone. I didn't think. Well, not physically anyway.

'I wanna get back with you, Jode,' he said.

This time I said nothing.

'D'you think there's any possibility?' he said.

That . . . was the million-dollar question.

'I've been with you two and a half years,' he said. 'That's nearly a thousand days. And on only two have them have I . . . lost it.'

Oh, so he'd become a spin doctor now. Interesting.

'So what, I'm due another smack in about five hundred days? I'll make sure I put it in my diary,' I replied.

He couldn't win. I had the upper hand, for once. And it felt good. I told him we couldn't go back to how it was. I told him I wasn't going to rush into anything either way. I told him it wasn't just about the violence, rare though it had been, it was about more than that. It was about him resenting my success. It was about him being fed up with always being my 'plus one'. It was about me not being sure what I wanted from life, and until I did things would have to be different. I proposed that, for the time being, we lived as flatmates. Separate bedrooms, separate lives, till I worked out what I wanted to do. He asked if this was a test, did he need to prove himself? I told him no, it was a holding measure. We had to keep calm and carry on till I decided what would make me happy.

'Anyway. Now for the good news,' he said.

'What's that?' I asked.

'Well, you've had your phone off,' he said.

'I know. I'm the one who switched it off,' I replied.

'And everyone's been trying to get hold of you,' he said.

'Who? Why?' I said.

'Coz you've made the shortlist for the Soap Awards. You're up for Best Actress,' he said.

'Oh,' I said, though I also have to add my heart skipped a beat and I felt like jumping up and punching the air, but I didn't want to display too much emotion in front of him: I was enjoying giving him the impression I'd turned into a deep-thinking, overly rational, centred queen of Zen.

'The ceremony's next week,' he said, 'and they want you on *Brunch With Bronwen* on Tuesday.'

Brunch With Bronwen. Everyone's favourite breakfast telly show. I had finally made it, I told myself sarcastically. He sounded so excited when he said it, like it was the most amazing thing in the world. Maybe he'd forgotten that I'd already been on it twice before and I found Bronwen grating, sycophantic and shallow, but hey, all publicity was good publicity, right?

'I think you'll win,' he said.

'Who am I up against?' I asked.

'That bird from *EastEnders* – Colette thingy.'

'Court,' I said. She was very popular. And never out of the tabloids with her fluctuating weight, on-off marriage to a footballer and her fondness for turning up at the opening of an envelope. Her autobiography, *I'll See You in Court*, had recently been published, and in it she'd confessed that she had been offered Sister Agatha in *Acacia Avenue* and turned it down because she couldn't face being parted from her beloved toddler daughter Chloee (yes, it is spelt like that), which was a bit embarrassing for me but never mind. She was a busty, blousy cockney sparra with a heart of gold, and even I had to admit the girl had star quality. I didn't stand a chance.

'Oh well, you win some, you lose some. Still, it's nice to be nominated,' I said.

'I'll never hurt you again,' he promised.

And in that moment I believed him.

'Hiya, Jodie love, are you OK? I've been going out of my mind here.'

'Yeah, Mum, I'm fine. Sorry about that. I just had to get away for a bit.'

'Where are you? Blackpool?'

Blackpool?

'South of France.'

'Where?'

'South of France.'

'In France?'

'Yeah, in the south.'

'Oh. What did you go there for?'

'Dunno, just felt like it. It's where the Cannes Film Festival is.'

'Have you met Tom Cruise?'

'No.'

'Now I don't know if you've heard, but you've been—'

'Nominated for Best Actress, I know.'

'Oh well, yeah, there is that.'

'Why, was there something else?'

'No. Well. Yes.'

'What? Mum, are you OK?'

'I'm fine, it's just you've been in the papers. I don't know who, but someone's sold a story on you claiming that Stu beat you up and you've had to take time off and you've got a drink problem and . . . Well, it's tomorrow's chip paper. That's what I say.'

Another spin doctor. My life was full of them.

My stomach turned in knots as I realized. Oh my God, I'd become a proper soap star. A full-blown one whose personal life matched the turbulence of the storylines they acted in. Ergh, I felt like throwing up.

'Are you still there, Jodie?'

'Yes.'

'They doorstepped us on Wednesday. Your father gave them short shrift.'

'Right. Stuart didn't tell me about that.'

'Stuart?'

'Yeah, he's here with me now.'

'You . . . you went on holiday with—'

'No, he just turned up. I didn't invite him.'

Maybe he hadn't told me because he didn't want to hurt me.

'Oh my God, he's stalking you. I think there's laws about that in that France, you know.'

'Mother, he's not stalking me. We live together. For now.'

'Are yous getting back together again?'

She sounded genuinely surprised. And I liked it that she assumed I had the strength of character to kick him to the kerb. It showed she had faith in me.

'No. Well, not now anyway. I'm not sure what I want to do. We're just gonna be flatmates for now.'

'He's telling all and sundry he's going for the counselling and that.'

I didn't know what to say to that really.

'So what's the latest with the papers?' I asked.

'Well, you know, Eva and that lot have issued a statement saying you'd had a nasty fall and were having two weeks off recuperating, so it seems to have died down.'

'Oh. Oh OK. Brilliant.' And it did, it made me feel a lot better.

'Though Val's not convinced. Keeps asking how yous two are getting on and that, you know.'

'I know,' I said, although I didn't really. I could only imagine. But now was not the time to split hairs.

'So when are you coming back?'

'Tomorrow. Stu's going to Liverpool, I'm going straight to London. I spoke to Eva today; she'd rather I went and did some publicity and came back to filming after the awards. They're putting me up in a nice hotel.'

'Oh that's nice. Coz I heard you were doing *Brunch With Bronwen* and all that. Oh I love that Bronwen.'

'I know.'

'She's dead . . . down to earth.'

'I know.'

'Even if I can never really understand a word she says.'

Bronwen is Welsh. I rolled my eyes.

'Jodie?'

'Mum?'

'Are you OK?'

I stopped. Thought. Then said, 'Yes. Just roaring.'

I thought it profound. Feminist. I thought it spoke volumes. I thought it said I may not have my mojo back completely but I'm getting there. I was very pleased with myself. I thought she might be, too. But she said, 'Y'what?'

'Yes, Mother, I'm fine.'

And I allowed myself a little smile.

THIRTY-ONE

Mrs B kindly drove us to the airport, despite claiming that autoroutes were the work of the devil. She'd been polite and civil with Stuart over dinner the night before, as if she knew nothing about what had gone on between us, and I appreciated her upper-class restraint. She'd made up an extra bed in one of the spare rooms for him, which she didn't charge for when I settled the bill. I'd asked her how come the place wasn't full. It was a glorious house; it should have been packed to the shuttered gills. She'd told me, 'I'm very choosy about who I put up. And there was something about your manner on the phone that told me we'd get on.' And we had. Hoorah.

She parked illegally outside the departures entrance and doled out hugs and kisses like we were her own children off on holiday. As Stu headed in through the zappy doors she grabbed me and whispered just one word in my ear: 'Roar.'

Somehow I knew we'd keep in touch.

My flight to London was half an hour before Stu's to Liverpool, and as I headed off to my gate we hugged. It was our first proper physical contact in weeks. He held me tight and gave me yet another apology, promising he'd never hurt me again.

Those words were meaningless, I knew that. Even if he never hit me again, we all hurt each other sooner or later, even if we don't mean to. It might be a look when you put on a new dress, or a roll of the eyes when you espouse an opinion. Anything really. We're all fragile beasts with an infinite capacity for pain, great and small. So promising never to hurt someone is like a bee promising never to sting. But now wasn't the time to point this out to him, so I just murmured, 'I'll bear that in mind.'

'We'll make this work, Jode. Promise. I ain't going anywhere.'

'Well, you're going to Liverpool.'

'You'll never get rid of me.'

And I wasn't sure if that was a promise or a threat. I kissed him on the cheek, pulled down the brim of his straw hat, and headed towards my gate.

Sitting on the plane I heard a text coming through on my phone. A bulldog of a stewardess pounced on me.

'Madame, you'll have to switch that off.'

'Yes. Sorry.'

She stood over me, waiting for me to do it. I assumed it would be a text from Stu offering a soppy goodbye etc., but when I looked it was Mandy, who said,

I see you're on *Brunch With Bronwen* tomorrow. If in London please come and collect necklace? I have found bag of your stuff in loft, too. Be good to c u.

Jesus. Did she never give it a rest?

Fortunately the bulldog was distracted by a guy fiddling about on his iPad, so I had time to write,

Cool. See you tonight. XX

Then I turned my phone off.

*

The hotel that Crystal TV had booked me into was in the heart of Soho, tucked away down a polluted cul de sac, with SUITE SOHO picked out in fibre optic lights on its frontage. The staff all looked like they'd just hopped off the catwalk in Milan, and behaved as if they were keen to hop back on it at any minute. Dressed head to toe in Armani, hair styled to within an inch of its life, all wearing identical orange blossom scent. To put it mildly, they were scary. But ask them a question and their stern expressions quickly switched to happy smiles for the duration of their answer, before retreating to the modus operandi of surly bastards.

I spent the afternoon shopping for an outfit to wear on *Brunch With Bronwen* and plumped for something white, sleeveless and floaty from Ghost, which would normally have made me look like a ghost, except that I was impressively sun-kissed from my time at Mrs B's. Well, impressively for me. I decided to team the floaty white thing with jeans and my strappy cork platforms. Even I had to admit I was going to look good.

The interview was the next day, Tuesday, and the awards were the same night. I didn't need to bother about an outfit for the awards as Ming had emailed me to say there'd be loads of free clothes to choose from tomorrow. Killing time in my humongous suite, I checked Facebook to see if Matthew had rejoined. He hadn't, so I read through all the emails I'd missed while I'd been in France and listened to the innumerable messages on my answerphone. Most of them were from Mum, wondering where I was and then panicking about what had been in the press about Stu. I deleted them all, then wondered what to do with myself that night, which was when I remembered my text from Mandy. Oh well, time to reclaim that blessed necklace after all these years. And whatever she'd found in the loft. Which was bizarre in itself because, despite living there for a couple of years, I hadn't even realized we had one.

As I luxuriated in my second bath of the day – I couldn't help it in posh hotels, I had to jump in the tub as often as possible – I thought about Stuart. The woman that roared would say enough is enough, but the Jodie I knew only too well wasn't sure she could. Maybe the anger management would work. Maybe the counselling would, too. Maybe he would never hurt me, physically, again. Was it worth throwing everything away because of that? But the more I thought about it, the less clear I became. One minute I'd be valiant – yes, I would get rid. The next – oh, but he looked after me when I needed it. The question was, what did I need now? All I knew was, I'd still not made up my mind.

I took a cab to the Oval and got it to drop me off outside L.A.D.S. I stood outside, remembering my first audition and how excited I'd been every time I'd climbed those steps. I also remembered staggering out, completely lost, when I'd suffered my big rejection. I looked up the street and saw the phone box where I'd called Stu. Bless him, he'd not given it a second thought that day, he'd just taken care of me and made sure I was OK. But then, that was a very long time ago now. I looked back at the red-brick building, hoping Rupert would come out. I wanted to tell him I'd done OK for myself, tell him I was nominated for an award tomorrow for my acting, but no one came or went. I turned and headed to my old flat.

I'd only met Mandy a handful of times over the years, when I'd been out on works dos with Stu's lot. Seeing her again I found it laughable that I'd ever considered her a rival for Stu's affections. She had a bit of an Elvis quiff and, as she showed me up the stairs, I wondered if she'd dressed up especially for me as the price tag was still attached to the back of her top. Her combat pants looked like they'd not long come out of the dryer. Everything smelt new.

'I've got a few mates round, hope you don't mind.'

Mind? Why would I mind? She could do what she liked in the flat, within reason, it was nothing to do with me.

But when I got upstairs and entered that which was once my love den, I realized she'd had a bit of an ulterior motive. She'd clearly got a few mates round to show off to them that she knew someone on the telly. She offered me a beer and was quite surprised when I asked for a cup of tea. As I sipped it genteelly her friends produced various *Acacia Avenue* memorabilia from about their persons and asked me if I'd mind terribly signing them. I posed for several photos, their arms round me like we were long lost friends, and there was general chit-chat about what I was going to wear to the awards and how I was going to 'kick Colette Court's fat arse'. They were quite sweet really, but it did feel like a P.A. rather than a visit to my tenant's. In the end I invented an appointment I had to go to and Mandy grabbed a plastic bag from the side and said, 'Here's your stuff. You could wear the necklace tomorrow.'

I smiled politely and had a quick look in the bag. I saw the emerald necklace – a present from Stu – and also a load of envelopes. I recognized the handwriting immediately. My heart seemed to stop. I felt faint.

'Where . . . where did you find these again?' I stammered.

'The loft. I was putting some shit up there the other day and found that bag in the corner. I hope you don't mind, I saw they were addressed to you.'

'Have you mentioned this to Stu?'

She shook her head.

'No, they're all addressed to you. I've not read them. They're not love letters from Stu, are they?'

I shook my head, tried to keep it together as I bid my farewells, then stumbled down the stairs and out onto the pavement. Although I'd not had a drink since I got back from France, right now I felt drunk. The street seemed to be moving around me. The traffic lights ahead appeared to bend towards me, forcing me out of their way. I was gasping for breath. I felt hot, then cold, and suddenly realized I was going to be sick. I was. In the gutter. I stood, feeling no better for it, and retreated to sit on the steps to the house.

No. This could not be happening.

I looked again at the bag and pulled it open. All those envelopes. I pulled one out from the middle of the pile and opened it. Inside was a birthday card. It had a picture of a nun on the front. I didn't read the logo, I just snapped it open. On the right hand side it said:

> Happy birthday, Jodie,
> Love Joey xxx

And on the left hand side it said:

> I don't care if you're not speaking to me. I'm going to keep
> sending you birthday cards and Christmas cards and letters
> until you give in and decide to be my friend again. I love you.
> I fucked up. I miss you.
> PS Off for a nightcap. Hope it fits xx

I looked at the postmark on the envelope. It was dated two years ago.

I pulled out another envelope. My hand was shaking as I ripped open the still-sealed envelope and pulled out a three-page letter. It was dated three years ago. For God's sake!

Dear Jodie,

    I just had to write to say I thought you were BRILLIANT tonight on the show. You made me and Paolo cry.

Paolo? Who the hell was Paolo?

He sometimes has difficulty understanding what they say on *Acacia Avenue*, but when I looked at him tonight he was sobbing his heart out. And so was I!

I rummaged in the bag and pulled out the letter at the bottom of the pile.

Dear Jodie,

    Well you can't say I didn't try. I get the message, and though it pains me I'll leave it at that. You can't blame a boy for trying. You reckon you're not speaking to me? Well guess what, bitch, now I'm not speaking to you. LOL. I respect your wishes. Take care and I hope life brings everything you wish it to. Dead proud of your success.

    Joey x

    PS I'm so over nightcaps.

Joey had been writing to me. Regularly. And someone had been intercepting the mail. Not even throwing them away, but saving them in the loft. Why? To throw in my face in the future and say, 'See how much I controlled you?'

    It could only be one person. I took out my phone to call Stuart, but I just couldn't bring myself to dial. I was angry. Outraged. Gutted. Bewildered. How could someone do this to me? How could *he* do this to me? I had written a letter to Our

Joey, had he not got it? And then I remembered. I was laid up in bed with a broken leg at the time, so I'd asked Stuart to post my letter. He must have thrown it away. Why? Did he want to control me that much that he wanted to kill anything I had with Our Joey? Was our potential friendship that much of a threat to him? It didn't make sense. And to keep the letters like this was just bizarre. Years and years of contact thrown away by his desire to control me. Missed chances, missed opportunities, missed happiness. And it was all down to Stuart.

I stood, invigorated suddenly. I had to see Our Joey. I had to find him. Tell him what had happened. Tell him I had no idea. I checked the address on one of the letters. I checked another. Two years ago he'd been living in Streatham. I hailed a cab.

My mind was racing, my heart was racing, sadly the cab wasn't. I was going to go up to his front door, bang on it loudly, throw my arms open, do a showbiz wiggle and scream, 'SHE'S BACK!'

He would collapse, crying into my arms, grunting, 'I never thought I'd see the day!' And everything would be all right with the world.

I had so many questions I wanted to ask him, but more than that I had a zillion and one that I wanted to ask Stu.

Why had I felt sorry for him? Why had I thought him worthy of my pity? Even when he'd hit me I'd still been in two minds about whether to get back with him or jib him? Even when he'd hit me for the *second time*.

I was a fool. I was an idiot. I was a loser. I was everything bad in the book of bad words to describe stupid people.

Or, put that in the past tense. I *had* been. Not any longer. I wound down the window of the cab and screamed out of the window.

My driver looked petrified.

'You all right, love?' he asked, eyes piercing me through the rear-view mirror.

'Fine thanks,' I said. I had roared.

Our Joey didn't throw himself at me like the wailing wall, nor did the nice woman in the burka who answered the door. At first I thought she might be his housekeeper, sticking a stew on for him after one of his crazy nights out on the London club scene. No doubt soon I'd be joining him on it, partying hard and wedging myself behind the DJ's decks like I understood what he was doing. Maybe he'd explain to me how it all worked. Maybe he'd get on the mic and shout, 'MAKE SOME NOISE, PEOPLE! SISTER AGGIE IN DA HOUSE, YEAH!' or something similar. That's the sort of thing I'd do if I were a DJ. If he was Mr Milk, I'd be Lady Cream. Oh dear, I was getting ahead of myself.

'Hello, is Joey in please?'

'Jo-eey?'

'Joey McGee? Joseph McGee? Mr Milk?'

She shook her head. Her veil shimmied. Jeez she had a lot of eyeliner on.

'I am Rashida. Have you come about widow?'

'Sorry? No.'

'Widow not opening.'

'No, I'm trying to find my brother?'

Oh anyway, to cut a not-that-long story very short, she eventually told me that she had been living there for six months and had no forwarding address for the previous tenants who, she informed me, had left a terrible mess in the bathroom. She didn't give details.

I'm not sure why, but I sprang to Joey's defence.

'Oh that wouldn't be Our Joey. He's meticulous about personal hygiene. I imagine that was Paolo, his life partner. Well, I assume it's his life partner. It could be his cat for all I know.'

'No. We not allowed animals here.'

'Sorry to have troubled you.'

I saw more white in her eyes. It was a bit unnerving. She pointed at me.

'You. It is you. Nun.'

I almost curtsied and nodded, giggling with embarrassment.

'Yup. Anyway, nice meeting you Rashida. Good luck with your window. I think that was the word you were looking for.' And then, just to be even more patronizing, I pronounced it for her again. 'Win-dow. It's got an 'N' in it. N-n-n-n-n-n. OK?'

'Keep your hair on, lady.'

She had a point. I backtracked down the path. It was a lovely location, a Georgian mansion overlooking Streatham Common. I could imagine him and Paolo sitting in their attic flat, admiring the view and saying stuff like, 'Aren't we lucky having a view like this?' Paolo was Brazilian, I decided, and did Brazilians for a living. They'd met when Our Joey had gone in for a back, sack and crack job and they'd fallen hopelessly in love over the waxing strips. God it was idyllic. I wanted their life.

But where was he?

I phoned Mum. No time for pleasantries.

'Mum, where's Joey?'

Although I was so overexcited it sounded like 'mum-wheresjoey'?

'Ibiza.'

'Again?'

Oh bollocks.

'When's he back?'

'Well, he's not. He's moved there.'

'WHAT?'

'Why do you want to know all of a sudden?'

'Mother, why haven't you told me this before?'

'Jodie. Every time I've mentioned your brother you've done the equivalent of sticking your fingers in your ears and singing Misty.'

'Ibiza?'

'D'you need to speak to him?'

'Yes. It's really important.'

'Has something happened?'

'Yes. No. I don't know. I just wanna speak to Our Joey.'

She gave me a mobile number and I swiftly hung up and called it. No reply. No answerphone.

Ibiza?

Something Mum said reverberated through my being.

'He said there was nothing keeping him here.'

As I walked across the common I could think of only one thing.

How much I wanted to kill Stuart Moses.

A plane flew overhead, spewing out a line of cotton wool behind it. I wanted to be on it. I wanted to go back to the villa. I wanted to go back to Mandelieu. Mrs B would know what to do. I'd ring her this evening. But first, I'd sit myself down on the common and read through all Joey's letters and cards. I devoured them like a good book. I laughed, I cried, I gasped and I laughed some more. And as the sun set I realized that a roaring woman would know what to do. A roaring woman wouldn't need to phone France for advice. She would follow her instincts, follow her heart, do what she felt was right.

I picked up my phone and wrote Stu a text, then sent it.

Jodie: Baby, make sure you watch *Brunch With Bronwen* tomorrow. XX

Ping! One came back.

Stuart: Wouldn't miss it for the world. XX
Jodie: Cool. Was hoping you'd say that.
Stuart: NGHYA (never gonna hurt you again).
Jodie: Indeed.

I sat on the famous nipple-pink sofa, readjusting my floaty top as a make-up artist coated my forehead in powder to stop it shining under the harsh lights. On the other side of the studio Bronwen was finishing off a cookery slot with Fabio, the show's resident chef. She was practically orgasming over his credit crunchy flapjack. I could see Ming sitting on a discarded stool in the corner, rapidly writing something on her BlackBerry – she came to all the high-profile telly interviews – when suddenly I saw the floor manager waving his arms in the air and, through a mouthful of oats, Bronwen turned to camera and beamed.

'It's so gorgeous! It's fab-luss, I love it! And coming up after the break, *Acacia Avenue*'s very own Jodie McGee, that's Sister Aggie to me and you, is here to tell us why she's so excited about the National Soap Awards tonight. I love her, she's fab-luss. Don't go away.'

The red light disappeared from the camera and Bronwen spat the flapjack onto the work surface, then glided towards me with outstretched arms, cocking her head to one side, as if greeting a long lost relative.

'Jodie! Fab-luss! How's you?'

I jumped up and we hugged.

'Good thanks, yourself?'

'Fab-luss! Take a seat.'

The make-up artist now descended on Bronwen, who closed her eyes and ran through the 'shape' of the interview.

'Soap Awards – what it means to be nominated, maybe talk about the serial killer. I know you can't say anything. And can we mention your recent leave of absence or should I keep my silly mouth shut?'

'No, that's fine.'

'HOW MUCH DO I LOVE THIS WOMAN?!' she called out, eyes still shut, pointing in my general direction. Nobody answered, the crew were too busy setting up the cameras and rushing around like headless chickens to care, but Ming was on her feet and rushing over.

'Actually dat's a no-go, Bronwen,' she barked. God she could be officious.

'I don't mind,' I offered.

'No, Jodie. You didn't have to deal with all the shiss when you were—'

From somewhere a voice called out, 'OK, and going again in five, four, three, two . . .'

Another wave, a red light and we were on air. Ming hurried back to her stool. Bronwen switched from 'off' to 'on' in a split second.

'Hiya! Bronwen here! And look who I've got on my sofa today! Way hey! Jodie McGee! How much do we love Sister Aggie?! Hi, Jodie!'

'Hi, Bronwen.'

'You're looking fab-luss by the way. Love the hair.'

'Thanks.'

We talked all the usual bollocks you had to talk about when you were on a soap: ratings, storylines, the fact that there was absolutely *no* competition between the different soaps and how we were one big happy family. Then she went on to praise me for my recent assisted-suicide story, blah, blah, blah. And then

I saw a look of devilment in her eye as she shifted in her seat and leaned in compassionately.

'Jodie, I know you don't like to talk about this . . .'

Out of the corner of my eye I could see Ming jumping up from her stool and waving her arms about.

'. . . but you've been in the press a bit lately because of certain personal problems. Is tha' right?'

'Well . . .' I started, then faltered. I looked towards Ming. She was shaking her head and giving me *huge* daggers. I looked away and back to Bronwen. 'Yeah, that's right.'

Coward.

'Some of the papers said you'd been in a bit of a fight. Others said you had a drink problem. Your producers say you had a fall and needed time off to recuperate. What's the real reason you had to have time off, my love?'

My mouth went dry. I discovered a frog in my throat. I coughed politely and took a deep breath.

'Well, it's all a bit embarrassing really. I . . .'

Ming seemed to be arguing silently with some of the big cheeses at the back of the studio. I had to get it out. I had to say it. It was a compulsion. But try as I might it just wouldn't come out. Bronwen had someone talking to her in her earpiece.

'I'm guessing you were just overtired.'

I nodded. My mouth was locked shut – try as I might it just wouldn't open – so Bronwen covered the excruciating silence.

'Long hours, lots of scenes, I'm sure it's a common problem in—'

Suddenly my mouth sprang open and I blurted out, 'My boyfriend hit me.'

The smile froze on Bronwen's face. It was clear she'd been

expecting me to say I was overtired and needed a well-earned break. Now it was her turn to be catatonic. So I said it again.

'My boyfriend hit me. Stuart hit me.'

'*Right.*'

It was clear she was taking instructions through her earpiece again, so I carried on.

'We've been going through some hard times and . . . he's never really coped that well with my success and . . . well, a few weeks ago, he hit me.'

Bronwen's expression hadn't changed.

'That's . . . quite a litigious thing to say. Obviously he's not here to give . . . his side of the story,' she said, and opened her mouth to change the subject, but I took out my phone from my pocket.

'I've got some pictures if you don't believe me.'

'I'm not saying I don't believe you, Jodie.'

'I was going to delete them the other day, but I'm really glad I didn't now.'

I scrolled through to one of the pictures of my black eye and showed it to her. A camera zoomed in, so I turned it towards that the camera.

'Did you report it to the police?'

'No, I got pissed.'

'I think Jodie meant to say she got drunk there. Apologies.'

'Sorry. Drunk. I turned up to work drunk and Eva, my boss, gave me two weeks off to sort myself out.'

'Right. Anyway, erm . . .'

It wasn't often I'd seen Bronwen lost for words.

'So I went on holiday, took stock and then decided. Well, I'm a bit of a coward, so I wasn't sure what I'd decided. But then something happened yesterday and . . . I decided if I did something on here, on your show, then I'd have to stick to my guns and ditch him.'

I could see her warming to the discussion now, realizing this was probably going to be viewed again and again and again on YouTube or shows like *100 Top Celebrity Meltdowns*.

'Because you're such a big fan of the show, right?'

'In the past I've pretended my problems haven't been happening. I've lied and said everything's OK. By doing this today I'm hoping to—'

'Did he just hit you the once?' she butted in, nodding, like she knew it was a one-off.

'Yes. That time.'

Her eyes widened. 'He's hit you before?'

I nodded. 'Ages ago. He can be really nice, but . . .'

The headless chickens had stopped running around. I glanced over to see Ming slumping back down onto her stool, her eyes closing in dread.

'Well I . . . really respect your honesty, Jodie. I think a lot of people will look at you and assume you've . . . got it all. But obviously things have been tough, would you say tha' was right?'

'Listen, I'm a really lucky girl. I am the official lucky bitch. And don't get me wrong. I wasn't being punched in the face every time he came home drunk from the pub. I've certainly not had it as tough as some women. But it wasn't easy, and personally I don't think I should have had to have put up with it. But I did. I was . . . I was probably scared of losing him. Does that sound mad?'

Bronwen shook her head sadly.

'I'm sure a lot of our viewers'll be able to identify with that.'

'I loved him but . . . I've got to love myself a bit more.'

Bronwen nodded. The floor manager was waving again.

'Jodie, we're going to have to leave it there, but thanks for sharing and good luck at the awards tonight. Our roving reporter will be . . . catching up with you then no doubt.'

She then turned towards the camera and perked up.

'Coming up after the break, health and fitness expert Gina will be showing you how to lose some pounds while getting the dreaded housework done. Fab-luss! Can't wait! Don't go away!'

When the red light went off the camera, Bronwen seemed in a daze, staring straight ahead of her. She wrenched the earpiece from her ear then turned to me.

'Jodie, that was so brave. I'm so sorry.'

I nodded, embarrassed now. I'd poured my heart out to the nation. Well, to whoever was tuned in to her breakfast show – God knows why it was called *Brunch with Bronwen* as it was on from 9–9.45 a.m. A shadow covered me: Ming. She was furious.

'Nice one, Jodie. You've made Eva look like a liar now.'

'Oh shut your face, Ming, you stupid bitch.'

And no that wasn't me, it was Bronwen.

I walked from the studios into the sunlight of the South Bank. The Vietnamese food van was still there, reminding me of my first date with Stu. A young couple were getting noodles. As they walked away he put his arm round her. I wanted to cry, but tried to hold back the tears pricking my eyes. The girl dropped some food as they trudged along in insouciant bliss. A seagull swooped to gobble it up. Life, I guessed, went on.

Everything around me seemed to be in slow motion, as if the earth had stood still. My focus was precision sharp one second, blurry the next. I walked slowly to the nearby pub, sat at the table where we'd had our first drink and drank a vat of wine. Very soon I was pissed. I'd not eaten breakfast and it was still only ten in the morning. Oh well. I could get a cab back to the hotel and sleep it off before the awards that night.

My phone rang. It was Mum. I ignored it, but saw I had eighteen texts. I ignored them. I sat and got wasted, feeling sorry for myself and victorious at the same time. Nobody around me seemed to care or notice. They were probably piss-heads, too. Their indifference was strangely reassuring. It was OK to drink. Drinking made you feel better. Drinking made you feel, full stop.

My phone rang again. I knew it'd be him, ringing to ask me what on earth had happened yesterday to merit the public out-cry. I took a deep breath and answered.

'Hello, Stuart.'

'You fucking bitch. What d'you go and do that for?'

He continued to rant, so I placed my phone on the table, reducing his voice to a cartoon comedy caricature, tinnily rattling away. I smiled and ordered some more wine. A bottle this time.

Ten hours later I was in a blacked-out car, war paint on, mahoosive hair, driving to the Royal Albert Hall. I'd sobered up and was going to be fine. I was going to get through the evening unscathed. I was never going to make a show of myself again. My big statement had been made and my drama-queen days were over. I just had to get tonight out of the way, get back to work tomorrow and then my life would be on track. Everything was going to be OK.

What could possibly go wrong?

Keep it all in, Jodie. Keep it all in. Deep breaths, you're going to be fine. Just get through this and then the rest of your life can begin.

I opened my eyes. I'd arrived.

EPILOGUE

Three months later

I checked my face in the back of a spoon, which wasn't the best idea as it made me look like a satellite dish with foetal alcohol syndrome. I placed the spoon on the table and tried to see if I could clock my reflection in the restaurant window. It still shocked me that I had short hair; I'd had it cropped shortly after losing my job. New look, new start, new me type thing. I wasn't wholly convinced. I'd wanted to look gamine, pixie like. Mum said I looked like I was in a prisoner-of-war movie. Still, that meant I was slim, right? Result!

I didn't just have butterflies in my stomach, I had a whole swarm, and possibly the net, too. I wanted to get up, pace about and do something with all this bubbling nervous energy, but it wasn't really the done thing in a well-to-do restaurant as people would think that either a) the Ladies' was locked or b) I had mental health issues and was about to break into a chorus of 'The Grand Old Duke Of York' before the men in white coats came to bundle me into the back of a van.

Oh I had mental health issues all right. Or I had had. Some of the things I'd done in the past had hardly been sane. But I was getting my life back on track, and today was another step on the race track. A race track littered with hurdles.

I saw people recognizing me, trying to be subtle as they informed other members of their tables who I was. So much for the new look bringing me anonymity. But then, I guess when you've been famous for having a bit of material on your head, it's the face they recognize. How your hair looks is pretty inconsequential. A middle-aged woman in her best bib and tucker walked past, returning from the loos. She slowed down as she passed me, hovered for a bit, then smiled.

'It's you, isn't it?'

I nodded. 'I believe I am me, yes.'

'Sister Agatha.'

'Oh right. No, I just look like her.'

But she wasn't listening. 'Oh we thought it was criminal killing you off. Criminal. I nearly wrote a letter.'

I just smiled and repeated, 'I just look like her.'

'You're a lot prettier in the flesh.'

Well, that compliment I could take. She backed away with a 'won't disturb you further' and then I decided I wanted her to come back. At least she'd distracted me temporarily from my nerves. Nerves! Why was I so nervous? This was worse than a first date. And it was ridiculous, it's not like I'd never met him before. I picked up my menu and scanned it for the umpteenth time, still undecided about what I might order. The problem with billboard-sized menus is there are so many choices I always end up going a bit food-dyslexic and just see a jumble of words. I put the menu down on the table again and looked out of the window. Over the road I could see the Philharmonic Hall, where they put on classical concerts. There was a poster outside with a picture of a man with a baton, who I took to be a conductor, only someone had graffitied the baton to make it look like he was holding a penis.

I looked back round the restaurant. It was pretty swanky and the clientele was mostly couples here for a special occasion. The woman who'd spoken to me earlier looked over and raised her glass to me; I nodded and saw her husband reprimanding her quietly. She rolled her eyes and took a sip of her drink.

I thought about the night before, when I'd seen Debs and Hayls at the Blue Lagoon. It hadn't been the easiest of meetings, but I tried to focus on it as it was taking my mind off my impending 'date'. Apologies had been uttered and hugs exchanged. We blamed our separation on Stu and his controlling influence. It was easier that way, even if it was only half true. We agreed that Greg was a bastard and Debs confessed she must have had a moment of madness. The words forgive and forget were bandied round the table, as well as promises never to fall out again. Hayls had been wearing an eye patch. I'd not asked why and she'd not offered an explanation. There'd been laughter and tears and I'd been sad to say goodbye to them.

I heard the chug of a black cab pulling up outside. I looked. It stayed parked there for what felt like ages, and then he got out. He was taller than I remembered, though he was still the shape of a boxer. He was wearing smart dark blue jeans, multi-coloured trainers, some kind of sports hoody in a startling turquoise and, on top of that, the campest fun fur coat you ever did see. Massive reflective sunglasses covered most of his face. He looked up at the name of the restaurant, then bounded in. At the doorway he shoved his shades on top of his skinhead – pur-lease, skinhead? Who was he trying to kid? – and his myopic eyes scanned the room. I waved, and his surly look of concentration burst into a gigantic smile. He practically cartwheeled over to me. I jumped up and we bumped into each other in our hurry to hug, and as we clung on to each other we both burst out laughing. And didn't really stop. That laughter felt like it would go on for ever. The other diners were looking at us like we were bonkers, but I didn't care. The laughter was like a conversation. We knew what we meant, and we knew what the other person was saying. Eventually a waitress approached with a menu and we squelched apart and threw ourselves on our seats.

'Bottle of champagne?' he said, excited.

I so wanted to say yes. I so wanted to think, Sod it, it was a reunion. We deserved a treat. But I remembered my promise to myself, and what I had to do to keep on roaring.

'Actually, I've given up booze.'

I expected him to laugh in my face, but he didn't. He nodded, looked at the waitress and said, 'I'll have a glass of champagne and . . . Jodie?'

'Diet Coke, please.'

One of the most disheartening things about giving up alcohol had been that no one batted an eyelid when I told them. Nobody seemed surprised or disappointed. No one said, 'Oh come on, Jodie, one's not going to hurt you!' But I suppose, mixing in the circles he mixed in, Joey was probably surrounded by people in recovery.

'And a Diet Coke for the lady.' He winked at the waitress. My God, he was flirting with her! He was so confident, poised, everyone's best friend no doubt. Even his confidence made me proud of him. As the waitress slunk away he did a little drum roll on the table and said, 'So, what's the goss? How've you been?'

Like it hadn't been documented in the papers. As we talked I realized just how alike we looked. Snub nose, freckles, sparkling eyes. His green, mine mismatched. Eyes aside, he was the male equivalent of me. As someone had said when we were kids, 'Jeez, yous two could swap heads.' I'd hated it at the time – who wanted to look like their kid brother? – but today, today it felt so fabulous I wanted to explode.

Two months later

I phoned her. I always phoned her every Monday.

'Hiya, Mum.'

'Hiya, love. Hang on while I light up.'

Scritch scratch scratch and . . . inhale! And blow . . .

'That's better. How's the weather?'

'Lovely, thanks.'

'Mrs B?'

'Yeah, she's good thanks.'

'You had a drink?'

'No, Mum.'

'Oh good. You're doing ever so well, love.'

'Yeah, I'm not doing bad.'

I'd spent the summer at Mrs B's, helping her with the B & B. Well, helping was a bit of an exaggeration, I mostly dusted the David Hockneys the night before new guests arrived. But I was living rent free and, even though I eschewed her beloved rosé, we were getting on like a house on fire.

'Oh we don't half miss you, you know, love. It's not the same with you over there and your brother in Ibiza. Is it, Alan?'

I awaited a muffled response. None came.

'Your father's recorded *Top Gear*.'

Say no more.

'Actually, Mum, that was part of the reason for ringing. I . . . I might be coming back.'

'Oh, Jodie!' She sounded elated. 'That's brilliant. When?' She gasped, 'Are you gonna do *I'm a Celebrity*?'

'No.'

I'd been offered so many celebrity shows since leaving *Acacia Avenue*, but had turned them all down as I thought I'd be asking for trouble. I just knew I'd end up getting pissed and making a show of myself. And I just knew that's what the producers who were approaching me wanted to happen. I couldn't let it.

'I had a phone call the other day.'

'Oh aye? Who from?'

'From the new producer on *Acacia Avenue*.'

'Go'way! What did he want?'

Eva had left the show a month or so ago after having a nervous breakdown on set. She demanded to be in one of the scenes and wouldn't budge till the director had to fireman's lift her out of the building.

'Well, he was saying what a shame it was that Eva got rid of me and so . . .'

'But you can't come back, Jodie. You've died.'

'I know. So he wants to talk to me about' – God it sounded so daft saying it – 'coming back as my identical twin sister. They reckon they've got a great story for me, and he thinks the publicity they'd get from it would be immense.'

'And would you do it?'

'I don't know. But I'll go and have a meeting with him.'

'Oh right.' She sounded excited. 'And would you come and live with us? For a bit, like, you know.'

'Yeah I . . . I probably would.'

The silence that followed was a wave of contentment.

'Hey,' she said eventually, 'I hear Stuart's walked out of his job.'

'Really?'

'Yeah. Fed up of everyone calling him a wife batterer. Moved back to London by all accounts.'

'Right.'

'So, you know, you wouldn't have to see him if you moved back here.'

'No. Guess not.'

The police had been in touch in the days after my appearance on *Brunch With Bronwen*, asking if I wanted to press charges. I'd declined. I felt Stu had had all the humiliation he'd deserved. That, surely, was some kind of punishment.

'Oh, and we got something through the post today.'

'Oh aye, what's that?' I was beginning to sound like her.

'Invitation to Greg's wedding.'

'Who's he marrying?'

'Someone called Keisha. I think that's how you pronounce it anyway.'

'Ah, that's lovely.'

'The name?'

'No, the fact that he's getting married.'

'I know, God love him. He hasn't got a mother, you know.'

'I know, Mum. We went to her funeral.'

'Oh yeah.'

I sighed. I didn't feel jealous or bitter or hacked off or anything negative. I actually felt happy for him. I supposed that's what you call progress.

'Hey listen, Mum, I was talking to Our Joey last night.'

'Oh yeah?'

'And he reckons if I do take this job, him and Paolo might move back to England.'

'Oh right.'

501

She sounded unsure, but I think that was more because she wasn't used to us not using her as a conduit through which to communicate.

'Is he fed up with Ibiza?'

'A bit, yeah. I think all the partying's doing his head in.'

'Well, let's face it, Jode. Maybe he's got something worth coming back for now, eh?'

'Yeah.'

Mrs B floated past and deposited a glass of pink lemonade on the table where the phone was. She gave an illicit wink and scurried away.

'Listen, Mum, I'd better get on. We've got a new couple arriving tomorrow and I need to get the room ready.'

'Oh, OK.' She always sounded disappointed when I said I had to go. 'When are you coming back for your meeting?'

'Next week. Tuesday. So I'll come back Monday night, if that's OK.'

'Your Dad'll pick you up from John Lennon Airport.'

They'd recently bought an Uno. No doubt Mum was dusting down her chauffeur's cap in anticipation of my potential return to the Avenue.

'Great.'

'I'll do a nice roast and get some of that fizzy water in. You like that, don't you?'

'Yeah.'

'Personally, I think it tastes like Alka-Seltzer. Oh, I can't wait to see you, Jode. Give our love to Mrs B.'

'I will.'

'Oh, and how's your friend in the wheelchair?'

'Matthew? Yeah, he's fine.'

'Any romance on the horizon?'

'No. No we're just mates. Neither of us is ready for any of that crap right now.'

'Oh well. It's always good to have mates.'

'Yeah. Yeah it is.'

'Right. Well, *Top Gear*'s finishing now, so I'd better get some food on. Take care of yourself, love.'

'I will. And you.'

'Thanks, love. Ta-ra then.'

'Ta-ra, Mum.'

I hung up. I stood for a moment, feeling that little pang of sadness I always felt after speaking to her. Then I headed upstairs to dust the David Hockneys.

extracts reading groups
competitions books new
discounts extracts extracts discounts
competitions events
books
new books extracts
events reading groups
extracts books
new titles reading groups
interviews
events extracts extracts
discounts events
new books events interviews new books
events new events books extracts
discounts extracts discounts
www.panmacmillan.com
extracts events reading groups
competitions books extracts new